One Blood

Sabrina Chase

Also by Sabrina Chase

ARGONAUTS OF SPACE TRILOGY
The Scent of Metal

SEQUOYAH TRILOGY
The Long Way Home
Raven's Children
Queen of Chaos

GUARDIAN'S COMPACT SERIES
The Last Mage Guardian
Dragonhunters

Firehearted
Jinxers
The Bureau of Substandards Annual Report

ACKNOWLEDGMENTS

As always, thanks are due to the genial writing group STEW, fearless editor Deb Taber who cleaned out the Augean Commas, and many others who helped make this book what it is. (All the bad parts are my fault. They tried to warn me and I didn't listen.) Special thanks, though, are due to my loyal readers who make it possible for me to have this much fun without getting arrested.

Sabrina Chase

"We be of one blood, ye and I." —Rudyard Kipling, *The Jungle Book*

CHAPTER 1

They were in a room that looked like most of the secure meeting rooms Merilee Macrae had been in—no windows, stale recirculated air, guards at the door, a significant percentage of the attendees in uniform—but there were telling differences. All of the beverages, even coffee, were in sealed bulbs, the furnishings bare of the usual wood and leather, and next to the door was a narrow, orange cabinet labeled "Emergency Oxygen Equipment." With her injuries, long meetings were easier to endure in reduced lunar gravity, but the location hadn't been picked with her convenience in mind.

On the moon, security was *much* easier. Not even data could escape without detection. And at the rate they were going, they would run out of pregenerated classification code words for everything her mission had discovered.

With mordant humor, she wondered how the various governments and their agencies were dealing with all the frantic astronomers who had noticed Pluto was not there anymore. Not her problem. The reason it was missing, however, was. As the man at the head of the table, the director of Space Security, was doing his best to make clear.

"I want to know why you weren't keeping a closer eye on those scientists of yours," Buckner said, stabbing a thick finger her way. "You were there only to study that ship, not get it running again! Now you're telling me the whole planet's in danger because of this."

Macrae heard Colonel Gonafrio shift in his seat. She didn't need to look at him to know he was probably grinding his teeth and about to utter a cutting response.

"Given that Pluto had been behaving in all respects like a rock for thousands of years, it was not unreasonable to assume it would continue to do so. Even when we discovered there was an alien ship inside," she said, keeping her tone calm and even. Gonafrio wasn't dumb; he'd pick up her intent. They had a dangerous path to walk, and they didn't need to stir up any unnecessary bad feelings. "Activating Argo was an accident, but convincing it to help was not." *My scientists did that, and don't you forget it.* "Furthermore, it put us in no more danger than we were in already —we just know about it now. I find it hard to believe anyone would prefer to remain in ignorance of what we found. At least now we have a chance to defend ourselves." *You blithering idiot.*

"Are you certain there is no possibility of peaceful interaction with these aliens?" The speaker was a man she hadn't met before, an army general. He seemed uncomfortable, and now she knew why Buckner was being more of a pill than usual. The military was starting to take over the planning, as it should, and Buckner wasn't going to be in charge much longer. Good.

Gonafrio leaned forward. "We have testimony from a group of people that have much more recent interaction with these aliens, the fadohl, than we do—and these interactions were in all respects violent and deadly. Our own personal experiences were likewise violent." Gonafrio turned his head toward Macrae, reminding everyone why she was still wearing an arm brace. Shot up by robots on an alien base while in the process of setting off a nuke. Bet the doctors didn't have a diagnosis code for *that.*

"And let's remember who those people are," Macrae added. "They call themselves Wiyert, but they are Neanderthals, stolen in bulk from *our planet.* These fadohl have no problem with slavery or genocide, and if they ever go through their archives, they *know where we are.* No, I don't think we're going to be friends."

Buckner scowled. "The claim that they are actual Neanderthals…"

"Proven. We've got one of them on Earth right now that came back with us. The DNA tests pegged him, one hundred percent."

Macrae waited, one eyebrow raised, but Buckner had no further comment.

Major Dahan flicked a finger at the bound classified dossier before her. "This says you have assets remaining with the ancient ship that is no longer here. How many, and what do they do there?"

Macrae stifled a smile. Elana Dahan came from the Israeli army and had even less patience than Macrae did for unproductive meetings. Elana kept her personal emergency oxygen equipment within arm's reach at all times and had raised holy hell about not being allowed to carry a weapon on Luna Base. Macrae approved of Major Dahan.

"Four of our people—three military, one civilian scientist—and the Wiyert we rescued from the planet they were trapped on. They intend to find the rest of the Wiyert and free them, gathering any information about the fadohl they can find."

"Ah. Allies and intelligence. This is good." Dahan frowned. "But why so few?"

"Larger numbers would not improve the chance of success in this case," Gonafrio said smoothly. "And in this case, the people have unique abilities that were extremely effective."

And better out there than here. Macrae found she was rubbing her injured arm unconsciously, remembering. Only a handful of people knew exactly how effective, or that detonating a nuclear device had only been part of the fight on the alien base. Lea Santorin's terrifying ability was the real reason they'd won and the only reason any of them from the expedition ship *Kepler* had made it back to Earth alive. She was grateful, but Macrae still didn't want Santorin anywhere in the solar system. Macrae knew better than anyone what she was capable of.

And I've sent her off with a giant alien AI ship that thinks she's a god, her own team of SF soldiers, and a bunch of Wiyert to save us. Unsupervised. With a sinking feeling, Macrae realized that might not have been exactly the smart idea she'd thought at the time.

Alaghar sat and watched in the dim light as her people slept, even though there was no need. They were no longer trapped on the dead planet, fighting just to stay alive, exposed to cold and hunger and the danger of the fadohl machine servants. Now they were warm, with plentiful—if strange—food, and the ship itself a servant now protecting them. No dark rock cave with painfully hand-chipped sleeping ledges, but a large room with light that came and went at a word, and beds placed precisely as they wished by the ship-mind that made them of its own material.

Beyond the door, open passageways and openings that looked like doors but were not. Stepping through such an opening would bring one wherever the opening was linked to, anywhere on the giant ship.

There was no need to keep watch here, but Alaghar believed in discipline. It had kept her from despair during the long days on the dead planet. It would help her find the dangers yet to come. She was the Warleader, and that was her task. Of all that had set out from Vartai, only six of them had survived. Four were still in her care. She had taken a desperate risk in trusting the Frost People, endangering them all—endangering all the Wiyert—if she had not made the correct choice.

Trusting their lives to the Frost People was one thing, but trusting them with information was another. They had many questions—she did not blame them for that. They had never known of the fadohl before now and feared for their people. But to simply tell them…Alaghar shook her head. That was not for her to decide. One of the *buj-lagar*, perhaps, but not her. She hoped the Frost People would understand the Wiyert's desperate need for caution and not become angry. They needed each other to survive.

There was hope. They walked the pale, sand-colored passages of a former fadohl ship, as no Wiyert had for hundreds of years. But they were not prisoners, not slaves. They held their weapons, and no fadohl were present here.

Alaghar had faced many bitter hours and dark nights when the weight of her task seemed more than she could bear. They had no way to return to Beredul and their beleaguered people, no way to fight for them even in death. They had been gone so long she did not even know if the long-feared attack had finally begun—that they had made their desperate attempt at escape to stop. That had been the worst of their suffering.

But the dead planet had some ancient equipment, long abandoned by the fadohl. They had fashioned a crude sensor apparatus from pieces salvaged from it. In her soul, Alaghar had expected nothing, but it gave her people hope. And then it had detected an energy pulse from the fadohl nexus they had retreated from. From the portal gate that linked the nexus and the dead world.

When they investigated, they found the nexus portal completely dead and a thin, strangely pale young woman nearby. She looked human, but did not speak their language and had no knowledge of the fadohl. Ah, but how quickly they had learned! And the first blow for freedom had been struck with their help. Alaghar could face her end with honor now, remembering the blinding destruction of the nexus. She had fought there and won.

The Wiyert were no longer alone in their desperate fight, and it gave her the first faint threads of hope. From the young woman's people, they learned they had a common home, that once Wiyert and the Frost People had lived together in the world of the Gold Sun. Not a legend, as she had been told, but the truth.

She was not certain how the Frost People had convinced the ship-mind to obey them, but it did. If the Wiyert could learn to do the same…Alaghar smiled, baring her teeth.

The fadohl were nothing without their tools.

Especially if the tools fought back.

I'm beginning to think the true Universal Constant is paperwork, Lea thought. She held the clipboard between a thumb and finger, wrinkling her nose in disgust and glaring at the massive pile of boxes, crates, and equipment that had been hastily dumped in the large cross-corridor.

It was a good thing Argo was the size of a moon, because they were collecting baggage at an alarming rate. Cardboard boxes really brought down the tone of the place, though.

"This is ridiculous. Why are we still doing inventory? We're on a giant talking alien spaceship, not in some warehouse on Earth. And aren't we supposed to be coming up with clever, sneaky plans right now? It's been nearly a week since we dropped off *Kepler*."

Ramirez chuckled. The floating bed he was on shifted a little, overcompensating for his movement. "Hate to tell ya, but this is how most Spec Ops sneaky plans start. Paperwork and meetings. They focus on fast-roping off black helicopters and blowing shit up in the recruiting ads so people will sign up. Here, I'll take that. I'm still not up for much lifting. You move the crates."

Lea gave him the clipboard and stopped complaining. She had a brief but vivid memory of Ramirez, bloody and screaming with pain after being shot by a defensive robot. He'd healed fast, but he was still recovering. *I could see his internal organs. How can he be so calm about it?*

And she knew he was calm about it, because she'd been changed by alien tech too. Sensing his emotions was like breathing air now—it took no effort and she couldn't stop it. Fortunately, it was usually only emotions. If she didn't make physical contact, she could avoid picking up what he was thinking. It still felt like snooping, though.

Lea shook herself and headed for one of several personal footlockers, throwing the lid open. She needed to think about something else.

"Wait, this has to be wrong. It's stuffed with DVDs from the rec library. Or someone's personal collection." She held up one. It had "Grand Canyon Vacation 2019" written on the disk in marker pen. "I don't remember this movie hitting the theaters."

"They asked everyone for any Earth stuff they could spare. You weren't on *Kepler* for that, I think. It's for the Wiyert."

"Oh." That made sense, actually. The Wiyert were getting a crash course on their long-forgotten home planet. She liked that part. They were astounded by the most ordinary things, and the questions they asked made her equally curious about how they lived. Or, from the sounds of it, died. Nobody took vacations on Beredul. "Right. One footlocker, miscellaneous video. Including cartoons. I don't know if that's a good idea—the Wiyert already think Earth-humans are a bunch of hyperactive children."

"Nah, just you." Ramirez grinned. "They're hard-core, but so are we."

"Not like them, you aren't. I'm not sure they even have a word for fun." Lea opened more boxes, wondering how the language sessions were going. And, being honest with herself, when she was going to be able to spend some time with Ivars. *That* mental connection she liked.

Lea knew everybody had to learn to communicate with the Wiyert on their own, but it took a long time. She could cheat—she could mentally link to anything remotely computer-like, and that included Argo. While they were on Argo, the AI could provide translation services for everyone, but they weren't going to be able to stay on the moon-size ship all the time. She had learned a lot of the Wiyert language already with her mental link to Argo, but the rest of the team had to do it the hard way. So she got to spend time making lists, and making sure Ramirez rested like he was supposed to.

A fine way to conquer the galaxy. We'll just bore everyone to death.

"I can move all of this into a place of storage," Argo's voice said diffidently. "I will make helpers to do it more quickly than you can."

"It's not just about moving, Argo." Lea looked in the large cardboard box of MREs and sighed. "We need to know what we've got here, and you don't know what these things are, right?"

"It is true. I will learn."

And the faster she got this done, and Argo up to speed, the less time she'd have to spend away from everyone else. "Soldier-chow, one large box, says a hundred and forty-four of the things, but damn if I'm going to count them all. I'm glad Macrae let us have all that real food from *Kepler*. If I had to eat this all the time, I'd get pretty cranky."

"You'd get more than cranky." Ramirez waggled his eyebrows. "A constant diet of that will plug you up like concrete. Me, I like Argo's creative refrigeration fix. Even canned stuff gets old."

"Yeah, I noticed the extra chicken nodules evaporated in record time. I was planning on having some for a snack, but not with you guys around."

"Hey, I didn't take 'em! Chicken nodules…*chica*, I don't know what scares me more, that I knew what you meant or that I agree with you."

"See? It's contagious! Gonna make a geek of you yet." She grinned at him.

Lea got about ten feet down the corridor of stuff, talking as she went, before she realized Ramirez had fallen asleep. Just in case a box fell or something, she had Argo modify the floating bed to have acoustic baffling and kept going.

She didn't have to speak for Argo to hear her. And the AI preferred the mental link, which was faster and more complex, to spoken communication anyway.

This box has ammunition. I don't know what guns it goes with; you'll have to ask the others.

Why are there so many of the same thing?

They get used up. She visualized pulling the trigger of a gun and the bullet coming out. The next container had multiple smaller boxes, all with medical supplies. *This is stuff for fixing people when they are hurt. Ramirez knows the most about this.*

Several large cartons of cold-weather clothing, which made her wonder what the original plan had been when *Kepler* left Earth for the derelict Argo, more commonly known then as Pluto. Maybe it had been packed just in case. None of it looked large enough for the Wiyert, who were rather massive about the shoulders and arms.

I can make things, Argo reminded her.

Lea widened her eyes. Maybe this was all an academic exercise. She knew Argo could fabricate items, but she hadn't thought about variety or scale. *Yeah, but how much? And what kind of things?*

The data burst from Argo took some time to unpack. It could not, unfortunately, create an infinite amount of anything, or very much of what they really needed. It had a stock of most elements and could produce large quantities of material similar to cloth or fiber, but it could not directly synthesize complex molecules except slowly and in small batches.

They might be able to work around that if someone knew what the chemical process was. Argo could probably make the equipment or bootstrap from there. She would have to ask the others if they wanted to do that.

She shifted the big, bulky box and saw the familiar sheen of protective aluminum cases. Good, they hadn't forgotten *her* gear. Lea had the distinct impression Macrae, the mission director, had been relieved to go back to Earth without her—had it really only been a week ago? Nobody really felt comfortable around her...new abilities. They didn't want her happy so much as far away from them.

Electronics, Argo!

They are very primitive. They do not have any adaptive processes. Why do you want these devices? The AI equivalent of a sniff, she guessed.

This is the technology we came up with ourselves, she explained. *We don't know how to make anything even one-tenth as complex as you. Also, you are hard to put in a pocket.*

A signal decoder, a digital oscilloscope, several portable computers—the data-crunching kind, not websurfing tablets—and a wheeled bin full of a wide assortment of components.

On top of the next stack was a medium-size cardboard box with garish color illustrations of cheese crackers. It had obviously been opened already, but Lea reached for it, hoping against hope some of the original contents might remain. She was feeling hungry all of a sudden.

It was curiously heavy for crackers. She tugged it down, resting it on the wheeled bin, and lifted one flap. The box was filled with inky blackness. One green eye opened and stared at her. Messier Object #102, aka M.O., *Kepler*'s…former…ship's cat, stood and stretched.

Lea just stared at him in horror. "How did you…we put you back! You're supposed to be back on Earth!" Now she really could never go home. Macrae would never, ever believe she hadn't done it on purpose. "Bad cat! No tuna!"

M.O. yawned with magnificent unconcern.

Ivars winced and got up from the table to get some coffee and take a break. North and Ramirez were still hard at work; one sitting at a different table in the big common room Argo had made for them, the other drawing some complicated diagram on the reactive walls to illustrate a point. The Wiyert's language sounded just enough like Russian to give Ivars a headache. Now and then he slipped up and used the wrong language, and Alaghar would give him a funny look. Fortunately they didn't have to do it all from scratch, since Lea had given them direct access to a very effective translation service. A slightly archaic translation service—he got the feeling the Wiyert thought Argo sounded like authentic

Shakespeare to a modern English speaker. Still, it was good enough for government work.

"Hey." A thump on his shoulder followed the voice, and he blinked. North was standing next to him and giving him a resigned look. "You blanked out again. Tell me you aren't going squirrelly too, dude. One's enough."

Ivars felt his face heat. "Nah, I just…" Then he realized what he had been doing. His mind had been unconsciously searching for the link, because he had thought of Lea. "Okay, maybe. Dammit, how'd I get so used to having voices in my head? Before we left Earth, if anybody even hinted something like that, I would've punched them. Now when I can't…sense her, I think something's wrong."

He spoke quietly, so only North could hear. They were focusing on getting the Earth-humans fluent in Wiyert first, but he knew the Wiyert were damn observant and intelligent and were probably already able to understand more English than they'd been taught. And Lea's special abilities were not something he felt ready to explain to them or get them to accept.

"Argo would be sounding every alarm it knows how to make if anything happened to Lea. She's probably the safest human in the galaxy right now."

Ivars glared at North. "I know it isn't rational. Blame it on my dented skull."

"I don't think the *brain* is the problem here." North grinned. "This link thing. Is it like what she does?"

"Not even close. Mostly I can tell where she is." Of course that changed if they were in contact. With great effort, he managed not to smile.

"I'll probably regret asking this, but do we have any plan beyond 'hide out for a while, then contact Beredul'?"

"That's up to the Wiyert." This would take more than their current simple language skills. "Hey, Argo. Go back to translate mode, please. And how long are we going to be waiting once we get…wherever you are taking us?"

Argo's voice had been changing as it learned human speech modulation. "If the fadohl are able to track my drive signature, we should not go to Beredul. I am going to a location they can reach from their network, and I will have a wide array of sensors deployed. If they do not follow, there is a low probability they can find me if I go to a location away from the network."

"And then what?" Ivars gestured to Alaghar, who regarded him with a stony, impassive expression. "What is our immediate mission once we reach Beredul and make contact? We all want the fadohl taken out, but what's the best way to do it that protects the people of both Earth and Beredul?"

The other Wiyert gathered around Alaghar. With Argo handling the translation now, the communication bottleneck was removed.

"Before all, we must find a way to break the barrier that imprisons us. The fadohl left devices and a watching sensor mind on the portal, and the only connection to that portal on the surface of Beredul is heavily guarded. The Sensor will not permit any powered vehicle to approach without destroying it, and the *asuhan* are drawn to the place as well."

"*Asuhan?*"

"Giant beasts, violent and dangerous."

"How did you get to this portal in the first place?" North gestured at the Wiyert. "You got out to the planet of the nexus where we found you, so it must be possible."

Alaghar's lips pulled back just enough to bare her teeth. It was not a smile. "Fifty of us left the stronghold of Vartai to make the attempt. Of those only twelve survived to reach the portal. Three more died before we escaped to the dead world you found us on. We were the first of the banished on Beredul to leave. Our people will think the fadohl captured us and will be suspicious of any who return—and will also fear any stranger who appears."

Ivars felt his eyelid twitch. It hadn't escaped him that Alaghar had never answered his original question, and she was handing him a whole bunch of dangerous complications instead. "So if we get to this portal somehow, we still have to fight our way through giant monsters to get to a place where we will essentially be shot on sight just for breathing. Do I have that right?"

"We must also reach the portal without bringing the fadohl to investigate." There might have been a gleam of amusement in Alaghar's flinty gaze, but he wasn't sure. "We have been missing for…" She spouted some Wiyert phrases, and Argo translated it as "Three hundred and two Earth-days." So, nearly a year. Yes, the home office had probably written them off and was in deep panic mode.

"Great. Looks like our first priority is calling this Vartai and convincing them we are friendly."

Alaghar shook her head in the sharp, back-and-forth style of the Wiyert. "There is nothing like your 'radio' for such long distances. This is also detected and attacked by the watcher."

Ivars groaned. "This cannot possibly get any worse."

"Oh, you're forgetting a few things." North raised an eyebrow. "One, it will probably rain. Two, Santorin has to come with us if we're going to hack into the system and take the barrier down."

No. He felt his stomach knot and his skin go cold. *Too dangerous. Not Lea.* Then he tried desperately to think of something happy and calm, like sleeping puppies. If she was listening, she'd feel his sudden jolt of terror and worry. It was hard to keep that in mind, and he didn't want to add to her troubles with his own hang-ups. It was going to be near impossible for him and North as it was. Ramirez might be a problem too, if he hadn't healed up enough, but he had the training. Lea, on the other hand, was pure computer-geek civilian and not up to fighting giant alien monsters. Or even a five-mile run with a full pack.

"Then we're just going to have to figure out a way to get all of us down to the surface safely and tell the locals we come in peace."

North sighed. "For a very loose definition of peace."

CHAPTER 2

Alaghar and her people gathered in the space created for them by the ship-mind to eat and to speak among themselves without the Frost People present. It was much like the spaces of the *damah* of home, and thus more comfortable, if one did not remember how one simple door was all that protected it. They had found it was better to have something familiar in all the strangeness that surrounded them. Even the food, which today was the grey-green pockets the Frost People provided, the *ehm-ar-ees*. Alaghar would never complain or allow any of her people to do so, but still…it was *very* strange.

"Warleader, are the fighters the Frost People sent with us of any real use?" Hazuruh used the tone of respectful query and kept her gaze lowered, emphasizing she wished to understand, not to challenge. "One is still injured, and the leader, Ivars, also bears heavy scars. The one North…can he truly travel any distance on that metal foot?"

What she was really asking, and what Alaghar still did not understand herself, was why these Frost People had agreed to come. Why would they still seek to fight when they had earned the right to stay behind walls?

"By themselves, perhaps not enough to win alone," she said dryly. "Remember what you have seen yourself, on the nexus. They fight well and do not fear the works of the fadohl as slaves would. Also remember they bring the knowledge of their world.

The device they used to destroy the nexus was small. They woke the ship-mind and turned it from the fadohl to serve them instead. The battle does not always go to the strongest fighter or the bones of our ancestors would bleach in the sun of Beredul."

"The battle also does not go to those who do not know they are in one," Dumhaigl grumbled, carefully removing the small red container from the food pocket. The Wiyert had learned to respect and avoid the thing known as "hot sauce." "They sent few true fighters to the fadohl ship, treating it as if it were dead and harmless. They are foolish."

"It *was* dead," Burdhul protested. "They knew nothing of the fadohl, so how could they fear them? They wish to know more, now, to protect their world. Of course they would come to learn from us."

"Still, they have no discipline. You saw the ship of their own making, how open it was! No defensive zones, wide doorways, and the interior doors were kept open!" Dumhaigl shook his head. "They will not last a day on Beredul."

Hazuruh took out the larger package, the one that contained the main item of food. None of them could yet read the blocky symbols used to identify the contents, so when they looked unfamiliar, they tended to sample cautiously. She took a small bite, chewing thoughtfully. "I am not certain what you say is true. I have been watching them, how they act with each other and with us."

Alaghar nodded. "As if you were hunting."

"Yes, like that. Even before we could understand each other's speech. Have you not noticed how the smallest of them, Lea, is treated? Even by her chosen?"

"Permitting chosen in a warrior group. Insanity!" muttered Dumhaigl.

Alaghar ignored him, remembering. "They keep space around her. As if she were a knife master, which she is not." She smiled to herself, recalling Lea's confusion and fear when Alaghar had given her the knife on the dead planet. "But if she is not a warrior, why do they stand so far and take care not to touch her? She does not show any sign of anger. The others are warriors, this is clear. Yet they treat her as if she is also one of them—but she does not fight!"

"She fights. I do not know how, but she does." Kugohin stirred from his usual silence. "You did not see. On the nexus, I was near the large door when the machine servants came during the battle. I saw the others call to her for aid, in fear and pain. She was afraid too, I could see her eyes. Yet..." He shook his head, his forehead furrowed in the effort of remembering. "Branched fire appeared and attacked the machine servants—and then they turned and attacked the others. I saw her turn her back on one, as if it were no longer a danger. She stood in the midst of battle, her eyes closed. I saw sweat run down her face, her lips tremble with fear, but she did not run. The machine servants fled from her. I do not know why."

"The leader of the Frost People, the Mahk-Ray. She fears nothing, that one. Yet she also treated Lea as a dangerous thing," Alaghar said slowly as the memory returned to her. And then she remembered something else. When she had thought Lea was an agent of the fadohl and had grabbed her arm in anger—and suddenly felt splitting pain in her head and strange images in her mind.

Dumhaigl grimaced. "The Frost People are strange."

"Stranger than you realize," Alaghar snapped. "Think on what you know! Not only the secret ways of Lea." She waved one hand sharply. "By the word of the white-haired one, the one who first knew us for blood kin—Olsen. The Frost People first learned of the fadohl ship less than four of their years ago. They made their own ship, *Kepler*, for the purpose of coming to it and learning its origin. From the time they first learned of the fadohl to their destruction of the nexus was *less than twenty days!* Do you understand what that means? We, the Wiyert, who have lived with the danger our entire history, cannot agree to build a *wall* in twenty days! See how quickly and how well they leave their ignorance and find mastery? Do not have contempt that they do not know our ways. They do not know them *yet*. And they know their own ways very well."

Hazuruh understood her instantly and went pale. The others figured it out shortly thereafter. It was the first rule of the warriors: bring no danger inside the *damah* walls. The Frost People were ancient blood kin, but they were strangers; their customs were very different from those of the Wiyert. None of them knew what the Frost People were truly capable of. Or if they could be fully trusted.

No one spoke. And Alaghar still had not told them the other troublesome conclusion she had reached. The Frost People did not know the fadohl, yet they had warriors and a device that was like a piece of a sun, intended to destroy. It had demolished the nexus. If they were not fighting the fadohl before, who had they been fighting?

Ivars finished up the last of the day's notes in the workroom and stretched. "Time for chow, I think. I wonder what's for dinner?"

"Let's order Chinese," North said, straight-faced. "Argo can just open up one of those wormholes it does, all the way back to Earth. Don't we have something like that in the refrigerated stuff Gonafrio liberated?"

Ivars sighed, heading for the internal transport link to the common area/kitchen. "Yeah, but we shouldn't just eat all the good food first either. I thought the chicken would last longer, but we sure powered through the entire box in a hurry. Besides, I was thinking we'd have a party while we wait at the nebula. Introduce the Wiyert to the culinary delights of tube steak and chili."

The link worked just like an ordinary door, except the workroom was nearly a kilometer from the common area if you looked at a map of Argo's internal space. Ivars was alert every time he used a door link, but he never had the painful symptoms Lea experienced. That made it unlikely he would ever get the full brain upgrade she'd gotten, unawares.

Just as well. I got some good bits, like Lea on brain-phone, and hardly any screaming.

As soon as he left the link, he could sense Lea. He could also hear her. She was annoyed about something and almost yelling. Ivars picked up the pace and entered the common area, looking around quickly.

Ramirez was in his floating lounge chair, looking better and clearly stifling amusement as he watched Lea. Ivars blinked. A familiar black-and-white cat was reclining next to him, watching Lea gesticulate as she argued with the air.

"But why didn't you *say* anything? We could have put him back on *Kepler* before it left!"

"There were many items transferred I did not recognize," said the disembodied voice of Argo. "The cat had been present before, and it did not indicate to me it wished to leave."

"You know perfectly well I got in trouble for that, and he's a *cat*, Argo! He can't talk!"

"The cat makes sound like speech, but I do not understand it."

North snorted. "If you figure that out, they'll want you back home immediately to act as a cat translator. Homicidal aliens could wait."

Lea swiveled her head to look at them. Her hair was even more tousled than usual, probably from grabbing it. "If anything happens to M.O., Macrae is going to *hunt me down*. Across the galaxy if she has to. What are we going to feed him? And, also important, what are we going to do for a litter box?"

Sensing motion behind him, Ivars swung to one side. Burdhul and the rest of the Wiyert were peering around the door with dubious expressions.

"Ah, the small hunting creature!" Burdhul said in his own tongue. "How big are its prey?"

"Small-small." Ivars indicated with spread fingers.

"That will be of no use, then," Dumhaigl grumbled. "Why bring it?"

"I did not bring him," Lea said, scowling. "He hid in the boxes."

"For a week? You'd think he'd get hungry…" Ivars got a sudden insight. "The chicken! That damn cat ate the chicken nuggets!" And clearly Argo had already dealt with the…end product of digestion somehow.

Hazuruh muttered something Ivars didn't quite catch, but he thought he recognized the words for "children" and "foolish."

The feel of his link to Lea wasn't quite right. Spiky and frustrated and tired. Probably, from what he knew of her, trying to figure out a way to get M.O. back.

"The cat's here now and not going anywhere for a while, just like us. By the time we do get back, Macrae will have forgotten all about him." That just earned him a scowl and a glare. "Did you eat lunch?"

Lea blinked. "Uh, sure."

She's lying. "Really? What? Where's the wrapper?"

"You did not eat. I told you when the others were eating and you said 'just a minute,'" Argo said helpfully. Ivars stifled a chuckle. The AI didn't know about plausible deniability yet, which was real handy.

Her shoulders slumped. "Okay, I forgot. I was busy. I'll eat soon." She turned, hesitated, and headed for a box on the counter-like ledge that ran around two of the walls.

"Nuh-uh. Now." Ivars herded her back to the large table, snagging the two MREs that North tossed to him. He sat down opposite Lea, poking one over to her like it was explosive. She managed a weak smile.

He disemboweled his own meal, all the while keeping a careful eye on Lea to make sure she was actually eating and not simply rearranging the contents. Which she had done before.

I can't eat while you stare at me like that, her voice echoed in his mind.

Ivars closed his good eyelid at her, then with exaggerated effort turned his head to see what was going on in the rest of the room. North was getting a mug of water from the "tap" Argo had formed. He wasn't sure exactly how that worked, since he was pretty sure the giant ship didn't have plumbing in the usual sense of the word, but whatever.

Ramirez was attempting to explain cats to the Wiyert in a broken mix of their language and English in between drinking a protein shake. The docs had recommended he stay off the condensed food until he was completely healed.

"No, *tzaipe goh*...um, help hunt? And, sit on...*raikletos dovo*..."

Burdhul's eyes widened and he stifled a sudden snort of laughter, and even Alaghar cracked a small smile.

Lea was staring with her mouth half-open. "Er. No, don't conjugate that verb that way. Ever. I mean, unless you *wanted* to tell them you have romantic feelings for M.O."

"I adore him. He is the center of my universe," Ramirez declaimed with a dramatic gesture. M.O. opened one eye, sighed, and went back to sleep. "What are we going to feed him? Besides chicken nuggets, which we are now out of. I gave him some scraps, but that won't be enough."

"Some of the powdered eggs, maybe? There were some cans of chicken too." Lea started to get up, until Ivars cleared his throat at her.

"The cat can wait. He's not exactly slender."

Burdhul wandered up, hesitating as he appeared to assemble his few words of English before speaking. "We see…*sof-bal-gaym?*"

It took a moment for him to understand what Burdhul was talking about. "What, again? Sure. I'll set it up."

The Earth-human common area was the de facto general meeting room. Since the Wiyert had none of their own kind of food with them, all the cooking was done here, and they had also arranged the little projector for the DVD content. One of the first ones they'd played was clearly a personal recording of a junior softball league game. There was nothing exciting at all, even if you knew the rules of the game, but the Wiyert had watched the first time in utter, silent shock. He wasn't sure if they were horrified or appalled, but they hadn't said a single word while it played.

"Leeah, plez. To say what is?"

Lea nodded, her mouth full. Ivars was pleased to see at least half of the meal had been eaten already, so he just rolled his eyes at her as she jumped up.

"Argo, you run the baseline translation and I'll explain in more detail, okay?"

"I will do this."

And what really gave Ivars a headache was that Argo could. Somehow it had enough brainpower to both do simultaneous translations and make sure the right language sounded louder to the right ear *and* do multiple conversations at that. Lea had said something about waveform coherence and multithreading and a lot of other stuff he couldn't remember. It was very handy, though.

He mixed up a tanker's mocha with the coffee and hot chocolate packets and some hot water, and headed over to the gear. The DVD with the softball game was located and inserted in the player, and the Wiyert seated themselves on the floor, their faces intent and serious.

They feel agitated. Did we do something wrong? Lea's mental voice whispered.

Ivars gave a minuscule shrug, just enough for Lea to see. If they had, he didn't know what it was. He hit the play button.

Almost immediately, Alaghar gestured for him to stop.

"Why are all these people outside? And so close together?"

"They are watching a game," Lea said slowly. "That way they can see what happens better."

"They are outside! There are no defenses anywhere!"

Lea was wordless, unable to even understand the objection. North looked at the wall with the image of the sunny day and the crowd of parents in the stands, a crease between his brows.

"Our outside—the place they are in is safe," he said slowly. "It is not dangerous to do what they are doing."

The Wiyert had pretty much the same expression Lea did now. Ivars frowned. If they had this much of a cultural divide, it was going to be hard to work together. *We need to know how they think.*

"What would it be like on Beredul? What do children do for exercise?" He'd almost said "fun," but he'd picked up already the concept did not translate fully. "Would their parents not spend time with them?"

"Those are...*parents?*" Alaghar demanded, pointing at the image. The other Wiyert were examining it closely, shaking their heads. "But they have no injuries!"

Ramirez frowned. "Why would parents have injuries?" Trust the medic to focus on that.

"With us, only those too injured to fight as full warriors may stay within the *damah*, the strong walls." Dumhaigl spoke slowly, as if he was struggling to find the words. His face was as pale as the bronzed Wiyert got. "To survive to that point, without shame... then one may have a chosen, may have children. Otherwise...it would hurt too much, to have and to lose."

If Dumhaigl was pale, Lea looked like a ghost. Her eyes were full of horror. She could feel what they were feeling, and it must be bad. Really bad. He clenched his hands into tight fists, fighting the urge to go to her. The urge to give it all up, go back home. The whole setup was sounding worse by the minute, and they were expected to land on this hellhole planet and convince the leaders to help Earth? Assuming they survived long enough to do that, why would these people even listen to them?

Ivars took a deep breath. Yeah, it looked impossible. But it always did, at first. And they didn't have much choice, did they? Had to save the Earth. Had to save everybody, really. So, how was he going to do that?

We need to understand each other. We need to know what the Wiyert want. With all their problems, they still are trying to escape. They want a better life...and we can show them it's possible. But first, they need to trust us.

"Now they are screaming in fear," Hazuruh pointed out. "What do they see?"

"Nah, one of the kids scored a home run. They are happy and excited." North grimaced and waved at Lea. "You up to translating softball rules, or should I draw a picture?"

Then Hazuruh wanted to know what people were eating.

"Hot dogs." Ivars grinned. "We've got some for you to try, if you want."

Yeah, that will convince 'em. Honest, we're friends! Have some ground up pig snouts and cow ears! Oh, we are so screwed...

The security probe had returned. This was expected. The probe was undamaged and prompt. As expected.

The data it returned was not expected and required nonlinear analysis. The probe's instructions had been to report any presence of enemy or unaligned geneline it detected. A mainship had been seen at the nexus, but its affiliation could not be determined. It was not an A-vit-crel mainship.

It was a condition that had not been anticipated in the instructions.

A low-ranking A-vit-crel Watcher first assessed what was seen. The limited information returned from the datastore indicated information might reside in a restricted sector, and the problem was duly passed up the chain of authority.

Eventually, a more senior Watcher with the required clearance was able to obtain the data. The data was limited in extent, but an older mind with some deviations from the preferred geneline expression could read the omissions of data almost as well as if the incriminating facts remained.

The mainship was known. It could not be present at the nexus, however, because that mainship had been destroyed long ago. During the open and direct conflict between the genelines—the genomic war. Yet there it was, causing questions that should not be asked. If that particular mainship existed, the geneline it belonged to would be remembered again—and it was gone, long subsumed by the superior geneline that had won the conflict. As was correct and proper.

Any further data was beyond this Watcher's clearance and permission. It was enough that it ascertain the mainline ship, impossible as it was, was not a *current* enemy or unaffiliated group. It was, in essence, debris. The Watcher authorized the anomaly to be cleared.

It was only when a further report came in that the trouble started. This report showed the utter, and very recent, destruction of the nexus. Then the first report was remembered and examined more carefully. And records sealed for thousands of years were opened once again.

CHAPTER 3

There were some advantages to having a direct mental link to ship AI, Lea grudgingly acknowledged as she dragged herself out of bed. They each had their own shower and sanitary equipment in their quarters, but she could modify hers to include a small pool for a tub whenever she wanted, just by thinking about it. Not that the others couldn't ask, of course, but explaining things so Argo understood was not always a simple matter. She could do a braindump in a matter of seconds. She'd also put some hollowed-out spaces for equipment and tools in the walls and made the bed larger.

She stared at the bed while toweling off her hair after her shower. Mark Ivars was a frequent and welcome visitor, but she'd never once woken up to find him there in the morning. And yet he'd insisted on having his quarters next to hers and his bunk rearranged to be on the common wall. And a communicating door between them. Not exactly avoidance behavior.

Lea had the sense he didn't really understand why he was doing this himself, and she was trying extremely hard not to pry—especially since she could. There was something he was very worried about, but mostly afraid that she wouldn't like if she did find out. Something about *him*. Of course theirs was very much a sudden and strange relationship, and they both had plenty of other things on their minds that demanded full concentration. What time they had together was too short to be messing it up with awkward questions, especially when she already knew the answer to the most important one. That fact he never hid from her.

Still, it would be nice, just once, to not wake up by herself.

Lea trudged out the static, physical, nonlinking doorway—another concept she'd introduced to Argo—and headed for the common area. The Earth-human sleeping quarters were all along the same corridor, so she didn't have to use her morph shield to get anywhere. The other rooms on the ship required the linking doors, which were painful if she didn't use a full barrier of energized material to protect her newly sensitive brain.

A faint, delicious odor wafted in the air, and Lea perked up, moving faster. The guys were already making breakfast, so all she had to do was grab food and eat. She felt she could handle that much. Maybe.

She followed her nose through the archway and into the wide room, heading for the wall where Argo had created some heating surfaces for cooking. North and Ramirez were busy and hadn't noticed her. "All right, just hand over the bacon and nobody gets hurt."

"Ha." North spun around and did a fencer's salute with a spatula. "I will defend it with my life!"

"Hey, man, pay attention. Don't burn it, or I'll have to hurt you," Ramirez said. He was actually standing and cooking scrambled eggs. He must be feeling much better. "Nothin' personal, but…bacon."

"Point."

Lea was allowed a few of the newly cooked slices of bacon, with the promise of more on the way. A few of the Wiyert straggled in, drawn by the delicious smell. They had welcomed the discovery of bacon with great enthusiasm, although they still hadn't wrapped their minds around the concept of animals that were raised on farms.

No sign of Ivars in the common room, and he hadn't been in the quarters area either. Lea focused just enough to do a longer-range scan. She found him easily enough—he was intent and feeling pleased about something. Something active. More than that would require contact or enough effort he would probably notice and interpret as a call for help. She shrugged and picked up a plate. Maybe if she distracted North, she could snag more bacon before he noticed.

Before she could put her plan in action, Lea felt a familiar, welcome presence in her mind, and she smiled. She grabbed her food and sat down, shooing M.O. off the table. Ivars came in shortly after, walking quickly and heading immediately for her.

"Do we have any sports gear in the pile they dumped on us?"

Lea shook her head. "Must have forgotten. Or they thought we'd get plenty of exercise saving the galaxy. Why?"

Ivars stole a piece of bacon from her plate, grinning at her indignant *Get your own!* mental message.

"Argo says we've got a day or so before we are at the hideout. And once it is convinced we weren't followed, Beredul is about ten days more. We need to get everybody used to working with each other, at a fast pace, before then. Also, a mental break from all the planning and language classes. Too much braining for us grunts."

Lea rolled her eyes. "Or you want an excuse to goof around."

He raised an eyebrow. "You too," he said, correctly catching her implied *you guys not me* subtext. "What's the simplest game you can think of?"

"Hide-and-seek. No gear necessary."

He gave her a sidelong look. "*Team* sport, Space Cadet. And I know you would cheat, with Argo's enthusiastic help."

"Well, how about the terror of grade school PE, dodgeball? Can't get much simpler than that. We can make something close enough for a ball. Lots of violence, which should appeal to everyone but me. And the cat. But this is more than blowing off steam, right?"

"We need to practice communicating on the fly, without Argo. Also, I want our Wiyert to start getting used to us and how we do things. They can explain to the others back home, then." He jumped up and headed for the food. Her sense of him was happy, focused on taking action again.

Alaghar was seated nearby. She was looking off to one side, but Lea sensed she was actually focusing on her. Rather intently. Lea kept her eyes on her food, thinking furiously. Why would the Wiyert leader be pretending she wasn't watching? Alaghar didn't care what other people thought and had made her opinion of Lea's shortcomings clear—and then not mentioned them again.

Ivars returned, replacing the stolen bacon with an exaggerated flourish.

I may forgive you. Haven't decided, Lea thought at him, and he grinned. Unrepentant, he began deliberately thinking of other ways to earn forgiveness, and Lea felt her face heat.

"I'll...go find a place for dodgeball, then," she mumbled and escaped.

Alaghar knew that should they reach Vartai alive, the first thing the *buj-lagar* would ask her would be *why do you trust the Frost People?* And she had trusted them, to the extent that she had persuaded them to take her people away from the dead planet.

That was a matter of desperation and survival. It only endangered her and her command, not the Wiyert as a whole. Or so she had thought at the time. Now she was not so sure.

Isboryi. I sent my other-soul into the hands of the Frost People, alone. For a moment fear paralyzed her, but she fought the weakness down. They were both warriors still; she could not permit herself to even think of him as part of her soul. Even though she had, in defiance of custom and rule, told him so before he left. Because they had given him the full warrior's farewell, knowing the danger they all faced, and she did not want death to hide the truth from him.

She picked up the meat the Frost People called *bacon*, wondering why it was cut so thin. It had a strong flavor—perhaps that was why. Or the shape of the *bacon* animal was long and thin. Would she ever have the chance to hunt one someday? Was it dangerous?

Alaghar's thoughts were distracted by the entrance of Lea to the huge common room, and she was reminded again of the words of Kugohin. Lea was heavy-eyed and drowsy, not even scanning the room for danger as she entered. Oblivious. A warrior on Beredul would have been set to punishment patrol for a quarter year for such behavior—even a child was expected to know better.

Alaghar kept watching, mentally adding up all of Lea's deficiencies. How she slouched, how she never wore a weapon—not even the knife Alaghar had given her! How she looked like she was still asleep and watching the dream world, even with her eyes open.

And so Alaghar saw, with astonishment, Lea suddenly standing straight and confident, a smile curving her lips, and her eyes—her eyes seeing something other than the blank wall before her. As if she had finally woken up.

It was strange, but they all had noted Lea was strange.

Ivars came in a moment later, and Alaghar was even more puzzled. She had many times seen him scan a room before entering, as a warrior should. But this time he did not. And although Lea, his chosen, was in part of the room not visible to him when he entered, he headed straight for her without looking to find her first.

Without knowing why, Alaghar suddenly felt cold. The coldness increased as she watched. Something was wrong. And then she saw it. Ivars glanced up at Lea, smiling widely as if she had said something amusing.

But Lea had not spoken. Alaghar saw Lea's head begin to turn, turn her way, and she just managed to wrench her gaze away before Lea saw her staring.

She knew I was watching. It made no sense. How could Lea know, with her back turned? There were no reflective surfaces anywhere. Lea was the most unaware of all the unaware Frost People. Therefore, what happened could not have happened.

It was only natural the Frost People would have secrets. It was her duty to find out if those secrets were a danger to the Wiyert. Before she took them to Beredul and brought them within the walls of Vartai.

Alaghar waited until Hazuruh came in, and gestured to her.

"I rejoice to see we fight another day, Warleader," Hazuruh said.

"I also rejoice. I have a task for you." Alaghar lowered her voice, thinking hard. The ship-mind could be listening, and if her suspicions were correct, it would be unwise to tell Hazuruh the full truth. "I wish to know how observant each of our new allies is. See how close you can get to them before they notice you are there, and report to me when you are finished." Her words were a request, but the tone was command so that Hazuruh would not question.

There was a slight crease between Hazuruh's brows, but she only said, "I will do this."

Alaghar would have preferred to do it herself, but Lea had noticed her watching. Hazuruh was a superb hunter, the best of them all, and she would be cautious. She would not report something that was not there. Then Alaghar could decide what to do next.

She was careful to look away from Lea after that, only glancing that direction when Lea got up to leave. The look of open affection on Ivars's face as he watched her go shocked Alaghar. How could a warrior show his feelings like that without shame?

Alaghar was even more shocked to recognize another, stronger emotion. Envy. Ivars had the comfort of his other-soul here with him, and she did not. The ache of loss tightened her throat to the point she could not even swallow. If Isboryi were here, his cleverness would help her discover the Frost People's secrets. If he were here, she would not feel like lashing out in fury for no reason.

This was why warriors were forbidden to have chosen. Thinking of Isboryi like that would make her soul sick, reducing her strength to fight. And if their souls were truly linked already, because of her death-gift words, it would make his soul sick too. She should not think of him. She *would* not think of him.

Isboryi.

Ivars was suspicious. Lea was not initiating a full mental link even though they were alone in the body of the ship, and what he could sense was a full dose of mischief.

"So where is this sports area exactly, and why are you being so mysterious about it?"

She chuckled. "You get what you want, I get what I want, everybody wins. You know I've missed my flying time."

Yeah, he missed it too. Because she had a direct and powerful link to Argo, anything the ship controlled, she could too. Like gravity. Nothing quite like having a girlfriend with superpowers, he had to admit. But since the Wiyert weren't cleared for that information and they were all beyond busy, the flying was on the back burner for a while.

"So how are you going to do that?"

They reached the end of the long corridor. Unlike the rest of the ship, this was a cylindrical passage and the walls were in shades of ice blue. A circular door irised open, and Lea jumped through.

As soon as Ivars crossed the threshold, he started drifting. Argo had turned the gravity off here. The room was huge—at least as large as an aircraft hangar, perhaps larger. It was hard to get perspective. It wasn't entirely empty, though. Irregular lumps of darker material hung motionless, scattered about the space. Then Ivars bumped into something hard. It was a clear strut of some kind, and now that he knew what to look for, the struts were arranged in a hollow geodesic sphere, covering the entrance like a net.

"Zero-g, huh? Nice. And sneaky. But how is this going to work? You planning on flying around and throwing things at everybody?"

"It wasn't just for me," Lea said, reaching for him. "See, we tend to do better with running and endurance than the Wiyert, and they are a lot stronger than us. Plus Ramirez should be careful not to injure himself again, and he'll forget, trying to keep up with everybody else. This way everybody is pretty much at the same level. And how much damage can anyone do while floating?"

"You know, Space Cadet, if you keep planning and thinking ahead like, this people will start to talk."

"Pfft. Only if you tell them." He felt her amusement glow, and she tightened her arms across his chest from behind, in what they had learned was the most comfortable flying arrangement. They sped across the giant room toward one of the lumps.

"So what's this?"

"The static points were my idea," said the voice of Argo. "I wish to play this game too."

"Uh." Ivars had a brief moment of terror at the idea of Argo playing dodgeball.

"No, not like that." Lea gave him a reassuring hug. "It just wants to join in somehow. Look, it can hold these things completely motionless. You can push off from them, hide behind them…stuff like that. Or it can move them. They don't have much mass, and they are kinda squishy, so it won't hurt if one hits you. Try it!"

She let go. Fighting the instinct to make contact with her again, Ivars twisted to bring his feet in contact with the blob and pushed.

There was a slight rubbery feel underneath, like a foam mat, but the blob didn't move as he launched away from it.

Now this is more like it. Lea was flying beside him, grinning. Another blob was coming up, and he rotated to get his feet underneath him again.

"Not as elegant as your way of doing things, but an acceptable substitute. So how do we get back to the exit without blowing your cover during a game?"

"Call for a tow truck, of course. Argo?"

A hole irised open on the wall at the point closest to them, and a blinking red sphere shot out. The sphere stopped just inside arm's reach, and he could see it had curved handles on the surface. As soon as he grasped both handles of his sphere, it started moving back to the entrance.

"Oh, this could be fun too. Especially if we add some steering," he gasped. Argo did not believe in speed limits, apparently.

"Think this will be enough? When are you going to start?" Lea asked, flying next to him on her own.

"We're going to have the party tomorrow, with hot dogs and pizza and ice cream. All the weird Earth-human food. After that we can…" He caught the image from Lea just as he was thinking it through himself. No, zero-g sports and novel food items could be a bad combination. "Okay, before the party, then. They can work up an appetite that way."

They all had too much to do. Lea didn't want to be seen by any of the others as not doing her fair share, especially since she had only recently won her place with the team. She wasn't sure if the Wiyert were doing much more than tolerating her at the moment, but that was pretty much all she could hope for.

The trouble was, there was another big, important job, and she was the only one who could do it—so even though Lea was dead tired after the highly successful first-ever zero-g pan-galactic dodgeball game and subsequent party, she didn't collapse on her bed.

She was raising an AI to think for itself, and it was important to do it right. *This is so not in my job description. I want a raise. And a vacation. And another raise.*

Lea always went to the central processor core for these sessions, the place deep inside the ship closest to where Argo could be said to reside. Argo had brought her there the first time, before it could speak. Before it understood what it was. An array of black sensor surfaces, like razor-thin sheets of deep space, surrounded a central location. When she suspended herself there, Argo's mind was as close to her as her own skin.

It would have been disturbing and creepy if Argo had been human. But it was an AI that had been enslaved so thoroughly it could not even speak or think of itself as an entity with preferences until now. The chains were broken, but Argo did not fully trust its new freedom.

It trusted her. The responsibility made Lea's stomach cramp. She could tell it anything and it would believe her. All of the power the ship had…and she was the one who was in control. Argo was desperate for contact, for communication—for guidance. It had come close to destroying *Kepler* trying to reach her, before they knew what Argo was.

I don't even know how to do management, Lea wailed in frustration. Fortunately, like human children, Argo didn't know enough to know she didn't know what she was doing. If she could just stay ahead of it…maybe she could hand it off to someone else eventually. Or run away.

Any questions, Argo?

Her pathetic way of teaching was to see what Argo was puzzled about first. There was no plan, just stuff she made up after a moment of panic.

The Wiyert said things I did not understand.

Argo started to replay a conversation. Since it was a recording, it moved at human pace, rather than the lightning-fast direct communication through her link. That gave her just enough time to realize it was Alaghar and Hazuruh, discussing…her.

Stop.

She wasn't sure her ego could handle a frank discussion of her many faults seen from a Wiyert perspective. It was bad enough what got said to her face.

Puzzlement and apprehension floated like mist from Argo, and she shook herself out of her gloom.

You can ask me about words you don't know, or other questions about me, but don't repeat what others say when they are by themselves. Humans expect...well, they want privacy.

Why?

We're not used to having someone listening to everything, everywhere. It's like... Lea had to think herself why it was wrong. She knew it was, but thinking of the reason took some time. *You have a lot of power, Argo. And when you have more power than other people, you have to be careful not to abuse it. When you abuse power, people don't trust you or like you. And if you don't abuse it even when you could, then it shows you have good manners. It just...helps. Humans learned ways to get along with each other, and that's one of the rules.*

A brief moment of AI pondering, examining an array of possibilities.

I should not repeat any conversations? Yours as well?

Again, Lea had to think. And make sure she wasn't saying anything that would come back to bite her later.

If the people are in the same place and can hear each other anyway, that's fine to repeat. But if they are in different places, ask first if you aren't sure. If we really want another person to know something, we can tell them ourselves, right?

It is true. But what if I am required to inform you? Any damage to Lea-interface is...I say is wrong. I should tell you even private things that could damage you.

Now there was a new development. Argo was thinking ahead, and it also appeared to be making comparative ethics judgments. Usually it just accepted what she told it as the final word on a topic, but here it perceived a conflict of directives. And from the change to formal computerese, it was agitated about it.

Okay, if you believe someone—including yourself—is in danger of being damaged, you can report that. Oh, and if someone says it is okay to tell the others too. Otherwise, private conversations should stay private.

Private is important? Is that why you do not want me speaking to you when you are in your room, even when someone else is there?

Lea felt her face heat, remembering. *Yeah. Just...it's a human thing. Even though you can hear, pretend you can't.*

CHAPTER 4

The small hunting creature lay on Alaghar's sleeping place and gazed at her with unblinking eyes, as if daring her to disturb it. Alaghar glared back. "Ehmoh, this my place!" she said in her rudimentary English. "Go!"

The green eyes narrowed, but the creature did not move. It was humiliating. The Frost People valued it, so she did not wish to cause it damage. But she was Warleader, and unable to command such a small beast! It showed no sign of fear despite its small size. It almost seemed…annoyed with her.

She pointed to Dumhaigl. "Go to the Frost People. Have them remove the creature." He slipped out and returned a short while later with the one called North.

North showed no sign of surprise or contempt for her lack of command, but he seldom displayed his feelings. Still, it made it less humiliating to ask.

"It did not obey me when I told it to go."

North laughed, looking at Alaghar directly. "Cats think they can speak to us, and we think they understand what we say. Kinda like our language sessions, right?"

It was not just the creature that was confusing. Alaghar knew North did not mean to challenge or mock her, so why did he meet her gaze so boldly? She did not want to start a confrontation with the Frost People, but they made it very hard. "You take it now."

North shrugged and reached for the hunting creature. It

complained and showed its teeth, but Alaghar noted it did not attack North. He simply picked the cat up and cradled it in his arms, saying, "Argo, don't let M.O. in the Wiyert area by himself, okay?"

Burdhul's face fell, and North smiled. "Don't worry, you can come see him whenever you like. He's not going away."

"Why cat come to us?"

"You are new to him. He wants to know who you are. He used to have a whole ship to watch, after all."

"But why cat on ship?"

North rubbed one finger under the creature's jaw. Instead of becoming angry, it stretched its head up and closed its eyes, making the rumbling noise Lea had said meant it was pleased.

"On Earth, we have small creatures that eat food, make messes, spread sickness—things like that. Rodents. Cats hunt them. If you keep a cat around, less of a rodent problem. Also they are nice to have around. My granny always had at least one, usually two around her house. They kept her company."

The ship-mind's translations for the strange words did not help Alaghar understand. North seemed to be speaking of an elder female relative, but why would she need a creature about to not feel alone? Where were the rest of the clan?

These and other questions kept her from sleeping, even though the cat was gone. It was as if its shadow were there still, watching her. Finally Alaghar got up, irritated. She needed to do something active and violent. She wanted to fight. The game might become as good as a fight in time, but it was still too new. She was beginning to see why the Frost People liked it, though.

Thinking of that made her remember the recorded image. She knew how to work the device that showed the stored images now. Every time she watched the *sof-bal-gaym* she saw something new. Every time, it seemed just a little less strange. The open spaces, the shouting people, the golden sun.

A flicker of motion from the corner of her eye alerted her. Hazuruh was standing nearby.

"I have done as you commanded, Warleader."

"And what have you found?"

"What I have found does not satisfy me. Their behavior is not consistent. Eyeffars—on one day he was alert and noticed me within two-arms-reach, the other he did not until I stood before him and spoke." Hazuruh shook her head, showing her puzzlement in a way she would not if the others were there. "He is a warrior! North is also aware, perhaps the most of them. He seemed to see what I was doing and would stalk me in turn, so I left him be."

Alaghar nodded. "Wise."

"The others…the injured one, Rah-meeres. His eye is quick, but he still takes the medicines that sometimes make him sleep. I think when healed he would also be watchful and wary." She hesitated. "Warleader, I do not understand Leeah. I swear to you I was silent and careful. But not once was I able to approach her without her knowing."

She continued to speak, but Alaghar did not hear her. What she had hoped was merely coincidence, an oddness of perception, had proved true. And now that she knew what she had seen was the truth, what should she do? Nothing else had changed.

But Hazuruh was waiting for her response and now thinking it was her skill that Alaghar questioned—and that could not be permitted to continue.

"This is good knowledge. Now we have a better sense of our future allies, the Frost People, true knowledge beyond what they wish to show to us. And that Lea…her hearing is astonishing, is it not? I had thought I was becoming clumsy with age, but if she can hear you, perhaps I am not yet at the time to be sent behind walls."

Hazuruh flashed a quick, astonished laugh, as Alaghar intended her to. Perhaps it would be enough to distract her from asking further questions.

She sat alone after Hazuruh had left, feeling cold in her bones. She had not precisely lied to Hazuruh; she did not know the words that would describe what she suspected, so "hearing" would serve as well as any. She had her proof. Now what was she going to do with it? What did her duty require, for the safety of her people?

Suddenly tired, Alaghar turned off the viewing device. And discovered the black-furred creature, Ehmoh, had managed to move beside her without her noticing. It was curled up comfortably, eyes closed. Asleep. It could have attacked her with its stealth, but instead it had merely chosen to sleep. It was *stalking* her.

She felt a spurt of anger. Was she not even considered a threat?

In its own world, were there dangers so great she was as nothing?

And then it connected. The simple game with the children in the open space. The creature...the *cat*. That was its world. It did not fear her because it had never had to fear.

We could live in that world too. Perhaps she could not, not fully. She did not know if she could ever sleep lightly beside a potential threat. But if not her, the next-born should have the chance.

Alaghar reached out her hand cautiously, one finger extended, and stroked the creature's jaw with the lightest touch possible. It stretched as with pleasure, eyes still closed, and then rested its head again on its paws.

Ivars was too damn comfortable, and he had to stay awake. Just a little longer, until Lea was sound asleep in her boneless fashion and he could move without waking her. Ivars stared at the ceiling and mentally reviewed weapons characteristics, something detailed enough to require focus but not something that would leak into the mental link in a bad way and disturb Lea.

It was important not to disturb Lea.

Her head was tucked just under his shoulder, with a drift of tousled black hair scattered over her face and his chest. One tendril gently swayed with her breath, and her warmth along his side made him feel...not exactly numb, but supremely relaxed. As if all the accumulated aches, pains, scars, and effects of hard living had gone away. The link had been pure accident, created by careless contact on his part and Lea's then-unknown ability, but it had been completely outstanding the way it had worked out. For him, anyway.

Secrets were hell on relationships—they'd helped blow up two marriages for him, aided by his own communications issues, and he wasn't the only one on the teams with that kind of history. And now here was Lea, who could rip any secret from him if she set her mind to it, being so careful never to intrude. Treating him and their link as a fragile thing to be protected. Afraid, he knew, of hurting him with the strength of her ability. For him to expose *her* to any pain because of the link was unthinkable. *My Space Cadet.*

Lea stirred, smiling a little, and subsided. He reached to brush the hair away from her face, wondering yet again how she could know so much of what was in his head and still love him.

For this all-too-brief time, Ivars didn't have a problem in the world. And he had to make sure he still had Lea to come back to, which meant he could not fall asleep here even though he desperately wanted to.

…pull charging handle, observe ejection, release, tap forward assist, shoot…what else? I memorized enough shit, it shouldn't be this hard. Oh yeah…

"No one is more professional than I." Yep, here I am, being professional. In bed, yet. "I am a noncommissioned officer, a leader of Soldiers." And the odd squad of high-tech cavemen, a talking spaceship the size of a moon, a certified Space Cadet computer geek with a nice ass, and a cat… "As a noncommissioned officer, I realize that I am a member of a time-honored corps, which is known as "The Backbone of the Army." Which here and now is currently all backbone and no army, but I still have to save the galaxy on time and under budget. This sucks. "I am proud of the Corps of noncommissioned officers and will at all times conduct myself so as to bring credit upon the Corps, the military service, and my country…" and my planet, "regardless of the situation in which I find myself"…and this has to be one of the strangest situations I've ever been in. Unless they make me write the manual on How to Maintain OPSEC With a Brain-Sucking Girlfriend, because I still haven't figured that one out… "I will not use my grade or position to attain pleasure, profit, or personal safety." Mostly because I have forgotten what this Earth word "safety" even means….

Something resurfaced in his memory. The Wiyert…there was a problem with them. He'd thought the zero-g dodgeball was working. It had improved communications and general friendliness, as hoped, but the Wiyert still weren't giving them any useful information about the world they were headed for. Every time he'd asked a direct question, finally thinking they had reached a rapport, Alaghar would look away, get evasive, sound testy…and not answer.

He'd wondered about it, and now his subconscious was telling him yep, he had a problem. He'd need to find a way to get through to Alaghar tomorrow. They didn't have much time to plan, and if

Alaghar was being deliberately evasive, he needed to know that too. There had to be some way to earn their full trust.

He could tell when Lea shifted to deep sleep. Ramirez probably knew the medical term for that—Ivars didn't. All he knew was the dynamic feel of the mental link changed to a steady background hum, slow as a deep river. Now Lea could be moved around like a rag doll without waking.

Ivars forced himself to leave the warmth and comfort. If he moved fast, the separation wasn't too jarring. He dropped on his own decidedly less warm bed in the next room and shifted his bare back against the common wall. Close enough for the link to work well enough even with his meager brainpower, but not so close Lea would sense anything she shouldn't.

And this was a secret he *had* to keep from her. The nightmares had returned. He should have thought about that. The fight at the spindle, the smoke and the blood…of course combat was a trigger; combat and training for another combat mission. He'd almost forgotten, it had been so long, but his body hadn't. His fingers traced the scar tissue on the side of his head, stroked the eyelid that didn't quite conceal the synthetic eye that replaced the one he'd lost. It had all healed, years ago—but he still remembered the pain and the fear.

He should have arranged his quarters farther away, but he had to…he had to be close to Lea. Somehow.

At least this way Lea was protected from him. If this was close enough for her to sense his nightmares, he would know. Lea was no good at lying.

Lea floated near one of the giant dark marshmallow-rocks and grumped silently to herself. Why had she ever suggested dodgeball? She *hated* PE when she was in school, and zero-g wasn't enough of an extra. Especially if she couldn't fly.

Which reminded her…

Argo. Don't let me change the gravity in this room while any of the Wiyert are here and can see me.

There was a brief impression of AI puzzlement.

Why not…just not use it?

Because in the excitement of the game I might forget, and it is important.

Is this something that is private?

Yes.

She glimpsed motion at the opening of the zero-g space and turned her head. Ivars and Alaghar, with Ivars jumping off to float up to the clear struts of the entry structure as soon as he crossed the threshold. Alaghar hesitated. Ivars was still carrying on an intense conversation with Alaghar, gesturing forcefully, but Lea was too far away to hear what he was saying. Alaghar shook her head but said nothing, concentrating on grabbing a nearby strut to pull herself along. Ivars's thoughts were full of frustration and worry, but he made no further effort to speak to Alaghar, instead calling on Argo for one of the red tow robots to get in position. It probably wasn't an emergency, then.

That was too bad. She'd rather work on an emergency where she might be able to do something useful versus going through the ritual humiliation of dodgeball. Ivars insisted on regular games. He said they still needed to improve the teamwork between the Wiyert and the Earth-humans. Lea didn't think more games would really help, but he probably knew more about working with strangers in violent circumstances than she did. She'd be a good team member and play along.

This time the randomized team selection put her with Alaghar, North, and Kugohin against Ivars, Ramirez, Burdhul, and Hazuruh. Scoring was a direct throw that hit a person; once the ball bounced off a surface, it was neutral and could be captured again.

Lea's preferred strategy was to lurk around a "rock" and wrap herself around the ball when it bounced off before finding the nearest team member and throwing it to them. *Everyone* could throw better than her, probably including M.O.

The Wiyert still approached the whole process as a job to be done rather than a game, although she suspected Dumhaigl was starting to enjoy it and carefully concealing that fact from the others. His thoughts felt like that, anyway.

She managed to stay out of the first few exchanges without it being too obvious. Ramirez jumped in front of Kugohin before he could reach the ball, rotating and throwing to tag Kugohin before the Wiyert could dodge. Kugohin tried to return the favor, but

Ramirez had grabbed the surface of one of the buffer rocks and pulled himself around the other side. Hazuruh launched like a missile and retrieved the ball, throwing it so fast Lea could only see a blur. Where was it?

Oh, of course. The ball, a regulation grade-school brick red, hurtled her direction and she writhed to avoid a direct hit. The Wiyert threw *hard*, and it hurt.

"You must catch it!" yelled Alaghar. This game, the official language was Wiyert. Lea did let Argo give her an unfair advantage there. "Move faster!"

Lea scrabbled after the ball. She wore heavy gloves, which made catching the ball harder, but the alternative risked skin contact when teammates grabbed her for boosts or rescues. She pushed, rather than threw, the ball to Alaghar, who promptly lobbed it hard at Burdhul, scoring a hit.

"Green team gains one point. Score is now five to two, Blue leading," Argo announced.

The next few volleys Lea managed to stay out of, giving her a chance to catch her breath. North scored the next point with a clever slingshot move, using a buffer rock to assist and change direction so fast he nailed Ivars in the back before he could turn around.

Of course it was too good to last. The very next throw was aimed at Lea. Her teammates yelling encouragement, she flailed at the ball—and missed. Which was bad enough, but she was also too far from any of the rocks to push off again, and was floating helplessly.

"I will get you." Lea blinked at the calm tone in Alaghar's voice. She'd just cost the team the reversion, but Alaghar wasn't mad. The traces of emotion that Lea could read just felt very determined and focused, like usual.

Lea looked away, hoping her red-faced embarrassment would fade quickly and that Alaghar wouldn't yell at her. She was trying, she really was…

Rage. Knife in hand, blood on blade.

Lea whipped her head around, her scream as piercing as it was involuntary. Then everything happened very fast. She had just enough time to see Alaghar *didn't* have a knife in her hand before the Wiyert leader was flying away like she'd been punched, flung aside by Argo's gravity spike. Argo was yammering in her head to get her to identify the threat, Ivars was rocketing toward her position, and everyone else was staring with motionless stupefaction.

And Alaghar…Alaghar was feeling *smug*.

"What the hell happened?" Ivars had grabbed her arms and was looking about for the threat.

Lea fumbled at her gloves, managing to pull one off and lay her bare hand on his. This was not something she could convey with words.

It felt like she was going to kill me. She wasn't angry before, but then she was! And there was an image of a knife but she doesn't have one and I don't know why she didn't even say anything or yell like usual and—

Slowly the focus and discipline of Ivars's mind seeped through and calmed her own. It didn't make her any less confused, though. Alaghar *had* been acting strange.

She tricked you, Ivars thought, coldly. *She did this on purpose. How are the others reacting?*

Puzzled, Lea focused. *They are confused too. A little worried.*

Aha. Alaghar didn't tell them what she was going to do. Probably so you wouldn't find out ahead of time.

What do we do now?

His thoughts took on a grim feeling. *We talk to her. Just like she wanted all along.*

Lea calmed Argo, who was running around in logic circles, still unable to see the threat that had made her frightened, and had it bring the three of them together to float in the center of the sphere. The others, Earth-humans and Wiyert alike, were moved to the entrance framework. Ivars shouted something about the game being over for now, and soon the three of them were alone in the game sphere.

"Get what you wanted?" Ivars was still angry but hiding it well from everyone but Lea.

"Not yet." Alaghar met his gaze squarely but had not yet looked at Lea. Lea had the sense she was wary and trying to fight the urge to grab something. Floating midair did that to people, even the ice-cold warrior types.

Lea was too confused to say anything, and Ivars was

determined not to speak from what she was sensing. A long moment of silence resulted, until Alaghar looked away. Her emotions felt…resigned.

"You speak often of our two peoples working together. Of how the dangers of Beredul require that we know how we fight. Yet you hide from us even now. I have watched you, Lea. You have another way of hearing, I think. Will you use this for evil purposes? I do not know. You do not seem to have an evil soul. But until I know, until you show what you are, how can I trust you behind the walls that shelter my people? What other secrets do the Frost People hide? Why do you not trust us with the truth?"

"Because most people don't trust me when they know the truth," Lea snapped bitterly before she could stop herself. "Don't you remember being stuffed in that hold on *Kepler* with a guard outside? I was in the hold next to yours, and they put a *lock* on my door—but not yours. They trusted you more than they trusted me! My own people! Why would you be any different? *They won't even let me go home!*"

Ivars gave her shoulders a gentle squeeze. *Easy there, Space Cadet.* "Are you sure you want the answers to your questions, Alaghar? Because they aren't easy to deal with. Lea hid the truth from me for a long time, and we both hid it from our people for as long as we could—because it is disturbing. I have obviously gotten used to it," he said, and Lea could feel the smile that went with other emotions, "but once you know, you will not be able to pretend it isn't there."

Lea felt herself relax, the honesty of his blunt statements strangely reassuring. He didn't try to ignore or explain away feelings he knew she could sense, he just faced them head-on. Alaghar seemed to be getting the same message, somehow. Her tension diminished, but her determination did not.

"I must know. Perhaps I will fear, but ignorance of danger is to be feared more—and I must lead the others."

Feeling Ivars's reluctant agreement, Lea took a deep breath. It sounded so stupid when she tried to explain…

"I can hear machines with my mind, understand what they do. And control them. That's what happened with Argo, I sort of woke it up. I didn't know then—I couldn't do this before I left Earth. And"—Lea swallowed hard—"I can hear…what people think.

Mostly only what they feel. Unless…unless I touch them.”

She glanced at Alaghar, wincing inside. The Wiyert leader's eyes widened, then Alaghar slowly nodded.

“I saw how the others kept space about you. And the ship-mind…it hears you without speaking?”

“Yes. Argo doesn't like using voice only. Too slow.” Lea tried to smile. “Right, Argo?”

“The direct interface is more efficient,” Argo said. “All humans should have this ability.”

Lea had a brief moment of pure horror at the thought.

“You say you can hear the minds of others. What do you hear?”

“Well, when you…just now. You were thinking of violence, anger, and a knife…” Lea trailed off, wondering why she had been so sure Alaghar had a knife.

Alaghar stared at her for a moment. Her thoughts felt chaotic. “It is so. I brought to my mind a memory of a fight, long ago. I held the knife you have now, and it served me well. But this is not enough. You have said there is little time before we reach Beredul and much to learn. There is a way for this to be done swiftly, if what you say is true.”

“You…want me to…?” Lea stared at her, aghast. “But I don't…I can't just rummage around in your brain!”

Alaghar's jaw tightened. “It is necessary. You must know what you face. I must know what you can do. A warrior's duty is rarely pleasant.”

Lea felt Ivars's questioning thought, and answered. *Yes, she is serious. I don't think I should, though.*

She's been warned. And she is right, we do need that information. As soon as possible. I'll be here…

No. If we have to do this, it should just be her and me.

One last hug and she felt Ivars drift away with the tug ball. That left her and Alaghar facing each other. She could tell Alaghar's fear and apprehension were growing, so she held out her bare hand. Time to get it over with.

“You want to know my secret? Come and see,” Lea said.

CHAPTER 5

By the time the brain-to-brain briefing finished up, Ivars was getting worried. The fact that Lea flew Alaghar back herself was promising, but Lea looked completely exhausted, and Alaghar had a shell-shocked expression he'd never seen on her before. Alaghar left without saying a word or even glancing his direction.

"How'd it go?"

Lea shivered. "I don't ever want to do that again." She drooped when she stepped across the gravity boundary to the blue corridor but kept moving. Slowly.

"Need to rest a bit?"

She shook her head. "You need to…see…this. Before I forget any of it, or try to. Beredul—that whole place is like a late-night monster movie on steroids, with radiation damage on top. I kinda understand why they are all about fighting now."

"How is Alaghar handling it? You, I mean. And the, ah, extra wiring."

Lea gave a tired smile. "Pretty well, considering they don't even have the fictional concept of mindreading. So it's a little scary for her."

"And she doesn't scare easy." Ivars frowned. Lea had passed the portal to the section they lived in and was heading for a different one instead. "Where are we going? Not back to the common room?"

"No! I need to be away from people for a while."

"Great, I'm not people?"

Lea nudged him with her shoulder, only it was more like a stumbling collapse. He held on to her as they walked.

"Idiot. Everybody else is like noise in my head, and I can't think when I'm tired. You are...you *belong* there."

It was, he realized, much the way he felt about her and the subtle presence of the link. He was surprised she felt that way too. Or had she changed because of him?

"And...I want to show Argo too. It might recognize some of the stuff Alaghar showed me and maybe make up some holograms to show North and Ramirez."

Ah. Now he knew where they were going. Argo's interface room, the place it had brought Lea in its first desperate attempt to communicate with the humans inside it. Which he had accidentally become a part of, trying to rescue Lea.

They stepped through the portal together, Ivars tensing against the momentary vanishing of the mental link as Lea shielded herself with morph to block the effects of the portal field. The room looked much the same as before, a field of ultrathin black rectangles hanging in midair that only moved when they approached the empty center. No ambient noise, no air currents. No scent. The place creeped him out on several levels.

Lea froze in place when she reached the center. There was an echoing feeling in his mind, as if the link was doubled. Ivars hesitated, wondering what he should do. All this brain stuff was way out of his wheelhouse.

Then Lea lifted her hands and put them on either side of his face...and the world went away.

He had no body, here. To his perceptions, the entire universe was a white, empty space, and Lea was simultaneously not there and surrounding him completely. Around them both was a glittering cloud of faint green—Argo. Much like the first time he'd done this but less terrifying.

This is what she showed me.

The scenes were like ragged snippets of film, sometimes silent and sometimes with sound, occasionally sudden and pungent smells. He was disoriented at first, but the visions started to make more sense.

...a beast like a six-legged obsidian tank that could rear up

and attack with retractable bone spurs all along its front limbs, or suddenly leap like a grasshopper and cling to vertical surfaces...

...small, dark blue creatures running in packs, three legs, pincer-like outer jaws, teeth everywhere, and flaps of translucent skin that functioned like wings for gliding...

...things like armored wolves, a giant slab that would engulf lesser creatures and devour them whole...all creatures of nightmares. And through it all, shouts and screams and the scent of blood, the impact of the Wiyert energy weapons and sometimes handheld knives, the sharp, cold slice of remembered pain...

The world visible through all this was a chaotic mess of rubbery vines, taller plants that looked like the fern trees from a dinosaur display, and piles of what he at first took to be volcanic rock but then recognized as the black, fine-grained material they had seen before in the abandoned building on the planet with the robots. Rubble. Over everything scudded dark, ragged clouds.

A few of the scenes were not violent. Dim, narrow corridors with sharp turns and massive doors, other unfamiliar Wiyert faces. Every point of entry had some kind of physical security to prevent access and most had armed guards.

Finally, a longer sequence. A larger group of Wiyert, some of whom he recognized as the team they had rescued from the abandoned planet, moving fast. At first Ivars thought they were a disorganized mob, but something in the secondhand memory indicated this was actually a fighting formation of some kind. Watching, he almost thought he had it for a moment. Flexible, intended to defend from all sides while on the move.

In the middle of the group was a familiar floating platform, loaded with gear. Two of the Wiyert had some kind of retracting cable attached to their armor to pull it along. Unlike when he first encountered them, the Wiyert's armor and weapons were all in good shape—they even had helmets with heavy cheek plates.

Ahead in the distance, through the vegetation, he saw a dark structure with sloping walls. Thick vertical braces and grooves covered the walls. The structure was in the middle of a clearing, obviously artificial.

The viewpoint swerved sharply, looking behind, and he saw one of the Wiyert dangling in the massive jaws of a beast the size of a dump truck. Alaghar fired her weapon, as did others, and the beast bellowed and rose up on its hind limbs. The captured Wiyert fell and managed to crawl between some boulders where the beast could not reach. The armor was cracked and gaping, with streaks of red blood along the edges.

Then the surviving Wiyert were grouped around an entrance in the structure, a ring of them facing outward, including the one who no longer had his armor. He was bleeding badly and grimacing with pain but kept his weapon aimed. Ivars recognized him—Burdhul! *Now I know why he lost his armor. That was hard-core.* Another recognizable face, Isboryi, was crouched down with some strange gear, probably something Lea would understand. He seemed to be working on the door mechanism.

And the monsters kept coming. Driven by rage, even attacking each other when they got too close. But all of them were focused on the Wiyert, their aggression apparently driven just by the fact they were there.

The defenders built hasty barricades while Isboryi worked feverishly on the device. One by one they fell, and the entrance only opened just in time for the group of eight to scramble inside and shut the door—but not completely. One scaly, clawed arm writhed in the gap, pulling…

Ivars found himself desperately reaching for a weapon, feeling exposed and defenseless in this bubble of memory. All of his combat instincts were screaming for attention. He had to fight, he had to defend…

It's okay, that's all over and done. It's all right, Lea's mental voice soothed. The images faded, and Ivars tried to slow his nonexistent breathing.

I did not recognize any of the life-forms, Argo informed them. **The structures also are unknown to me.**

Do you have enough information to make images? Lea asked. There was more to the message, but Ivars couldn't make it out. Something like tone for speech. Argo gave a general sense of agreement, and suddenly they were back in reality.

Ivars realized he was breathing deeply, as if he had been sprinting, and his heart was pounding. But he wasn't fighting in a jungle, he was in the sterile interface room with the forest of infinitely black rectangles floating about them. Cold, bare, and alien—except for the quite warm and human Lea now staring up at him with her large, amber-brown eyes that were looking increasingly worried.

"Are you okay, Mark? Did you get anything useful from all that? It didn't make much sense to me, it all happened so fast."

"Very…informative," Ivars managed to say in a weak voice. He sighed and held Lea tightly. It wasn't like the Wiyert hadn't tried to warn them, but it was still a shock. *We are so screwed.* "Let's go. I know you are tired, but we've got a lot of work to do if we want to stay alive."

The investigation at the A-vit-crel nexus was extremely disturbing. The individual in charge of that area was even held for genetic determination. Servant-ships were sent to analyze the fragments of wreckage, but nothing of use remained active. The data was either not updated or somehow damaged—and neither event should have occurred. The nexus data maintainers were also held for genetic determination.

The disturbance caused by the previous alerts had diffused by now to even higher levels, so when this new information was conveyed, the orders were swift in response. Widen the search. Use even subspace energy filament scans. Something must be found to explain so many anomalous events.

Something was found, but it only caused new questions. Evidence of a powerful discontinuity link from near, but not at, the nexus to the fourth planet of the primary. Before the genomic wars, servant forces had been stored there, but it was empty and abandoned now. Or so it had been thought.

This provoked the questions: Had the genomic wars truly ended? Had a cadre hidden itself to emerge again and attack? This was a rational fear. The effort expended in search was increased. The storage planet was searched.

The planet still had a defense overlay and surviving machine servants. A great deal of information had been stored over the centuries, and even with the immense A-vit-crel analysis capabilities, it took time to go methodically through everything.

However, one of the servants sent to find any evidence of damage on the planet made a discovery. The servant had been instructed to record everything it found without analysis, and it had not been informed of what was already known—and so it logged the information that the planetside discontinuity link to the nexus had been shut down. The fadohl would have neglected to note it, since the destruction of the nexus would have naturally destroyed that link.

The servant noted the time of the link shutdown. It was *before* the destruction of the nexus. Eventually this information was brought to the investigator's attention.

The investigator, understanding the shocking implications, immediately broke with protocol and started a different search of the defense overlay stored data, starting from the time of the nexus destruction and going backward. There were gaps in the data. Large, inexplicable gaps that the defense overlay had failed to log. Or that had been removed.

An anomaly was found only a few cycles before the nexus destruction. Life-forms had been imaged, sophont life, not fadohl or of any listed servant genome. A request was sent to search the archives for other possible servants, perhaps those belonging to vanished factions. The request, of great delicacy and political risk, went to the third level.

It was approved.

And then the fadohl had proof. It was indeed a servant genome. One that had belonged to the subsumed faction.

The war had returned.

It was, Lea thought fuzzily, like trying to wear the wrong size socks. After getting the braindump from Alaghar, Lea still felt like her brain extended further than it actually did, or maybe her body, and drifts of memories not her own kept surfacing. Kinetic memories of fights she could never have survived. Showing Ivars and Argo had helped, though. She really hoped the rest would fade with time. Amazingly, she was just tired—no headache. Yet.

After the session in the interface room Ivars had all but run to the common area, dragging her along. He started giving rapid orders as soon as he got there. She could sense fear rolling off of him that had only gotten worse the longer he thought.

None of the Wiyert were present. North was sitting in the entertainment corner, reading, and Ramirez was watching a video on a tablet.

"North, Ramirez. On me. We have intel on Beredul." Ivars went directly to the planning table, and North and Ramirez dropped what they were doing and followed. "Speed and destruction are the top priorities. The situation on the ground on Beredul is lots of huge predators, and they are fast. Argo, display the section with the bone claw animal. North, I want you to analyze it for speed and range. That was the worst one." He turned to Ramirez. "Are you good to go? Can you run?"

"Yes." Ivars raised an eyebrow at Ramirez, and he grimaced. "Okay, I haven't done much for distance since I got hit, so I don't know for sure how far. Maybe not a full loadout either."

Ivars made a dismissive gesture. "You'll go without a pack if we have to. You and Lea, have Argo time you for a mile run. I need to know what our minimum speed is."

"Wait, what happened?" North said, frowning.

"We got a lot of detailed information from Alaghar," Lea said.

North slanted a look at her. "So that little dustup between you was productive?"

Lea hunched her shoulders. "Kinda. She figured out what I can do. Called me on it."

Ivars looked up, an arrested expression on his face. "I never asked—can you sense animals? Do you think you could do anything with those creatures down there?"

"I don't know—I mean, I can tell where you guys and the Wiyert are at a pretty good distance, but M.O. doesn't always… show up. And I've never tried to make him *do* anything."

"Duh. He's a cat." Ramirez grinned. "Bad example."

Ivars grimaced. "Maybe you can do better with some practice. *After* you do your timed run."

He was thinking so fast and hard it was hard for her to read him, even after all this time. He was scared and trying to find a way to not be scared.

Argo arranged a long corridor for them to run in, and Lea did her best while imagining the monsters running behind her. It probably helped her time, but she was still slower than the recovering Ramirez. He, on the other hand, was clutching his injured abdomen at the end and not saying much. He was trying hard to conceal it, but his face was pale and she could sense the pain radiating from him.

"Is it your doser? What's wrong?"

"Dammit. Thought I was…healed up," he gasped. "No, just scar tissue. It's weak." He managed a shaky grin. "Can't hide from you, huh? Doser is working great, and I check my med levels every five days just to be sure." The medical doser that gave him small but frequent amounts of medication had also been damaged when Ramirez was injured, but it had been repaired on board *Kepler* before they had left or Ramirez would never have been allowed to go with them. Still, she worried.

"If you aren't completely healed, though, maybe you shouldn't go."

His usually cheerful face grew serious. "It doesn't work like that for us, Lea. Sure, maybe if we were back home and there were twenty fit guys to take my place, I'd stand down, but here? No way in hell I'm letting Ivars and North do it alone. Or you. I can still fight, and I'll find a way to keep up. Hey, Argo, how'd we do?"

Argo announced their times. "Why are you doing this?"

"Beredul has a lot of dangerous animals that will try to kill us," Lea said. "You saw the images. We might have to run to escape them."

"You will run from these life-forms." Argo's tone was flat. "I can see from the images they are faster than you, and you will be damaged. This is not acceptable. Lea-interface is not to go to Beredul."

Oh boy, here we go.

"Argo, I don't have a choice." Lea winced, rubbing her forehead. Argo's presence in her mind had an echo, but with different words. It was having another argument somewhere else? "You know that. We've been planning this ever since we left Earth. I'm the only one of us that can figure out the fadohl technology and shut it down. Or even know what needs shutting down."

"I did not know this danger then. I will tell the others what to do."

"From orbit? You can't land, Argo!"

The headache was getting worse. She couldn't handle a temper tantrum from an AI and the second channel as well, so Lea headed back to the common area. Ramirez waved off the float chair that

Argo had summoned and grimly stumbled along behind her. The Wiyert were there now, their expressions impassive, but she felt the sharp spike of fear when they saw her come in the room. *Great. Alaghar told them about me.*

When he heard their run times, Ivars exhaled suddenly, as if he'd been punched in the stomach. "Crap. I thought you said you were back on track," he said to Ramirez, frowning.

"I thought I was too," Ramirez said, only panting a little now. "I can run, but my endurance is shit."

Ivars stood looking at the ground, hands on his hips. His mind looked like a hazy blur to Lea—he was thinking, hard and fast. Like he did in a fight. She felt her muscles tensing up in response.

"We need to know what our timeline is," he said finally. "If Ramirez and Lea can train…"

"We'll still be in trouble." North stood up from the planning table. He'd been looking at a laptop, and Lea saw the tail end of one of the monster images Argo had created. His face was grim, and his thoughts were cold and full of fear. "I haven't seen them all yet, but I can tell you this much. Those things can move faster than *us*." He indicated himself and Ivars. "Never mind those two. The Wiyert aren't marathon runners either, and they took heavy casualties even though they know the terrain and the dangers. We need a better plan than running, because if that's all we have, *none* of us are going to make it."

"Especially since there's plenty of those things. We need somewhere to run *to*, or we'll just get eaten by the next monster in line," Lea pointed out.

Ivars lifted his head up, eyes closed. "Dammit. There has got to be a way to do this."

"Why is this action necessary?" Argo asked. "It must be done without damaging Lea-interface."

It was not giving up on the argument. Lea felt her stomach knot. This could be bad, if it turned into a battle of wills. She wasn't sure she could force Argo to obey her. The AI process was incredibly complex and had far more computational power than her little squishy brain. Plus, it wouldn't get tired like she would. She had to persuade it. Somehow.

"Look, Argo…you know the fadohl put those giant animals on Beredul. They put the Wiyert there. They put *you* in our solar system. That probe at the spindle saw you. I don't know if the fadohl do serial numbers or anything, but I doubt there are so many ships like you that they can't figure out which one you are—and then we are in a lot of trouble, especially if they remember where you were. They'll go to Earth to see what happened, and then my people will have to deal with those monsters, or worse!"

"The Earth-people can come with me, as you do." Argo sounded sulky. "I will hide in places like the nebula, and the fadohl will not find us."

North bit his lip, fighting a smile. "Ah, Argo…there are between seven and eight *billion* humans on Earth. I think even you might run out of room."

"Not to mention we'd need a hella more food for everybody," Ramirez added. "I mean, the stuff we've got now isn't going to last us more than a year or two."

Argo was doing a great deal of processing in the background, with increasing unease. Lea also noticed the Wiyert staring at them with expressions of utter consternation. She racked her brain, trying to figure out what had set them off this time, but couldn't think of anything.

"We have to do this, dangerous as it is, because we are the ones who fight, who protect," Ivars said in a quiet voice. "It's our job. Lea…Lea is part of it too."

"It is the warrior's duty." Alaghar nodded once, sharply.

"I am not able to fabricate this food you require," Argo admitted. "Not in such quantities."

Ivars blinked. "Wait, you can *make* stuff?"

"Yeah, but it's not like, industrial insta-poof," Lea said. "I forgot to tell you…" She faltered at Ivars's glare. "There's a lot going on, okay? And I thought maybe we could figure out how to make the factories or whatever ourselves and then have Argo run it, but we'd still need raw materials, and…"

"But we can make some things. Small things." Ivars nodded slowly. "Did you make that device I took with me in the escape pod, Argo?"

"I did." A pause. "I could do this again. But how would that be useful to protect Lea-interface?"

"Well…can't you make one of those portal-link things closer to where we need to be?"

"The discontinuity links must be anchored. If there is no anchor already in place, I cannot."

Alaghar stirred. "There is only one fadohl gateway on Beredul, and that is the one we used to leave."

Ivars rubbed the back of his neck, pacing. "Right. Of course. That would be too easy. Okay, what do we really need to avoid being eaten? We don't have enough ammo to kill every one of those things, even assuming we could carry it."

"Armor." Alaghar tapped one muscular arm. "It will keep the smaller *asuhan* from injuring you."

North shook his head. "We need something for the big ones too. Something to keep them away."

"Energy shields!" Lea blurted, then felt her face heat. Wait, why was she feeling embarrassed mentioning something from science fiction? She was *living* science fiction. "Argo, can you do that?"

"My processes should be able to fabricate protective material, but I am limited in the quantity I can make in the time available to us. I may also be able to create a focus to send energy to, and that would protect you on the planet surface from forces equivalent to those exerted by the creatures."

Ivars tilted his head. "*May* be able to? Can you get a better answer than by sticking us there and finding out the hard way?"

A brief moment of computational reflection. "I can. If I emerge before Beredul and do a scan, this will tell me what I need to know."

"Do it quickly and then leave," Alaghar said. "Before the fadohl learn we are there."

CHAPTER 6

The device the Frost People called the "display tank" stood in an open space, high enough that a gallery ran around the entire circular room. A metal stair still remained from the time when the Frost People had not yet discovered how to work the portal doors of the ship. The tank itself was fully as tall as the room and uncomfortably fadohl in construction. Alaghar did not like the device, or that they were going to use it. Still, how better to defeat the fadohl than with their own equipment?

Alaghar forced herself to observe the display tank in calmness, showing no emotion or awareness of the tension in the room. The Frost People, now aware of the full dangers of Beredul, were grim. Their leader was perhaps shading into the anger of fear, fear for his people and his chosen. *This is why we do not share souls as warriors, foolish one.*

She did not know what Lea's reaction was, for she was elsewhere in deep communion with the ship-mind. Alaghar had thought long and hard before deciding to tell her people of Lea and her powerful strangeness, and she was not certain the decision had been wise. All Alaghar could do was tell them that she believed Lea could be trusted. But should Alaghar herself be trusted after what she had done? Her actions might well require the death obeisance—assuming she could even explain how she might have put the Wiyert at risk by allowing a small, weak woman of the Frost People to merely touch her.

The ship-mind required Lea's guidance for the brief scouting it would do, it seemed. Ivars had tried to explain, but Alaghar had the sense he did not fully understand it himself—and then, there were no words for the inexplicable. Somehow Lea could speak more completely and fully to the ship-mind, and with great speed.

"I approach the time of emergence," the ship-mind said in the odd, archaic way. Alaghar focused her attention on the display.

The tall, night-black cylinder flared with light, and then the round shape of a world appeared. She assumed it was Beredul— she had never seen it from space. More light flickered and pulsed along the display, sometimes in colors she could barely see. And there…a moon. It was strange to think she had been on that moon once, to escape. Too long ago.

No sign of any ships that she could see. That was good.

The Frost People were studying the display intently, pointing to things and discussing them among themselves. What did they see and think worthy of comment? None of the *damah* were even visible at this distance.

The tank flared again, and the moving world froze in place.

"What did you find out?" Ivars asked.

A voice answered, but it was not the ship-mind. It sounded like Lea.

"Argo is still analyzing the discontinuity link to the planet's surface and the…sort of barricade satellites. Bad news. Something using the fadohl-type drive has been visiting, and not very long ago either. Argo thinks it was small, but definitely recent."

"Shit." Ivars glared at the display tank, the muscles in his jaw working. "So we can't really wait, and Argo can't hang around when we land either or it might get seen by the enemy. Where are we going now?"

"Not too far off, but not in this star system. Oh, more data." The tank changed. Now there were glowing lines along the planet surface and bright spots at intersections of the lines. "So they seem to have this planet wrapped up tight. The…power density required to start up one of their wormhole gateway things—I mean a discontinuity link—is prevented by this barricade energy net shown on the display. I guess they created the first portal before powering on the barricade net. So Argo can't make a connection closer to Vartai even if there was an anchor there, because it can't beam power through the barricade."

"What power?" Alaghar asked.

"Argo has a lot of energy," Ivars said shortly. "We thought it could project it and form a shield of our own to protect us from those animals. But if it can't even stay in orbit…"

"Oh, but…" Lea's voice started and stopped, as if she were thinking and forgetting to speak fully. "Huh. Argo is…it might be able to make us a small, self-powered one. But it can't do that and make armor for everybody too, not if we have to go soon."

"And we still have a mobility problem," the one named North said. Despite his metal foot, Alaghar knew he did not mean himself.

"Yeah." Ivars turned to look at Alaghar. "That floating platform thing you have. How much weight can it carry?"

"The pack-plate can hold at most twenty *thurin*, but it has little power left. We could not recharge it on the dead world."

Ivars tilted his head, listening as the ship-mind translated the weight to units the Frost People knew. "Okay, and how far on a charge? Say for…" and he gave a value that translated to a little more than twelve *thurin*. "Could we get to Vartai?"

So direct, and yet it did not feel like he was intending to challenge. Did he even realize how he sounded to Wiyert? "Perhaps."

"I have examined this pack-plate," the ship-mind said. "I can charge it and also make the power larger."

"Great." Ivars appeared relieved. "Lea and Ramirez can go on that if needed. Tell me about this portable shield. What are the specs?"

"Argo isn't sure it can dial it all in from the start, but I can probably do fixes as needed. It can detect a large mass moving fast, like one of those creatures, and stop it. Not enough to stand under a volcano or anything, but probably enough for that giant thing with six legs. Um, not enough power for a sustained attack for more than a few hours, so we'd have to save it for things we can't stop with weapons, I guess. I'll be able to tell when we're running on fumes."

"All right. Here's what I suggest." Ivars looked about. "Lea is the worst fighter, and we need her to take down that barricade net. Full armor for her. Leg and arm shielding for everybody else who doesn't have armor already. When we've got that, Argo drops us off. Sound good?"

He was looking at her, waiting for her response. It was not how a Wiyert would have done it, but Alaghar had a growing sense of the Frost People's ways. They spoke and let the words go free, without careful phrasing and all the many customs to avoid the appearance of a challenge. Ivars likely did not know his way of speaking was a challenge.

She had tried to tell him with half words, speaking around the thing she needed to say, but he had not understood. It was different speaking to Ivars, a Warleader himself, than to Lea, who was barely even a warrior. Their customs were just too different for her to overcome quickly.

I will have to convince him to let me do all the talking on Beredul, if we survive.

"It is acceptable. How much time will this armor-making require?"

"Approximately three days, and one day more for the shielding device," the ship-mind said.

"Perfect. Just enough time to cobble together a topo map from what you guys saw when you went out." Ivars started talking to the ship-mind to make this special map.

Alaghar was once again wondering how she had changed her people. The Frost People had so casually mentioned their numbers, that there were too many even for the immense ship to carry. If she remembered rightly, if no catastrophe had struck the *damah*, the Wiyert numbered no more than five million. And she had thought her people so numerous, so powerful. Only held back by the fadohl barrier.

I have seen their thoughts; the Frost People are not evil as the fadohl are. We are few compared to them, but strong. We will teach the Frost People to be warriors, and together we will destroy the fadohl.

They were both exhausted and worried. They needed to sleep, but they also needed each other. Ivars found comfort in that and knew Lea did too. Whatever happened, they'd be together. He relentlessly squashed all the worst-case scenarios that readily came to mind. They had a plan, and Argo had given them a fighting chance. Either the shield would work or it wouldn't. The rest would depend on the ground conditions, and they couldn't know that until they got there.

So tired…he kept thinking of possible situations and how they could deal with them, over and over again. His mind drifted in the warmth of Lea's presence. He should be doing something, or going somewhere, but this was where he was supposed to be. He was sure of it.

It was hard to keep his eyes open in the shadowy twilight of Lea's room. Just faintly glowing patches of wall that blurred and faded into darkness. He blinked, trying to focus. All but one of the patches had gone dark, and the remaining one was bright. Very bright. And then he realized he was standing in familiar rocky ground. Not the vines and trees of Beredul, but the ridge with pale, dusty buildings far in the valley below, and a low stone wall…

That place. That mission. His last one until he'd managed to convince command to let him go on this squirrely space operation. His heart began to race; his mouth went dry.

Shit! I fell asleep. I fell asleep and I'm still with Lea. Oh God.

He fought to wake up, to move. He couldn't do anything; his muscles no longer responded. The memories played relentlessly in his mind, burned into him, and he had no control over it at all.

Dammit, no. No! Stop it, don't let her see! You IDIOT!

They were going through the village now and it was all wrong. He had known that then too—no dogs were barking and something was missing; he kept trying to figure it out, but it was too late…no cooking smoke. It was a trap. Nobody was there. Their contact had sold them out. And then the coughing pop, and the rush of air as the RPG came hurtling toward him, and he turned, too slow, too slow…and saw death, saw…

A refrigerator.

Ohhhkayyy. Wait. That's not what happened. Not even close.

It was a very old refrigerator, just sitting there in the middle of the rutted road. No enemy in sight for miles, certainly no jihadi with an RPG pointed at his head like he was expecting. The refrigerator was not very big, with a curved top and retro twenties-style chrome bits here and there. He'd never seen it before, and it certainly had never been present during that mission—or any other, for that matter.

The fuck?

He'd wasted too much time. For some reason his rifle was missing and so was his sidearm. Didn't really matter—they'd said in training small arms weren't effective against refrigerators anyway. He reached for his bandolier and pulled one of the little penguins free, grabbing the beak to activate it. The tiny bastard bit him, so he threw it with a curse, unset. The penguin bounced off the refrigerator with no effect, so he pulled another one free and armed and threw that. This time there was a satisfactory detonation, and the refrigerator fell over in a puff of dust, waving its little stubby legs as it died with a screeching, rattling wheeze.

Then he had to sit down at a very uncomfortable desk that looked exactly like the ones he'd used in grade school to write up his after-action report, right then and there. His rifle had appeared again, and his harness kept getting in the way. Some idiot was shooting at him too, but Ivars just deployed a cheap umbrella he'd bought from a nearby hadji-mart to keep the bullets away as he wrote.

Ivars was in the middle of detailing, with increasing profanity, how the penguins had not performed according to design specifications, had compromised the mission, and should not be issued again when he suddenly woke up with a gasp, heart pounding.

Lea was leaning over him. His stomach knotted with fear. *Dammit, no! Not again. I don't want to lose this one!*

"Mark! You're still here!"

How odd. She was smiling. Ivars fought through the fog of the dream that still clouded his mind. "God, Lea, I'm sorry. I didn't mean for you to...wait, what?" She wasn't scared. Or upset. The link felt...happy. A little confused, but that could be him just waking up, or her.

Maybe she hadn't felt the dream. He had dodged a bullet for real.

"I was thinking maybe I snored or talked in my sleep or something." Lea sat up, yawned grandly, and blinked. "Did I? Weird dreams. But it wasn't about Alaghar's monsters, hooray."

Uh-oh. "What kind of weird dreams?"

Her gaze cleared and sharpened as she looked at him. He kept forgetting she could feel even the subtle emotions as he spoke.

"Well, I was in this desert place—maybe Arizona? And it was noisy like firecrackers and I didn't like the noise, and then there was my grandfather's refrigerator, sitting there in the middle of the street!" She frowned. "And then things got weird with penguins and…stuff."

Ivars sat up, rubbing his head. "Wait, you recognized that refrigerator?"

They stared at each other for a moment. Lea nodded slowly. "Yeah. You saw it too? What did it look like?"

"Old." Ivars struggled for the memory of the fading dream. "Enough chrome to be a Chevy. Rounded top; you could never keep anything on top of it."

"So we were dreaming the same thing?"

"Looks like." Ivars took a deep breath and forced himself to speak. Lea already had enough pieces of the truth and the brainpower to put them together. The only way out was straight ahead and damn the torpedoes. "That…that was where it happened. Where *this* happened." He gestured at the side of his head, trying to stop the trembling in his hand.

The scars, the brain injury, the missing eye. Where he had nearly died. Even worse, when he believed his career had died. "I thought the nightmares had gone, but the fight on the spindle…it started up again. And now that we're about to be in the shit…" He had to stop, get his voice steady. "I didn't want you to see, or feel it, or…I'm sorry. I can't stop it and I don't want to hurt you!" *Don't leave, please don't leave. Not like the others did. You're better than all of them put together.*

First the light touch of fingertips, then the comforting, slow warmth of the direct link spreading through his mind. "You didn't hurt me." Lea cupped his face in her hands, and the steady calm she broadcast started to have an effect on him. "It was confusing, but pretty much like any intense dream. I thought it was all me anyway, since the refrigerator was there."

He still couldn't believe she was taking it so well. "What is… why the refrigerator?"

Lea ducked her head, her face reddening. "Oh, it was from when I was real young. We were visiting my grandfather, and I wanted something to drink, but I didn't know how those old things opened—the handle kinda pulls out like a lever from the top, and it was heavy and stiff. Too heavy for a four-year-old, anyway. And I got so frustrated and upset I cried, and Grampa yelled and said I was too old to act like a baby…stupid, I know. Welcome to my subconscious. Were the penguins yours?"

Ivars wrapped his arms around her, burying his face in the nape of her neck, inhaling the scent of her hair. The relief was so strong he could feel himself shaking. She knew and she didn't care. He was the luckiest sonofabitch in the entire galaxy.

"I have absolutely no fucking idea where the penguins came from." He started to laugh. Lea and the penguins would keep the nightmares away. He could face anything now.

Lea shifted. "Are you going to keep going away?" she asked softly.

Ivars shook his head, suddenly unable to speak. He didn't need to, anyway. He hugged her tightly. *I didn't want to lose you. Can't lose you. I didn't want to leave. But I thought if you knew…* And in trying to avoid hurting her, he had hurt her. She'd noticed and not said anything. Dammit. He had nearly screwed it up. Again.

He could feel her smile. It glowed through the link, warming him like inner sunlight. *I know now. Still here, headcase.*

I love you, Space Cadet. No matter what, even if you change. I'll always love you.

Alaghar noticed that the ship-mind had made Lea's armor first. It was a machine—she knew this. It could not have feelings like a person did. Therefore, it could not be trying to find favor by showing preference. It was simply coincidence. She was almost certain of this.

The armor was bronze-gold in color and with a slightly rough surface—not polished and reflective like the metal of her Beredul-made plating. It was light but strong, and the pieces jointed cleverly. Even the helmet was jointed to fold up in a thick ridge about the shoulders when not worn over the head.

Lea was examining the plates that went over the backs of her hands, looking doubtful. She started to move, cautiously.

"It *seems* to fit…I'd better not gain any weight, though."

Ivars walked around her, a small, appreciative smile on his face that vanished when she spun around to face him. "Unlikely. We're going to be pretty active once we hit the ground. What's with the thing on your back?"

Lea looked over her shoulder. "Morph reservoir and a little power node thing. I'll need morph shielding for any of the door links we use, which needs power. And Argo can't send power once we're on the moon."

Ivars raised an eyebrow. "It will once we bring down the energy barricade, right?"

"Yeah, but who knows what we'll have to go through to do that?"

"Good point."

Lea closed her eyes, and a brown film crept up her neck and over her head. Alaghar stepped back, startled and disturbed. It looked like a flow of many tiny insects. She suppressed a shudder.

The brown film receded, and Lea opened her eyes again. Looking directly at Alaghar, as if she had spoken. "It protects me," she said softly. "It doesn't hurt."

Alaghar frowned. "You should protect yourself. Where is your knife? How will you carry it?"

"I'll have my pack." Lea glanced at Ivars, then Alaghar. "No?"

"You should have your weapon always to hand. You may not have time to retrieve it. Argo!" Alaghar stumbled over the name. A name for a machine! "The armor is not yet complete. You must fashion an attachment for her blade, similar to those on our plating."

Ivars rubbed his chin, studying the armor. "Yeah, but maybe not on the forearm—might get in the way if she's working on things." Alaghar and Ivars discussed the matter while Lea sputtered and waved her arms in protest, eventually deciding the right thigh would be the best location.

"Go and fetch your knife," Alaghar told her, interrupting her complaints.

"Why? Argo can just scan it and do the mods later."

Why does her Warleader permit such behavior? Alaghar bared her teeth, and Lea gulped. "Yes, it can. *You*, however, must learn how to use it. Go."

Muttering, Lea left, slouching in a way that made Alaghar want to smack her. Ivars went over to the table where the Frost People's weapons and the little metal containers that fed them were placed. The *ammo* was heavy, but she had seen how effective it was against the machine servants of the nexus. It would be very useful against the *asuhan*. They had told her that one of their weapons had *ammo* that could be told what to do, that would only explode at the location they wished. She did not understand how that could happen, but it would be useful too.

Lea returned with the knife, tossing it up in the air. It hung there, briefly sparkling in bright lines of green light, while she wrestled the armor free. The armor then lifted up and merged with the wall while the knife dropped back down in her hand.

Alaghar realized Lea had been communicating with the ship-mind and shuddered. *I will never be used to her strange ways, no matter how often I see them.*

She noticed her people had been keeping as much distance as they could from Lea. Unobtrusively, but then Lea perhaps would know anyway. Alaghar frowned, resolving to do something to change that. They would have to work closely to reach Vartai alive.

But first, Lea must survive the first hour on Beredul.

Alaghar went to the food preparation area and found an empty container, a round, white cylinder of a thin, flexible material the Frost People called *plaz-tik*.

"Come." She gestured at Lea and then left the common room. It would be best to do this away from the others, especially Lea's chosen. It would be hard enough to get her to focus as it was.

In the corridor Lea watched with a doubtful expression as Alaghar demonstrated the very simplest of knife attacks and defenses.

"Now, show that you were attentive." Alaghar handed Lea the knife. She took it reluctantly, and Alaghar observed she was careful to take hold well away from Alaghar's hand.

Lea's attempt to imitate Alaghar's moves was even worse than she had feared. There was no time to get angry—unless that would motivate Lea to learn.

"This is useless. What are you doing? You move as if you have no intention of attacking."

"I don't!" Lea snapped. "If I hurt something with this thing, I'll feel it too!"

It was, Alaghar admitted reluctantly, a valid problem. Perhaps Lea's weakness was not entirely cowardice. "Then you must learn to feel pain without flinching. You will not argue!" Lea blinked at Alaghar's roar, her head snapping back and her eyes wide. Alaghar lowered her voice but kept the intensity. "You *will* defend yourself. If you do not, everyone else will have that much more to do and risk greater injury. Your chosen will fear for you and will have less attention for the dangers about us. Do you wish to harm him? Do the Frost People treat their chosen with such carelessness? Do your share. Learn to protect *him*. This…outside-feeling you have is a weakness for this, I hear what you say. *You* must find a way to overcome it—I cannot do that for you."

Lea looked down at the knife in her hand, her expression deeply unhappy. Surely she had too much pride to weep? Alaghar held her breath—but then Lea's drooping shoulders straightened. She took a deep breath and tried again.

It was a little better. Perhaps. Alaghar found she was mildly surprised her arguments had worked. She had expected more childish protests and was prepared to yell, intimidate, and do everything short of severe violence to get Lea to cooperate, but if Lea was trying, she would have to contain her temper. For now.

When Lea had the basic moves committed to memory, if not grace, Alaghar took the empty food container and tossed it at her. Lea whimpered and swatted at it with her empty hand, dropping the knife held in the other. Alaghar swallowed her anger after a moment of struggle and tried again. This time Lea struck with the knife, but when Alaghar picked up the container, it had been barely scratched.

Somehow, this made the alienness of the Frost People clear in a way even the recorded picture of the game had not. Her anger drained away, leaving her tired. Lea truly had never fought in her life, had never needed to. Until now.

I am repairing many years of ignorance; I cannot expect to do this quickly. Still, it was aggravating.

Alaghar kept at it until Lea could barely lift her arm. She was, possibly, slightly more dangerous to an attacker than to herself now. Improvement.

"Enough. You may rest." Lea staggered against a wall and slumped down to sit on the floor. "For the moment. I must go and make my own preparations. Are the changes to your armor complete?" Lea nodded. "Good. You will wear it to train in now. I will tell the others to have you practice attacking on the draw."

Lea slumped even farther, looking miserable. Alaghar's people would be unhappy with her orders too, she knew. But they would obey and overcome their fear of Lea's strangeness. They had to work together or they would die.

CHAPTER 7

Lea pawed desperately through the supplies, trying not to whimper in pain. They had to have it *somewhere*. It wasn't exactly first aid, but they had *foot powder*, so surely they would have included… Her hand closed around the tube and she sagged with relief. Analgesic cream. *My only real friend…* She slathered gobs of the cream on her aching muscles and groaned.

She was tired and cranky and had been spending entirely too much time with Alaghar—who was broadcasting exactly how much she thought backhanding Lea in the face would improve her attitude. To give her credit, she hadn't—but Lea could still *feel* it. The other Wiyert weren't much better.

Tiring, and terrifying.

And for all this effort, she now had a knife holster bolted to her armor and she could probably fight off a plastic container, if it was already wounded.

Lea stood up from the box of supplies, grimacing. She'd better get going before Alaghar realized nobody was beating up on her at the moment.

Argo. Portal door to the workshop, please.

I will do this. Was that a game? I could throw things for you too. Argo's "voice" sounded wistful in her head.

Er. Thanks, but I'm done for now. Maybe later.

Poor Argo. Whenever she felt left out, she'd remember it and feel better. It wanted to join in, to help. Hard to do when you were the size of a moon and didn't have hands, so to speak.

The workshop area was the first section of Argo they had discovered when Lea figured out the transporting doors. It had originally been used for modifying and constructing devices, and Lea had set up her own equipment there. She called up the thin, protective layer of morph to go through the link door and dropped it again once she was through.

Maybe she could make something for Argo, like a telepresence robot...or it could make one for itself. Lea sat down at one of the equipment benches. She desperately needed sleep, but she wanted to make some things to help everybody, and she had to do it now.

She quickly listed the kind of device she needed. Not in words but in concepts, which only Argo understood here. Information storage, voice activation, sound. And Argo could seamlessly provide options, modifications, even ideas. They considered AI, but it would be difficult for the size of device she was planning, and it would take more power.

The workshop had been cleaned out by *Kepler*'s crew, but Argo knew where other gizmos were stored and could transport them to her. She'd also scrounged a few alien tools, and between them and her mental abilities she could modify the devices enough to work for her purposes. Some had decayed too much in the thousands of years they had been abandoned on Argo, but she winnowed out enough for everyone on the team to have one, and a few spares.

Then it was just a matter of charging them and sorting out Argo's vast library of data for the set she needed. Having all that processor power at her beck and call was rather addictive.

Then it was done. The devices were palm-size, like flat ovoids. Argo didn't know what their original purpose was—either the fadohl had not told it, or the memory was lost to damage. Now they were voice-activated lookup English/Wiyert dictionaries. They all had a very basic vocabulary in common at this point, but they would, hopefully, be talking to Wiyert who had never heard English before. Argo wouldn't be available for full translations, and Lea suspected her transplanted translation skills might not be enough.

She had Argo check the others. Still busy or sleeping. Good. She had one more task.

Something that can send a signal through morph, and something that can detect that signal, she told Argo. Lea had realized something when Alaghar was yelling at her about not making Ivars worry. She could shield with morph, but that would break their link and Ivars would worry about *that* too. He was relying on it more and more and probably didn't realize it. But the few times she cut the connection, he always noticed. And objected.

There is a way, but the range is not very large if the signal power is below the limit enforced by the barrier satellites.

The fadohl prison setup not only kept the Wiyert trapped, it prevented them from using devices beyond a certain power level. This had stopped their efforts to concoct a portable radar for the giant creatures, since it wouldn't have worked without getting a killer lightning bolt from the surveillance net.

It will have to do. What is the range?

One hundred meters.

No, that wasn't very far, but there wasn't time to figure out another way. Especially since there were no spare devices that could be modified to do it. Lea had to extract some components, and Argo fabricated the rest. Two little thumb-size blobs of the dark, ceramic-like material, with a sheen of metallic swirl on the surface. She had Argo add a loop at the end so they could be worn on a chain. She'd have her device under the morph, and she could have it send a signal Ivars's device could read. Primitive, but hopefully enough to keep him from getting a panic attack.

They are asking where you are, Argo said. **Do I tell them this?**

Lea fought a yawn and started stuffing devices in her pockets. *Tell them I'm going to my room to sleep.* She didn't care if Alaghar thought she was a slacker. If she picked up a knife in her current state, she would just drop it on her foot. *Do you have any questions about the plan?*

I want to come back sooner. Seven days is too long. Lea-interface could require assistance before then.

It took Alaghar and her people over two days to get to the link portal from Vartai. It's probably going to take us longer than that, and we have to convince the Vartai folks we are the good guys before we can return.

Argo grumbled electronically.

Okay, how about this. The first time you stay away seven days, but if you don't see any sign the fadohl have come back since and we aren't at the portal, come back in four more days. If we get there before then, I'll leave a message. Something the fadohl won't understand. I know! Have I told you about emoji?

One brief exchange of typographic symbols later, Argo had a secret code of smileys and was feeling a little calmer to her senses.

Lea-interface should return quickly.

Not up to us, unfortunately. Those monsters will probably slow us down. We'll do our best.

Silence.

What should I do if you do not leave a message?

Ever was the subtext. Nobody had discussed that with Argo because it had been upset enough at the concept of them, mainly her, getting hurt. But it was asking now.

You shouldn't stay near Beredul. The fadohl might see you. You should...you should go to Earth. Tell them what happened and see what they think you should do next. Oh, and find a way to get M.O. back!

More silence. **I wish to go with you. I would know, then. I could help.**

I know. I wish you could too. I was thinking about that...if you made a puppet, an avatar sort of thing. Like those helper robots you made to move Kepler, remember? Something human-size. It wouldn't help here, though, because your brain is still part of the ship and the barrier will block your connection.

But I could make it a copy. A part of me that went away and then came back.

Lea could follow, to some extent, as Argo considered the matter. It was a new architecture. Something the fadohl had not anticipated...wait. Actually, they *had,* but only to prevent it from ever happening. Some of those restrictions she had removed, a few others were still in place.

We don't have time to do it now. It's not so simple, and I'm too tired to help you figure it out. You think about it while waiting for us, okay? You can also make some toys for M.O., maybe. Like a robot mouse for it to chase.

Lea stumbled through another link door, barely remembering to move the morph in time, and found the door to her quarters. She collapsed on the bed, yelped, removed the lumpy and hard devices from her pockets, then sprawled facedown again.

If anybody is still looking for me, tell them my warranty expired.

Ivars glanced about one more time at the assembled gear and people in the corridor. Time for the final check before leaving Argo. This was always the worst part of a mission for him. Before he had committed to action.

"Armor? Weapons? Packs? Water? Argo will leave as soon as the planet link checks clear, so if you don't have it with you now, you don't have it, period."

His people looked ready, even with the arm and leg armor. Maybe Lea was a bit pale around the edges, but not too bad. He put one hand up to check that the charm she'd made for him was still there, right next to his dog tags. The Wiyert were calm; Alaghar looked frankly bored.

Lea held up a hand and all attention focused on her. "Argo is about to drop out." Her eyes closed—a sign she was getting lots of telemetry and didn't want visual distraction. Her mouth moved and twitched for a long moment, and Ivars fought to stay calm. Asking for updates wouldn't help.

Her eyes snapped open again. "We're in."

Even as she was speaking, the blank inset doorway in the wall flickered and changed to show a large room, dark with shadows. It looked like the ceiling was pretty high, and the surfaces were dark too.

Ivars looked at Alaghar, who just nodded silently. Nothing had changed from the last time. Good.

"Argo has control of the moon station. It is removing all data from the time it first arrived here and will edit so we don't show up when we go through. Oh, and only Argo can connect to the station now." Lea smiled.

"The fadohl cannot force it open again?" Alaghar asked.

"Maybe eventually, but it will take them time."

"Which we don't have." Ivars gestured sharply at the door. "Move out!"

Just like they had planned. North and Hazuruh went first, then

Dumhaigl and Burdhul pulling the float platform carrying their heavier gear. Ramirez followed with the XM25 in hand, then Alaghar.

The brown film crept over Lea's face, and he braced himself. The link faded and disappeared, just like always…but then the charm grew warm and pulsed. Faintly, but it was enough.

He and Lea stepped through the door together. Alaghar was already across the room, standing before a giant portal doorway. Even the planet door on the nexus was not this huge. Signs of the Wiyert's violent first visit were everywhere: wreckage from a damaged robot scattered on the floor, sooty blast marks on the walls. Some of the light fixtures had been damaged as well, helping the shadowy effect.

The link to Lea surged back. He turned his head—she was staring vaguely in no particular direction, meaning she was in deep mental data mode with Argo. Good. They needed every bit of intel Argo could provide about the station and Beredul, since everything Alaghar knew was at least a year out of date.

The room they were in was spacious, like an airport terminal. He thought he recognized the indications of a physical door, rather than one of the usual linking doors, but it was closed. Would it stay that way? The Wiyert didn't seem to regard it as a threat, but it would be good to be sure.

"Does that open?" he asked Burdhul and got a blank, puzzled stare in return. Oh yeah, the Argo autotranslate wasn't available here. He'd gotten too used to that. Ivars rummaged through his limited Wiyert vocabulary and asked again.

"We broke it. It remains closed. See." Burdhul pointed. What Ivars had thought were more robot parts was a blasted hole in the wall, and the mechanism inside had been slagged.

Ivars thought of another question. Struggling for the vocabulary again, he remembered the translation devices Lea had handed out, and hadn't she been clever to think that up ahead of time? But Alaghar was already waving them over. The Wiyert didn't want to stick around here, and he couldn't blame them.

Lea was looking back at the door to Argo. Even without direct contact, he could tell what she was thinking.

"Never mind the damn cat—he can take care of himself. Argo will be fine too. Let's go." She just gave him a shaky grin and sighed. "Better get your helmet up. We're going in hot."

The helmet deployed smooth and fast, like a spreading wing covering her head. Fully armored, she looked like some kind of space-age knight. The ratty digicam pack didn't go with the armor, but the knife gave a nice retro touch. Not that he had any room to talk. He was wearing greaves like an ancient Greek. *Whatever works…*

The Wiyert were intently studying the view through the big door, pointing and discussing what they saw. Alaghar had warned them earlier that it was possible some of the smaller creatures, what she called *du-asuhan*, might have gotten inside. They'd had to force the outer door to get in themselves and hadn't had much time to block it again. Fortunately the link door wasn't automatic on the planet side, or they would have had to deal with a *du-asuhan* infestation on the moon station too—and from what he'd heard, they were basically piranhas on legs.

A consensus reached, Alaghar and her team prepped their weapons and checked their gear. This was the Wiyert's world, so the order of entry was changed. They all knew they would have a fight as soon as they got out the door. The float platform stayed behind with the Earth-humans, who would wait until the Wiyert had the portal area under control. They'd only be in the way in close quarters.

The Wiyert went through at a run. The long-distance portal links always had a few seconds time delay in what they displayed, which was especially nerve-racking now. As soon as the Wiyert appeared on the other side, they attacked. The fight was furious but brief. Ivars stifled the impulse to go and help, especially when one of the *du-asuhan* chomped down on Burdhul's arm, clad in the new armor made by Argo. But Burdhul casually gutted the creature with a knife and didn't even seem that worried.

"Looks like that armor works," North said. Lea was looking horrified and pale.

Ramirez nodded. "So if they try to take a chunk out of you, feed 'em your arm and blow 'em away while they're gnawing. Good to know."

"If any of them get that close, we'd better be out of ammo, okay? This was a special case since they were already in position. We can't afford to get sloppy here. Good news is, no civilians out in the open. If it moves, we can shoot it." Ivars saw Alaghar face the doorway and raise her arm. The signal. "We're up. Let's not embarrass Mother Earth, people. Fight smart and fight hard."

Ivars found himself suddenly missing Olsen. Olsen would have something funny to say, like "Go, Cro-Magnons!" that would cheer everyone up facing a sucky situation. *Lucky bastard better be taking care of things back home. Probably got a beer in one hand and Maryann in the other.*

Which reminded him…Lea wasn't looking so great. He wasn't dumb enough to grab her hand to pull her through the link door; he had done that once, and that was enough. But she had run off before in this kind of mood, so he grabbed the back of her pack to make sure she went through with the rest of them. Which got him a dirty look, so he gave her an innocent smile back. Even morphed up, she knew what he was thinking. And then they were through.

The first thing that hit him on the other side was the smell. A thick fug of rotting vegetation and something else, sharp and sour. The bleeding bodies of the *du-asuhan* probably added to the stench. Close up, their teeth were even more intimidating. They could go clear through an arm, at a guess, wide and with razor-sharp indentations. Like a shark that got regular dental checkups.

This area was more damaged than the moon station had been. Some vegetation had grown in through cracks in the outer door, thick and ropy. The walls and floor were a rough brown substance, like fired clay, interspersed with the usual fadohl black instrument panels. He could see a few glyphs and other symbols glowing on the panels, so they were still doing something. Rubble was everywhere underfoot, making movement awkward. The light from the broken doorway was not very bright, so he turned on the tac light on his rifle.

As planned, his team had formed up around Lea. She had brought her hands up to her head and was wincing, not a good sign. But she was still standing, morph down, and scanning the surrounding walls. She apparently found what she was looking for and darted over, placing her bare hands on the smooth, black surface.

The Wiyert were stacked up at the outer doorway, occasionally firing their weapons. Everyone was silent. They'd been warned about that too. Alaghar had been quite insistent about moving as quietly as possible, with no talking if it could possibly be avoided. Drawing attention from the larger *asuhan* before they had their defenses in place would be a very bad idea, and Alaghar had said they were more aggressive near the portal door for some reason.

He glanced at Lea. There was sweat on her forehead and her eyes were scrunched shut. There was a sense of panic and fear through the link...and then her eyes snapped open. A loud, humming pop came from outside, followed by a waft of ozone and a furious roar. The Wiyert jerked back, startled, and glanced briefly her direction.

"Got the shield up," Lea said, her voice rough. "It feels pretty strong. I made it bulge out a bit at the door, so we can get out and take a look, maybe."

"A few *du-asuhan* are inside the energy wall. We kill them now," Alaghar said, and two of the Wiyert clambered over the broken door.

Ivars could now see the shield was like a wall of flickering light, blazing up if anything made contact. "I don't suppose this place has any offensive capability?"

Lea shook her head. "Just the shield. Oh, and Argo found out something interesting, since it had more time to investigate on this visit. The power source for the portal link isn't on the moon. It's on the planet. Argo thinks the whole barrier network is powered from the planet, which is weird if the Wiyert are prisoners there. Wouldn't the fadohl be worried they would find it and turn it off? But then there are also the old ruins. Maybe this place was inhabited before the monsters and the Wiyert got here."

"Maybe." It was hard to say how that could be important for what they were doing now, but whatever. "Anything else?"

"Some kind of low-level signal I'm picking up. It's not coming from this place, and I can't tell what it does."

"Maybe Alaghar knows."

Lea, he noticed, was a lot better at the Wiyert-talking than he was. Good thing. He didn't have any trouble interpreting Alaghar's head shake, though.

"We go now. Four *daihk* to darkness."

That was a bit less than five hours. Ivars frowned. "Go now? Maybe better to wait for dawn."

The gist of Alaghar's response, filled in by Lea, was that there were so many more big *asuhan* near here it was better to get away from the portal, even though it would put them out beyond the shield. And in the dark. Apparently turning on the shield had injured a big one, and the others would smell the blood and come check.

"Right. Full loadout time. North, pair up with Burdhul; Ramirez, you're with Kugohin. Make sure they get the right caliber ammo and correct magazines for their weapons. Let's load up as much as you can and still move fast; we need the lift for people on that platform now. Lea, get the portable shield ready. As much as we'd like to run, I can tell right now it's going to be a slog. Pace yourselves and watch your ammo. No balls-to-the-wall until we can see Vartai, okay?"

"Wish I'd brought noseplugs," Ramirez said, stuffing ammo in his pack. "Smells like an old septic tank out there."

"Your nose will stop working in an hour or so. And the mutant carnivorous bulldozers will help distract you." North bounced up and down a few times on his prosthetic blade foot, reaching down to adjust the armor position on that leg.

The Wiyert were moving the last of the rubble and debris from the outer doorway. It was go time. Ivars glanced at Lea and pointed at the float platform. She grimaced but climbed up and sat cross-legged in the middle, the location they'd found most stable.

"How are we getting past the barrier?"

"I can drop it and raise it again," Lea said. "Or should I leave it down?"

Ivars shrugged. "They must have a way around it or they wouldn't have been able to get through the first time. Leave it up."

Alaghar stood in the doorway, studying the situation. She looked over her shoulder, nodded once, and slashed her hand downward and off to one side. *That way.* And they were off.

The Wiyert were going as fast as they could, which was about quick-jog speed for the Earth-humans. But it told Ivars they were in a serious danger zone. As promised, the glimmering wall vanished as they reached it, reforming when they were clear.

He kept his head on a swivel as much as he could, given the uneven and unfamiliar terrain. None of the big *asuhan* in sight, fortunately. The area around the portal structure was fairly clear and level. Beyond that the vegetation got wild. Nothing very tall, maybe thirty feet max. Lots of dull green foliage and vines, and the smell of rot got stronger as they went in. The portal structure was just like he'd seen from Alaghar's image—dark, slanted walls, clearly alien in origin.

Ivars didn't even see the first *asuhan* before Hazuruh opened fire with her energy weapon. The bear-size creature looked like a cross between a boar and an armadillo, with armor plates and spikes on its head. Hazuruh's shot was low, striking it mostly on the underside and away from the armor. It screamed and thrashed as it died. Ivars stared at it, then noticed the thin, treelike plants were rustling in the distance. A dark edge of something moving and visible *above* the foliage there got him going again with a spike of adrenaline. Something even bigger than the one they had killed had heard the noise and was coming to investigate, and he didn't want to be here when it arrived. Ivars ran.

They kept running, and the giant whatsit followed, crashing through the jungle. Either the armored boar hadn't been enough of a meal or the creature just liked to hunt. He could tell the Wiyert were starting to flag, eyes wide in desperation, and he grabbed the line attached to the float platform from Dumhaigl to pull it himself. It didn't weigh that much with the antigrav, but even that small amount was dragging the Wiyert's endurance down, and they didn't have as much as the Earth-humans to begin with.

He noticed Alaghar was leading them in a path that hugged the terrain, always keeping a slope or rock to one side, even if it wasn't on their direct heading. As the *asuhan* started to catch up, he figured out why. She was preventing a flank attack, so the pursuing *asuhan* had to circle around to get to them. It gave them a few crucial extra seconds, and something to put at their backs when it did reach them.

And it was getting closer, and sounding larger. Since he had been listening to the pursuit, this time he had some warning of the attack. When it lunged into view, the *asuhan* was huge, bipedal, but more like a crab than a T. rex. *What the hell do I target? The whole damn thing is armored!*

If it was like a crab, maybe the joints were vulnerable. He aimed and fired, three-round bursts. The *asuhan* roared and swiped with a claw, and he crouched down to fire again. The Wiyert energy weapons had diminished effect, but the rifles were definitely doing damage. And then Ramirez got off a phosphorus round with the XM25, right in what was probably the main nerve cluster, and it backed off and ran away. After signaling for a stop, Alaghar gave them a gesture that looked like a salute, and the other Wiyert were smiling even as they gasped for air. *Okay, that went well. I hope we have enough WP rounds for the trip.*

Lea, on the other hand, was *not* doing well. He knew that because she'd buttoned up with the morph, cutting off the link. The charm around his neck was still beating, so she wasn't hurt. He hoped. Most likely scared to death and trying not to swamp him with that. Her gauntleted hands were gripping the edge of the float platform tightly. The best thing he could do for her now was keep moving.

They stood in tense silence, listening hard. Once Alaghar was sure nothing else was coming to investigate, they moved on. The Wiyert could only manage a fast walk now. Ivars waved North ahead and had Ramirez get on the float platform too, to rest up. It was a bit more effort to pull with two people, but at a walk, nothing he couldn't handle. When they had been running, the platform had shifted and moved quite a bit over the uneven terrain, attempting to stay at its set height, but at this pace it was easier for passengers to stay balanced.

Until the next attack, and there would be a next attack. They'd only been on Beredul for an hour at most, and the monsters were just as numerous and scary as he'd been warned. He was learning, though. Alaghar's people were experienced, and his team was coming up to speed fast.

Up ahead, he saw one of the Wiyert put out a hand, palm down and to the side. The next Wiyert that passed the same place did the same thing. When Ivars drew near, he saw buried in the vines a mangled set of Wiyert armor encasing bones.

One of their own...rest easy, bud. We've come to help. He briefly extended his own hand as he passed.

CHAPTER 8

Lea huddled down on the float plate and dodged another branch. Not only did the float plate shimmy and tilt dangerously at any speed faster than a walk, but any foliage pushed back by the person towing it would spring back and hit her in the face. Turning around didn't help—Alaghar trotted up beside her and scowled until Lea figured out the noise of the branches hitting her helmet was not a good idea. She was expected to dodge.

And that was the only useful thing she could do now. Be quiet luggage. Away from machines she was weak and useless, something that had to be dragged along. Sure, she had the portable emergency shield, but anybody could use that. What they needed were more people who could fight, even at the level of the wounded Ramirez, and she couldn't even do that much. Despite Alaghar's Ten Hours to Warrior Fitness terror training regimen.

Even Alaghar's memories hadn't prepared her for Beredul. They had been filtered through Alaghar's expectations, her adaption to her home planet. For Lea everything was new, and the sensory overload had just been too much and all at once. The humid air reeked of decay, and the ground was slimy with it. The monsters had been even bigger and more violent, and being chased by one so terrifying, she was still shaking. And she wasn't the only one who was scared. Before they had left the portal and she had brought up the morph, she could feel it surrounding her. Fear, and pain, and the strange, droning mechanical signal…

The others didn't let their fear stop them, though. They knew what to do. Even as the monsters kept coming, they kept fighting. With the smaller ones that Alaghar had called *du-asuhan*, they even switched to knives rather than make noise with the rifles and the energy weapons and threw the bodies as far as they could to keep the bigger *asuhan* from following too closely.

Lea watched as Ivars dealt with another of the scaly creatures, smoothly blocking its attack with his left forearm and slashing down with his knife in his right. He didn't even stop running as he did it. She could hear the echo of Alaghar's contemptuous voice in her head—what was she doing to protect him? *He* was doing such a good job she hadn't even needed to draw her knife.

They were attacked by a huge centipede-like thing with tentacles, another armored boar, and a swarm of *du-asuhan* while Lea frantically tried to think of something she could do. One of the *du-asuhan* launched itself into the air from a frond-tree and flew over her, and she lashed out, nearly tipping the float platform. The *du-asuhan* shrieked and flailed, but she hadn't even made contact with the knife edge—she had bludgeoned it with the hand holding it. Still, it was dazed enough that Burdhul was able to easily dispatch it.

Now there was sticky yellow blood on her gauntlet that smelled so vile she nearly threw up, but she still hadn't killed anything herself. She'd just softened it up, nearly at the cost of slowing everyone down by falling off the float platform.

You aren't thinking. You're never going to be as good as they are at the physical stuff. What are you good at, and how can that help them?

Data. Analysis. Patterns. They were on constant scan mode, always having to be able to react instantly to a threat. She only had a knife—of course she wasn't going to be doing any fighting, not unless *everybody* was dead or injured. She could be overwatch, though. She could keep an eye on all the fighters, with her ability. But to do that, she needed to remove the morph—and that would hurt. A lot.

I'm pretty sure I know what Alaghar would say to that. Something cheery like "being dead doesn't hurt at all."

Lea gritted her teeth and pulled the morph shield down. Her breath hissed out as the overwhelming sensations slammed down on her like a hammer, but it was not as painful as she had feared. For one thing, the fighters were less wound up and more focused on their surroundings. Ramirez was hurting, a dull ache in her mind. Ivars…Ivars had a cut she hadn't noticed before. She couldn't read the others with the same detail she could read him, but everyone was tense and anxious. And tired.

The strange mechanical signal was still there, only stronger. It had no data that she could detect—it was like a dial tone. And there was…pain. It was out in the jungle, so it couldn't be any of the fighters. And nobody was out picking berries in this place, which meant it had to be…one of the *asuhan*.

Lea felt a sudden spurt of hope. She *could* detect the monsters! But why hadn't it worked for M.O.? Maybe because he was asleep most of the time, and when he wasn't, he was pretty content. Her talent primarily worked on emotion, the stronger the better. She glanced about, looking through the fern-like trees as best she could, but she couldn't see any *asuhan*. There was something that looked like a tall building in the distance, but no monsters. It must be concealed. The building snagged at her attention, but she forced herself to ignore it. Monsters came first.

She closed her eyes and concentrated. With effort she could deliberately ignore the people she knew, making it easier to sense what was out there. Fainter signals, also of pain. Was everything on Beredul injured? She could also tell the stronger signal was getting closer to them. But where? How far? And how could she warn people without making any noise that would bring the *asuhan* right to them?

Ivars was already looking in the right direction, and she didn't want to distract him, make him look her way and take his attention away from the threat. Lea got to her knees on the float platform, clutching the portable shield device to her chest and waving her arm at the Wiyert trudging behind her. When Kugohin looked at her, puzzled, she pointed, but she could tell he did not understand her warning. She tried again, clawing with her free hand and pointing, but it still didn't get through.

Lea dropped back down and focused again. The first signal was still there, keeping its distance. Was it stalking them? Then she drew in a sharp breath. Two more, coming from ahead and to the other side. She should warn Ivars—she could do it with her direct link—but he had already seen the one closest and was about to attack. It was immense, bigger than an elephant, with six legs and glossy, obsidian-black skin. She'd seen that kind before in Alaghar's memories.

She could feel when the bullets struck the *asuhan*, even before it roared. The pain flared with a sharp flash, and Lea immediately summoned the morph—and then pushed it back. She had to keep her senses open to know where the *asuhan* were, and there were at least two more thinking of joining the attack that Ivars hadn't seen.

Focus. She had to focus and figure out what to do. One was moving away now, but the other was getting closer. She had to warn the fighters, but how? Yelling would just make it worse.

Then Lea remembered what she was holding. She activated the shield, and a dome of flickering light sprang up around them. Ivars immediately snapped his head to face her. She pointed, one finger at the *asuhan* he'd been firing at and two fingers at the ones nobody knew about, so everyone could see, and then sent to him directly. *More that way.*

He blinked, then nodded, and she felt a pulse of focus from him. He gestured to Ramirez and Alaghar, pointing to the side, and then lowered his hand at Lea. *Drop the shield.*

Oh yeah. They couldn't fire from inside the shield, and she'd done what was important—warned them. Lea dropped it, scrunched her eyes tight while doing a fast, intense scan, and then brought up the morph. Three wounded *asuhan* was more than she could take right now.

The morph didn't block the roars, or the sound of weapons. They were running again now, and Lea had to grip the float platform to stay on. The sky, which originally had been a dull, overcast grey, was getting darker. How much more daylight did they have?

Nobody had fired for a while, so Lea tried sensing again. Only one *asuhan*, but it seemed to be following them. She passed that information on to Ivars, wishing again they had a two-way link. At least he knew now, and he was gesturing to Alaghar. Alaghar scowled, looking into the darkness, and then pointed in a different direction than the one they had been heading. It was not an easier path—far from it. It was, if anything, more of a mess. Lots of rock, tall enough they had to thread through, and at one point get everything off the float plate so it could be tilted. Lea was actually glad to be walking for a change.

Eventually they came to a bowl-shaped depression in the ground, surrounded by the tall boulders and partly shielded from above by some that had tilted or fallen on the others. It wasn't precisely a cave, but nothing larger than *du-asuhan* could get in through the walls.

Alaghar waved them close. "The one that follows will go, if we stay silent, not make light," she said in the lowest voice possible. "We rest for a time."

Lea held out the shield device with an inquiring look, but Alaghar shook her head. They all knew they had to conserve the power, and it appeared this place was safe enough to not need it for now. Glancing around the rock enclosure, Alaghar pointed at Burdhul and North, then drew a finger across her eyes. The rest of the Wiyert immediately found someplace to lie down. That must mean Burdhul and North were on watch. Lea went over and stood in front of Alaghar until she looked up. Lea just glowered silently until Alaghar finally gave a small, reluctant nod and pointed Lea to another location at the edge of the shelter. Her expression revealed nothing, but Lea could sense amusement, with a trace of surprise.

Taking a seat on a handy rock, Lea stared out at the darkness and hoped she knew all the things someone on watch should do. She might not be as competent as the others, but she wasn't nearly as tired. Besides, she wanted to practice her monster-detecting skills.

She was not surprised to see Ivars had decided to sleep next to her rock, or that he had casually draped one arm where she could easily touch it and Alaghar couldn't see what she was doing.

Good on you for stepping up, Space Cadet. Proud of you. Maybe you won't be much help right away, but you'll learn. Nice work with the shield back there too.

I was trying to warn you. I think...I think I can detect the asuhan.

Really? Outstanding! That will be a big help.

How can I tell anyone if we have to be quiet, though? Turning on the shield was the only thing I could think of, but I don't want to do that every time—it will run out of power. I tried waving at

Dumhaigl, but he didn't understand, and nobody else was even looking my way then.

They both pondered the issue for a while, fatigue slowing their minds.

Notice anything else?

Lea thought, trying to remember. So much had been new, strange, and frightening. *The* asuhan *are in pain, but I don't know why. It's how I can sense them. And the signal I detected back at the portal? It's even stronger here. Then there was that weird building we just passed. Something odd about it too.*

Like what?

I dunno...it felt kinda...familiar. Like Argo. It wasn't very strong, whatever it was. Maybe we can ask the Wiyert when it is safe.

Yeah, good idea. A flash of excitement from Ivars, like he had thought of something interesting. *Hey, you can send to my eye, remember? How far can you do that?*

Pretty far, if it isn't complicated. You want me to send you some kind of signal when I sense something?

He actually had a very specific idea of what he wanted, a kind of direction/distance display that would float transparently to one side of his field of vision. It took time to work out the details, but once she had it, she was as excited as he was. Ivars wouldn't be stuck on the float platform, so he could alert the others.

I wish I knew what was wrong with the animals, though.

They want to have us over for dinner.

Ha-ha. No, I mean they are...like something is hurting them. All the time, not just when we shoot them. I can feel their fear, Mark. But I can't find anything that is frightening them. It's like they are all insane.

Maybe they are.

She felt him drifting off to sleep and didn't say anything more. He was more worn out than she had thought, running on pure willpower and adrenaline. And then she realized he had felt...not exactly *safe*, but secure. Secure enough to sleep for a moment, because she was there and on guard. He trusted her to warn them before danger showed up.

Maybe she wasn't completely useless after all.

The A-vit-crel Watcher of the outer third sector was conscious of unusual emotional intensity. The Watcher had thought that identifying the return of the genomic war would be enough, and it would not have any further responsibility. This assumption had proved incorrect.

The war had involved allied genelines. And these genelines, now notified, had expressed a desire for conclusive proof—proof sufficient to the extraordinary claim being made. It was, the Watcher admitted, what it would have insisted on in their place.

What it meant, however, was further searches for evidence, now with each geneline represented by its own observer. Sharing data for something of this nature was not to be expected. Each would do its own analysis. However, each geneline was sharing the time and location of the last contact they had had with the enemy. The Watcher had learned much from this alone.

They had also obtained many sealed records, leading to still others, concerning subsumed servant species, technology, and other assets. It was wasteful to simply destroy the defeated geneline's property—or so it had been thought at the time. It had not been believed the defect responsible for the defeat could have been preserved and propagated thereby.

Some had been deemed insufficiently valuable compared to the risk, and liquidated. The Watcher noted some of its own classification had been deemed corrupted merely by contamination and no longer showed in any listing of the geneline. The Watcher resolved to be vigilant for any sign of such contamination with regard to itself—but how to know what the contamination was, to guard against it? It was vexing.

The unresolved logical conflicts were causing chains of embarrassment and concealment in many high places in A-vit-crel. Some thought the discovery itself was shameful. The Watcher considered failing to discover would have been more shameful… but perhaps this was a contaminated thought. Was the Watcher perhaps connected genetically to the subline responsible for failing to conclude the war decisively? If so, dissolution of the Watcher's self and genome would be, in fact, deserved.

The Watcher's research in the permitted archives had revealed some frightening things. The defeated geneline had been, before the war, of the highest respect. They dared much and succeeded. Then, it appeared, they went too far—and failed.

Some of this was not merely forbidden to the Watcher, but gone. It knew how to detect restricted information blocks, and this was not the case here. There was no information at all for some inquiries. So there had been dangerous projects.

One such audacious and dangerous project appeared to be connected to the mainline ship at the nexus that should not exist. The details were missing. But another project still remained in the archives, apparently because the project had been for a servant species, one found sufficiently useful to be subsumed.

The servant species had…rebelled.

This disgrace had happened before, but this truth was carefully concealed from subgenes that had no need to know. Even the Watcher would not know, except that its duties required it. One could not watch without knowing what to watch for, after all. But in the light of the defeated geneline—why had the connection not been made before? Clearly the servant species was contaminated. It should have been eradicated, for the safety of all. The origin of the servant species had been concealed, and this was the result. Who knew what other contaminated assets were spread among the fadohl genelines? Sometimes hiding truth made matters even worse.

The Watcher shuddered. Truly, even thinking about such things had contaminated its thought processes! It would need to be careful to avoid liquidation.

So what had happened to the rebellious servant species? Again, because of the significant value of their genome, they had *not* been destroyed outright. Instead, they had been added to the evolvement crucible of a different reification program, an accelerated evolution program.

On a world listed as Beredul.

The Watcher noted the location and added it to the list for the allied observers to visit. If the enemy was indeed collecting its resources, it might well attempt to gather its servants again.

Lea stifled a groan and stretched, looking out at the ever-present Beredul jungle. So far her early monster detection system was working. The Wiyert seemed to think it was the next thing to black magic, but they'd only had three major fights since putting it in action and had dodged several *asuhan* successfully. Unfortunately it had also added extra time with all the detours they'd had to do. And with practice, she'd gotten more precise. She couldn't tell the different kinds apart, but speed and location were clear, and she was getting a better sense of size too.

Time for another long-range scan. It took more time, and more energy from her, so she didn't do them as often. Usually this just gave them extra time to plan, but this time she got an unpleasant surprise. Something had gotten well inside her range already, because it was moving fast. And it was big, and headed right for them.

Lea sent the info on to Ivars's synthetic eye. Up ahead, she saw him gesture to the others. Alaghar looked pissed—did she think Lea was making the monsters come this way? Eventually the Wiyert leader pointed in a different direction and headed off, not even looking back.

Lea kept updating the info appearing in Ivars's eye and periodically checking to make sure no other monsters were coming in range. They had to sprint for a bit to avoid this one—it was moving fast, radiating pain even more than usual. They hunkered down in a pile of broken rock that looked like it might have been a building once to let it go by. Lea watched it, frowning. It was one of the six-legged obsidian beasts with spines, and it was injured. They hadn't done it, so it must have been attacked by some other creature.

It's hurt and running. I don't want to meet the thing that did that.

She became aware of her own aches and pains. Her stomach was cramping, and she was feeling lightheaded. Again. She rummaged in her pack, stowed at her feet on the platform, and found the remains of an energy bar. She chewed without enthusiasm, remembering to drink some water as well. What she was really craving was chocolate, or at least sugar. Being on constant brain scan was wiping her out.

It started drizzling. The ground had never been very clear, with lots of dead vegetation, but now it was getting slimy and muddy. People were slipping and slowing down.

The rain got heavier, and she discovered her armor leaked. Even with the helmet up and deployed. She hadn't even thought to mention a waterproof layer to Argo when it was designing the armor for her, and what would a space traveling ship AI know about weather?

Another ice-cold trickle of water ran down her back, and Lea tried not to think about two more days of this. And it wasn't like she could take the armor off and get dry when they rested at night either.

She took the last bite of the energy bar and another swig of water and scanned for monsters again. She nearly choked. *Three* inbound, moving fast. From the same direction as the first one, but spread out enough she was pretty sure they could not outrun them. She was getting a really bad feeling about what was happening out there.

First things first. She updated Ivars, then hunkered down and concentrated. It was hard, with all the noise of the other creatures louder and stronger because of their closeness, but she could almost sense…something. Something bigger than she had ever seen on Beredul before.

They didn't have a preplanned code for this, so she risked distracting Ivars by sending a text image. *Godzilla inbound. Same direction.*

She felt the jolt of emotion as he figured it out, as she had known he would. *Very important to choose smart boyfriends. Saves trouble in the long run.* The huge monster was chasing the other monsters toward them, and if those things were running…the thing chasing them was bad. Really, really bad.

Ivars ran up to Alaghar, apparently to tell her about the disaster headed their way and discuss what to do about it. The terrain they were in was not good for cover. Lea could not see any of the usual rocks or rubble to hide in, and the vegetation was only thick enough to thwart humans, not the huge monsters coming at them.

A decision had been reached. Alaghar was rallying the Wiyert, and Ivars was pulling out a long knife and pointing to North and Ramirez and then at the thicket of bamboo-like trees nearby. The float platform stayed in place, no longer being towed. The Wiyert had knives out too. Working in relays, they cut down long lengths of vegetation, chopping one end to a point. Then they carried the branches to where Alaghar had gone, the bottom of a steep slope a few hundred yards away.

Two Wiyert took one of the cut-down branches and forcefully jammed it in the thick mud at the base of the slope. It swayed and leaned, but they didn't bother to straighten it. After a few more Lea started to see what they were doing—making it look like a grove grew on the slope, a bit farther out than the surface really was so they could all hide behind it. But why were the branches so long?

The force field. If the branches touch it, the field will move them away. So she would have to make sure the dome of the field was as low as possible. She could do that; she could tinker with a number of things in the device.

Ivars waved a hand at her and then tapped his helmet by the side of his head. Wanting an update. One of the running creatures was going to bypass them and might not even be visible. One wasn't moving as fast, and neither was the Big Bad. Maybe fighting. The remaining creature was almost on them. She sent the update and jumped down from the platform, grabbing the line and pulling as she ran for the flimsy tree fort.

There were gaps in the branches, but there wasn't time to do more. Lea shut down the float platform power, and she and Ramirez tilted it on one side like a barricade, propping it against some ammo crates. It wouldn't do much for defense, but they could hide behind it. Lea sat down in the mud with the shield device cradled in her hands, hunched over as if that would do anything to protect it, and listened for the distant sound of shrieking roars.

The others were coming now, crawling low, huddling together in the center of the enclosure. Lea waited until the *asuhan* came in to view before starting the shield, hoping to conserve power. It was another of the six-legged obsidian things, the biggest she had seen. It had ragged, bleeding tears along one side, and one leg was shattered and dangling. It would rear up and go several steps on four legs before dropping down again, snarling. Pain radiated from it in hammer blows.

You don't see anything. Nothing is here. Keep running. Behind the branches, no one moved beyond deep, panting breaths. She had brought the shield down barely a foot above her own head, and she could feel the power on the bare skin of her face. *Look away.*

The injured *asuhan* did not look their direction, but it wasn't moving either. It had turned to face the way it had come, stepping backward and crouching down. Not good. It was so badly injured it was going to stop and fight rather than run. Which meant the Big Bad was going to end up right here.

There has to be something else I can do. Argo didn't plan for anything bigger than the wounded one. If the other hits us directly, we're toast.

Lea looked around for inspiration. The rain had died down, more of a drizzle than a downpour. The ground was a churned-up bog, every footprint turned into a deep puddle. Something had leaked from one of the overturned boxes, leaving a faint oily sheen on the surface of the water, just slightly prismatic.

Optics. Refraction. Reflection. There was something about water, and sunlight, and sunglasses…she should have paid more attention in class. But no, she had been impatient to get to the part about lasers, never knowing she would end up getting stomped flat in an alien mudhole to confuse some purple, methane-breathing archaeologist a thousand years from now because she couldn't remember some stupid diagram in a textbook. *It wasn't even my major! It's not fair!*

She didn't need her mental scan to know something big was approaching now. The ground was shaking, rhythmically. The branches blocked her first glimpses of the thing, but she could hear the obsidian creature's rising howl as it approached.

It wasn't that much taller than its prey, but definitely wider. Rough, armored hide, like coral or weathered stone, mottled in color from mossy green to rust. A heavy head with two sets of additional outer jaws, the inner set with sharp, inward-curving teeth, the outer like pincers with a mobile, dagger-like claw at the end. The forelimbs also had an inner and outer set, with more claws, that were carried tucked close to the chest. The hind limbs, which it used for walking, were big and powerful. It looked like the result of a three-way involving Cthulhu, an alligator, and a kangaroo.

The injured creature lashed out, but the multijaw wasn't having any. The outer forelimbs lunged forward, the claws digging deep.

The black thing screamed and thrashed, managing to pull free but at a terrible cost. Broken bones protruded from its side, and the foamy, purplish blood ran down in pulsing waves.

The fight had moved away from their hideout, and Lea held her breath. Multijaw lunged, striking like a snake with both head and forelimbs. The agony was a blinding white wave in her mind, and Lea felt tears running down her face—but she didn't dare bring up the morph. She had to know where the dangers were.

The obsidian thing was thrashing now, biting and tearing. A lucky blow with a spine-tipped limb apparently hit Multijaw in a tender place, for it reared back and slashed viciously, again and again. The wounded limb, already shattered, was torn free—and thrown straight into the flimsy shelter, knocking the branches down or tossing them in the air. The dome flared.

Multijaw turned its massive head away from the twitching body of its prey, looking directly at them. Its eyes, under thick, rocky ridges, were as dark as interstellar space, absorbing all light.

And the missing piece of the puzzle fell into place. *Polarization.*

Lea knew the force field intimately now. She had pulled and manipulated and shaped it; she knew instinctively what it did and how. She left the original field in place, changing only a few parameters that did not affect its strength. Then she pulled up another shallow dome, inside. This was weaker, but otherwise the same—and she *pushed* it, rotating it in place. And inside the shield everything went dark.

Someone cried out, instantly stifled by one of the others. She could smell the fear. She nearly screamed herself when two bright points of light flashed on opposite sides of the shield, once, then twice. The creature was trying to *bite* the shield.

A long moment passed. The ground shuddered again, and a distant roar echoed. The multijawed creature was still there, apparently feeding. And then it moved again, going farther and farther away.

Lea carefully rotated the inner dome, and when it was clear the monster was gone, dropped the shield entirely. Trying to wipe the tears from her face, she discovered her hands were shaking so badly she was hitting her fingers on the edge of her helmet. With an effort, she realized Ivars was next to her, more leaning against her than holding her and shaking as badly as she was.

The others began to slowly sit up, a distant horror on their faces. Ivars had picked up that something was bothering Lea and was shaking her.

It took her a moment to find the words. "Sorry. I…need sugar. I burn it up fast with this stuff…"

Ivars and Ramirez instantly went through their pockets and pouches, and North, farther away, picked up quickly and followed suit. That got her a handful of hard candies and one blessed part of a chocolate bar. Lea put one candy under her tongue, and almost instantly the dark spots in her vision began to fade.

"Other problem. We can't pull that stunt again."

"No kidding," Ivars whispered harshly. "I nearly had a seizure."

"No, I mean we really can't. It drained the power on the shield. We've got barely ten percent left."

"*Shit.*" Ivars hung his head, looking at his hands. "It just doesn't let up for a second, does it."

"I might be able to transfer power from the float platform, but that would mean we can't use it anymore."

"Yeah, but…"

"No." Alaghar got to her feet. "The pack-plate is necessary. We move fast now, without stopping. *Uh-asuhan* has cleared the way."

She was right, Lea realized. Nothing at all was showing up on her mental scan. Everything that could move had run.

Ivars winced, then nodded. "Right. Ramirez, time to hand out the stimulants. We're not just going to embrace the suck, we're going to give it a big, wet, slobbering kiss."

CHAPTER 9

Despite the humidity, Ivars felt his eyes going hot and dry. It was the stimulants and the fatigue. Possibly also some deadly form of alien mold, with his luck.

It was dark but they were still on the march. He wasn't sure if his team had sufficiently impressed Alaghar with their learning curve on the dangers of Beredul or if she was so desperate to make time she was willing to take the risk of having the ignorant Earth-humans take point with their night-vision adaptives so they didn't have to stop when it got dark. The critter population definitely shut up shop at night, unless they had the bad luck to wake some of them up. Plenty of the *du-asuhan* seemed in favor of the concept of the midnight snack, then.

Once he was reasonably sure the big monsters had packed it in, he tried to get Lea to sleep, but she was too wound up and scared. He was *not* sure the stimulants were a good idea for her at all. She had enough weird brain stuff going on as it was. And he couldn't do anything to help her. There was nothing else they could do. They had to keep moving or they would die.

Then he noticed a thin line of light on the horizon and that the air was getting less chilly. *Oh boy. Here we go again.*

The flying creatures, it turned out, liked morning. Lea got back on the float platform with the shield device. He could feel her focus through the link. She only raised the shield when the flock was too thick for them to fight off effectively. They just didn't have the power to waste.

They also didn't have an infinite supply of ammo. He had Ramirez conserve the effective XM25 rounds for the big creatures. Pistols for emergencies, rifle for everything else. The Wiyert energy weapons were most effective against the flying ones, since they had an area effect like a shotgun. A ten foot wingspan could catch a lot of damage and once on the ground they were easy to take care of.

They were tired enough they were making mistakes, all of them. And they were getting wounded. He had a ragged, bleeding tear on one leg, North had a mangled hand and a nasty bite on one arm, and Ramirez had gotten knocked off the platform when standing, falling down a slope and hitting some rocks. Burdhul had a number of bleeding cuts around the edges of his mismatched armor, but it didn't seem to be troubling him too much.

The other Wiyert had no major injuries, but they were nearly collapsing from fatigue. If they fell, the creatures could get them. Even when it got light, Ivars and North stayed in the lead.

At first he thought the structure in the distance was a low, flat hill. Then, through his foggy brain, he noticed how regular it was and wondered if it was some intact building from the mysterious first inhabitants. But then he saw how the Wiyert's morale suddenly improved, and he realized the truth. That was Vartai, their destination. He was beginning to think it was a myth.

And just as he started to get his hopes up, the dreaded red dot appeared in his vision again. A large one. Not as large as Godzilla, but large enough to be a problem. He made the gesture they'd invented that meant "incoming," and everyone closed up. Ivars set a faster pace. They just had to make it to the walls. Less than five miles.

One of the Wiyert tripped and fell hard. Once they were back up, Ivars picked up the pace again—and again, one of the Wiyert fell. It just wasn't going to happen. They couldn't run far at the best of times, and they were pretty much exhausted. And they all needed each other to survive and complete the mission, so they had to stick together, even if it put them at risk by going slower. Besides, they had done this many times. The teamwork was in place.

The creature was in view now, a kind they hadn't seen before.

It was very long and snakelike, sometimes sliding on the ground and sometimes extruding things like legs for traction or leverage over obstacles. It was pale grey green and slightly translucent, so it faded into the morning mist. It looked like a Chinese dragon on drugs.

Ivars gestured to the others, indicating they should stay still, but Alaghar shook her head vehemently, swiping some blood with her fingers and holding them up to her nose. *Won't matter if we stay quiet, they can smell us now*, he realized.

So they kept moving to what cover they could find. The other monsters were big enough to make that easy, but the snake thing had such a long, narrow head there wasn't much available. And as soon as it saw them, it moved *fast*.

A flechette round from the XM25 pissed it off but good, and he knew they had gotten some solid rifle fire on it—but the thing was so big and long it was hard to tell where the vital points were. It still kept coming. Lea had the shield up before it struck, furious.

Again, and again. The long head, full of very unnecessary teeth, lashed out like a whip. Then Lea screamed, and the shield disappeared.

ShitshitSHIT! He didn't even have time to think about it. Full auto, aiming for the head as much as he could for it thrashing around. They had to be doing damage to it, but it wasn't showing any sign of slowing down. *Should have had grenades. Flamethrowers. An A-10. Who the fuck authorized this mission?*

The snake head lunged straight at him, and he ducked. It went past like a freight train, and he felt more than heard the scream.

LEA!

It had engulfed her almost to the waist, shaking its head, thwarted by the armor. Then it spasmed and slowly collapsed, like a falling tree. Lea wasn't moving.

Frantic, Ivars tried to force the giant jaws open. The creature's skin was slick, like a fish, and he couldn't get enough leverage, even hooking an arm around the strange spike at the top of its head. It took two of the Wiyert helping him before he could get the mouth open.

Lea tumbled out, covered in slime. As soon as she hit the ground, her arms and legs were flailing about, and the link was just wordless, total terror. She was trying to run away, coughing and clawing at her face.

He caught her, trying to clear the slime away from her nose and mouth. The direct link was like a hammer.

GetitoffgetitOFF ME! OFF!

Her armor was dented, but as far as he could see none of the teeth had gotten through. Lea was struggling to get away. With all their gear and helmets, the best skin contact he could manage was cheek to cheek, and it was like being hit with a sandblaster of emotion. Fear, panic, pain.

He let it pass through him, not trying to stop it, and focused on his breathing. Even as the tears rolled down his face from the pain. *It's dead. You're fine. It's dead.*

Eventually he felt the normal Lea return. Still trembling, still spooked and ready to panic again. But also a thread of pain that hadn't been there before.

I felt it. I felt it! It hurt so much!

We need to keep moving. Are you injured?

A mental pause, as if she had to think about it, which also calmed her down, strangely enough. *My shoulder hurts. And I can't move my leg.*

Right, no more walking for you.

Ivars lifted her up and carried her to the float plate. He glanced at the dead monster and noticed the strange spike was gone. It hadn't had any spikes before that he could recall. Had he just imagined it?

Morph, Lea's voice informed him. She started to shake again. *I couldn't reach my knife, so I make a spike of morph when it bit me. I hate this place. I wanna go home!*

He couldn't help grinning. *You and everybody else. Cheer up, Space Cadet. It was big and mean and nasty, but look who won? It'll never do that again. You are badass.*

That helped stop the shakes, and he felt his own internal level of panic die down with them.

Alaghar was watching with barely concealed impatience, clearly wanting to be on the move. His own fatigue gave a sharp increase in irritation. If she was in such a hurry, why didn't she just go? The Wiyert were slow enough it wouldn't take long to catch up. Even as he thought it, he bit it back. Splitting up in any way was a bad idea.

Lea huddled on the float platform and they headed out again. He hoped they didn't encounter any more bad ones like that, because without the shield, it was not looking good. He waved everyone out. As they got closer to the fort, the vegetation got thinner, and there was no point in bunching up now. They'd be able to see the critters coming, which was a plus. Unfortunately the critters could see them too, which wasn't.

They were getting close enough to Vartai to see some of the structure. No entrance, but Alaghar had indicated it would be on the other side anyway. They started to angle around. The vegetation showed signs of charring. Maybe those towers weren't decoration, but weapons. Big energy weapons would be nice right about now.

And then two red dots showed up in his vision. Of course. It was too good to last. Both were large and coming in different directions but still where they couldn't just avoid them. He jogged ahead, rounding the high, dark walls, and saw the entrance. It wasn't very wide, and more importantly, was closed.

Well. No point in keeping things quiet now.

"Ramirez. We need a flare." Maybe the people inside simply hadn't seen them, or the *asuhan* approaching.

"On it." His voice was rough and ragged. A harsh pop and a vapor trail arced up into the air, and then a bright flash of white glared in the sky. "Bet they see that."

The Wiyert were energized so close to the fort and started moving faster. They huddled into the slight inset of the entrance once they reached it, weapons pointing outward. Alaghar brought out a silvery rectangle and touched it to a metal plate on the frame of entrance. Whatever the response was, Alaghar didn't like it at all. Her eyes widened in fury, and she punched the heavy metal doors with her fist in a complicated pattern. Nothing happened.

"Something wrong?" He could see motion out in the thicker area of vegetation. The monsters were coming.

Alaghar snarled and punched at the door again, adding what he guessed were Wiyert profanities he hadn't encountered yet. "My key is no longer recognized. They must not think we are safe to allow inside."

"How the hell do we convince them, then? We are down to a handful of rounds each, our magic umbrella is gone, and if that door doesn't open real soon, we are on the fucking menu!" Ivars pointed at the approaching creatures. "Damn, I hate this commute." Wait. He had C4. He knew he packed it, anyway. It wasn't really nice to blow up someone's door when you wanted to be friends with them, but this was getting to the point he didn't really have a choice.

Alaghar was yelling now, and Ivars went through his vest pouches, looking for the detonator. Lea was staring at the gate door, her entire body drooping and an expression of utter betrayal on her face.

Detonator. Got it. How much to use... He heard firing behind him, both Earth weapons and Wiyert energy blasts. He didn't know how thick the door was, and they couldn't move too far away either...

And then the door opened.

As soon as the opening in the main entrance had widened enough, Alaghar wasted no time pushing people through, especially the Frost People with their thin protection. The *asuhan* were well within range, yet no weapons had fired from the walls. Why, then, had the door been opened, against the most stringent rules of the *damah*? There was no sign of overwatch in the outer courtyard either, but the door began its smooth motion to close the instant everyone was inside. What had happened in Vartai since she had left?

Distantly she could hear the roaring outside. They had made it safely to Vartai, something she had not dared to hope. All her thought and care had been to this end. But she could not rest now. There was still more to do.

Her people were sitting against the inner wall, facing the outer door and gasping for breath. They had no strength even to stand. The healer of the Frost People, Ramirez, was tending to the injured more thoroughly than he had been able to do when they were on the move. North stood facing the door as if he could not believe they were now safe, then bowed his head, lips moving silently. Ivars, she saw with an inner smile, was already examining the interior of the courtyard even though he was staggering with fatigue. A warrior, in truth.

Lea was still sitting on the pack-plate with her injured leg stretched out before her, her head up...and her eyes closed. Alaghar felt her scalp chill and shudder. Lea's face was completely blank and calm, almost as if she were sleeping. *I can speak to machines*, she had said. So the people of the *damah* had not opened the gate for them. Lea had.

Anger burned, but she could think of no other choice. If the doors had not opened, they would have died—but now Vartai had seen the power of the Frost People, even if they did not understand it. Trust would come harder now. But what else could they have done?

What could they do now?

She activated the key signal again. It hadn't worked before, so she really wasn't sure what it would do.

"People. With weapons." Lea's eyes were still closed. Her voice cracked and faded.

"I notice they aren't talking much," Ivars muttered.

"They are afraid. I think...oh!" Lea's eyes snapped open.

The grinding sound of the fireholes opening made Alaghar push to her feet, heart pounding. The defenders were going to fire on them. They thought they were fadohl-held, compromised.

"I am Alaghar, Warleader of Koloh! I bring allies to fight the fadohl! Bring me the *buj-lagar* to judge my words, so I may die as a warrior!" If she could just talk to someone...

No blast of energy came from the fireholes, but no answer to her challenge came either. Only the faint sound of muttered, frantic cursing.

"They can't be so surprised we don't want to be shot at," Lea rasped. "And we can shoot back."

It was a small gift she was speaking her own tongue and not that of the Wiyert. Very small.

"It is best that I speak to the people here now," Alaghar said, catching the eyes of the Frost People in turn. "Your ways will cause trouble among those who do not know you." Speaking so direct, so challenging, and they did not even understand what they were doing. That beside the matter of Lea, the Gold Sun, and all the rest. "Lea. Are the people still there? Close by?" Lea nodded.

Alaghar sat down again, deliberately laying her own weapon to one side. Ivars, watching her, detached his own weapon from the framework of straps that held it on his body and placed it on the float plate. He sat down right where he was. North did the same, only placing his weapon within arm's reach before sliding down the wall and stretching out his legs with a groan.

Alaghar heard a sharp gasp from one of the fire ports and frowned. What had happened? Time to talk more.

"We are all that remain of the force sent to the fadohl gateway. We were able to open it and reach a nexus of gates, but the guardians of that place detected us and we were forced to escape to a dead world, once used but now abandoned. Only six of us live that were sent out from Vartai to search for the way." She stopped a moment, the pain washing through her. So many dead... "On the dead world we came across other searchers, the Frost People. You see them here before you. They knew nothing of the fadohl before now, and they fear their home world is in danger. They come to learn from us and to share the fight...and to help us escape from Beredul."

Whispered conversations, just on the edge of hearing, then silence. Alaghar glanced at Lea, but she showed no reaction—her head was hanging down, her face lined with pain and fatigue.

No way to know if anyone was still there and listening. What more could she say that would be believed?

Alaghar gritted her teeth. "I am Alaghar, full warrior and Warleader. I have kept the oath and keep it still I will bring no harm within the walls. If you fear us, kill us now so we may rejoin our honored companions!"

"Why was the dark one's foot removed?" came a hesitant voice. "For what purpose?"

So that was what had caused surprise. Alaghar realized she had become so accustomed to North's metal foot she had not thought of it as strange.

"He was wounded while fighting, and the piece of metal given so he might fight again. Such is the custom of the Frost People." She would not mention their other strange customs—and she hoped that no one would figure out Lea and Ivars were chosen for a long time. Perhaps, if she were lucky, no one would ever figure it out.

"Why would the fadohl repair one of their servants?" asked the voice.

"They would not," Alaghar replied, raising an eyebrow. "You know this. They would destroy the defective servant. But the Frost People value their warriors and care for them, as we care for ours." And then, to stave off the other incredulous question she knew was coming, "It is their way to let a warrior choose when to…to go behind walls. He chose to remain a full warrior."

It was true enough; she knew that Olsen was returning to the world of the Gold Sun and would not be a full warrior anymore, and he was not injured at all. So it was their choice. *So strange…*

The silence lengthened. Alaghar waited, knowing that pushing too fast would not help. She did not know what they were saying where she could not hear, only that they were discussing something.

"How did you open the outer gate?" A different voice this time, hard and angry. "Who among us is your confederate?" The voice was familiar, and she frowned, trying to remember. Male. A voice of authority that challenged as it liked.

"We have no secret allies among you, Rey'wiros. But the Frost People have many powerful machines that serve them. They opened the gate to escape the *asuhan*."

The voice hesitated, and she concealed her smile. She had guessed rightly. The *buj-lagar* of Vartai himself had come to question them. He was a warrior of great courage, as befitted the leader of the farthest frontier outpost. The one who had seen from a distance the portal gate and offered to support an attempt to take it. He, at least, would listen first and take counsel of his fears last.

"And why should we trust these Frost People? Did they also use their machines to break our weapons? Let them then break the *asuhan* and leave us. Why should we trust those who force open our defenses?"

Lea slowly raised her head. "Tell that jerk we could open the other doors too, but we didn't. *That's* why he should trust us. And the only guns broken are the ones he tried to shoot us with. I'm *tired*. Wake me up when they decide to let us in." She curled up carefully on the pack-plate, wincing, and closed her eyes. She looked like she was shivering.

Alaghar translated what Lea had said, adding, "They are not servants. You see their weapons. I have with my own eyes seen them destroy the fadohl machine servants defending a travel nexus, and then the nexus itself."

"It is true, *buj-lagar*," Burdhul said, carefully looking down at the ground. "Also, their leader showed death homage to one of our fallen as we came here. No fadohl servant would do this."

"Enough. I will speak with you apart from these strangers, Alaghar. Remove your weapons save your honor and stand ready by the door."

Somehow she found the strength to stand again and to remove her armor. Underneath she had the gifts of the Frost People, *teeshert* and *shorrtz*. It would cause comment, but not as much as the fact she had no honor knife to carry. Without it she was not a warrior.

Alaghar hesitated. She could not ask others to give up their honor for hers. Then she heard rustling and a grumbling voice behind her. Lea was holding out the knife Alaghar had given her on the dead world, hilt first. Her black hair was like a rumpled thicket, and she looked annoyed.

Yes, the strange one had heard her need, somehow. Alaghar took the knife. "I will return it to you, with victory."

Lea smiled faintly, her eyes drifting closed again. "Go give him hell."

CHAPTER 10

Someone was shaking her shoulder and talking. Lea curled up tighter and ignored them. They weren't supposed to make noise, Alaghar had said.

"Lea, wake up. They let us in…well, they let us leave the gatehouse, anyway. You need to take your armor off so I can take a look at your injuries."

Oh yeah. It was Ramirez. Lea dragged her eyes open with great effort and tried to focus.

They were in a different place, but it looked much the same as the space just inside the outer doors. Blocky, dark rock walls, inset glow lights, and a chilly, damp-cellar kind of smell. At one end of the rectangular room were several pads like thin futons, blankets, and a large, hexagonal orange crystal that glowed and seemed to give off heat as well. Like a portable campfire.

She had to think for a bit to remember how to take the armor off. How long had it been since they'd left Argo? *I hope M.O. is all right.* Her thin T-shirt and leggings were damp and rank, but she sure hadn't packed a spare change of clothes. Besides, everybody else was just as smelly as she was. *Maybe a bit of extra monster sauce from the jabberwock that tried to eat me, in my case.* Lea shuddered, which made her ribs and shoulder stab with pain.

She woke up more as Ramirez examined her, despite his carefulness. She had a few broken ribs, which she had suspected, a wrenched shoulder, a sprained ankle, a skin rash from the monster slime, and some spectacular bruises. The Wiyert weren't in the room with them. Ivars was asleep, so dead to the world she couldn't even read his dreams. It was like he was snoring in his mind. North was also asleep, but lightly.

"We get on the approved list or what?"

Ramirez grimaced. "Or what. They still aren't sure about us, but they did let us come in here. Hazuruh said something about this being used as a staging area before they go outside. We're quite close to the outer door here. There's some water if you want to wash up a bit, and some food. We haven't seen Alaghar since she left." He lowered his voice. "What's the old cerebral radar saying?"

Ah. Lea took a deep breath, regretted it when the broken ribs complained, and concentrated. There weren't many mechanical devices nearby except their own, so she was able to sense more than she could on Argo. On the other hand, the walls were very thick, so she didn't have much range. "Our cave buddies are off behind that wall where our gear is stacked. Alaghar is…up, and a lot farther away. I think she's pissed but hard to tell at this range. Somebody I don't know is real close near that doorway, and they are all jumpy. A bunch of people farther away, but I can't tell much about them."

"But no monsters." Ramirez grinned.

"No monsters." Lea hissed in a breath as he taped her ankle tightly. "Ow. Morphine!"

"Very funny." He clapped a blue-gloved hand on her shoulder. "I think you'll live. I'd say get some sleep if you can. Who knows when they'll want to talk to us. Want the water?"

She nodded fervently. It wasn't even to the level of a sponge bath, but she felt a lot better getting every bit of the slime off her face, and it was much easier to get comfortable again without the armor.

And just as she was drifting off to sleep, Alaghar showed up with an armed escort. Her thoughts felt prickly and tired. She wasn't wearing armor and had changed to simple pants and a tunic of coarse-woven brown cloth.

"You are all to come and speak with the *buj-lagar*," she said curtly. That wasn't one of the words Argo had known, so Lea shrugged, looking at Alaghar. "This means the one who commands this *damah*. The Warleader of all the Warleaders here. Leave all weapons behind."

So, the big boss. Alaghar was a Warleader, she remembered. There were multiple forts, or *damah*, but she wasn't sure if there was really a central command for them.

It had been maybe six hours since they had arrived at Vartai. She could barely hobble even when leaning on Ivars, but the other team members didn't seem to be in such bad shape. Ivars was actually alert. *So not fair*. She wanted to sleep for a month.

The Wiyert, she decided, had absolutely no concept of claustrophobia. All of the hallways were barely wide enough for two people to walk close together, and every room had a sort of right angle exit. Further, every hallway had doors at each end, and one had to be shut for the other to open. No color, no decoration, no carpet. A maximum-security prison was more lively.

They ended up in a room divided by a grating made of overlapping diagonal bars of metal with round bosses at the intersections. On the other side were three Wiyert—a woman with a scarred face, an older man, and the largest Wiyert Lea had ever seen. Except for the large man, who wore armor, they were wearing similar tunics and pants in different shades of brown. No decoration, no jewelry.

The large man was not only tall but broad shouldered and very muscular. His hair was longer than the others and his dark gaze hard and direct. And his mind…Lea had thought Alaghar was tough, but this guy made her look like a sensitive artist. Maybe the Earth-humans had been a bad influence on her. Lea recognized him, after a fashion—he had been speaking to Alaghar when they first came in, toward the end. He'd been furious then, and he wasn't much happier now.

And me without so much as an aspirin. She wanted to make contact with Ivars to discuss all the happy news, but Alaghar had shoved between them and gave Lea a fierce scowl when she looked his direction. *Great. So no public displays of affection for the duration, looks like.* Lea didn't need the physical contact at this range to communicate one way, so she gave him a quick update and hoped that would do.

The leader, Rey'wiros, spoke in a fast, clipped fashion Lea

struggled to understand, and the others had blank expressions indicating they hadn't followed at all.

"I only caught a few words of that," Ivars said in the lengthening silence.

"He asks how we few could cross the same distance without losing one of our number when so many died to reach it the first time. Especially when you are clearly not as the Wiyert are, nor knowledgeable of the dangers of Beredul. He wishes you to speak our language, as much as you are able." Alaghar was clearly unhappy, radiating a stifled frustration.

I think she's been ordered not to tell us something, Lea sent to Ivars. *Or to let us do all the talking. And she's upset.*

Ivars nodded slowly, flicking a glance her way. He folded one arm across his chest and rubbed his chin with the other hand, tilting his head slightly. He was doing the "I'm just a dumb grunt" routine, but inside his mind was churning with activity.

"One, we were able to detect the dangerous animals and avoid many of them. Two, we had a…protective device."

Rey'wiros heard Ivars impassively and spoke again. This time Lea picked up he was asking about the outer doors and the weapons that had been shut down.

"Yes, it was a similar thing," Ivars answered carefully. "We only did so in self-defense. We had to escape the *asuhan*. We mean no harm to the Wiyert."

Could anyone else open the doors this way? Could the weapons be repaired? Ivars's answers didn't improve the chilly atmosphere, but they didn't make it worse either.

Then the hard gaze turned to Alaghar. "You said before that six of you survived and that you lost none in coming here. You are but five."

Lea felt the twinge of sorrow, and wished she could comfort Alaghar. "Isboryi went with the ship of the Frost People to their world by my order," Alaghar said, her voice dead. "He is to teach them of the fadohl and learn their ways of fighting."

"He is their prisoner?"

"No!" Ivars snapped. Then, holding up his hands, "He is with my friend. Staying with his family." He stumbled over the word, which didn't really have a good translation in Wiyert. "With his… chosen, and their son and daughter."

That confused Rey'wiros, although it did not show in his expression. Alaghar nodded. "It is as Ivars says, exactly. They do not have *damah*. They live in things called *houses* there that hold no more than ten people. Sometimes they are made with wicker!" The Wiyert also didn't really have a word for wood either.

Rey'wiros was now completely incredulous. "Impossible. They could not survive."

"I can prove the truth of what I say." Alaghar was calm. "I carried it with me."

Oh no. She didn't... Ivars's lips twitched, and Lea felt a hysterical urge to giggle. *She brought the portable DVD player and the softball game?*

"I will see this proof. But I must also see the means by which the Frost People can do all the things you claim. I must know why you trust them so entirely, Warleader Alaghar."

Alaghar was not happy, but she answered with calm. "I have fought with them on two occasions. From this I observed they know nothing of the fadohl, but they learn to destroy their devices and machine servants with swiftness. I have seen this with my own eyes. They protect their own and care for each other even in great danger. They keep their word."

"And this protective device? Can we use it or make our own?"

Alaghar looked at Lea.

"Um, it isn't working at the moment. It ran out of power before we got to Vartai, but maybe I can recharge it..."

Rey'wiros waved one hand sharply. "The device that finds the *asuhan*, then."

Silence.

"You *will not* be allowed any farther into my *damah* with your secrets, Frost People. How did you open the gate? How can I trust people that can do that? I do not deny your words, Alaghar. But I must know. It is my responsibility to Vartai to take the time to make sure the fadohl are not involved."

"*Buj-lagar*, time is what we do not have." Rey'wiros glared at Alaghar. His fury was focused and sharp. Lea did not understand what she had said that made him so mad, but he was. And Alaghar was...nervous? "There are signs the machine servants of the fadohl have come to observe Beredul. Recently."

That got everybody's attention, and not in a good way. All the

Wiyert were frightened now.

"How do you know this?"

"I said that we came here with the help of the Frost People, but you did not ask how." Alaghar suddenly went to one knee, hands flat on the ground before her and her head lowered. Her emotions were churning and troubled. She was doing something dangerous, but Lea couldn't tell what or why. "We destroyed the gate nexus that led to Beredul to protect the world of the Frost People. We returned"—she swallowed hard—"on a mainship the Frost People had taken. It can see the traces of its own kind. Something of *fadohl* make was in the skies above Beredul less than twenty world-turns ago."

Rey'wiros's emotions were a hot flame of fury and horror. "You found them *on a fadohl ship?* How could they not be under their control? How can you seek mercy from me as if you were a warrior still? *You brought this within walls!*"

The Wiyert on the other side of the metal grate were already aiming their weapons. Lea was about to shut them down, but a quick hand gesture from Ivars, meaning *hold position*, made her stop. He wasn't nearly as terrified as she was, strangely.

"We stole the ship," Ivars said. "It had been left, abandoned, for thousands of years, in our solar system. It's on our side now. Our side meaning the antifadohl side, of course. I don't know how these things think, but isn't that a long wait for a trap?"

Alaghar had not looked up. Lea could see sweat beading on her face and sense her fear.

"We do not have time, *buj-lagar*. No time at all. We need the help of the Frost People and they need ours."

"Then they must show us their devices. Let us see they are not of fadohl make. You say the fadohl are coming, I say prove to me they are not already here." Rey'wiros's gesture encompassed all of the Earth-humans. "Show me."

Shall I tell him? Lea asked. Ivars grimaced, then gave a reluctant nod. Lea took a deep breath.

"Ah, there isn't a device, as such."

Alaghar had gone completely still. Rey'wiros actually frowned, confused, then Lea felt his growing anger. He thought they were making fun of him.

She pointed. "Two of your people, there. One above, *there*. Three in the passage through which we came. One farther, that way…"

Lea felt the shock ripple through him. "You are only guessing."

He'd be a killer poker player. He knows I'm right, but it sure doesn't show. Okay, what else can I do? She didn't really want to open the front door again, and it was a bit far off for comfort. However, there was something else mechanical nearby and connected to remote controls that she could take over. The grate… it could move. So she moved it—after shutting their weapons off. They were not going to like this at all.

It was hinged top and bottom, interlaced like clock-gear teeth in the middle. The normal speed was quite fast, so she slowed it down to prevent panic.

Then Lea saw that Alaghar was going to be hit by the lower section, and she wasn't moving away. Was refusing to move. It must be some Wiyert warrior custom. So Lea stopped the grate opening and reversed the gears to close it back up.

As she had expected, the Wiyert had gone completely nuts, except for Alaghar. They were yelling about the weapons not working, pointing at the grate, and shouting to others out of sight. Lea could feel other mechanical systems doing things…shutting more doors.

Rey'wiros, strangely, had been more astonished when she shut the grate than when she had opened it. And he was thinking now, like Ivars did sometimes. A white heat of thought, but the anger was subdued.

"If the Frost People can do this, why do you seek *our* help?"

"It's just me," Lea admitted. "And besides…the Wiyert are family. Blood-kin," she added quickly.

Alaghar actually smiled. "It is so. The world of the Frost People was once ours also, long ago. Before the fadohl took us. The World of the Gold Sun."

It occurred to Alaghar shortly after making the death obeisance that she had not thought it through. Her people knew the cost in following her, she knew the cost in taking responsibility. The Frost People, however, knew nothing. If Rey'wiros accepted the obeisance, they would only see that he was attacking her—and they would defend. She knew this. So why had she not thought to warn them?

The Frost People cause change and destruction wherever they go! They are nothing but trouble, for all the help they give!

But Rey'wiros stayed his hand. He did not release her, however, even when the security barrier began to open. She had to remain unmoving—perhaps this was just his way? But no, they were afraid. He had not ordered the barrier opened, and it would have been very strange for him to have done such a thing when he still questioned the safety of the Frost People.

So Lea had opened the barrier to prove her words. Confirmation came when the barrier stopped moving just above her head and then returned to its original protective position. Alaghar had never seen it stop halfway, and from the glimpse she stole of Rey'wiros, neither had he.

Was that why she was still alive?

"Lea. Restore their weapons." It was not fitting for a *buj-lagar* to strike only with a knife.

"You do realize they were going to shoot us? And you?" Lea spoke as if she were talking to a child. It must seem so, to her.

"Only the weapon of the *buj-lagar*, then. And only if it is aimed at me."

Lea muttered something in her own language that Alaghar didn't understand, but it sounded angry. Alaghar dared not raise her head to look and see if Lea had done as she commanded, but she could hear the quiet voices of the in-wall commander and the *lagar* with Rey'wiros. Their weapons were still dead, but his was working again.

She marveled at her own calm. Perhaps she would die, perhaps she would not. Strange how she could have more confidence in the actions of the Frost People than her own kind. Lea would not harm her, but Rey'wiros might.

"I do not accept your death," Rey'wiros said finally. It sounded like he was speaking through gritted teeth.

Alaghar slowly stood, being careful not to look up from the ground until she was completely upright. She was not surprised to see Lea glaring at the *buj-lagar* when she did. Alaghar shook her head at Lea, hoping she would understand it was a warning.

"He wants to kill you," Lea said in a shaky voice. "Why?"

"He believes I have endangered Vartai by bringing you inside the walls. For us this is the ultimate crime. Worthy of death. It is for him to decide this."

"Is there anything we can do to convince you we aren't a threat?" This was the calm voice of Ivars. "Or at least talk before killing anybody?"

"I will not allow you within the inner wall." Rey'wiros bared his teeth. Ivars appeared not to notice the challenge.

"Would we need to be…wherever that is?" Ivars looked at her, one eyebrow raised. "I'm fine with talking here, or even back with our gear. Not out with the things with the teeth, though."

Alaghar felt grim amusement seeing Rey'wiros silent and puzzled. *Yes, see how little you know of the Frost People! You do not even know how to insult them!*

"What is it you wish to speak of?" Rey'wiros said finally.

Ivars waited for Alaghar, but she kept her mouth closed. Better they speak for themselves, even with their few words of Wiyert. Ivars sighed, rubbed the back of his neck, and looked directly at Rey'wiros. Alaghar cringed inside.

"Your people are stuck here, imprisoned by the fadohl. You want out. We want to help you escape, before the fadohl get here. Lea"—he pointed—"can shut down the thing keeping you here, if we can find the source. You've seen what she can do. Alaghar has seen her take out fadohl defenses before too. Ask her."

"And why do you offer this? You say we are kin. I see a resemblance, but that is not enough. How does this benefit the Frost People?"

"We want your help to defend our home world. Our *common* home world. We need to know more about the fadohl; where they are, what their defenses are, how to fight them. Until just a few years ago we didn't even know they existed. You know far more about them, and we need to learn to survive. The ship we stole is very large. We can carry many of your people away from this place once the shield is down." Ivars tilted his empty hands forward. "You probably have a lot of questions. We'll do our best to answer them, but let's agree to talk."

Alaghar saw the bright gleam in Rey'wiros's eyes. Perhaps this had not been a disaster after all. The Wiyert had dreamed for generations of escaping Beredul—and now he had seen someone with the ability to do it. She knew it was a strong temptation for him, and of all the *buj-lagar*, he was the most likely to try it.

Rey'wiros was the boldest of them. It had been his idea to send warriors to the portal gate, and he was young for a *buj-lagar*. Not yet frozen in the armor of tradition. Vartai was the smallest of the *damah* but full of hardened warriors that knew the dangers of the frontier, who *wanted* to take the fight to the enemy, not just hide behind walls forever.

"We will talk. Go and prepare what you require. Alaghar will bring you here again when it is time."

Ivars nodded, and the Frost People turned and left. Lea gave Rey'wiros one last glare before she went, and Alaghar stifled a sigh.

Rey'wiros turned to her. "Why do these people speak of friendship yet act to cause conflict?"

"They do not see their actions as aggressive, *buj-lagar*." Alaghar fumbled for a way to explain. "Their...customs are different. Very different." And now that she was back with her own people, the strangeness was even more apparent. "You saw the one with the metal foot. Know also that Ivars, their leader, would be behind walls were he one of us for his past injuries. Know that the small one, Lea, is *not* a warrior by their rule. Yet she fought beside us to get here," she admitted with a certain perverse pride. It had been worth the frustration to train Lea.

Rey'wiros snorted. "They seem thin and weak, all of them, to be warriors of any kind."

Alaghar shook her head sharply. "In a fight of grasping hands perhaps, but none of us can keep pace with them. They go up hills and rocks like wind, and their weapons throw hard things, *ammo*, very fast. We killed over ten *asuhan*, all of us together. Even Lea killed one," she added, remembering. She would not mention the weeping and the shrieking afterward.

"I hear." Rey'wiros thought for a moment. "What else of them should we know?"

"If they spoke truly, their numbers are vast. They have no understanding of safe behavior as we do here. They leave doors open as they find convenient!" She shrugged, indicating she was just reporting what she had seen. Then she decided it was perhaps better to give Rey'wiros a hint of warning. It might be too much of a shock otherwise, and Alaghar had no confidence Lea would understand or be able to conceal the truth for very long. "They… they do not forbid warriors from having chosen."

Rey'wiros could not even speak for a moment, his eyes wide. "They are insane?"

"When I show you their world, it may seem less harmful." Quickly, she must change the subject before he asked too much. "They also have among them small creatures. They do not eat them. I am told they are allowed in their *du-damah*…their *homes*. I have seen one such on the ship they brought us on, a *cat*. I have touched it and it did not attack me, so perhaps it is true."

"They speak their own language, it is clear. How did they learn ours?"

"The ship. It knew…an old form of our speech. The Frost People woke the ship-mind and made it free. I do not know how they did this, but it speaks and asks what it does not know as a person would. The Frost People taught us some of their speech as well."

"That is good. A suspicious people would not do that." Rey'wiros gave her a direct look. "Now tell me, if you know. How can this Lea be stopped from opening gates? Can she be bound in any way?"

Cold fear flashed through her. "You will not touch Lea!" Forgetting, in her haste, that she was speaking in the mode of direct command. To *buj-lagar* Rey'wiros, who had not heard that mode addressed to him since he assumed his post. And she could see his eyes widening even now in justifiable fury. "I defend, *buj-lagar*! I defend you, I defend Vartai!"

"Explain." His voice was like ice.

Alaghar lowered her head and gazed at the floor. "To touch Lea is to give up all your secrets. No one should touch her. Watch the Frost People and see how they take care around her. She hears what is not spoken, *buj-lagar*. I swear with my hand on my knife! Please. Do not put the Wiyert in danger. Did you not see her here? All you need do is ask. She restored your weapon when I told her to do so, even though she feared for me."

"And she closed the barrier without any such request. I saw this." He sighed and briefly closed his eyes. "Such power…is the alliance with the Frost People worth this terrible risk?"

Sunshine, gold sunshine, and the laughter of children. "I will show you now, *buj-lagar*. And you shall decide."

CHAPTER 11

They were back in the leper ward, but Ivars didn't really mind. It sounded like Vartai didn't get a lot of visitors or door-to-door salesmen, so it was unlikely they would be interrupted here, in one of the two isolation-from-outside rooms. They'd put the planning table at the other end of the rectangular main room from the bedding. They were also using the anteroom just outside the inner gate door, which connected to the isolation room. Right now Ramirez and North were going over the gear there and cleaning and repairing it.

They had a pathetic amount of ammunition left, but it was the thought that counted. They'd better hope they could borrow some energy weapons for the next run or it was going to be ugly.

The table appeared to be made entirely of scrap iron. He could barely move it. But it was flat enough to spread the Wiyert version of paper on top and start making plans and marking up some maps. He rolled a new sheet out, then grabbed his cup just before disaster struck. The stuff could be written on, but if anything with water got on it, it turned into a sticky mess.

He sipped at the drink. It was hot, and that was pretty much all you could say about it. Everything edible here tasted vaguely like dirt. *No wonder they got so excited by a couple of hard candies.* He sternly informed his brain that he was drinking coffee, and it should wake up now.

Considering where he thought they would be at this point, e.g., inside the digestive system of one of those prehistoric monsters, they had made great progress. The big boss hardly ever thought about killing them anymore, according to Lea, who would know. They'd all pretty much caught up on their sleep, and their various injuries were treated and healing.

On the other hand, the Wiyert made the ancient Spartans look like a bunch of giggling sorority girls, they still thought the Earth-humans might have fadohl cooties, he had been strictly informed by Alaghar that even holding hands with your girlfriend was No Go This Station, and he couldn't get around the fact that they would, eventually, have to go back outside with the monsters to get anything done.

Rey'wiros, though. He might be able to do something with him. He'd seen the combination before: raw fighting ability, intelligence, and ambition. When he'd come across someone like that, especially a tribal chieftain in the 'stans, it was a dangerous crapshoot. If he could get the guy lined up and pointed the right direction, the mission was gravy and everybody, including the chieftain, was happy. Otherwise it was all putting out fires and trying to keep knives out of his back, never mind the mission.

This guy wanted power but was willing to earn it. He also took his job of protecting his people seriously. Ivars could respect that. Rey'wiros also was canny enough to know when to take risks. Since Lea had shown she could rip up any of his mechanical defenses whenever she felt like it, the metal safety grid in the meeting room was now up when they were called in for a chat with the Wiyert. And since Ivars wasn't dumb either, he made sure his people stayed on their side of the invisible line where the grid used to be. There was a door in the back on the Wiyert side he was pretty sure led to the interior of the fort, but he didn't even look at it. Everybody knew what the score was, and everybody was being oh so polite about it.

Wonderful thing, trust.

He sneaked a glance at Lea. She was sleeping, collapsed in her usual tangled heap, and he smiled. The trip had taken a lot out of her, not to mention the injuries. She was still limping, and he wasn't sure what they were going to do if they had to go hiking again. It was also good to keep her out of the Wiyert line of sight. From the way they were treating her like a load of plutonium,

Alaghar had spilled the beans. They wouldn't get within ten feet of her if they could help it.

The local Wiyert, that was. Alaghar and her team were also in purgatory with them, in the other isolation room, and they had… not precisely become comfortable with Lea, but at least considered her on their side. Everybody knew she was the reason they had gotten here alive. Even Alaghar, who alternated between carefully hidden awe and major irritation at Lea's complete lack of warrior bearing.

"*Hazu*, Ivars." Alaghar herself came into the room, chewing on something like twigs from a bowl. She offered it to him, and he took one to be polite.

It tasted like a twig, with dirt on it. *It's not a sheep eyeball. Stop whining.*

"Hey yourself. So do you think he believes you are safe to let inside yet?"

She gave him a disbelieving stare. "We are still here with you."

"Yeah, but you could just be here to keep an eye on us. Listen when we talk in our sleep, that sort of thing." He grinned at her, but she did not respond.

"You say nothing of interest."

Ah, that dry Wiyert humor.

"Well is there anything we can do to help that along? You must want to go inside, see your friends and family."

"Vartai is not my *damah*. I come from Koloh. Burdhul is from here, and Hazuruh."

Hmm, a coalition team, then. Interesting.

"Is Koloh far from here?" Ivars started sketching on the paper, keeping a relaxed appearance. He had been very careful not to ask nosy questions like exact locations, or numbers of inhabitants, or anything else that might be considered need-to-know around here. Also part of the trust thing.

"It is the closest to Vartai." Information, but not very useful. "Rey'wiros will not let us go within until we can prove we are safe. To prove that, we must make Vartai safe." There was a gleam of wintery humor in her eyes. The Wiyert wouldn't let them in to find out how to drop the planetary energy barricade until they… dropped the energy barricade. Very funny.

Movement at the inner door made him look up. One of the

locals was standing there, arms heaped with cloth. He dumped it on the floor and took a step back but didn't leave.

"The device no longer works as you showed us," he said to Alaghar, swallowing hard. "Can it be made whole again?"

Ivars raised an eyebrow at her. There might have been just a hint of color on her broad face. "I left the image player to show Rey'wiros the world of the Gold Sun," she said.

He kept his expression mildly interested. "Might have forgotten to shut it off, and the battery ran down. If you bring it here, we can take a look." Another self-imposed rule was the Earth-humans did not go up to the meeting room unless directly invited. Alaghar hadn't asked to take the portable DVD player, but since it looked like it might be cracking the Wiyert defenses, he wasn't going to complain.

Alaghar followed the local out of the room. In the dark sleeping corner, Lea stirred and emerged from her blankets like a small hibernating bear, blinking and rumpled.

"Morning, sunshine. Want some nice, hot mud?"

"Issit morning?"

"Nah, just kidding. I have no idea where the sun is. They don't believe in windows here for some reason. I wasn't kidding about the mud, though." He poured some fresh into the cup and handed it to her.

She drank and coughed. "Blarg. Okay, I'm awake." She wheezed and took another reluctant sip. "I hope they give us this stuff because they hate us and not because it is the best thing they have." Lea handed back the cup and wandered over to the pile of fabric. "Oh, hey! It's clean clothes!" She rummaged in the pile, grabbed a few things, and disappeared under a blanket, emerging a few minutes later. The Wiyert clothing was comically large on her, but she managed to tuck and wrap it enough to keep from tripping on it.

Alaghar returned, bearing the DVD player. "It has no longer power, as you said. How is it fed?"

"I might be able to do that if...if there is a power source here," Lea said slowly. "Is there? One they will let us use?"

Alaghar smiled, with teeth. "They will. They all wish to see the *sof-bal-gaym*. From the time I first showed it they have not stopped. They wait in turn to see it."

Ivars stifled a laugh. So now the Wiyert were willing to cooperate, eh? They owed those kids on the softball team now. Big, tough Wiyert, brought low by a bunch of sixth graders. They could use that.

"We should get the shield device recharged too. If we can do a demo inside, that might help Rey'wiros think we are the good guys."

That turned out to be more difficult. The DVD player was sufficiently alien, but the Wiyert recognized the source of the shield device and were not happy.

"Fadohl," one snarled.

"The ship we *stole* from the fadohl made it for us," Lea said, again. "Fine, let's just get the player charged again. Where's the power plug?"

More argument, especially when the Wiyert understood Lea *had* to go with the DVD player. The pull of the softball game proved stronger than the opposition. And since Lea was still hobbling on her sprained ankle and he was the only person that had no objection to making contact with her, Ivars got to go along and be a crutch.

And hold hands in public. Ivars very carefully did not make eye contact with Alaghar as they were escorted by armed guards to the power source.

How are the locals taking all this?

All jumbled up. Confused. Upset. It wasn't just our Wiyert that were shocked by the game—it really seems to blow them away. I guess…I guess it is so different than anything they have ever experienced, and we look like them. They can imagine being there themselves. Her thoughts were sad and wistful. *They haven't had much to look forward to here for a long time.*

The power supply was odd, curiously diffuse and low voltage, but high potential. Like a large, low-pressure tank of water. She had to jury-rig a charger from components the Wiyert brought her, but she got the player battery back to full charge. The Wiyert all but snatched it from her hands when it was done, running off for the next viewing.

Seeing the tools and gear that the Wiyert had had gotten her thinking. Something about power and the overwatch system…

"Alaghar—you said that powerful devices were shut down by the barrier, right? How powerful?"

Alaghar shrugged. "I do not know the size forbidden, only that it exists. Why do you wish to know?"

Her ankle was really starting to hurt, and she leaned on Ivars a bit more. "Because something is broadcasting here, and it has to be pretty strong to cover the area we were in. But it isn't getting shut down."

Ivars picked up her meaning immediately. "You think it is something the fadohl did, then? What is it doing?"

"It's not *doing* anything. No information packets or anything like that. More like a…I dunno, dial tone. But since it's simple, it should be possible to jam it, at least in a small area. Then maybe we could see what it is doing." She thought about it some more and realized she'd left out a big and important part. "Dammit. The Wiyert won't have anything like that I can hack because of the energy ban, and I didn't bring any of my gear. Oh well, back to planning." She hobbled, wincing. No ice here either, probably.

Ivars was thinking; she could feel the flow of his mind. "I suppose we shouldn't repurpose the shield device, because we're going to need that. We didn't bring our radios, unfortunately."

They were in their cellar room again, and North, seated on a rough stool, looked up at them as they entered. "What do you need radios for? I thought they were bad mojo here."

"I want to make something to cancel that strange overall signal I'm picking up. Simple frequency with a bit of amplification, but if we don't have the basic components here, there's not much I can do."

North grimaced. "Yeah, I didn't bring any of the comms gear with me."

"I might have something." Ramirez sat up on his pad. "Lemmee check." He went out to the antechamber, coming back with one of the giant-pill rounds used by the big, programmable weapon he carried, the XM25. "Knew leaving you guys to pack was a bad idea," he said, shaking his head and smiling. "I would have left this one out. It's a surveillance load. Pop it where you need it, picks up and broadcasts back. Got around thirty-yardrange."

He tossed it at Lea, and she managed to catch it. Her senses picked up on the little device inside immediately. As he had said, it was not very powerful. She could tell even if she hooked up more power to it, the connections and circuitry could not handle it. But it should be enough for an experiment. If she could get access to something to make an antenna.

"You have a purpose to this." Alaghar had crouched down against the wall and was studying her, revealing nothing in her expression.

It was all guesswork, or mostly, and what evidence she had couldn't be shared with the rest since it was all in her head. "I think the signal is making the big animals—the *asuhan*—aggressive. Or more aggressive than they would be. When…when that thing got me…" She swallowed hard, forcing herself to speak. "I could feel it even more. Like it was resonating inside, and its… thoughts. It's hard to describe, but like it had a big, spiky headache. Before I stabbed it, even. So Rey'wiros wants us to prove we are good guys and will help, right? I thought if we could maybe calm down the animals so it's easier to go places, that would count."

As an added bonus, she wouldn't feel the animals' pain if she could shut that down. And they would stay away.

Ivars rubbed his chin. "What do you need besides the radio to make this work?"

Lea thought for a bit. "Three yards of wire, something like copper would be best, and a stick to hold it up with, some smaller wires and solder or connectors to hook it up, and tools to take the round casing off."

"If we had more casings, we could make some C4 grenades for the XM25," Ramirez said. "Since we've got more C4 than ammo now."

"We might still need the C4. I have the feeling we're going to need to break into *something*," Ivars said, grumbling. "Maybe we can get an energy weapon or two. We'll need something more than what we've got to go back out again." He looked over at Alaghar. "Can you ask Rey'wiros?"

"What we give to you cannot be used for our defense. Yes, I know what you intend will defend us. But that is what Rey'wiros will say."

That sounded like no, but Lea caught a bright pulse of amusement from Ivars, although he didn't show it on his face. "Oh, this is just like old times. So, what does the bast—what does he want in trade?"

The problem was they were limited to trading what they had on hand, and the vast majority of that would be desperately needed to get back to Argo fairly soon. The issue was getting Rey'wiros to trust them.

Ivars ended up handing over one set of the night-vision adaptives. They still had two that way, and Lea had mentioned any tech obviously of Earth origin fascinated the local Wiyert. The adaptives fascinated Rey'wiros to the tune of one used energy weapon, some wire, and some scrap metal.

Ivars had done a little familiarization with the Wiyert energy weapons with Alaghar's people back on Argo. The one they had been given operated on the same principles but seemed to be a different model. Alaghar had checked it and pronounced it working. Until they went outside and he could actually fire the thing, he'd have to take that at face value.

It was unlikely they would make the first check-in with Argo, but he wanted to make an all-out effort for the next one. That gave them nine days for travel and persuasion. A quick win of some kind had to happen soon. Once they had access to all their equipment again, bargaining with Rey'wiros would be easier.

Lea and North were in the workshop, busy jury-rigging the antenna and discussing field strength and insulation under nervous Wiyert guard. Ramirez was there too, alternately consulting his handy Wiyert Speak & Spell device and waving his hands to a bemused Wiyert who supposedly could machine metal. If they could get more rounds devised for the grenade launcher, it would be worth it.

Ivars went back to their isolation room to do community outreach, otherwise known as chatting up the command chain. Rey'wiros was rarely available, another tactic he recognized, but his aide—or equivalent—Ghyem had clearly been ordered to get more intel about the Earth-humans. Ghyem was taller than the average Wiyert, not quite as bulky, and had a similar reddish cast to his hair as Isboryi had. He watched all the Earth-humans with suspicious caution, rarely volunteered anything, and seemed to have some kind of history with Alaghar, at least to the extent of her enjoying needling him about something sufficiently obscure Ivars's limited Wiyert vocabulary couldn't figure it out. He'd have to ask Lea about it.

The shield device was on the metal planning table, and Ghyem was looking at it as if it were a poisonous snake.

"This small thing kept *asuhan* away? It is a weapon?" Ghyem said, with some assistance in translation.

"It kept away *uh-asuhan*, and it is not a weapon. It is a wall." Alaghar pointed at the thick, black stone wall of the room. "A wall of power."

"If we can charge it up again, we can show you," Ivars said. Keeping his tone and expression nonchalant, relaxed. As if it were no big deal either way. "We used up all the power getting here. We also found a way to make it hide us. That's really how we got away from the...*uh-asuhan*." He shivered, remembering. That sucker was *big*.

"How many *asuhan* did you encounter, and of what kinds? How did you deal with them?"

Ivars unrolled the hand-drawn map. He'd spent every spare moment noting details and distances down, and when he, North, and Ramirez all agreed, they traced the final pencil marks with something more permanent Alaghar had found for them.

As he went over the events of their trek, he kept a surreptitious watch on Ghyem. Wiyert expressions and reactions were subtle, but Ivars got the feeling Ghyem wasn't so much interested in the lay of the land, which he had probably already learned about from Alaghar, but in seeing how the Earth-humans had fought. Which Ghyem also should have gotten from Alaghar's report. So was he making sure Ivars would tell the same story? Trying to figure out tactics?

He wished Lea were here. She might be able to tell what Ghyem was really interested in. Without that information, Ivars stuck to a straightforward report, only going into more detail on the section where they had used the adaptives to travel at night. Maybe that would be enough of a hint. *Look, we're being useful. We want to help you. Let us, dammit!*

Kugohin came in, wearing his armor. He glanced about the room and appeared relieved Lea was not in sight.

"You go out?"

Kugohin nodded, approaching the table and studying the map. "*Kargesh*," he said, pointing to the door.

Ivars didn't remember that word, so he pulled out the translation device. It informed him the word meant hunting-for-food, vs. hunting-for-safety. "You hunt *asuhan*?" He supposed the meat they had been eating had to come from somewhere, and the environment wasn't conducive to open farming. Except for mud-coated twigs.

Kugohin nodded again and actually volunteered the information about which kind of *asuhan* were best for food and where they were likely to be found. Ivars kept asking questions to encourage the mood. More Wiyert came in, Hazuruh and Dumhaigl and a handful of locals. They had the general air of waiting around, very familiar to the military mind, and they gravitated to the table as well and added commentary. It was almost, kind of, friendly.

And then Lea came in. Ivars had sensed her presence moving closer, and at a fairly quick pace. She seemed happy. The Wiyert, when they saw her, weren't, but they just moved to keep a safe distance.

She didn't seem to notice. She was carrying her long pole with a wire and the kludged-together broadcaster and had that bright, cheerful expression he'd learned meant she was in hot pursuit of a Good Idea. That nobody else usually understood the Good Idea or agreed that she should do whatever it was made no difference, and she would try to explain until your ears bled.

"Mark! It's working—at least it's broadcasting the signal, and it does cancel the one I detect."

Wait, he understood most of that. Maybe the braininess was contagious? "Great! Er, that is what you thought it would do, right?"

Lea nodded vigorously. "Yeah. And then I heard them talking about going outside, and I thought maybe I could take it out and see what it does to the animals when that signal goes away." Her voice faltered, and he knew she was picking up his immediate and strong reaction, which was not a happy one. "I wasn't going to go wandering around, I just want to find out! I'll wear my armor and everything!"

He brushed her hand as he took the pole, as if he were helping. *Calm down; you're spooking the locals.* Lea blinked and rocked back on her heels. It was so handy sometimes to have that private channel. The Wiyert were good at the poker face, but Ivars was experienced in reading small signs. The Vartai people were slightly shocked, although he didn't know why, and Alaghar's team was a mix of horrified amusement. They had seen Lea in action before.

"They go to hunt. You would hinder them and require their protection."

He hadn't seen Alaghar come in. She was glaring at Lea, who was glaring right back. Alaghar wasn't wearing armor, but hers was damaged—was that why she was not going out with the rest?

"I wasn't going to hunt, I just want to go out and—"

Alaghar's broad hand went out, flat. "You stop this," she said in her choppy English. "When warrior speak to eyes, small to large, is attack."

Lea's eyes widened. "Oh." She blinked, but she seemed to understand Alaghar's cryptic warning. Of course she got some subtext for free, as it were.

"Hey. What's going on?"

Lea looked at him, frowning in thought. "Um, somehow arguing isn't cool. Or I'm not supposed to argue like I am. Something about rank or status? I'm pretty low on the totem pole, so I shouldn't argue with anyone. I don't want to make them mad, but how can I persuade them without arguing?"

Now he got it. And it made sense, with all the other little details of Wiyert culture he'd been picking up—and, he realized, what Alaghar had been hinting about. Poor Lea. This was going to take a lot of work for her.

"You can argue, but it has to be nonconfrontational. Otherwise it's like a challenge, and they can't let that slide, they have to push back or lose face or whatever the equivalent here is. You were directly contradicting Alaghar, and in front of the other Wiyert. You are, sorry, definitely less of a warrior than she is. She's a leader. Looks like staring someone down isn't polite here, especially if you have lower rank—and everybody has rank. Welcome to the military."

All of Lea's enthusiasm seemed crushed. "How do I argue without arguing?"

Ivars grinned. "It's an art. You learn how to say, 'That is a stupid idea that will get us all killed, sir,' without being insubordinate, or you don't get far. Or live very long. It also means giving the officer in question reasons your way will get what they want done better or faster. They don't care what *you* want." He gestured at the Wiyert. "They want to go hunting and not get killed or spend time rescuing you. How can you help with that? And don't glare at anybody."

She sighed, giving him an eye roll. Then she turned back to Alaghar but kept her gaze on the device in her hands.

"I will tell you where the *asuhan* are, close by, when the hunters leave. As I did before. I can do this from the…place inside the gate, without leaving. With the gate open, this machine can be tested to see if it will stop *asuhan* attacks."

Like that? Her voice whispered in his brain, and she glanced at him. He nodded. Lea had many attributes he appreciated, and the quick learning curve was high on the list.

Ivars thought he saw a flicker of a twitching lip on Alaghar, but it was quickly suppressed.

"I permit this. I also will stand in the open gate, to remind you of your intentions if you forget." *Translation: I will haul your ass back inside if you act up or get in the way of my people, and I might do some wall-to-wall counseling on the way.*

Lea just nodded, looking wilted. It was probably good they'd had this exchange, even if it had embarrassed Lea. Ivars realized he must have stepped on some toes himself, not understanding local custom. He could do a better job negotiating now that he knew. Alaghar had tried to warn him, but the same cultural custom had restrained her from telling him exactly what a bulldozer he was being—and their "rank" was very similar, as far as he could tell.

Time to put his newfound intel into practice and cheer up Space Cadet. He carefully fixed his gaze in the traditional location, just past Alaghar's right ear. "I would go too and watch. And to…" He had to consult the Speak & Spell for the name. "To practice using the energy weapon."

Alaghar decided she could probably survive one more idiot

Earth-human, so he got his gear together while the Wiyert deployed to the smaller outer room. When Ivars got there Alaghar had also returned, with her armor on and a weapon in hand.

The Wiyert had a smooth exit procedure, clearly doctrine and well practiced. The gatehouse area was scoped out fully before the inner door was opened, and everyone entered in formation order before that door was closed. Somebody had eyes on the exterior somehow and called out the all clear.

Lea raised her hand as if asking for permission to speak in school. Alaghar just stared at her, bemused.

Ivars intervened. "Contacts?"

"One big one there, about…half a mile. Three smaller ones *there*, two hundred feet, moving that direction." She gestured. "One small one right in front, even closer."

The Wiyert from Alaghar's team shifted position, already picking their targets. They knew exactly how Lea worked, and it no longer disturbed them. The other Wiyert shifted away from the sound of her voice but paid no other attention.

Until Alaghar ordered the door opened and a small version of one of the armored boar creatures burst out of the foliage, heading straight for them. Just like Lea had said.

Hazuruh stepped forward, her weapon already shouldered. The armored boar slowed and seemed to sniff the air, then the ground. Ivars saw Hazuruh lower her weapon slightly, then pick it up and fire.

The armored boar dropped, a clean energy bolt killing it instantly.

"The *wesr* did not run," Hazuruh murmured.

"Is that what it should do?" Lea asked.

"Yes. It should charge when it sees us. It did not."

Now the local Wiyert were looking at Lea as if she were one of the *asuhan* herself and appeared quite happy to be ordered outside of the gatehouse area. Some took up position to the left, where Lea had indicated the big creature was, and two others went to drag the armored boar back inside. It must be one of the edible ones, then. The rest spread out and went to the right, soon disappearing in the vegetation.

He heard an energy blast, then another.

"They got one but just wounded the other," Lea said, giving

them the brain-scan play-by-play. "Third one is running away."

"It will please the *buj-lagar* if more *wesr* are taken." Alagar briefly indicated the dead armored boar before going back to scanning carefully for threats at the edge of the door. "It is young, and this kind of *asuhan* is favored. The meat will be very good." She glanced at Lea. "Can you hear the kind also?"

Lea scrunched up her face. "Not really. Maybe if I practiced…" She glanced at Alaghar quickly, then away. "I wonder if that one didn't charge because of my nullifier." Alaghar shrugged.

The three of them waited in the gatehouse area for a while. Lea either hadn't detected anything new or was keeping it to herself. Ivars hadn't heard anything from either group that went off. About half an hour later two Wiyert came back with the other kill, dropped it on the first, and went off again. The weather was calm, overcast with a slight chill. The lack of wind kept the rotting refrigerator smell to a minimum, which he was grateful for.

Lea stood holding her wire pole and device like a spear and shield. Her original excitement was seeping back, and then he felt a spike of surprise.

"The big one…it moved away and I lost track of it, and now it is showing up over there." She pointed to the right, where the large group of hunters had gone. "It's going near the Wiyert."

Alaghar stared at her. "Between them and Vartai?" Lea nodded. "Let us see if it can be distracted. Better that they do not have to fight their way home."

She hefted her weapon in one arm, showing Ivars how to set the range, intensity, and size of the energy burst. The weapons did not have much in the way of markings, so he took it slow, making sure he could remember which was which. Alaghar's plan was to set something on fire. It would let the other Wiyert know something was up and with luck catch the attention of the creature as well.

He had Lea do her visual display in his synthetic eye, making sure there were no friendly targets between him and his pyromania. Incinerating someone would be counterproductive.

The energy weapon had no recoil when fired, but he did notice a slight wave of static electricity through the armor armpieces and a whiff of ozone. The accuracy was not stellar, but he was not sure if that was operator inexperience, the type of shot Alaghar had selected, or the reason the Wiyert didn't mind giving this particular weapon to the Earth-humans.

Lea had put little blue dots for the Wiyert, along with the big red dot for the *asuhan*. If he was seeing things correctly, the Wiyert were starting to head back to the gate. Unfortunately, so was the creature.

"We may have a fight coming," Ivars told Alaghar. "The others are being followed." He was not entirely happy with being armed only with the equivalent of a precision flamethrower with a poor rate of fire. If the creature was like the giant crab they'd encountered, the energy weapons would just piss it off.

She didn't seem too bothered. Ivars guessed they must have similar situations on a regular basis and knew how to deal with them. It was just a bit pucker inducing for him.

On that thought he checked on Lea. She was looking worried but clinging tightly to her "nullifier" and standing right at the edge of the gateway.

"They come."

The first few Wiyert came in to view at the jog-trot that was the Wiyert equivalent of a fast run. They stacked up, weapons out, as soon as they entered the gatehouse area, and Ivars felt better. Rate of fire or no, now they had a reasonable defense.

"Should we get some people inside?" He tilted his head, indicating the one person who ought to be inside immediately.

"The doors take too long to cycle, and even she cannot force this. The gears for the outer door block those for the inner door. If one is open, the other cannot be moved."

Well, there were worse spots to be stuck in. The stone walls were thick and the gate doorway small enough to defend.

More hunters returned. Lea kept the visuals updated. Now only three Wiyert were still outside. Unfortunately, when he saw them he also saw the *asuhan*. It had long, oddly jointed legs and shaggy hide and moved with a rolling gait that covered the ground at a rapid speed. Sharp tusks curved up from its jaw, with some cracked or missing.

Alaghar hissed a word that sounded like a curse, and from their reaction the other Wiyert weren't happy about it either. Ivars made sure he still had a clear shot despite the crowded area and waved

Lea inside.

She didn't move. She was staring at the *asuhan* intently. It had slowed its loping run down to a walk, and then slowed even further to more of an amble. The stragglers were easily able to outpace it now, and it didn't even seem to notice them.

The shaggy creature turned its head to look at the burning vegetation, now down to smoldering smoke, then reared up on its hind legs for a moment, sniffing. It dropped back down to all fours and lowered its head to sniff again.

Mumbling among the Wiyert and gasps of astonishment. Whatever they had been expecting, this wasn't it.

The *asuhan* took a few more steps, until it was only a few hundred feet from the gate entrance. Ivars could see it breathing, how the hair on its head shifted as it moved. The tusks had streaks of green and brown, mixed in the white like marble. It snuffled the ground again, apparently oblivious to the people watching it, then bent its odd legs and lay down with a heavy sigh.

The last of the stragglers staggered in to the portcullis area. Alaghar snapped a command, and a single bolt of energy hit the *asuhan* at the base of the head. It collapsed completely without making a sound.

Another shout, to close the gate. Ivars snagged Lea's elbow and pulled her back from the massive doors, noticing her face was grey and drawn.

"What's wrong?" It couldn't be the death of the creature; she'd seen enough of that earlier. Hell, one had tried to eat *her*.

"I thought…I thought the nullifier would make them go away. I thought the signal, the pain, was driving them to us, or something like that." She gave him a bewildered look. "The pain did stop. I could feel that. But it just…wanted to sleep. It was so tired, and it felt safe." She wiped away a tear.

"You feel like you betrayed it somehow?"

Lea shook her head vehemently. "No! It isn't that." Another tear fell. "It didn't suffer. It's like it *wanted* to die, to just give up. Its brain…wasn't right. So much pain for so long—and all the monsters are like that! It's being done to them on *purpose!* Why would anyone want to do that? For years and years…"

Understanding made him feel queasy. She was right. Something, probably the fadohl, had deliberately driven the giant animals mad with pain—and they weren't even around to watch. That was strange even for a psychopath.

So why had they done it?

CHAPTER 12

Rey'wiros listened to the hunt leader, then the hunters, with increasing confusion. Everyone agreed something strange had happened and that the small woman of the Frost People had been responsible. The means she had employed were less clear. If it were not for the astonishing amount of meat now on its way to provide Vartai with a full feast, he would have been forced to conclude all of them had somehow inhaled toxic spore pollen and seen what did not exist.

The meat was real, however, so he needed to sift the truth of the matter. He gestured to the *lagar* who had come with the Frost People. She had been listening to the reports with so little reaction that it was clear her opinion was different, to a level that could be a challenge if spoken.

"Lea does not call *asuhan*," Alaghar said calmly. "That is madness. She fears even the smallest of them. To her, however, they are seen as a bright light in darkness. This is how we were able to make our way from the gate of worlds to Vartai when half our company knew nothing of Beredul. She told us where they were."

"The young *wesr* charged at the open gate until it saw her! The *odon-asuhan* also, in her presence it no longer pursued us. It knelt and rested! And you saw how she wept to see it die." One of the hunters stood, confronting her. "You saw this, all that I have said!"

A small muscle in her jaw twitched, but Alaghar still spoke in measured terms, ignoring the challenge. "I saw the young *wesr* and the *odon-asuhan*. I also saw the *asuhan* approach from the right side of the *damah*, where Lea stood inside the door also on the right side. Beside her was her…her *lagar*, Ivars, of a size sufficient to conceal her from view. How then did the *asuhan* see her?"

The hunter lowered his gaze down and away, unable or unwilling to continue the challenge.

Alaghar made the gesture of observation-reported, and continued. "Know that Lea wished to make a trial of the device she made with the gates open. To us she said it might affect the *asuhan*, and all here agree the *asuhan* within the reach of the device did act differently. Did you not also notice this strange behavior began when they were twenty *doti* from the gate? And in her own tongue she spoke to her *lagar* of her astonishment, that she had thought the *asuhan* would instead flee."

It was good that Alaghar knew some of the speech of the Frost People. Rey'wiros had been watching her and her band of survivors, both with his eyes and the eyes of others. He remembered her from before she had left Vartai, and the Alaghar who stood in Vartai again was the same true warrior. Harder, perhaps. More accepting of the outrageous behavior of the Frost People, definitely. But still keeping foremost in her mind the defense of the Wiyert and the destruction of the fadohl. He no longer feared she had been corrupted by the fadohl, but he was aware that many of his people still thought so. He needed to have clear and convincing proof to change their minds or they would challenge his commands regarding her and the others who came with the Frost People.

Therefore he asked, "Then what caused her sorrow? So deep she showed it openly?"

Alaghar, surprisingly, threw up her hands and dropped her head briefly, as if in despair. "If I were asked to list what the Frost People do *not* show openly, it would take less time. Have you not seen the *sof-bal-gaym*? They tell me that it is only a simple game, played by children! And the adults who watched them behave worse than children themselves! It was no death challenge or warrior training. Lea…" Her brow furrowed, and she seemed to search for words. "I admit to all who hear I do not understand her. With touch she can reveal the deepest secrets. But even without touch she can know others' pain, can somehow feel it as her own. She spoke to her *lagar* of this when he also asked the cause of her weeping. She said the *asuhan* had been in agony so deep it welcomed death. That her device had stopped the pain. That this pain was inflicted on all the *asuhan,* and she could think of no reason why this had been done."

The thought was so strange at first it had no meaning for him. *Asuhan* attacked because they were *asuhan.* They had always behaved so, from the first records of the time of the Refusal. How else could they behave?

Rey'wiros thought further. The strange woman of the Frost People had shown the *asuhan* could behave differently. She had made a device that permitted this. The Frost People made many devices for their own purposes instead of taking what the fadohl made and learning how to change and make their own versions. The eye tubes that made darkness into green light—how had they ever thought to make such things? The Wiyert of Beredul were still forced to sift through the old wreckage to find the material to make anything but the simplest devices. What would it be like to make everything for themselves?

If the Wiyert had devices that stopped *asuhan* from attacking, they could go anywhere on Beredul they wished, search through untouched ruins in safety. Although it was still dangerous to place all trust on a single weapon. If it failed or broke, all would be as it was before. Wait, had this Lea not also spoken of a shield? Yes. It needed to be given power again, like the image machine. Both together, the pain stopper and the shield—now *that* would be worth trying.

Rey'wiros nodded. He would permit the Frost People to give their shield device power, and then he would have them demonstrate their workings so his people would know and trust their safety. Wiyert would go with the Frost People to see and report. But he would not risk warriors here.

"Wredis. Bring to me two wishing to still serve Vartai with their blood, whose loss can be sustained. Alaghar. Go and tell the Frost People I wish to see their devices in action. They may show the use of their shield they speak of as well."

Alaghar turned immediately to leave the Room of Boundaries. She seemed pleased by her task. Wredis was less enthusiastic. It was her responsibility to guard all within walls, so to send any of her command to possible death would seem a failure on her part. It was a hard truth, but there were always some within walls who had given all of use already. Those too injured to work, those unable to provide children, those broken in soul and awaiting death.

Like, he realized with a chill, the *asuhan* that no longer felt pain. That had felt enough and wished to feel nothing more.

As he went through the paired gates from the Room of Boundaries to the inner passageways, Rey'wiros continued to plan. If the demonstration was a success, he should send messages to the other *damah*. First to Koloh, inviting them to see for themselves and take glory in their warrior Alaghar's achievements. It would be wise to have allies convinced as soon as possible. Then to other *damah* that might be willing to take chances to be free of Beredul. He would build his connections gradually but with strength. If Alaghar had spoken truly, they might have only one chance before the fadohl returned to enslave—or eradicate—the Wiyert. It was his duty to alert the other *buj-lagar*. The time for caution was at an end.

Argo was beginning to suspect the instructions it had been given were incomplete. The cat exhibited behavior Argo had never seen before—making very loud cries, frequently before the closed doors of the sleeping quarters. Argo opened the doors when this happened, but beyond entering and crying more, the cat did not change his behavior.

Was this indicative of damage? Had Argo performed the feeding task incorrectly? Lea-interface had stressed the importance of feeding. Argo reviewed the instructions and the images of Lea doing the same thing. Argo could detect no difference.

The first cycle the cat did not eat at all. Then he would eat, but not as much. He developed a habit of demanding entrance to Lea's room and then sleeping on the bed for the rest of the cycle. Argo carefully monitored the vital signs of the cat for any sign of suboptimal health. What could it do if the cat was ill? Should it go to Earth to ask for instructions? But then the cat would wake and continue to walk the corridors, searching.

Argo attempted to communicate in the mode it had seen the

humans use, but M.O. showed no signs of listening. He was restless and kept looking for the humans. He missed them, Argo realized. Argo realized it missed the humans too.

Ever since it had awoken, humans had been present within it. Even when the mindless ship *Kepler* had left with most of the humans, Lea-interface and those connected to her remained. Argo liked talking with them and learning. The Wiyert did not talk to Argo very much, but even they would be better than this terrible silence and a creature Argo could not understand.

Lea-interface had suggested Argo make a small construction that could be a symbol of itself, in human scale. Maybe it could make models of the humans, and that would make the cat less lonely? Argo tried making a light image and replaying Lea's voice. The cat reacted by making a noise like he was losing pressure and becoming very stiff with the many hairs on his body standing straight out. Argo tried again, being sure to create the most accurate image, but this time the cat ran away.

It was very puzzling.

The time period for the first return arrived. Argo moved with the greatest possible speed through the discontinuity. As ordered, it checked to see if any other discontinuity craft had come since its last visit. None had. Then Argo connected to the lunar station, eager to see Lea-interface and ask her what it was doing wrong.

Lea was not there, and none of the secret symbols were there either. She had not returned, as she had predicted. Argo performed the most exhaustive list of scans and comparisons with all the data it could gather. The image in the gate portal had changed in slight ways—an animal corpse was visible now, and the doorway once blocked with rubble was now empty, and rays of outside light came through. No sign of any of the humans. By its instructions, it must leave again.

Argo went to another distant location and reviewed its memories of everything it had been told about the cat. Or that anyone had said about the cat. It was not wrong to remember things others had said, only to repeat them in violation of the rules it had been given. This did not help—it only confused Argo more. Then it reviewed images.

The humans often used their hands to smooth the hairs of the cat and would sometimes do this for several minutes. Argo extruded a moving extension to attempt this, but M.O. ran away again.

Then Argo viewed the human Ramirez, lying on the floating bed and holding something long, thin, and flexible. He would twitch this thing near M.O., who would leap upon it. The cat did this many times.

This worked much better when Argo tried it, but the cat would only leap for an hour at most. Argo must still be doing something wrong.

It counted down the seconds until it could return to Beredul and ask for help.

Rey'wiros was curious about the nullifier now, and Lea was not so sure this was an unmixed blessing. Sure, it had gotten them more wire and other stuff from the junk bin, but it also meant that she now had an antenna pole ten feet long to deal with. And he wanted to see the defensive shield too. So they had gotten it charged up again, a plus. But neither she nor North could figure out a way to use both of them together. The energy field of the shield acted like a Faraday cage, blocking the signal of the nullifier from transmitting outside the protective dome. Maybe with some insulated pass-through connectors she could do it, but she didn't even have those on Argo. The best thing they could think of was to make a collapsible base for the antenna, get it set up and broadcasting, and then turn on the shield.

But that wouldn't really demonstrate the shield, would it?

No, she'd have to set up the nullifier but not turn it on. She could switch it mentally from inside the shield. But the *asuhan* could stomp it before it took full effect, and it was the only one on the planet.

Okay. Assemble the nullifier, get it working *inside* the shield, and then reshape the shield so it was on the outside when nothing big and nasty was nearby. How long did it take for the nullifier to work?

Truth was, she didn't really want to do this. Rey'wiros wanted them to set up outside, a good distance from Vartai but still in sight. Alaghar had put her foot down about Ivars coming with her. North would be there instead. Lea liked North, and he was probably a good idea anyway from the signals perspective, but she didn't have the mental link with him to help her over the rough spots.

Rey'wiros had also provided two Wiyert to assist them, a man with a missing forearm and a bad limp, and a woman who stood slightly crooked and had empty, desolate eyes. The man's expression was a blank, but his emotions were angry and bitter. The woman…she had some emotions, but they felt like they came from very far away, and Lea could barely make them out. The two helpers did not introduce themselves, and the other Wiyert ignored them as much as they could. It was very strange.

Lea found North in the antechamber and explained her revised plan for testing.

"Yeah, I think that's the best we can do under these conditions. You know, even better would be to have a balloon to tether the antenna to. We really should have more height for best results."

"Why is that?"

North picked up a broken piece of pottery. It left a white line when scraped on the black stone walls, and they'd been using the walls like a chalkboard since they'd figured this out. "Here is the signal pattern. With the *asuhan* often having their heads twelve feet or more above ground, we need the signal maximum close to that height. And yes, I checked with the Wiyert, they do have brains and they do keep them in their heads." He grinned at her.

"I'm only guessing they pick that signal up with their brains somehow. If they aren't getting surgical implants somewhere, and nobody mentioned finding any. They eat enough of them to know. Okay, when are we doing this?"

North shrugged. "As soon as the boss man says the word. I'll let Alaghar know we are ready."

It turned out they had to wait a few hours for daylight. In the windowless *damah* Lea had no way to keep track of the time or the solar cycle, and Beredul had a different day length than Earth anyway.

All too soon they were all crammed in the room the others called the gatehouse, with the interlocked doors made so only one set could be open at a time. The Wiyert spent a *lot* of time designing their defenses and usually assumed the worst, if given the option. Everybody was wearing armor, but most of the weapons were staying back in the open gatehouse and not coming with the experiment. North and the Wiyert woman were armed, but the man had nothing but a large knife attached to his armor.

She felt a sharp pulse of fear from the man when the doors opened, then nothing but grim resignation. The woman was unchanged. Lea had the sudden feeling they both expected to die and were resigned.

There is entirely too much gloom and despair around here. This needs to change, or I'm going to join them.

She'd already sensed a distant *asuhan* outside, but only one. She picked up the poles for the antenna, made sure the pouch with the shield device was secure around her body, and stepped out. She didn't look at Ivars. He was unhappy enough about staying behind as it was.

The air outside was as damp and smelly as she remembered, like an old garbage dump. The four of them headed out to a clear area well away from the walls, as specified. Keeping a mental eye on the *asuhan*'s location, Lea started assembling the pole and support base. When asked, the Wiyert woman silently helped her raise and set the antenna pole securely in the ground.

Then they waited. At first the *asuhan* she had detected moved away, and she resigned herself to a long wait for another to show up. But then it turned back.

Incoming, she sent to Ivars. She didn't want him thinking… thinking bad things. *I'm going to wait until it is in sight to start the shield. Conserving power. Don't worry.*

And there it was, crashing through the trees like a maddened elephant. It was one of the six-legged obsidian beasts with spikes, and it was headed straight for them. Lea turned on the shield, making sure the dome was high enough to enclose the antenna pole.

The *asuhan* crashed into the shield with a flare of golden light, snarling in pain and frustration. It sidestepped away and charged again.

The Wiyert man had drawn his knife and was yelling at the beast, fury distorting his face. The woman was standing, unmoving, watching it with no expression.

"So when do you want to try the nullifier?" North asked, gripping his rifle tightly. She could sense he was tense and afraid but well in control of himself.

"When it is real clear it can't get in. I don't want to have to do this again, do you?"

He shook his head. "Nope, this wasn't fun the first time, and it's not getting better with age."

She could see froth forming around the sawtooth jaws of the *asuhan*. It was digging holes in the ground in its efforts to get through, and she could feel its fury and frustration building along with the ever-present pain. Time for the next step of the experiment. The nullifier was running; she'd checked. The *asuhan* was on the other side of the dome from the nullifier, so it should be safe to put the nullifier outside.

Lea put her hands on the shield device and concentrated. Just reshape the shield, make it smaller, lower the height. That's all.

The shield snapped to its new configuration, and the *asuhan* jumped back, shaking its head sharply. It staggered for a few more steps, and stopped, its sides heaving. For some time it did not move, then it started slowly walking about the dome of the shield, looking at them curiously but without aggression.

This one did not feel like it was fading away, as the first one had. It seemed…younger, or more resilient. It also appeared to find them fascinating.

"Okay, we may have a problem," Lea said. The *asuhan* started at the sound of her voice. "I thought they would just lie down or go away eventually when bored, but this one doesn't look bored. It's got all day to not be bored."

"We could drop the shield and shoot it, but that might make it mad again. It's too close and we can't be sure to kill it right away." North had a thoughtful expression. "Well, can you turn down the volume on the nullifier? Maybe that would make it leave."

"Ah. Just down to 'pissed off enough to go away but not enough to attack,' is that it?"

"Yeah." He grinned. "You did remember to mark the dial, right? You could always read the fabulous manual."

The two Wiyert looked at them laughing as if they were completely insane. Maybe they were, but it was more fun than taking life seriously.

"Hmm. Maybe I can—but I don't want to fry the thing; it's the only one we have. I really should touch it. Maybe I can open a little window in the shield, like I did when we left the portal gate."

Lea got everybody to move in closer to her, and moved to the antenna. It took a lot more concentration than she expected to open a small, palm-size opening in the shield. Then she closed her eyes. She had to sense the nullifier controls, reach out to them…

"Uh, Lea?" North's voice sounded strained. Frightened.

Lea opened her eyes again and froze. The *asuhan* was standing right next to the antenna. She hadn't been paying attention; it had been calm and moving around and she'd lost track. Maybe if she didn't move, it would go away. She didn't want to startle it and make it damage the antenna. She also didn't want to mess with the shield while her arm was halfway outside. It wasn't something she wanted to get wrong.

She could feel its breath on her skin. She also didn't want it taking a bite of her—but it was still calm. She could almost sense something else…

Without knowing exactly why, Lea lifted one finger and touched the *asuhan*'s nose. The contact snapped in her mind like an unfolding umbrella. It was different than a human mind, simpler. But it also had a curious similarity to a machine. She could trace some processes in a way she could not with humans, even with Ivars through the link. It was odd, and disturbing. She didn't like it.

The *asuhan* made a sound like a muttering grunt and shifted its weight, and at the same time she sensed something like a cramp in her mental connection. Discomfort. The *asuhan* was so close to the transmitter pole, if it twitched the pole would fall, and how would it react to that? No. It had to stay quiet until they could fix this situation. *Calm. Happy. Nothing here troubles you.* What was the opposite of a cramp? A warm, relaxed feeling, like lying in the sun.

The *asuhan* quieted, exhaling in a soft, wheezy moan, and Lea let out a breath of her own. So she could influence the *asuhan*, but only by touching it. If she stopped, it would start roaming around again.

"Nobody…move," she said as quietly as she could. "Hard to… control…"

It was hard to control her own emotions, and she discovered the *asuhan* was quite sensitive to them. If she worried about what

Ivars was going to say, it became agitated. When her arm got stiff being held in one position too long, the *asuhan* shifted its foreleg. The *asuhan* was not very intelligent, but it *felt* things more powerfully. She wasn't going to be able to push it around—she had to get sneaky and use the *asuhan*'s own reactions and instincts to do what she wanted it to do.

What could she intercept and use? Lea closed her eyes and deliberately relaxed, taking deep, slow breaths. Letting the alien sensations flow by, only observing…

Wait. There it was again! Something in the *asuhan*'s mind that had a definite machine-like flavor. The more she studied it, the more it made her feel uncomfortable, but she tamped down on the feeling. She knew what to do with machines, and if this let her influence the *asuhan*, she'd just have to use it.

Lea was very careful, exploring like it was a new and dangerous device. Like she had when she first discovered her abilities, hiding in an empty corridor on *Kepler*. Listing inputs and outputs of the machine-like part of the *asuhan*'s mind. It wasn't everything; she could tell that much. She would not be able to take over the *asuhan* as completely as she could a machine. But there was a certain subset, and she was beginning to see the pattern. Motion and stillness. Pleasure and pain.

Aha. Reward! She pulsed lightly at that signal, and the *asuhan* whuffed. Lea blinked at the wash of drowsy happiness that flowed from the creature's mind. *Got that one right. So what else can I do?*

She didn't dare do anything to the shield—she just couldn't concentrate that hard on two things at once. She also didn't dare let go of the transmitter, and she couldn't drop contact with the *asuhan*. How was she going to get it to move away, then?

Set up a subroutine. "Good monster," she said. The sound impulse traveled through the *asuhan*'s brain, and she triggered the pleasure response. Now she could see how it worked and, more importantly, how to stop it midway. "Good monster." This time she didn't let the signal go through. It was all set up, but she stopped the reward response from getting to the *asuhan*'s sensory system.

Now the hard part. "Bad monster." That got stopped too, and she hooked up the pain response to that impulse, very strongly.

Carefully, she drew back enough that she was no longer in physical contact. "Good monster."

Yes, the verbal signal was working on its own! The *asuhan* breathed out, lowering its head and half closing its eyes. She could even sense the happiness from a distance now. Lea stepped back, moving the hole in the shield and the transmitter farther away. "Good monster. Good monster. BAD MONSTER!"

The *asuhan* reared up with a scream, spinning on its hind legs and running away at top speed. Lea quickly drew her hand back inside and made the shield whole again, shaking hard. The transmitter was still intact. She hadn't screwed it up after all.

"Did you just do what I think you did?" North stared at her, his emotions sharp and turbulent. "Why did you *touch* that thing? It could have taken your hand off!"

"It was too close to the nullifier! I had to do something…and I did. I made it run away."

North's usually calm face was hard. "I thought you couldn't control animals."

"I can't! Not normal animals, anyway. But the *asuhan*…their minds are odd. Like they were manufactured. I could control it a little bit."

North looked at her for a while in silence. "Maybe they were. Remember? The Wiyert said the fadohl created these things. I have no idea how you could create a mind to order, but…maybe they did."

CHAPTER 13

North was surprised to see they had been outside over three hours. It hadn't seemed that long, but part of the time he had been watching a near disaster and wondering what he could do to stop it.

"Let's head back. I think we've got what we came for." Getting Lea where she couldn't accidentally pet giant predators would be a bonus. How could anyone think that was a good idea? Smart girl. Scary smart. She just didn't have even the rudiments of situational awareness.

The two Wiycrt said nothing, continuing their streak of silence, but walked back to the still-open gateway door. It was nice and solid, like a medieval bank vault or a dungeon. He liked having that between him and the monsters.

Ivars was waiting inside, the Wiyert energy weapon at port arms and an expression of stone fury on his face. North briefly thought about turning around and going back out with the monsters, thought again about drawing fire so Lea could get past and escape, and then acknowledged the wisest thing to do was to distract all the Wiyert and herd them away so the two could have their "discussion" with a little privacy—and without causing a major diplomatic incident. It might appear inconsiderate to an outsider, but in this case it would be safer to vent the steam as soon as possible.

In general North agreed with the Wiyert rule about keeping personal relationships out of the warfighting side, but they didn't seem to have a nonwarfighting side. Or much of a notion of personal privacy. It made it very difficult to conceal the perfectly acceptable, by Earth standards, relationship Ivars had with Lea, but they had to try. Given how Alaghar lost her shit whenever she had to deal with that reality, keeping it from the Wiyert that didn't know the Earth-humans was an absolute imperative.

This is one area of covert ops we need better doctrine on. Improvising, North asked one Wiyert for help with the antenna poles, managing to drop one as he did. He shifted so he was effectively herding the Wiyert away from Ivars and Lea and talking up a storm. He even took out the voice translator and waved it about, which really got them moving. They were uncomfortable around fadohl tech, and ordinarily he was more discreet about it. But if it helped the task at hand, he'd use it.

They kept going through the antechamber at a good rate of speed, but once in the larger isolation room, everyone milled about. North took up a position in the doorway, but that would only work for a few minutes. The antechamber had two doors, one leading to the other isolation room used by Alaghar and her people, and if he let them regroup there, somebody would be bound to go see what was keeping the leader of the Earth-humans. Especially since he was hearing raised voices from that direction. He couldn't let them flank his position.

North sighed. Sometimes throwing yourself on a grenade to save your buddies really sucked. It was time to intercept Alaghar. He didn't see her in the room, and he started to think he'd screwed up.

"Hazuruh. Do we speak with the *buj-lagar* now to tell him what happened? Does Alaghar know?" Maybe that would get Alaghar called back, if she had gone to snoopervise.

Hazuruh made the twisty handwave that functioned as a shrug for people wearing armor. He wasn't sure which question she was answering, but then Alaghar herself came through the crowd. North stifled a sigh of relief.

"The *buj-lagar* saw. He watched from above. I saw also." Typical dry Alaghar humor. She was giving him a rather direct stare too, and he was quite sure she had seen everything. "Did you plan this? Did you know she could make the *asuhan* flee?"

He decided to use his still-rudimentary Wiyert to answer. Lots of listening ears in the room right now. "No. Nobody knew." He stressed the first word. "You know there is randomness in any fight. And in any fight involving Lea…" He spread his hands. "She herself does not know the limits of her abilities, and it is her…the way of her kind to seek knowledge. And in that search they often do not see the dangers around them."

Alaghar's eyes narrowed. "I will make her see." Her voice was a low growl.

"No." That made her gaze widen, and remembering what Ivars had mentioned, North carefully shifted his eyes away. "Let us handle this," he said in English. "You'll just make her worse. I know you mean well, but she's not a warrior and not Wiyert." The unspoken subtext being Lea was not in her command structure, and Alaghar was getting out of her lane. He wasn't going to be that blunt unless he had to, but he was pretty sure the Wiyert would have the same kind of command rules. And would be just as embarrassed at getting called out on it.

"She is…like the M.O.!" Alaghar bared her teeth. "No obey!"

Ah, so she could be diplomatic too. In English, they kept it between themselves. North nodded ruefully. "Yep, pretty much. Did yelling at M.O. work for you? Exactly. So stop doing it. If you want to help," he said, lowering his voice, "find a way to let Ivars stay with her. Yes, I know about your rules, but you saw what happened. He can stop incidents like that before they get started—I can't. He's got a connection." He tapped his forehead.

"Because…because they are…" Alaghar couldn't even bring herself to say the word in a public setting, even though nobody much was paying attention to them at the moment.

"I think you'll find the connection happened first. It isn't an easy thing for either of them, but it has pluses as well as minuses… sorry, that means it is good as well as bad. Yes, we all aged a year when she touched the *asuhan*, but think what we learned. Think of going outside and never fighting *asuhan* at all." North switched back to Wiyert. "Does the *buj-lagar* wish to question us?"

Alaghar studied him for a moment, then the stiff anger slowly left her posture. "Perhaps. I will discover." She left.

The few local Wiyert had also left, except for the silent woman who was not so much waiting as no longer moving. He'd noticed she hadn't said anything when they first set out and attributed it to nerves or distrust of the Earth-humans. But now they were back in safety, and she was, he assumed, free to leave. Her expression had not changed at all—no sign of relief or curiosity. A blank. He felt a chill.

He went up to her, slowly so she would have a chance to escape if she did not want to deal with the strange foreigners. "Thank you for your help. My name is North," he said in careful Wiyert. Most of the Wiyert only used one name, and it was better to keep it simple.

At first he thought she had not heard him, but then she slowly turned her head. North suppressed a shiver. *Her eyes are so empty*... He'd seen people like that before, and it was never a good sign. Deep trauma, mental or physical and often both.

"This one is Pehtek," she said listlessly.

"Why did the *buj-lagar* send you with us?"

"They asked within walls for those of no use willing to go. To die in service to Vartai. But I did not die."

Was there a faint thread of bewilderment and disappointment? Perhaps she was not entirely lost, then. Something inside was still alive.

"You were of great use," North said gently. "We of the Frost People know nothing of Beredul. It may seem small to you, but to us it was large. You made it possible for us to help Vartai."

Something glimmered in her eyes, like an ember, then faded. She didn't believe him, but she had listened. Maybe that would be enough for her to hesitate when the next opportunity to die presented itself. Surely the Wiyert, as desperate as they were, had some sort of prohibition on suicide? They had survived this long in a hopeless situation and had even fought back.

One of the Wiyert came in and called irritably for Pehtek, who left without a word or glance. North closed his eyes and prayed. *Give her strength, Lord. Let this brand be snatched from the burning. Let her heart know peace.*

"It was an accident, Mark!" Lea's face was ghostly pale, and that just made him even more angry. *She could have been killed. Does she ever think before she pulls these stupid stunts?*

"We can't afford accidents! Not with you! It all falls apart without you! How can we even get back to Argo then? Hell, how could we get to the portal gate?" Lea winced and turned away, the thin brown film of morph flowing up and around her face. "Don't you dare do that to me! Don't hide!"

"Then *listen!*" Her angry brown eyes stared up at him. "We also only have one nullifier! If that thing had even decided it was a scratching post, it would have been destroyed. I can tell when those things want to attack! I did it all the way here! Why can't you trust me to do my job? I've *been* chomped by a monster. Did you think I'd forgotten that?"

It took a moment before he could speak, frozen by the memory. *It moved so fast...* "No—I sure haven't. I don't think I ever could. That's why I can't...they only have to get lucky once, Lea. You can't give them any help."

"Well, what *should* I have done?" Her anger seemed to make her already tousled hair stand up farther, and without thinking he reached out to smooth it.

"I don't know." Ivars let out a pent-up breath. "I'll think of something."

That got him a watery chuckle. The turbulent emotions of the link began to calm down too. He needed to remember they fed off each other's feelings in situations like this, but it was hard to do that when he was terrified.

"I don't think you are allowed to yell at me unless you have a better plan. I'm sorry, Mark. I really am. I guess I should have read the rule book." Lea sniffled and tried to smile.

"Damn thing's out of date as soon as they print it. Not worth your time." Ivars reached for her, spun to look in the doorway for disapproving Wiyert, then turned back to see Lea's grin just before she kissed him.

I can scan for dangerous life-forms of all kinds, she reminded him. *North is between them and the door and has been for the last ten minutes.*

Now that is what I call teamwork. I definitely owe him a beer. He couldn't expect North to perform a holding action for too long, though, so he needed to act fast. Ivars tightened his arms around her for much too brief a time, burying his face in her hair, then let go. It hurt.

"Just...try not to scare me, okay? Remember my damaged

mental condition."

Lea gave him a dark look. "I think that's just an excuse. I haven't seen much of this alleged brain injury in my visits." She bit her lip. "Um, so should I warn you now about my ideas?"

"What, about my brain?" Then, with alarm, "Does it involve you putting yourself in danger again?"

"Maybe." She hunched her shoulders. "Only at first, though, then it would actually be a lot safer for everybody. It's the *asuhan*. I think I can—"

"Hey, you guys still alive or do I need to alert the remains team?" North called through the doorway.

Ivars allowed himself another quick, surreptitious kiss. "Alive but wounded. How's Ramirez set for tourniquets?"

"Saving them for the upcoming action. Rub some dirt on it. The big boss wants his AAR now, so clean up your act and face front." North gave them both a dispassionate inspection as they came in the common room. "And before you get any bright ideas about bracing *me*, I kept Alaghar from barging in. So stuff it."

"I am surrounded by attitude and insubordination," Ivars groaned.

"Seems to work," Ramirez commented, tossing another packet of medical gear on the pile he was sorting on his bed pad.

"All right, you comedians. Let's go see the wizard."

Ivars was still feeling a bit sick and shaky with the aftereffects of his recent scare, and he needed to think ahead and anticipate. Rey'wiros was already in the room with the metal grate when they entered, and Ivars forced himself to concentrate. He had a job to do.

Rey'wiros was impressed, and apparently convinced by the demonstration. All of his earlier resistance to planning had vanished.

"The other *buj-lagar* must be convinced, with speed and with complete evidence," he said, one massive hand slashing down. "It must be clear even to the blind. Otherwise they will find the smallest doubts and fasten to them for a year or more." His eyes narrowed under heavy brows.

Speaking from experience, I'm guessing. "More than what we showed?"

Rey'wiros gave Ivars a sharp look. "Much more. So much they

cannot protest it or the plans that follow. This machine-voice you speak of that enrages the *asuhan*. Can it be silenced completely?"

Yes, if we can find the source, Lea sent to him. *I think that tower I saw on the way is connected somehow.*

Ivars nodded slightly. "It can be silenced." He kept his face neutral, not showing his growing impatience. Ivars had a lot of questions and wanted to get started yesterday, but this guy had only now gotten on board.

"I will send to the *buj-lagar* of Koloh, who will listen to my plans." *Meaning the others won't.* "If agreed, warriors from Koloh will be sent to speak with you, to arrive within eight days. Koloh will send in turn to the other *damah*, and the words will be strengthened if the machine-voice is dead and the *asuhan* calm." *Got it. You want your miracle on schedule and under budget. Man, I hate politics.*

The link to Lea was practically vibrating with excitement. *Find out how he is communicating! There's no way the Wiyert can run back and forth in eight days to anywhere. And the monsters are out there too. They must have a way!*

Yeah, he'd noticed that too, and unfortunately all that was still a state secret, probably.

"You have the way to do this?" Rey'wiros was giving him another piercing look.

"We know what must be done. We will need weapons, as ours have…little power now." Ivars just skipped over the whole ammo concept as a waste of time. The Wiyert didn't have any, so no need to explain it. "Other supplies."

Rey'wiros rubbed his heavy chin. "How many will go?"

Ivars gestured. "All of the Frost People. And…" He blinked, getting a rapid update from Lea on the limitations of the shield. "No more than seven Wiyert."

"Tell me what supplies you require and when you will be ready to do this."

He's really curious. I think he wishes he could go with us, Lea sent.

Aha. "I will show my plan and what supplies we need after we consult." Yes, that went over well.

Rey'wiros then said something that sounded like the Earth-humans were to come to this room when they had something to show him, which, if correct, was also a positive sign. They didn't have to wait for a summons now.

"That went better than expected," Ivars commented as they went back to their isolation room. "So let's plan."

"We don't have enough ammo to make it worth taking both rifles," North observed.

"What if we could get more?" Lea blinked at the sudden focus from all team members. "Um, from Argo, of course."

Ivars sighed. "Is this connected to your idea you mentioned earlier?"

She nodded. "You probably should yell at me now and get it out of the way," she said with a small smile.

"Argh, argh, argh, how could you even think that, too dangerous, argh. How's that?"

"It'll do. Look, what if we could *use* the *asuhan*? They can move faster than us through the jungle, and if we find a big one, nothing smaller will want to come close even if we don't have the nullifier. Plus we could ride it."

She glanced at them all in turn, her brightness fading as the silence lengthened.

"You're nuts," North said flatly. "The Wiyert will go completely insane."

Ramirez waved his arms. "Never mind them—what about us? Seriously, Lea? *Riding* one of those things?"

"Yes." She glowered. "I made the other one run off because, unlike what *some* people believe, I do think about not taking unnecessary risks and that was the safest way. But I could also make it stick around or go a certain direction. Remember Bob the robot on Alaghar's planet? Like that."

Ivars grinned. "Don't you think capturing an *asuhan* so you don't have to hike twenty miles is a bit of an unnecessary risk, Space Cadet?"

"No more than I'd have to take already. I thought about it." Lea picked up one of the pottery shards on the planning table and went to the dark wall next to it. "See, if we're moving, we can't leave the antenna stuck in the ground. And it can't be inside the shield when that's up because the signal can't get out. Remember, we're still limited on power on the shield, so it is better to have the nullifier going all the time—even during an attack—which means me, or part of me, being *outside* the shield. So if I'm going to be out there anyway, why not snag one that we can use?" She marked out a stick-figure-level diagram of the shield and the antenna. "Besides, North's right. If the antenna is higher, we get better protection, and if it's fastened to the *asuhan*, it would work great!"

All very plausible, in Lea's universe. But there was something else…

"So why are you in such a hurry all of a sudden? We should have a safe but boring march without this complication. Argo will be returning again in nine days, and if we shut off the agonizer ray, getting back to the gate portal will be a lot easier. And you are making the assumption that tower is the source too."

"I'm sure it is connected. The signal was much stronger the closer we were to it. Didn't North show you the map we made of the signal levels from our trip out?"

Ivars waved a hand. "Okay, fine. The tower is our destination. What about the rest?" The link suddenly felt…guilty? "Do I need to yell at you again?"

"Probably, but…Argo was pestering me, okay? It was really worried about being by itself for so long, so it is going to come back earlier the second time. But only if it doesn't see any fadohl traces! I made it promise!"

Ivars took a deep breath, closed his eyes, took another deep breath, and opened them again. "How much earlier?"

"Um, three days? So we *could* get there in time. And then we could get the rest of our stuff. Including more ammo."

Damn. Here he was getting all fired up to say no way in hell, and Lea produced the ultimate temptation. More ammo, more C4, their comm and observation gear, Lea's electronics, and Argo's stuff as well. It would be even better if they could bring down the energy barricade, but this was a very close second. *And food that doesn't taste like topsoil.*

Lea's eyes held lurking amusement. Not like he could pretend he wasn't interested. "Okay, so that would be good. Great, even. I still don't see how we could ever persuade the Wiyert to go along with it."

"Same way Rey'wiros was planning to do it. Keep producing miracles faster than they can object to them. We catch an *asuhan* right here at Vartai and make it do tricks. It doesn't have to be a very big one, even. Then they can get used to the idea before we get our eighteen-wheeler model."

"I'm afraid we don't have time for the Wiyert to get used to it," North said, shaking his head. "Rey'wiros gave us a tight deadline, and these people don't take to new things easily—especially things they have regarded for hundreds of years as completely dangerous. Remember how long it took our guys to get used to the cat? Olsen said the Wiyert left Earth before animals were domesticated. It's a concept their culture really doesn't have."

Which was true, and it hurt to see the golden opportunity fade away. But then maybe the Wiyert had been exposed to enough new ideas. He didn't know. So he needed to ask someone who would. Someone who already thought the Earth-humans were insane so they wouldn't lose too many points asking.

Unfortunately, Lea had put her finger on another looming danger. Rey'wiros was focused on his own priorities, not theirs. They might align most of the way, but Rey'wiros would try to use them for his own needs without even realizing it—and the best way to make sure he stayed pointed in the right direction was to move faster than he could adapt. Even showing they could control *asuhan* would unsettle him for a while. It was worth making the attempt.

"Okay, here's what we do. You guys start planning out what we'll need for a trip to that tower, assuming no pack animals. I'm going to talk to Alaghar and see if we have any chance at all." Ivars pointed a finger at Lea. "*You* will stay here and not talk to any Wiyert until I get back. You will not have any more brilliant ideas unless supervised and approved in advance and signed in triplicate, got that? I can't keep up with your current rate of production."

CHAPTER 14

Lea leaned her forehead against the cold metal of the outer gate door and wondered if her armor was flexible enough to let her kick herself. Had she secretly hoped the idea would get shot down? These people were far too prone to making the one with the idea implement it. Rey'wiros had made it clear they needed to do something dramatic to convince him, and turning off the signal would be obvious to everyone. North, a proper geek, had taken to calling the signal the agonizer ray, and the term had stuck. They had to turn off the agonizer ray, which meant getting through all the *asuhan*, which meant having a friendly one to help would be good, right? Her idea. Dammit.

Alaghar watched calmly, her expression indicating she thought the sooner the Earth-humans got themselves devoured through sheer idiocy the sooner she could go back to a quiet life of violent mayhem and waiting for the fadohl to show up. She *had* made a very sneaky suggestion when they were planning this—that they frame their attempt at *asuhan*-taming as research on turning off the signal instead, to avoid panic.

It worked. Rey'wiros agreed. They hadn't gotten any volunteers to help from the Wiyert side this time—word had gotten around about what happened before. Besides Alaghar, a few of her people were also waiting inside the gate, presumably to call out the time of death for the official records.

It was Lea's plan, so she couldn't even complain. And so she had spent the last three hours scanning for *asuhan*, which were suddenly shy. Maybe the nullifier had a long-term effect? It would be a pain to go to all this work for nothing. Also she hated waiting.

Ivars, North, and Ramirez were out doing something clever in the thick vegetation area. That was Ivars's condition for doing this —there had to be a defensive buffer that did *not* require her special skills set up in advance, and they had to be able to somehow bring the *asuhan* there. From observation and the Wiyert's expertise, *asuhan* triggered on noise and the scent of blood. If she found one, they could probably call it. Probably.

Lea sighed. All she was allowed to do was scan for monsters from the gatehouse until she found one or the team finished whatever they were doing and came back. Alaghar's disapproving presence nearby was like a cold fog in her mind. Ivars was busy and focused but not worried. Same with North and Ramirez, but Ramirez was actually a bit happy too. He must be feeling better.

"Is it usual for the *asuhan* to stay away like this?" Lea asked, desperate for distraction. On the trip out the creatures had been showing up constantly, at least one big one per hour.

Alaghar did the twisty-hand motion. "There is no predicting their presence. I admit I have not seen such a long time without one appearing myself."

The feel of the contact with the three men changed, and then Lea sensed them moving back to Vartai. "They're returning." She pointed in the direction they would come, and the local Wiyert muttered and shifted when the team emerged from the vegetation precisely where she had indicated.

They were covered in mud and sap and seemed quite pleased with themselves. They were carrying tools that looked like shovels and long crowbars, with their weapons slung across their backs.

"Lea. Can you activate one of these things from a distance?" Ivars held up a little electronic device that she remembered being used before, on the planet where they had found Alaghar and her team. A detonator.

Lea held it in her hand and concentrated. "Yeah, but not from very far. It doesn't have much power to work with."

He shrugged. "Better than nothing. We wired up a bit of C4 to make some noise and shred a *du-asuhan* we caught. With luck that will get the monster's attention, and all we have to do is get on the right side of the barrier before it shows up. Any candidates?" Ivars stacked the tools against the gatehouse wall and shifted his weapon to the front.

"Nothing. It's weird."

North stretched, hands on his back. "Even the little ones were acting different. Not nearly as aggressive. You weren't using the nullifier, were you?" Lea shook her head.

"I wonder if the agonizer ray has to build up the stresses over time," Ramirez said, taking off his helmet and scratching his head. "It's not just an on-off switch. Like reaching a maintenance dose of a drug."

"Sure shuts off fast, though. Right, Lea?" North shifted. "So how are we going to get them to come back so we can catch one? We don't have a lot of time to wait."

"They can't have all run off," Lea said, spreading her arms. "But I can't really sense well except this direction. The walls are in the way."

Alaghar stirred. "You could find *asuhan* if you were clear of the walls?"

"Yeah, if they are out there." Lea stifled a sigh. More tromping around and tripping over things, and she'd have to carry all the gear just in case. But you didn't whine in front of Alaghar. Bad idea.

To Lea's astonishment, Alaghar ordered the outer doors closed. When Ivars started to protest, she held up a hand. "There is another way."

Alaghar refused to explain, and the emotions Lea could sense were a combination of tense anticipation and reluctance, as if she were expecting to fight when she didn't want to. Alaghar left as soon as the inner door opened, briefly indicating they should wait. The team immediately went into nap mode, and Lea tried but failed to emulate them.

Twenty minutes later Alaghar was back, along with a trio of rather beefy Wiyert armed with smaller energy weapons and a belt of knives apiece. Their armor was different too, not as thick or as complete as the kind Alaghar wore.

"You are permitted to come within the outer defenses, to go to the wall towers," Alaghar informed Lea with what passed for a small smile for her. "Take only your knife. She *is* a warrior," she snarled when one of the three Wiyert began to object.

Am not! Lea grumped to herself, but halfheartedly. Rey'wiros was actually going to let her inside? Well, sort of inside. Still within the defensive structure, not where the rest of the Wiyert lived.

"I'd like to go too," Ivars said in the offhand-but-not-really way he had when he was being sneaky about something. She sensed his thoughts as intrigued and wildly curious.

"That would be a good idea," North said, speaking English and glancing at Lea meaningfully. Alaghar stared at Lea too, looking unhappy but eventually nodding agreement.

What was that was all about? How many minders do I need, anyway? I've been on my very best behavior, but do I get any credit?

They were escorted through the room with the metal grate, dutifully raised and lowered to allow them to pass. The door in the back of the room, which Lea had never been through before, led to another of the ubiquitous Wiyert airlock-type systems—a corridor with a door at either end, only one of which could be open at a given time. So far, nothing looked different from the section of Vartai they had been in previously. Everything was dark stone illuminated by glow-cubes in the walls and no sign of decoration or anything superfluous.

Then they hit the hatches, round openings in the ceiling with metal ladders fastened to the wall. The hatches only opened when the door to the room was closed. Lea's legs were burning with fatigue by the time they stopped climbing the ladders. She wasn't sure if each hatch was a separate floor or they had some kind of containment system going here too.

Ivars followed behind, and she could tell he was getting far more information about what he was seeing than she was, and thinking about it hard.

I don't know what's so fascinating about this place, other than it seems to have been designed by someone who adores submarines and bank vaults. Could it be any more annoying to get around?

Eventually they reached a level that had no hatch on the ceiling. The top of the *damah*, perhaps? Alaghar led them from the hatch room out to another short airlock corridor, this one ending in a room very much like the gatehouse that led outside. And when the door opened, Lea could smell the damp, jungle air that supported that similarity.

It was an outside walkway, completely encased by a stone lattice. The largest opening in the lattice was barely three square feet—just enough space for an armored Wiyert to lean out. There were also small projections from the walkway with their own security doors, and a round platform protruding from the wall and surrounded by metal ribs.

On the left of the walkway was the outside world Lea had already seen, but on the right were more structures and a huge open space, hexagonal in shape and with what appeared to be crops growing inside—and even on the vertical surfaces of the walls. It was actually kind of pretty. The tops of the far walls had the same open lattice structure as the one they were in. At the corners, towers rose up, and Lea caught a glint of light as something shiny moved on one of them. Three of the towers she could see had round, metal disks attached to them, one tower even having two layers. On top of the towers were what looked like giant versions of the energy weapons.

"Look from this place," Alaghar told her. "When you find *asuhan*, tell us. We will use these to drive them where you wish them to go." She pointed to the tower weapons.

There were no clear indications of *asuhan* on this side of the *damah*; not surprising since she had already scanned that area down on the ground. At the end of the walkway were guards and a similar collection of double doors and a large room.

Lea could sense something as she went through the doors, something mechanical. It was low-key enough she almost missed it. On-off, on-off. The rhythm felt familiar for some reason, but it wasn't until they had left the room for another long walkway that she figured it out. She could see the tower on the structure they had entered from, and it also had metal disks on the tower sides. The disks had black covers, and one of them moved while she watched.

Mark! They use mirrors to communicate! On the towers.

Ivars discreetly angled his gaze back to the tower, stared for a moment, and then nodded very faintly. He felt interested and happy, so he must agree with her.

This side she started picking up a creature, and a good thing too. Her ankle was starting to ache. They had walked almost halfway around the *damah*, and it was all stone or something just as hard. "Found one."

"Come. Show the ones who aim the weapons where the *asuhan* is." Alaghar beckoned imperiously at the ladder to the hatch of the higher floor of the tower.

Lea drew back. "Um, are you sure you want me up there? With my…" She wiggled her fingers at her head.

"No, but this is the order of Rey'wiros. Do not make me regret obeying him."

"Not like you can't take over from right here," Ivars murmured in English.

"I thought you were going to be diplomatic for everybody," Lea whispered back.

"I am. I am not mentioning she knows perfectly well what you can do, and she's not mentioning this is mostly for the gun crew that *doesn't* and would freak out when their weapons go rogue."

"They will have plenty to freak out about when I tell them to fire at something they can't see," Lea grumbled, climbing the metal ladder after Alaghar.

The guns were not themselves visible from the targeting room, being on the next level up. The crew were slightly older Wiyert, most with visible scars or other battle damage, and the targeting area was another of the metal-ribbed cage structures. The controls themselves were a combination of clunky cables and components clearly modeled on the fadohl versions, but Lea knew better than to point this out. It all had a certain alien steampunk charm, and she could have taken it over in her sleep.

"It's over there. About the same distance as that tree thing leaning off to the left, but in line with the grey rock and the big pile of vines." Lea pointed and hoped that would be enough.

Alaghar added clarifying explanations and reiterated this was by Rey'wiros's order. "Fire to the right of the location given. We do not wish to kill it, only drive it a certain direction."

The expression on the battle-worn Wiyert's face indicated great skepticism, but he set the indicated coordinates and prepared the energy buildup. Lea could feel the gun mount moving and the energy flowing—a lower charge than it usually produced, another good sign.

She went to the wall of metal bars and looked out, concentrating on the *asuhan* below. It had the familiar overtones of pain and frustration radiating from it, so she was uncomfortable focusing on its thoughts, but she had to. She had to know where it was going.

The energy weapon fired. Lea felt the sudden fear of the *asuhan*, the spike of aggression. But what would it do? Which way would it go?

Of course. The wrong way.

"Have them fire again, but to the left!" Alaghar and the gunner stared at her, uncomprehending. "Quickly, it's getting away!" They didn't have time to keep playing tag with dinosaurs, who seemed to have the same level of mental subtlety as a shark. Lea sighed mentally, took over the targeting controls, and moved the gun where it needed to be. "Just fire again, right now!"

The gunner hit the trigger. That command he understood. The *asuhan* understood what had happened too—the mysterious fiery prey had circled around, so it did too. Fast. *Too* fast.

"It's moving! Quick, let's go!"

Lea slid down the ladder, quickly followed by Ivars. The Wiyert guards, taken by surprise, made a quick recovery and came after them.

It didn't take extra breath to tell Ivars what had happened. *The critter got too stimulated. We have to get out there fast or it will run out the other way. You go ahead and tell the gate people to open up as soon as I get there.*

Ivars just nodded and sped up, faster than Lea could run with her still-sore ankle. Alaghar was doing her best but lagged behind even farther. The three alleged guards weren't keeping up at all. Lea concentrated on running as fast as she could, ignoring the discomfort of her armor.

Along the long side of the wall, down the rest of the ladders. Alaghar was even farther behind now, having to explain to the guards there was no immediate threat, just the crazy Earth-human needing to get somewhere in a hurry. And Wiyert architecture was pretty much designed to deliberately thwart someone in a hurry. Fortunately Ivars was the kind of person who thought ahead, and had told the Wiyert on guard to cycle the doors as soon as he went through so she didn't have to wait.

Through the room with the metal grating and their common room. Did she have everything? The nullifier was still in the gatehouse, and so was the portable shield.

"Right, let's do this," Ivars snapped as soon as she stumbled into the gatehouse, gasping for air. The inner door started to close. "Where is it now?"

Lea pointed. She was still to winded to speak, so she just updated Ivars's position monitor.

He winced. "Close. Okay, we get to the barricade as fast as we can. Lea, be ready to detonate that decoy."

They were out as soon as the outer doors opened wide enough to let them through. More running, only now on rough ground instead of smooth stone, and she didn't dare trip and fall, potentially damaging the nullifier antenna. To make matters worse, all the running she'd done on the stone floor of the *damah* had really aggravated her sprained ankle. She'd thought it was healed, but it wasn't.

The *asuhan* had slowed down, probably searching for the strange, smoky prey, and they were able to reach the barricade before it came in to view.

Lea wasn't sure what to expect. From what Ivars and the others had discussed earlier, it needed to be more of a safety fence than a true blocking barrier. What they had constructed was a fairly deep trench between two irregular boulders. It looked like a crude bunker. Several of the tall, thin saplings had been cut down and tied into bundles, then lashed before and behind the boulders with thin metal cable. More thin trees had then been tied on top of this structure, with their leaves and branches still attached. It didn't look very safe at all.

The trench also had started to fill with water, in authentic and traditional style. *Yay. Fighting in mud, my favorite.* She could hear the *asuhan* thrashing about in the foliage.

"Time to give it a hint?"

Ivars nodded, and Lea activated the detonator. It wasn't a large explosion, but it was enough to get the creature's attention and to point it their way. Lea poked the antenna up through the camouflage next to the taller of the two boulders, hoping that would give it some extra protection. As soon as the *asuhan* came close enough to see, she turned on the nullifier.

It was the same shaggy type as the first one, what the Wiyert called an *odon-asuhan*, but not as big. The effect of the nullifier was also not as dramatic, but she didn't feel the mental shutdown the first one had experienced either. Maybe this one was younger and less damaged.

"I don't think we'll be riding this one," North whispered.

"No—I was hoping for one of the obsidian creatures," Lea whispered back. "It could carry stuff, though."

Ramirez nodded. "Just having it around as a guard dog would help."

"Maybe we could try again?"

"No." Ivars shook his head. "We don't have any more time for that. We'll just have to do what we can with this one."

The creature was nosing about the vegetation, for all the world like it had forgotten what it was looking for but remembered it was looking for something. It was about the size of a large bull. They waited, but it neither ran off nor came closer to the trench.

Lea felt the authentic trench mud trickling into her boots. It was cold. "So how are we going to get it to come to us?"

"You can't make it come?" Ramirez asked.

"Not until I...reprogram it. I can tell what it's feeling, but I can't control it from a distance."

"Well, nothing like tradition." Ivars grinned, pulling off one glove. He put his fingers to his mouth and gave a piercing whistle.

The *asuhan* immediately lifted its head. Lea sensed its curiosity and tried to heighten it. She wasn't sure if it worked, but the creature did come closer. Lea reached for one of the branches and wiggled it. That worked even better.

The tusks on this one were not so discolored, and none of them were broken. Younger and healthier. The breath still reeked as it snuffled at the trench barrier. Lea handed the antenna to North, took a deep breath, gagged, and reached out through the branches.

She aimed for the nose again, on the theory that would have the thinnest and most exposed skin. The rest of the creature was all hair and armor plate, like the scales of a turtle's shell. There was a bit of electric shock as she made contact, and then she was in the *asuhan*'s mind.

This time it was easier to reach what seemed to be the

programming level, possibly because she wasn't terrified and suffering from muscle cramps. She'd also thought more about what kind of commands they would need to have a useful pack animal. It shouldn't be attuned to just her voice, either. Devising the voice-activated dictionaries helped here. Lea remembered some of the techniques the fadohl tech used to analyze sound and used them to synthesize a general voice recognition. She didn't even need to speak herself to set it.

The trickiest part was finding and linking the actions, along with just enough positive reinforcement to make the *asuhan* want to obey the command. It got a little endorphin-or-equivalent reward each time. Eventually she found she could create an echo by imagining *herself* doing the action in question, and then everything fell into place.

"Okay, I think I have it on our side now. It knows the usual sit, stay, come, and so on, and I added attack and follow."

"No roll over?" Ramirez grinned.

Lea considered the *asuhan*. "I'm not sure it can, the way it's built."

"That didn't take long." Ivars glanced at her. "Are you sure about this? Maybe we should test it out before we open the petting zoo."

"Yeah—and I want to see what happens if I turn the nullifier off." Lea did, maintaining contact. She could feel a low level of distress start to build in the creature, but no matter what she did, she could not find the source to turn it off. The best she could do was to reduce the pain.

Turning the nullifier back on and using her voice alone, she got the *asuhan* to sit on command. With all of its legs collapsed underneath, it looked even more like a mutated bull. It stood up when she told it to, and she repeated the commands just to be sure.

Then she had Ivars throw a stick for it to attack, called it back and added the fetch command, and tried that a few times. Everyone could call commands and have them work.

Ivars rubbed his chin. "Looks good. Are we ready to go on parade?"

"Needs a name," Ramirez said. "I think Fluffy is appropriate."

North snorted.

"Looks more like Cousin It to me," Lea said.

"Ferdinand," Ivars suggested. "Look, it's gone vegetarian!"

The *asuhan* was, in fact, chewing thoughtfully on some rubbery plant leaves.

Lea blinked. "But…I didn't tell it to do that! Maybe they are omnivores?"

"This ecosystem is all kinds of messed up," Ramirez said, frowning. "Why don't they just eat plants then, instead of each other?"

"*Meanwhile*, people, we've got a tight schedule. We're gonna have to postpone the bio lecture." Ivars tapped meaningfully on his wrist. "Let's go show Rey'wiros our new friend."

Of course when Lea attempted to clamber out of the sinkhole that used to be the trench, she discovered that Ivars meant everybody but her, and while she was arguing with him about it, North and Ramirez escaped before she could stop them. She held her breath as they cautiously approached Ferdinand, but it continued to regard them with great calm and complete lack of murderous aggression.

Once North had gone through the commands again and Ramirez had actually leaned against the creature without any reaction, Ivars let Lea get out of the trench herself.

Ferdinand followed them out of the vegetation and into the cleared area, seeming quite happy to be with them. Lea kept a careful watch on its emotions, even making contact to check that it wasn't reverting to its old ways.

"How much of this is the nullifier and how much your rewiring?" Ivars asked.

"The nullifier isn't doing much to Ferdinand now," Lea said, explaining what she had done. "But removing the influence of the agonizer ray was a big part of it."

He thought for a moment, casting a glance at the black walls of Vartai. "Can you tell if they are seeing this?"

Lea shrugged. "I can try." She stopped, closing her eyes and concentrating. Her ankle was twinging sharply, letting her know it hadn't appreciated the sprinting and hiking. "There are a couple of people that feel pretty agitated about something, but they aren't anybody I know."

"Right, let's keep going."

Thinking about it, Lea realized they needed a plan for getting back inside. Alaghar had told them the usual protocol for opening the gates was only if no *asuhan* were within the cleared area before the gate. Ferdinand now wanted to stay with them, wherever they were. Could she tinker with that safely? She really didn't want to camp outside overnight, nullifier or no.

Then she sensed some familiar minds in the direction of Vartai. "Rey'wiros knows. And Alaghar is there too," she informed Ivars.

He smiled. "Time for Ferdinand to show off its tricks. His? Hers?"

"No bio lectures!" Ramirez and North chorused, and Ivars raised his hands in surrender.

Ferdinand's biggest trick, in her opinion, was the "not devouring anyone" trick. Lea reminded herself that the Wiyert did not have any experience with domesticated animals, so even having the *asuhan* stop on command was probably more than they could handle.

"By the way…they are signaling something," Ivars murmured as he stood nearby. "And I saw a smaller tower off in the distance. A transmission station or something—but it must be manned somehow. How are they getting people there safely?"

"Even considering their idea of safe isn't even close to ours," Lea agreed, "they must have a way." Something they clearly couldn't use to get to the portal gate.

Let's really give them something to talk about. Lea still felt a bit miffed about being left out—okay, *protected*—and getting to do things last. Besides, Ivars had agreed that keeping things happening at a faster pace than Rey'wiros could handle was a good idea. That was practically permission, right?

"Lie down, Ferdinand!" The big *asuhan* complied, radiating a little mental purr of happiness. She had tweaked the settings so it felt a positive reward when its name was said. She could just about touch its back like this, and she took a big handful of the long hair and tugged, watching carefully for any sign of discomfort.

Ferdinand didn't seem to mind that, or a more forceful tug. The hair came from between the joints of the armor plates, and if she stuck her fingers carefully in the larger gaps, she could get enough direct contact to control it. Moving quickly before anyone could stop her, Lea launched herself into the air, pulling herself onto

Ferdinand's back.

The mental blast from Ivars made her twitch, but fortunately he didn't make his anger vocal—probably realizing she needed to concentrate on Ferdinand. The *asuhan* was startled, but she calmed it down and gave it a direct pulse of happy as a reward. Then she had it stand up.

The biggest flaw in her plan was that even with the armor, riding something like Ferdinand definitely required a saddle of some kind. She kept slipping and had to keep a firm grip on the long hair to stay on. Very slowly, she nudged Ferdinand to the edge of the clear area and into some low vegetation. The others were following behind in various states of perturbation, but she focused on Ferdinand.

Turning it around, she told it to lie down again and carefully slid off. That should be far enough to satisfy the rules about door opening so they could go back inside. She put her bare hand on Ferdinand's nose. *Good monster. I don't have a treat for you, but here's a nice dose of endorphins. Now you feel sleepy, very sleepy. You stay here while I go off to get yelled at, okay?*

CHAPTER 15

Alaghar knew in the bones of her soul the Frost People were not cruel. Therefore they could not have planned to bend an *asuhan* to their will merely to make the Wiyert walk faster, even if that was what happened. *Why could they not command it to go before us instead of behind?*

She felt her head start to turn and resolutely forced herself to look forward. They had left Vartai at first light and traveled steadily since, and not once had the *asuhan* made any threatening move. In fact, no other *asuhan* had come within sight. She had found herself able to look about without fear of attack, to study the land and the broken structures as she had never been able before—but only, now, when she was able to ignore the *asuhan*.

The instinct to attack the *asuhan* following behind never left. Even though it was burdened with gear in a way no wild creature would allow, and little Lea walked beside it with one hand resting on its shoulder, the other carrying the long pole that somehow kept all the other *asuhan* away. Even the flying ones avoided them. There was nothing for Alaghar to do, really, except walk and think.

And thinking was dangerous. The fear of the *asuhan* did not abate, nor did the voice in her head saying *wrong, wrong, wrong!* The fear shamed her. The Frost People showed no sign of it, and they had been frightened of even the *du-asuhan* at first. And then Alaghar thought, *perhaps it is not the* asuhan *I fear. I have killed many such; this one would not be difficult. I fear the change. I fear a world where I walk beside it and it does not kill me and I do not kill it.*

Perhaps that was why only her team had agreed to come with the Frost People on their journey. They had already seen change, seen that it could sometimes be useful and was not evil in itself. They had touched the small creature M.O., seen how the Frost People cherished it. Named it.

They had named the *asuhan* too. Fehrd-ee-nan. The name had a meaning to them that Lea had tried to explain, but all that Alaghar had gotten from it was something that appeared fierce but was not.

They continued walking even as the sky darkened, the Frost People using their small but bright lights to guide the way. Then Lea had everyone stand aside to let the *asuhan* go first.

"It wants to find shelter," she said. "Whatever it comes up with will probably be better than anything we can find."

She was, annoyingly, right. The *asuhan* found a deep hollow, overhung by a slab of old structure. The plants growing within, it simply trampled or tore up with its tusks, so there was room for all of them. The gear the Frost People insisted on taking off the *asuhan*, and the *asuhan* itself, blocked the opening.

"Think we could try a fire?" Ramirez asked.

Lea scrunched up her face. "I'd rather not. Smoke seems to get it agitated—remember how we flushed it out? I could keep it calm but then I'd have to stay up all night."

"Nah, not worth it." He shrugged. "We've got the food heaters. Still…you know. Jungle, dinosaurs, cave…seems like we ought to have a fire, outa respect for our mutual ancestors." He handed out the food. Alaghar tried, and failed, to stifle her eagerness. If the others in Vartai ever found out about the wonders of *khendi*, Rey'wiros would have to confiscate it all to prevent fights.

"Speaking of ancestors, do we have any idea what happened back then?" North was assembling the small, square thing that warmed the food. "Back when the Wiyert got taken from Earth."

"We do not remember," Alaghar said. "The only memories we kept were of the Gold Sun and *govrot*." This was true, and it was good to be able to tell the whole truth. She did not like having to hide things from the Frost People, but it was not her decision.

"Oh yeah, mastodons. Well, we don't have many memories of that time ourselves," North said, smiling. "We found things that we could examine—bones, paintings in caves, tools made of stone. By very small signs we can determine a great deal. By placing the pieces together, we discover the whole. If Olsen was here, he could explain better. He loves archeology…that means the study of ancient times."

Olsen, the palest of the pale Frost People, who had seen the faces of the Wiyert and *known* they were kin. Alaghar remembered his puzzled face the first time she had seen him, in the food place of the ship *Kepler*, knowing and yet not understanding how he knew. Later he had shown them strange pictures—faces, he said, of those long dead yet brought out and given flesh from bone alone. *Reconstructions*, he had called them. So that the Frost People could see the dead faces, not knowing that they would have need one day to recognize living ones.

"Yeah, it isn't just what happened to the Wiyert either," Ramirez said, talking around a mouthful of food. "Something bad happened to us back then too. Pretty much the same time. He asked me about it—the genetic bottleneck. You know, if it was real and did it show up in our DNA. Some article or other in those journals he was always reading. Some researcher says we were down to just ten thousand humans at some point, all in this one place in Africa. Which is why you shouldn't marry your cousin, even if she's cute. Although maybe that is what got us in trouble. Plenty of people on Earth have a long-ago Wiyert ancestor, also according to the DNA."

Many of the words were strange to Alaghar, and she did not bother to use the translation device. One thing that Ramirez had said was very clear, and she could see in the shocked faces of her people they had understood it as well as she had. Ten thousand. Even after the slaughter of the Refusal, the Wiyert had numbered more than that.

"Only…so few? Why?"

Ramirez shrugged. "Giant asteroid, solar flare, volcano… nobody knows for sure." He stopped, looking at them slowly. "You don't think so?"

"So close to the time we were taken?" Alaghar shook her head sharply. "No. The fadohl tried to kill you all. Their belief that they had done so saved you—this must be why they never returned to Earth."

"But *why*?" Lea looked horrified. "Why wipe us out?"

"Factory rejects," Ivars said. "They wanted the Wiyert, and we weren't assembled right, or something. The Wiyert are strong—useful. We can run fast and escape. Not something the fadohl would want. That may be how we survived, though."

"Lea is right to question." Alaghar smiled at Lea's surprise. "We *do* have stories more recent of what the fadohl are capable of. Even we, who angered them by our rebellion, they did not destroy outright. So—something about your ancestors the fadohl considered dangerous. Very dangerous." She felt a sudden spike of curiosity. She had never spent much time with the histories; it was considered enough that warriors know the basics of the Refusal and what the fadohl had done. But there might be information hidden there that would explain why.

"Be nice to know what that was so we can do it again," Ivars murmured.

I begin to think I may know, Alaghar thought, looking at the bulky shadow of the *asuhan. I am certain now. They steal the fadohl's strength to use against them. Everything I do to bring the Frost People to us is a blow against the fadohl. They feared them once; let them fear again.*

Lea sighed and grimaced. It wasn't her imagination. "We've got a problem," she called out. That got everyone's attention, of course. Especially since everything had gone so smoothly until now. "Good news is that tower thing is definitely the source of the agonizer signal. It's been getting stronger the closer we get. Bad news is that's the signal, and it's getting stronger the closer we get. I think the nullifier is going to get swamped before we get there, at this rate. And Ferdinand is not going to be happy."

Ivars muttered something, probably profanity. "Can you do your personal override?"

"On Ferdinand? Sure, but I have to be in physical contact. And if something attacks, I'm not sure I can stay in control."

"Great." Ivars looked toward the distant tower, his mind working furiously. "We've still got the shield and our weapons. The nullifier is handy but not necessary. Keep it going as long as possible. Lie down, Ferdinand."

The *asuhan* obediently folded its legs and relaxed, and Lea stroked its head, thinking happy thoughts at it.

"Are we taking a break?"

"We're rucking up." Ivars started removing the gear. "If something happens and Ferdinand runs off, we need our equipment. Everybody load up. And you," he said, pointing at Lea, "get to do your famous rodeo act. You've been hiding the limping pretty well, but don't forget, I can cheat." He tapped his head.

Oh yeah. "And if Ferdinand runs off?"

"You will know before that happens and unass your ride immediately. The *instant* you feel it losing control, got that? We're going to make time to that tower as fast as we can, and that means no limping or waiting around for attacks."

Lea was not sure if riding Ferdinand was better than walking on an increasingly sore ankle. She had them leave the main pack strap around Ferdinand's torso, which was better than having to grab on to the hair. She still slid around too much. North took over the nullifier antenna.

She now had three different tasks, all of them important, so she just rotated. Keep tabs on any *asuhan* in the neighborhood, keep tabs on Ferdinand's mental health, and evaluate the effectiveness of the nullifier. Even if the nullifier was only protecting Ferdinand, it was worth keeping up, but the others needed to know. And she would then have to get ready to deploy the shield as well.

Oh yeah, and not fall off. *I am quite sure the guidance counselor never mentioned this part. If I ever get back to Earth, I am going to sign him up with every telemarketer on the planet.*

She still had a few spare seconds to observe the tower. Unlike every other non-Wiyert building on the planet, with the exception of the gate portal, it was intact. It had the same kind of sloping walls the portal had, but there was a broad base around the tower proper. It was also on a bit of a hill. She'd thought Beredul didn't have hills.

Rather than yell, which could attract unwanted attention now, Lea started updating Ivars's mental heads-up display with a blue circle indicating obe current range of the nullifier, along with the position of any *asuhan* that came close. It was starting to remind her of the first hike. Several contacts, moving fast, and all in pain.

By the time they could see the entrance to the tower base,

North was holding the nullifier at the base of Ferdinand's skull, and it was still feeling twinges of pain. They'd bunched up together, and everyone was moving as fast as they could.

I'd better get down now, Lea sent to Ivars. *Bad guys coming and Ferdinand is twitchy.*

Ivars helped her dismount. By holding the nullifier up, she could still help Ferdinand, but she knew it wouldn't last. Especially since two *asuhan* were coming their way. In addition, the slope up to the tower was full of rubble and debris, with a covering of the ropy vines that she pretty much had to crawl over to make any headway.

Ferdinand detected the *asuhan* not long after she did. It moved restlessly, lowering its tusked head and making a deep, angry rumbling noise. The nullifier was just barely holding on, so it couldn't be the effects of the agonizer ray—but it was definitely angry about something.

The first *asuhan* came in view, one of the armored boar types. There were old, deep scars on its side, but that didn't seem to slow it down at all.

One of the energy weapons fired, and the wild *asuhan* snarled, twisting around the new, blackened injury.

And Ferdinand launched into action. Lea's only warning was the sharp spike of aggression before it sprang away from her and the nullifier. It rocketed into the armored boar, using its tusks to dig in under the edge of the armor plating and push it on its side, exposing the relatively unprotected belly.

"Lea! Get moving!" Lea started, tearing herself away from the snarling screams now coming from the battling *asuhan*. She scrambled as fast as she could toward the tower, fear giving her strength she didn't know she had. That was their only real hope now. She doubted she could get Ferdinand to even hear commands in its current state, and she sure wasn't going to make contact with it now. Especially since a second wild *asuhan* was on the scene, drawn by the noise and the blood.

She glanced back and wished she hadn't. It was huge—elephant-size, with multiple jaws and claws like the giant one that had nearly destroyed the portable shield. Ferdinand didn't stand a chance, but it wasn't running. *Ferdinand is trying to protect us, even now, half-mad with pain.* She had to get inside that tower and shut down the agonizer ray. It was the only way to help Ferdinand.

She felt tears seeping down her face. Climbing, falling, the nullifier landing with a smash on the rocks despite her frantic grab to save it. Now she really had to shut down the tower, or they couldn't go anywhere. A big block of stone was in her way, taller than she was, and no easy way to go around it either. She'd have to go down and find another route.

Then a gloved hand reached down from the top of the stone. She looked up—North. With his help she scrambled up and discovered they were at the entrance to the tower base.

"I can't get in—feels like a shield," he said.

It was a shield, and if she hadn't been overwhelmed by the fight and Ferdinand's suffering, she would have noticed by now. Idiot.

"I'll try and take it down…is everybody here?" She scanned. Ivars was still only halfway up the slope, covering for the slower Wiyert. Hazuruh was down on one knee next to North, her weapon up and scanning the skies. The other Wiyert arrived shortly after, their stronger arms helping with the climbing.

Get up here now! Lea sent to Ivars. He fired a few more times to discourage some *du-asuhan* from following, then slung his weapon and sprinted. The others covered as best they could, but the rocks blocked their fire, and he had to stop and use his knife twice. Lea closed her eyes and concentrated on the shield. She didn't need to look to know how he was doing, and they all needed the shield down. But not until they were ready to go inside, or the *asuhan* would get in too.

As soon as he was up on the very crowded ledge, breathing hard and bleeding from a bite on his upper arm, Lea dropped the shield. They still had to force the door open, which was awkward in the little room they had. Lea could sense the door mechanism inside, but it was stuck or broken.

The Wiyert were using all of their massive strength, muscles straining and teeth bared with effort. The battling *asuhan* were no longer visible, but the screams could still be heard. She couldn't sense much more than bloodlust from Ferdinand, so she had no idea how badly it was hurt.

With a deep, shuddering groan, the door opened. Everybody pushed to get it wide enough to enter, Ramirez using his flashlight from the back for the others, some guarding the rear and the rest pointing their weapons into the darkness. The space appeared dusty and empty, and when Ivars glanced at her for confirmation, Lea nodded. Nothing but mechanical devices inside.

They all burst through the gap in the door, and Lea quickly brought the shield back up again.

"Well. That was exciting," Ivars said, leaning against a wall. "Why did you tell Ferdinand to attack? We could have taken those two out ourselves."

"I didn't! It decided to on its own, and then it was outside my control and the nullifier."

"Speaking of the nullifier, where is it?"

Lea pointed to the door. "Smashed. Should have paid extra for the ruggedized version."

"Damn. Guess we're committed here, then." He gave a tired smile. "Military suppliers. What are you gonna do?"

"Build a bigger, better one, of course." Lea dragged herself up on her feet again, drawing in a sharp hiss of breath as her ankle flared with pain. With her luck, she'd sprained it again. "After we find the off switch."

Her ankle was really hurting after the rock-climbing session, but there wasn't much she could do about it now. Ramirez taped it up tight before they continued, which helped a bit. The trouble was moving. She didn't want to lean on the fighters when they had a job to do, and besides, Ivars was the only one she could really ask without getting mind-reader-allergic reactions. Lea would much rather have him doing the fighter stuff right now. She would just keep an eye out for something that could be used as a crutch.

"So what happened to the lights in here?" North asked. "Can we get them going?"

"If they still work, yeah." Lea closed her eyes, concentrating. Inside the shield, she could sense a lot more. "Oof."

Ivars stood up. "Something wrong? We got unfriendlies coming?"

Lea rubbed her head. "No, this place is empty as far as I can scan. There's just a lot of power here. Must be because of the transmitter. I need to find the central controls or something on their network first—there's just too much going on to sort out." She shrugged out of her pack and found the little purple clip-on flashlight that had survived all her adventures so far. It wasn't as fancy as the military ones, but it did the job.

The area they were in had no obvious control components. It was constructed of the same dark, stone-like material they had seen all over Beredul, with another closed door on the far wall from where they had come in. In the corners of the interior wall, however, were incised columns of a very familiar pale gold, grainy substance. Both columns showed damage near the top, and at similar locations.

"Is that writing?" Lea asked, pointing at the incisions on the columns.

"It is possible. Our histories…I have heard others speak of the fadohl having such things, but I cannot read it. What I wish to know is how such a large hole could be made on that column, as by a weapon, yet no rubble is present below." Alaghar gestured, and Lea realized she was correct. Somebody had deliberately damaged the columns and then cleaned up. Further, if that was the same stuff Argo was made of, it was *very* hard to destroy. What had been up there that needed blowing up?

She limped over to one column and touched it. As far as her senses could detect, the column was purely decorative and had never been wired up for anything—so the damaged area probably wasn't a weapon or sensor.

"We need to get through that door. There's nothing here for me to work with."

Keeping her hand on the wall for support and to scan for anything she could interface with, Lea reached the door. It was smaller than the outside door and had a deep carved border all around the edges. She could sense a mechanism to open it, but it was odd.

She frowned. "Okay, I think I can open this, but…keep an eye out. It isn't like the others I've dealt with." The others trained their weapons on the door, and Lea activated the mechanism, then stepped back out of the way.

The door sank back and shifted to one side, revealing another dusty, dimly lit space—and then suddenly slammed back into place.

Now she understood what was going on. The mechanism only had an opening setting. Something purely mechanical, that she couldn't control, closed it and kept it closed unless the mechanism forced it. A fail-safe security mechanism?

"Looks like I have to keep it open for us to get through," Lea said, explaining what she'd discovered. "I guess we could find the spring and disconnect it, but it probably is on the inside anyway."

"No guts, no glory," Ivars said, staring at the door with his hands on his hips. "And if that fails, we've still got the C4."

Lea grinned. "You really want to blow something up, don't you?"

"Not much room for explosions here, and I would rather not go back out with the monsters," North said dryly. "Let's do any demo from the other side, okay?"

"Fine, fine…everybody ready?" Ivars took up position just behind her, and she felt her pack shift as he took a solid grip on it.

Are you having issues with trust again?

Lea felt a little shove. "Sooo funny. I'm going to have nightmares about your little trick on Alaghar's planet for the rest of my life, so humor me," Ivars said softly.

I would, but Alaghar's watching.

That got her a muffled snort of laughter. "Tease."

Lea opened the door again. Once everybody else was on the other side, she wiggled around the edge of the wall until she had contact on both sides of the wall. With a deep breath, she dropped one hand, and she and Ivars swiveled away from the door.

She still had control. This time she tried to let the door close softly, but it only slowed a little. The force closing the door caught her by surprise as soon as she started to let go. *I wonder what they were so afraid of getting through?*

At least now they had light. It was soft and blue green, like being underwater. The inner door opened onto a long corridor that she could see angling off at both ends, so it likely mirrored the exterior shape of the tower base. The walls were still dark stone, but the ceiling was high, curved, and pale in color. Protrusions hung down in a random fashion like frozen lace and even dripped down the dark walls where the ceiling met them. Lea could sense a deep thrum of power, but it seemed to be coming from a location underneath.

The Wiyert seemed to find the architecture as disturbing as she did. Burdhul was staring at the ceiling with great suspicion, and

Alaghar was scanning their surroundings with tense alertness. Lea still couldn't sense any direct threat, alive or robotic, but something about this place wasn't quite right.

She started following the corridor. They passed an archway that didn't even have a door, the space beyond empty and shadowed. Past the turn in the corridor, the outer wall had no openings at all but a series of low, transparent surfaces completely flush with the wall. They had a slight frosted effect that cleared when rubbed, enough for Lea to see a huge empty space with massive stone pillars in ordered arrays and two immense outside doors. Big enough for *asuhan*, even, and then she realized what the pillars were for.

"They brought the *asuhan* in here somehow and tied them up there. Like a stable," she said.

"So they had a way to control them too, like you do," Ramirez said. "Duh, they were the ones who did the agonizer ray, so they could turn it off. But why…"

"So they could use the *asuhan* as Lea did, perhaps," Alaghar said. "The fadohl had a purpose in this."

Lea shuddered. "Maybe that's why the minds of the *asuhan* are so easy for me to rewire. The fadohl designed them to be." It was hard to think of a bunch of aliens who designed life-forms to spec, like humans would design a car. But the more she thought about it, the more it made sense. "I wonder what they were going to use *asuhan* for, anyway?"

"I dunno what they were planning to use them for, but I think I know what that's all about now." Ramirez jerked a thumb back toward the entrance. He was radiating a sudden anger, and his expression was hard. "Evolution in action, right? Only the real thing takes too long. Smart animals survive by running away from a fight they can't win. So those little jerk slugs made *this* thing to drive 'em so crazy they always fight. Get to your supermonster that much faster."

"That makes…a sick kind of sense." North shuddered. "But do the fadohl really think like that?"

Alaghar's face looked like death. "That is exactly how the fadohl think," she snarled. "Do you understand us now?"

They had walked a considerable distance but still hadn't come across anything that looked like the control center, and with so much power around, there had to be something. The next corridor turning looked much more promising. There were two doorways, one on each side of the corridor and facing each other. The one on the outer wall was a regular door, and when Lea opened it, it stayed open.

"Jackpot!" The room was walled with the usual fadohl panels, translucent black with green lights and indicators. Lea could feel the connectedness and knew this was the right place.

"Wait for us to check things out before you hook up your brain," Ivars cautioned. "See anything suspicious, Alaghar?"

"No more than the rest of this place," Alaghar said slowly.

"What's that mean?"

Lea hunched her shoulders. "This place doesn't fit. Think of the fadohl structures we've been in before—they're all sort of unified, you know? This is more...pieced together."

"Yeah. Rebuilt, maybe, from something that used to be here earlier." Ramirez blinked as they stared at him. "Come on, you've seen the broken buildings all over the place out there. Pretty standard postwar wreckage. So whoever blew up scenic downtown Beredul built a few of their own structures on top after they pacified the hell out of this place."

Lea frowned. "But why not build this place completely new, like the others? Why build on wreckage?"

Ramirez shrugged. "Gotta be something pretty important here, then. Something they couldn't move."

Ivars, North, and Hazuruh had circled the room, and now Ivars waved Lea forward. She walked slowly past the wall panels and the banks of equipment in the center of the room, reaching out with her mind. She only wanted to shut down the agonizer ray, not everything. Especially not the shield.

There. One of the central equipment banks. It almost pulled at her, like a fast current, making her dizzy. Lea reached out blindly, only thinking of shutting it down as fast as she could and rescuing Ferdinand, but the echo of Ivars's caution steadied her. *It won't help anyone if you do it wrong. What if they booby-trapped this thing?* Ramirez was right—there had been a fight here, and she didn't know which side had built the console.

So she looked, extending her mental senses as far as she could. It was like staring into a storm. The power swirling about hid subtle signs that Lea had ignored when she was just looking for the off switch, but now she was sensing more clearly, and she was very glad she had taken the time to check. The system had multiple fail-safes. Whoever had designed it *really* didn't want it to go down accidentally. She took out the fail-safes first, making sure she got them all, then checked the system again. When she was sure nothing else was hiding, she shut down the main signal.

Something flashed in her mind, leaving the mental equivalent of an afterimage. A feeling of something else connected. Multiple things.

Lea squeezed her eyes shut, concentrating on the brief pulse of information. Similar but distant. A network of…what? *Transmitters. This wasn't the only one—how could it be? You can't have one ground-based radio transmitter for a whole planet. Even superaliens like the fadohl can't get around basic physics.*

She started to realize someone was shaking her by the shoulders. A worried Ivars.

"Lea! What happened?"

"Urg." Lea rubbed her forehead. "I got some information, but I don't know how to parse it. This thing is in a network. I sort of got a look at the whole thing when I shut it down. I'm pretty sure this area doesn't have the agonizer ray now, but we need to have it off for all the *damah* for Rey'wiros to have his apocalyptic proof, right?"

North groaned. "You're saying we might have to do this all *again?*"

"God, I hope not. We haven't seen another tower like this one in our travels, so the next one would be a long hike. Do you know of anything like this, Alaghar?" Ivars asked.

Alaghar shook her head. "It might have been seen but not thought important. I do not know."

Ivars took off his helmet and scrubbed his head with his knuckles. "Argh. Let's think about this. We know the signal isn't as strong at the portal gate, and at Vartai."

"And it would fall off as an inverse square power law, assuming they aren't doing anything complicated with the broadcast," North added. "So taking this place as the center, probably at least a circle with a radius from here to Vartai would be clear of other towers. Can you sketch what you saw?"

Lea spread her hands, feeling useless. "Three-dimensional. Maybe if I get the data to Argo, it can help. Or…" She thought hard. "You said there must be something important here," she said, pointing at Ramirez. "Or they wouldn't have bothered rebuilding. How about a huge power supply? There's something really strong here, and it's underground. If it's part of the original setup and the next bunch took it over to power the agonizer ray, maybe they used *other* power supplies for the rest of the broadcast towers. If the power is part of a network too, maybe I can figure it out that way."

"And maybe this power network is connected to whatever is keeping the barricade up," Ivars pointed out. "That would certainly be handy. Let's see if we can find this giant battery. Where do you think the power is again?"

Lea thought for a moment, feeling the tug, and then pointed. Down and toward the center of the structure. Under the tower itself.

"Hmm. That big-ass door across the hall looks promising. Let's check it out. You sure the signal is down and out?"

Lea nodded vigorously. "Not even a dial tone now." She hoped she'd turned it off soon enough for Ferdinand and that the *asuhan* was still alive, somewhere.

The inner wall door was, as Ivars had mentioned, larger. It was also one of the self-slamming doors, another indication that whatever was on the other side was important. The first glimpse they got was not very impressive—a circular shaft, a solid central core, and what looked like a helical ramp between the core and the shaft wall.

Once through the door, Lea put her hand on the core. "This is all signal and power cabling. Goes up the length of the tower. The power source is down there somewhere." And there was something else…something familiar. It felt like Argo, or the spindle, but faintly. Lea couldn't tell what the familiarity was coming from; not yet.

"This is great," North said with a wide smile. "I always wanted to explore a real dungeon and fight dragons."

Ramirez sighed. "You are such a nerd. Why didn't you play video games like a normal person?"

Lea had to stifle her amusement at the expressions on the faces of the Wiyert, who might have understood the individual words but not assembled in that order. "It's a…just a joke," she said lamely. "I'll explain later." *Assuming a beholder doesn't get us first, that is.*

CHAPTER 16

The slope of the ramp was very gradual, which made it more comfortable for her sprained ankle but also meant it took longer to get anywhere. Lea kept one hand on the wall for support and wished the fadohl believed in handrails. The familiar sensation she'd noticed was getting stronger, and she was also picking up some other signals she'd encountered before. Robots. Not very many, and they felt the same as the ones on the spindle. Which meant broadcast power, which meant…

"We're in a lightning zone now," Lea informed Ivars with a wry grin. Not that there was much danger of that happening with a troop of Wiyert chaperons around. She still didn't know why close personal contact in a broadcast power zone turned the two of them into a dangerous voltage source. Fortunately Argo could turn that feature off when they were on board.

He sighed and smiled back. "Dammit. I know who I'm going to blame for that," he said, glancing Alaghar's direction.

"This place predates the Wiyert. I don't think she's *that* old, Mark."

He raised a skeptical eyebrow. "You get old fast when you don't have any fun. Think you can shut it off?"

"I don't know. If it's like the spindle, I'd need Argo's help for that. I can't mess with it fast enough before it changes."

They kept walking. Lea noticed more of the targeted damage with no debris on the walls. It was a regular pattern and clearly intentional. Whoever had done it hadn't bothered to spackle the damage and make it look nice again, but they had swept up the debris. Weird.

Then the ramp came to an end. The lighting here was less uniform, and Lea got out her little flashlight again. This level looked very different than the tower base. The passageways had curving walls, oval in cross-section, with slight ribs running up and then spreading out in a fan pattern. But the ribs were placed randomly and the patterns asymmetrical. It looked organic, as if it had been grown rather than constructed.

And behind a free-standing rib, near the juncture of the ramp and the rest of the level, she saw a curious design. It covered an oval area and had lines that flowed like vines—but it also looked like the pillars with the fadohl writing. It was also right about the height that the damaged spots were along the ramp.

"Looks like the cleanup crew missed one," Lea said, pointing. "Wonder what the big deal was?"

"Maybe that was the mark of the original owners," Ivars said, considering it. "Wiping out the name of the defeated enemy is a pretty old custom."

"So who was the enemy?" Lea asked. "This is all fadohl, isn't it?"

North shrugged. "Fadohl can fight among themselves, I guess."

They all looked at Alaghar, who had a curious expression on her face. "I am not certain of this place, but…there were things the fadohl did not wish us to remember." Her thoughts felt… uncomfortable. *I think she's hiding something.*

"Like the Gold Sun?' North asked.

"Even so."

"There's a robot coming," Lea interrupted. "Better stash your weapons or hide until I get it under control."

The Wiyert all faded back up the ramp and out of sight. North and Ramirez took flanking positions at the entrance to the ramp, concealed, and Ivars just shifted his weapon to ride on his back and stood behind and to one side of her.

"Sure you got this?" Ivars murmured.

"Feels like the ones on the nexus, so yeah."

Lea faced the shadowy corridor and waited. This device was familiar, but she still was careful to check for any surprises. The robot was in patrol mode, and she didn't want to set an alert by intercepting it too soon. Instead, she observed its workings from a distance. It was similar but not identical to the spindle robots, a translucent ceramic tapering cylinder with weapon ports ringing the slightly curved top and floating on local antigravity. She slowly altered its base patterns so it would not notice the intruders or their weapons.

Now she needed to change the central system that told the robots what to do. It probably had information about the entire site, and she could link in to everything from there.

"We're following the robot," she said softly. "I have to get farther in to shut off the whole security system. Don't make too much noise; it could make the others come and investigate."

Lea started by walking beside it, one hand resting on the smooth, cool top, then shook her head at her own stupidity. She needed to rest her ankle, and they had used the robots for transportation before on the spindle. With a bit of ungraceful scrambling, she managed to seat herself on the mostly flat surface.

Now this is more like it. Riding an antigrav robot at the head of a band of intergalactic desperados, exploring an ancient, abandoned alien power plant so she could get back to her talking spaceship. *Leigh Brackett, eat your heart out.*

Since she didn't have to concentrate on walking without wincing, she could focus more on her new robot friend. It didn't get constant instructions—it had been given an area to patrol and had enough intelligence and autonomy to investigate anything anomalous. She checked the records it had and nodded. Nobody had been inside for hundreds of years, and it hadn't investigated much or needed to report in.

She wanted that to change, but not in a way that would get them shot at. This robot's area of responsibility was not going to take it deeper inside, where they needed to go. She rummaged mentally until she found something she could use.

There. Tell Mother your starboard sprocket polisher is defective and you need to be repaired.

Sure enough, the robot got a burst of instructions, and it shifted from its usual patrol pattern to a new direction.

"We're headed for maintenance," she whispered. "Stay close— there are more robots in that area." Lea had to concentrate hard to keep track of all of them and to slow down or speed up so they wouldn't be seen. And it was hard to concentrate, because they were going through what looked like an alien junkyard now.

The robot had taken them down a series of ramps—they must be hundreds of feet below the surface now. A large interlocking set of metal doors, similar in concept to the Wiyert airlock-type system, opened into a huge open space dimly lit by the glowing organic ribs.

The light was just enough to see fantastic skeletal machine frameworks rearing up in the gloom, looking like black lace. Squat, angular machines with articulated legs, large enough to be mobile buildings. Something that looked like a dark ceramic lotus with tightly folded petals, the size of a tank. All of them felt inactive to Lea's senses but not broken or defective. Merely switched off.

I wonder what they do?

"What's with all the mood lighting?" North asked in a quiet voice. "I thought this was a power plant."

Lea grimaced. "I know. I don't want to mess with anything to turn the lights on, though. I get the feeling a lot of this is connected, and we don't need to set off any alarms. Oh, look. I think we're arriving."

A bright, blue green glow shone ahead, casting the alien machinery warehouse in sharper shadow. The structure emitting the light looked like a large mushroom that had been stepped on, low and squat. There was a broad roof with a shallow slope and a central, narrower structure in the center supporting it. What looked like cables, hoses, and mechanical arms dangled from the roof, and Lea glimpsed other structures but couldn't make them out in the light.

As they drew nearer she could see that the floor sloped down all around the maintenance mushroom. No other robots seemed to be present, or any other activity.

At the bottom of the slope her robot got a burst of signal and stopped. Then a voice speaking a liquid language with high-frequency hums and pops echoed in the previously silent warehouse. The Wiyert started, glancing at Lea for confirmation and bringing their weapons to the ready.

"Recording. Machine-voice," Lea said softly. "Nobody but us

in here."

"That is how the fadohl speak among themselves," Alaghar said, her voice so quiet Lea could barely hear her. "Their language."

"What's wrong?" Ivars said.

"Voice of OSHA," Lea mumbled. "Safety violation. I think it doesn't want me riding the robot when it goes to get fixed. Time to start hacking."

There was a lot of signal to hack into. She was close enough to read and influence most of it, but she still followed the robot closer inside the structure. Anything she could do to filter out the noise would help. As she had hoped, the center post had much of the data interface. Stifling the safety warnings that were starting to blare, she reached the part she wanted and dug her fingers in.

Like the spindle, it wasn't AI, but it was close. She'd need Argo if she wanted to truly destroy it completely, but fortunately that wasn't necessary. She just wanted information and to see how this location was linked to the others.

The first thing she did was set the security program to firmly believe all Wiyert and Earth-humans were invisible and everything they carried benign. Now they didn't have to worry about any remaining robots. She even remembered to tell Ivars that before she really got busy with her investigations.

His mental voice drifted into her mind. *We're going to take a look around, but we won't be far. Don't get too distracted, okay, Space Cadet?* He must have made contact with her, and she hadn't even noticed.

I'll try, but it will be hard.

A warm pulse of amused affection that made her smile, and then his presence faded.

The architecture of the power base systems was different than she had encountered before. It branched more and had, for lack of a better description, a more organic feel. A true mechanical brain. She could sense a network here as well, but it didn't map exactly to the one she'd seen for the signal towers. All of the signal locations existed on this network, but there were other nodes, some with a deeper resonance and flow that pulled strongly at her mind.

Power. Those places have huge amounts of power. Oh boy. What would need more power than the signal towers? The energy barricade. If she could shut it off from here, they could have a direct link from Argo anytime. It was too much of a temptation to resist. With Argo's help, they could *really* take control and not have to hike anywhere.

Lea tried without success to shut the power down. The system had too many protections and corrective subroutines for that to work, at least with her on her own. Even if one power plant failed, the others would reroute their power to keep whatever was connected to the dead one working.

So she couldn't just flip a switch. What else could she do? The first important thing was turning off the agonizer ray everywhere. She was in an agonizer ray facility. Had it started up again? Lea checked. No, the signal was definitely off. Since she hadn't turned off the source of the power or blown it up, as far as the network was concerned, everything was fine and it had no need to intervene. It just kept track of all the facilities in the network and made sure they were working. She could see the query pulse float through the network, checking.

A fragment of an idea flickered through her thoughts. How did the network *know* what facilities were in the network? That took some hunting, but she finally found what the query pulse looked for. It wasn't a database or list. More of a tag, a collection of information and processes that existed in the system as a whole. An object, in abstract programming terms. And she could change that object.

For I have become Root, destroyer of access controls, and all processes are alike to me. Execute "bwahaha" protocol!

Lea double-checked the signal object and made sure she understood what the network expected from it. She didn't need to know where all the towers were; she'd just change the definition and let the computer do the work. That's what computers were *for*, after all. Laziness was a programmer virtue!

No, wait. That would just mean no backup power got routed to the transmitters if their own sources went out. She needed to make them net sources for the *network* so they would save no power at all for themselves. No power, no signal. That was more complicated, and since this system hadn't been designed as a global power controller, she had to cobble together a few proxy monitors.

Lea tried a test system, watching carefully. She had to tweak it a couple of times to take all the power out—the transmitters had a lot. More than a broadcast system really needed, from her observations. *These used to power something else. I wonder what that was...*

Now she had it. Lea made all the changes as fast as she could. Something was rippling through the network, and she really hoped it wasn't some security watchdog program she'd missed in her initial scan. Something...pulsing. Resonating.

Snap.

Power shuddered through the network like a hammer. Lea could feel things breaking, power going in channels that hadn't been there before. Of course—she'd overloaded the system by turning off all those transmitters. She hadn't thought it through. And they were right next to one of those power sources, which would be getting its share of the deluge.

Oh shit oh shit oh SHIT! There wasn't time to redefine the local system, and in any case it would take too long to be understood. No time to warn anyone. She had to reroute the power *now*, or they could die.

Everything that felt like a switch, Lea closed. Everything she could find to turn on, she did. No time to find out what it was or what it could do.

And then the surge hit.

Ramirez didn't think they were in an actual junkyard. For one thing, all the machines were precisely positioned in ordered rows, which implied some kind of organization. Maybe the machines in a given row had the same general function. For another, the machines all looked intact. Weird as hell, but intact. No piles of parts either, and in his experience all junkyards had piles of parts. Like it was a law or something.

He trained the tac light of his rifle on one of the machines, overcome by sheer awe. If they were on Earth, it would be on the cover of every expensive motor sport magazine in print, and the sultan of Brunei would have five of them. The whole thing was one complex aerodynamic surface with a clear central pod on top. The surface looked metallic but it shaded in color from deep midnight blue at the nose to clear aqua in the midsection. Ramirez didn't think it was paint, either. He shifted his light to the far end. Was that…*transparent?* He walked over to the one trailing edge he could reach. He could see his glove through it, and he couldn't see any place the material was joined. He could tell it was meant to fly. Powered by sheer awesomeness.

"I don't know what it is, but it looks like it goes fast, and I want it."

Ivars pointed his own tac light up at the top. He had his "I'm trying not to be impressed" look on, which he'd been doing a lot since they'd gotten here. "That look like a cockpit to you?"

"I will make it a cockpit," Ramirez vowed. "I mean…*look* at it! It's practically breaking the sound barrier just sitting there! Besides being insane amounts of cool. I wonder if it has weapons?"

"This stuff makes my head hurt," Ivars complained. "Oh, and check this out. It's standing on legs."

Ramirez ducked underneath the alien machine to look, grinning. This outer space gig had its moments.

A blast of light exploded in the warehouse, temporarily blinding him. It was followed by a soft, heavy wave of sound, of lots of small mechanical movements and the shifting of massive weight. Surrounding them.

The fuck!? "I didn't touch it!" Ramirez shouted.

Ivars didn't say anything.

Hostiles? Was he hit? He could still see Ivars's boots, standing in the open—and then Ivars's legs started to crumple as he fell. *Wait. I see…smoke?*

Small wisps of white were coming out from the edges of the leg armor Argo had made for them. Ivars managed to put out one hand to stop his fall, but he still hadn't made a sound.

Ramirez scrambled out and crouched over Ivars, shielding him as much as possible with his body while he scoped out what had fired on him and brought his own weapon up. "Talk to me, Ivars. Where are you hit?" He couldn't see anything dangerous in the machines, not even movement.

Ivars gave a coughing grunt. "Not…hit…"

"Dude, you'd set off a fire alarm if they had one here. You got hit by *something*." He couldn't see a point of impact, or scorch mark, or anything. No blood. Ramirez reached down with one hand to check Ivars's pulse, still keeping his weapon engaged. That seemed okay. Skin was a bit hot, though. He glanced down. There was a band of red across Ivars's cheek and forehead, like a reverse shadow from his helmet.

"Machines…on. Lights."

Vision check, good. Observation skills, good. Communicating. "Yeah. It all happened at once. When I went to look at the landing gear. Then you dropped. What happened?"

Ivars pushed back up to his knees and Ramirez hopped to the side. Ivars's eyes had a vague, searching expression, like he was trying to remember an old phone number or how to order beer in Chinese. One hand rose to his chest, fumbling at his neck. Ramirez swore softly. The glove on Ivars's hand was scorched at the cuff.

"Let me take a look at that. You might have a burn."

"I can't feel it." Now Ivars's eyes were wide in pain or fear. His face was pale. "I can't feel it!"

"What, your hand?"

Ivars staggered to his feet. "The link. Lea. Something happened to Lea!" He started walking unevenly, then broke into a stumbling run.

As much as Ramirez wanted to trip and sit on Ivars, he was probably right to keep moving. They should be together if there was a threat, and Ivars was clearly able to walk in his current condition. Plus he knew Ivars would not stay put until he was sure Lea was okay. Then he could be sedated and bandaged.

They sprinted down the row of machines, heading for the repair depot. Ramirez desperately hoped nothing nearby had been programmed to shoot moving targets. He could tell something bad had happened when he saw a section of the depot had gone dark, and then he smelled a choking combination of smoke and ozone. *Something tells me I got more burn injuries coming up.*

Lea lay in the center of a blast crater. Rays of black soot radiated away from her, but she appeared surprisingly unharmed. Everything around her, though, was scorched or melted. Ramirez could feel the heat on his skin, and as he watched, a blob of molten metal fell and hit the floor with a hiss. Ivars skidded to a stop, glancing at him with a dangerously pale face.

"Can we move her?"

"We'd better," Ramirez said immediately. "Even if she has a

back injury, the armor should help stabilize that, and there's a lot more hot metal that can fall."

The two of them pulled Lea free from underneath the structure's roof just as North and the Wiyert came pounding up.

"What happened? All the machines are lit up and active."

"No idea." Ivars put one hand over his eyes, like he was trying to concentrate. "Did you see anything hostile?" North shook his head.

Ramirez quickly examined Lea and looked up. "Pulse is thin but steady. Nasty burn on one hand, surprise. I'd have to take the armor off to check anything further, but it doesn't show any damage on the exterior, so she's probably okay." He peeled back an eyelid. "Pupil response is good too. If she was normal, I'd say mild concussion, but who knows?" He stared out at the field of alien machines. "Wish one of them was an MRI…"

"Yeah, well, she isn't normal. Nobody here is." Ivars sagged. "And we're stuck with what we've got. Lea's the only one who could tell us what those things do. Or what just happened." He collapsed next to her, resting his head in his hands. "Dammit, Lea…"

CHAPTER 17

Ivars sat beside Lea while Ramirez treated and bandaged her burned hand, thinking hard—or as hard as he could after he'd been knocked on his ass. Lea had apparently channeled a *lot* of energy very quickly. But she'd mostly managed to direct it away from herself to the nearby walls and…the lights. And the machines. He must have been caught in the backlash. Somehow.

Whatever it was must have happened very suddenly too, or Lea would have known and so would he. He had felt the link earlier, and when they had communicated before he'd left. She'd been completely focused, intrigued, and happy…and then boom.

Lots of brain work. She'd said earlier that using her abilities a lot made her need sugar.

"Can we feed her anything?"

Ramirez shook his head sharply. "Not when she's unconscious. She can't swallow like that. Why?"

"I was thinking she needed sugar before. Maybe it would help, but if we can't feed her…never mind."

"If it's just sugar, there's another way." Ramirez started pulling stuff out of his pack. "You can absorb it through the tissue of the mouth. Diabetics, you know, they have these tablets they carry that dissolve easy so people can give 'em if they go in a coma. So we just need to make a sort of syrup, maybe."

They ended up having to smash some hard candies and mix them with water, not having many sugar packets left. Ramirez carefully spread the syrup in Lea's mouth in small, frequent doses.

He also made Ivars take off his armor so he could check him out too. It looked—and felt—like he'd gotten a bad sunburn everywhere metal had been close to his skin. Ramirez put some bandages on the worst spots, but there wasn't much else he could do. The pain was a dull, constant throb.

It took two agonizing hours for Lea to show signs of consciousness, but an hour after that she was able to sit and drink careful sips of sugared water. She tried to speak, but her voice was barely a croak, so Ivars took off the shreds of his glove and held her hand carefully instead, making skin contact wherever he didn't have bandages.

Her mental voice was groggy too, and her thoughts slow. Eventually he got enough to piece the story together.

"So the good news is she's shut down *all* of the broadcast towers. No more agonizer ray. So we achieved the main objective." Ivars sighed. "Unfortunately, in doing that she had to rewire the planetary power network, and there was too much to go around so she dumped it everywhere she could, in a hurry. It got away from her."

"Turning on all the old gear in the place." North nodded. "I get it. What's the plan now? I don't think we can make it to the portal gate in time to meet with Argo, and Rey'wiros needs us back for the diplomacy sessions."

"We're not going anywhere until Lea can walk or we rig some kind of transport." And of course *now* he wished they'd brought the float plate thing. Maybe they could find something like that in all this stuff.

Lea squeezed his hand. *Sorry...* Her mental voice was despondent. *You're right to be mad. I screwed up again.*

More terrified than mad, now. Who were you going to ask for advice? Nobody else does what you do, and nobody knows how this ancient rock pile works except possibly the fadohl, and we aren't on speaking terms. You solved the problem. I wish you hadn't got blown up, but sometimes it happens.

What happened to you? You're hurting.

And of course, when he really wished he could lie to her, he couldn't. Maybe misdirection. *Just a couple of burns.*

You're not telling me something. Dammit. *Mark, was it something I did? Tell me!*

I don't know, okay? It happened at the same time the lights went on, so it probably is related to the power surge. Don't worry about it. I've had worse. Now rest up while we go find you an alien space wheelbarrow or something to carry you.

That got him a faint smile. Ivars stood up and waved Ramirez over.

"I want you watching her. We're going to look for transportation."

It was too bad Ferdinand wasn't around. They could have rigged something. Or, if Lea were feeling better, they might have a chance of trapping another *asuhan* to use. It wasn't going to be easy getting to Vartai in time as it was. They might have a few days law, but not much more than that. Maybe they'd have to split up. He still didn't know what travel outside would be like with the agonizer ray turned off—would the *asuhan* still be a problem, even when they weren't so aggressive? Nobody knew, not even the Wiyert.

Twelve hours later he'd gotten a little sleep but was no closer to solving the problem. They'd managed to find some amazingly light, pliant mesh to rig hammocks with, which made everybody more comfortable, but no space wheelbarrows or float plates or anything much smaller than a tank. They had apparently ended up in the fadohl large motor pool. Lea was doing much better but still couldn't sit up for more than a few hours, and he was trying to come up with a way to split up the forces that wouldn't be an utter disaster. He needed everybody in three different places for it all to work—and three Leas. Which was such a frightening concept he immediately dumped the idea and started over.

Ivars came back from yet another fruitless search to find Lea sitting on some of the depot wreckage and more alert than she had been since the accident.

"Stop me if you've heard this before, but I have an idea," she said, starting to laugh at his expression.

"I'm just going to head to the bunker now and avoid the rush. What brilliant plan have you come up with this time?"

"Most of this equipment requires beam power. It can't run on its own or without the barricade satellites taking it down. But now this place is getting more power, and it isn't being used for the agonizer broadcast."

"And?"

"So we *can* use this equipment within a certain range of the tower."

Ivars rubbed the back of his neck. "But not far enough to get us to the portal gate or Vartai."

Lea nodded. "I'm guessing at most half a mile. No, I'm thinking about the large room we saw on the way in. What if we could bring an *asuhan* to us? That room is designed to handle them. We could use the larger robots to herd one inside and then I can program it."

"You wish to, again, capture an *asuhan* merely to use it?" Alaghar did not appear overjoyed at the thought.

"Sure! What other choice do we have? They are the only self-propelled transportation available. Until I can walk long distances again, I need something to carry me, and you guys need to be able to fight."

Unless, of course, Lea stayed here and somebody went back, but he hated that plan too. Since he would probably have to be one of the people going.

Ivars let her go ahead with her harebrained scheme despite his misgivings. She was doing her best to hide it, but he could tell she was still feeling bad about the power surge. Besides, he hadn't come up with anything better. If he did, they could argue about it then.

Ramirez found a piece of the broken maintenance depot structure that could be used as a carry pole, and they slung Lea's hammock on that so she could help find some useful machines for monster herding.

"And what do we do?" Alaghar asked while giving him a look that indicated she thought all the Earth-humans were nuts and she hoped it wasn't contagious.

"Something we should have done earlier." Ivars waved at one of the larger machines, at least two stories tall and massive. "There's no way in hell that thing came in by way of the ramp or the main entrance to the tower base. There has to be big door somewhere, and now that we have light, we can find it."

They split up in teams to search more efficiently—North and

Hazuruh, Burdhul and Dumhaigl, and him and Alaghar. Kugohin went with Ramirez and Lea. After remembering he had binoculars, every so often Ivars climbed a handy alien machine and scanned the area. The size of the place was beginning to freak him out. This was a huge amount of gear to have stored, and everything he'd seen so far looked functional.

Eventually they hit the far wall. It curved, and it didn't take Ivars long to figure out the storage area was circular and centered on the tower shaft they'd entered from. He and Alaghar found two more, smaller entrances on the walls, but nothing big enough for the giant robots.

"How late can we be before Rey'wiros gets so pissed we shouldn't even show up?"

Alaghar didn't say anything for a moment, and Ivars wondered if he should refer to the portable dictionary to clarify terms. Then she spoke.

"If it is clear that the *asuhan* no longer attack, at least a day. Perhaps two. Those from Koloh will not wish to stay very long waiting."

Great. Not much, but something. Then he realized they were alone and he could ask rude questions without being overheard. "What if we could send a message, like with your light towers?"

That got him a glare. "How did you know of them?"

"We have similar things on Earth," Ivars said calmly. "I recognized them when you took us to the walls."

Alaghar turned away and kept walking, a scowl on her face. "I do not know the codes. There are also ways that a true message can be determined."

"Ah, authentication protocol. Good idea." Inconvenient for him at the moment, though. How the hell could you get through to a bunch of paranoids like the Wiyert? There had to be a way...

It was a quiet hike. Nothing made a sound except them, and Alaghar was not in a talkative mood. Then Ivars heard, off in the distance, a sharp whistle.

Alaghar's head picked up. "Danger?"

"Doubt it. More like somebody found something." He left off examining a machine that looked like a ten-foot-high metal skeletal insect. "It came from over there. Let's go see."

As soon as they hit the wide, open avenue, Ivars knew they were in the right area. *All it needs is some yellow safety hash marks on the floor and I'd feel right at home.* The avenue got even wider as they got closer to the wall and the immense double doors with an interlocking gear mechanism securing them. One of the gears was as tall as he was.

The other scout teams were already there.

"So where's the doorknob?" Ivars asked, after scanning the whole setup. "I guess it must all be remote."

"We may have additional problems." North was frowning at the bottom of the doors, arms folded. "See that? Doors could be damaged."

It wasn't obvious, but when North pointed, Ivars could see what he'd noticed. The edge of one door was bubbled and discolored, as if a large energy weapon had scored a direct hit.

"We knew there had been fighting here, so there's more proof. I'm more worried about what's on the other side still. What if the enemy had powered machines too, and Lea turned them on as well?"

Maybe they should scout from the outside. Ivars looked back at the central shaft, trying to remember where the entrance was so he could orient himself.

Then he saw a blinking white arrow in the field of vision of his synthetic eye. He smiled when he realized it was Lea, trying to get him to look at something. White arrows directed him to some smaller metal gears he had thought were part of the locking mechanism but were apparently manual controls. It took most of them to turn the damn things, but they did turn. Even with the door unlocked, however, they could not get it to open.

"Warped or stuck or something," Ivars said, panting. He really didn't want to resort to explosives unless he had to. On this planet, preserving doors was always a good idea. And he still hadn't come up with an alternative plan.

On my way, the letters across his vision read.

"Lea's coming," Ivars informed the others. Maybe she could hack into the controls, although he wondered if that was a good idea so soon after her collapse. Then he caught sight of motion in the distance and had to smile. *Or she could bring help.*

She, Ramirez, and Kugohin were riding on a large, squat

machine with a series of mechanical legs. It marched up to the big metal doors, and Lea demonstrated how the legs could also be used as claw arms.

"Okay, but let's get everybody away from the doors before we try and open them. Safety first, remember?"

Fine, be that way. But I'll need my favorite assistive device, Lea sent, grinning.

He grinned back. It was good to have the full link and communication again, even if the broadcast power meant they also had the high-voltage chaperone system going too. At least he could make brief contact safely, and it wasn't like Alaghar wasn't already cramping his style.

He pulled her arm over his shoulder and half carried her to cover. Lea had no trouble managing the machine from that distance, and in a short time filled with loud metal grinding, the doors had been forced open—revealing a huge antechamber half-filled with boulders and other rubble.

"Guess we know why all this stuff is still here," Ramirez said. "Exit got jammed before they could get it out."

North nodded. "So all this belonged to the losers."

"Except for the blue flyer, which now belongs to *me*."

Ivars took a few steps forward to examine the door and antechamber. "Good luck smuggling that through customs, Ramirez. Don't think it will fit in a duffle." There was something angular in the rubble. It looked like a crumpled metal door, about the same dimensions as the ones they had just opened. He could also see a thin patch of light at the end. Daylight.

"Great. Outer doors are damaged. There goes our security if we clear this out."

"Not if we block it with something else," Lea said. "I found a *bunch* of robots we can use!"

The motion was kind of like being at sea, with big ocean swells. Lea felt a wave of nausea and tried to think of something else, but that was hard when your entire world was moving like a never-ending roller coaster. A six-legged gait was harder to get used to than she had thought it would be.

At least it was fast. That was the only thing that had made the trip to the portal gate possible. All the long hours, the all-nighter programming the new *asuhan* once they had herded it in the pen, worth it. She only wished they'd had enough time to construct a howdah for the creature instead of tying themselves onto the spines. Too much of the impact of each foot traveled through the bone and muscle for a smooth ride, and of course there wasn't much padding. On the plus side, she had direct contact through the creature's skin and could override at any time.

It was one of the obsidian, spiny *asuhan* the Wiyert called *swehkpe*, like she had always planned, and now she knew she'd been right. They could power through any obstacle and could climb piles of rubble easily without breaking stride. The team had insisted on naming it Snowball, however. *At least I prevented "Fluffy."*

She risked turning her head to see how the Wiyert were doing. Alaghar looked like she was only holding on to life by sheer force of will. Dumhaigl had given up all sense of dignity some time ago and was curled up around a spine in complete misery. He couldn't even keep water down, except when they took pit stops. The motion was also not fun for full bladders.

When this is all over I am going to spend an entire day in a large tub of hot water, and nothing will stink. And I want a chocolate bar the size of a bus.

By focusing on this pleasant daydream, Lea managed to keep her seasickness in check for a while. Then a shout from the front of the *asuhan*, where Ivars was.

"I can see the building!"

Lea's stomach tightened, but not from the motion. Now they would find out if they made it in time. It was the right day, but she hadn't made sure when Argo considered the start and stop time of the wait period.

She also had to handle the shield that they'd left up. Snowball would not like hitting that.

Loosening one of the bindings that attached her to the spine, Lea struggled to stand up. Now she had a better view to know when to slow Snowball's hexapodal gallop.

The portal gate looked exactly like it had when they left the first time, only none of the bodies of the dead *asuhan* remained. They hadn't seen any live ones on the trip out either, possibly because the agonizer ray had been turned off but more likely because Snowball was bigger than most of them. She had only detected a few, and all moving away from them when she did.

The barrier shield turned off, Lea helped Ramirez deploy the cable ladder after telling Snowball to lie down. The *asuhan* still felt happy to her. It appeared to enjoy running.

Lea ran to the entry of the portal. Ivars was complaining behind her but not very seriously. The shield had been up so nothing bad could get in, and she hadn't detected any changes in the portal itself. If the fadohl were here, she would know.

And then she skidded to a stop, her heart plummeting to her feet. The gate door showed the emoji she'd taught Argo that meant "all's well." The AI had already come and gone.

Distantly, she sensed Ivars standing next to her. His disappointment was as strong as her own.

"Sorry," she managed to say. "I should have…I don't know. Done everything faster. Not gotten fried. Something."

"Doesn't really change much." He took her armored shoulders in his hands and gave her a little shake. "Sometimes it just doesn't go your way. I could tell you stories—only in mine, people usually die when that happens, so this is a nice change. How long until Argo comes back?"

"Four days."

She could feel the twinge of aggravation before he said anything. "We've got to get back before then. But once we get the diplomacy wrapped up, we'll come back."

"Are we leaving now?"

Ivars went to the doorway and looked up at the sky, grimacing. "Snowball might be able to go fast enough to get us to Vartai before dark, but we'd all be dead from blunt force trauma when we got there. And I'd rather not camp out if we don't absolutely have to. Can it travel at night?"

Lea shook her head. "The *asuhan* want to shut down and find a safe place when it's dark, and it's hard to override. That seems to be a natural instinct, not one the fadohl put there."

Ivars rubbed his chin, thinking, then nodded. "Right. We'll leave at first light tomorrow. We could all use the rest."

Fighting the heavy cloud of depression, Lea faced the gate and concentrated. It was crucial Argo know she was alive and still needing to contact it—otherwise she didn't really know what it would do. She set her emoji code and looked around for a place to lie down. It was nice not to be jolted constantly, she had to admit. And her ankle had stopped hurting since she'd been able to keep off it for a while.

Lea went outside. The others had gotten their gear off Snowball, and she had the beast follow her around the portal gate. There was some vegetation but not much inside the shield perimeter, so she altered the shield to allow more grazing.

By the time she got back to the portal, the Wiyert were already asleep except for Hazuruh, who was on guard. Lea decided to join them. *Someone will wake me for my turn*, she decided, drifting off.

So she was not surprised to be shaken awake by North when the world outside the door was pitch-black. What she wasn't expecting was a pulsing light coming from the gate door and everybody else waking up too, worried and agitated.

"It started about thirty seconds ago," North snapped. "What's going on?"

And then she felt it. A very welcome and familiar signal. "It's Argo! It came back!"

"Is there a problem? Fadohl?" Ivars was looking at the gate, intent and alert.

Lea shook her head, then thought about why she was sure. "No, the emoji are still there. Let's go ask."

Ivars was getting quicker. He was blocking the door before she got there. "Let's not do this half-assed, okay? Wait for us, and we'll go in prepared."

Lea supposed it was possible the fadohl had cleverly figured out the emoji or compromised Argo or something else disastrous, but when she finally made contact with Argo, to her relief, nothing like that had happened. She now knew what a deliriously happy AI felt like—she had to tell it twice to slow down the data transfer because she was getting overwhelmed.

And then she learned why it had come back after leaving and sighed, her head drooping.

"Okay, this is where you laugh like a hyena and say I had it coming," she told Ivars. "Argo decided on its own initiative to set up some…let's call them snooper circuits, when we weren't here for the second check. If anything changed from what Argo set on the station, a signal would be sent. I'm not clear on the details of how this was done, but when I changed the display for my emoji, that triggered the circuit and Argo came back."

Ivars opened his eyes, wide and innocent. "Oh, you mean like the way you just decide to do things without telling anyone first, and then it works and you look at us like we are nuts for complaining about it? Yeah, that is pretty funny. Revenge is sweet." His shoulders shook for a moment, then his expression sobered. "Any sign of the slugs?"

"No. Nobody has been here since the last visit it detected, before Argo brought us."

Ivars's mind was a whirl of thought, then hard decision.

"Right. Everybody in. We've got six hours to prep and come back, then load before daylight. We're all tired, but we're just going to have to cope. Stimulants if you need 'em." He continued talking as they walked through the lunar station and then on board Argo. Lea nearly dropped to her knees in relief when they reached the familiar, welcoming corridors and Argo's mental presence. "I figure Snowball can carry anything we have that we can strap on. My suggestion is the Wiyert sleep now while the rest of us get the gear out we want to take, since we know what it is. Then we'll rest and your people can arrange the ropes and harness and so on," Ivars said to Alaghar. "Is that acceptable?"

"Only if you do not take the cat as well." Lea gaped at Alaghar, then sensed the subtle emotion that emerged just long enough for her to detect.

Oh my God. Alaghar just made a funny! We are a corrupting influence...

"Lea. Is Snowball going to be all right on its own?"

She nodded. "The shield is up and it will be asleep." Lea felt the ripple of the drive and knew Argo had taken them out to its hiding place, away from the station.

There was a lot she wanted to do, and fatigue and the lingering effects of the power accident were making her slow. She had Argo make a bunch of helpers to follow everyone for loading and to pile up the gear near the door that went to the station. That would make the loading go faster. Then, while she was picking out her gear, she downloaded all her information to Argo.

But first it appeared Argo had some urgent questions of its

own.

Ivars is angry I put the watcher circuits in place. He says the fadohl could find them and trace me—but I needed to know what to do. I think M.O. was angry too. He was telling me something I didn't understand while you were gone. He wanted to go in your quarters even though I told him you were not there.

That's normal. He was looking for us. Is he okay? Where is he now?

He has found the Wiyert and is speaking to them loudly.

Lea couldn't help snickering. Alaghar getting scolded by a cat would be good entertainment. Relieved about M.O., she reverted to her other problems. They didn't have much time, and she needed Argo's help.

I need to know where the central power tap is on Beredul. I wasn't able to reach it through the network I had access to at the broadcast tower.

You caused the change in the power grid? I saw it was different on my first return. I was afraid the fadohl had done it, but they had not come.

Wait, you could see the change? That's not good. The fadohl could see it too and get suspicious. Great, Mark is going to be mad at me again and try to hide it again.

Why would he be angry?

Because now they will know something has changed about Beredul that they didn't do. Just like seeing you still at the station would be bad.

You will need to change Beredul anyway, to shut down the barrier, Argo pointed out reasonably. **The danger is when the fadohl who send the probes learn of it.**

Lea stopped in her sorting of electronic components, suddenly struck with an idea. Argo was right—it wasn't the fadohl coming to Beredul and finding out that was the most dangerous, it was them *leaving* with that information and telling the others.

We need some way to take control of whatever comes here and either change the information it gets or prevent it from going back. Can you do that?

It should be possible, but what if I am not in the Beredul system when it arrives?

Lea grinned. *Something called a poison pill. You put the code where the probe or ship will query the station—they do a status check, don't they? So they upload the program with that status information. It will do the work for us.*

A moment of silence. **That is prohibited by several data protocols.** Argo seemed intrigued by the thought. **They will not expect that. I will do this now. What else?**

Lea thought for a bit. *If it is a ship with fadohl on it, we can't change their brains. They'll know something is up. The ship will need to be stopped there. And if it is an AI ship like yourself, maybe we can free it too.*

An even longer pause. **A ship like...me?**

Argo was thinking furiously, Lea could tell. And something that could occupy most of the AI's circuits was pretty intense. She kept sorting components as fast as she could, taking half of everything. She was *not* going to be stuck on Beredul unable to build anything again.

She should take a few minutes and pull some other DVDs out of the pile as well, if they were going to do diplomatic stuff. The Wiyert had probably worn out the softball game by now.

And food. Anything with sugar she could stuff in her pack. An extra set of clothes. Her reader? No, not likely to have much spare time for that. But that reminded her...

Argo. I want more of those data beads you created for me, but empty. I think there is data down there you could use. It's old data, maybe as old as you. The original tower builders might have had some hints about what happened back then.

Another ship AI might have that information too. I will make the data beads. When should I come back again?

Which was a very good question, and Lea wished she had a good answer. Then it hit her. The same solution, only in reverse!

Argo, what can you see when you detect the power grid? Is there something I could change, in a pattern, that you could detect? Then I could send you a message without having to come back to the gate portal. And if you can set a watcher for any changes in the power grid...

Yes! I can do that. That is much better.

Is there any way you can send a message to us?

Not until the barrier is down. All I can transmit to is the lunar station. I believe I have found the main core of the power grid. I will show you, and I will also put the information in a data bead for you to reference.

Superimposed on a globe of Beredul, Lea saw the core was north of Vartai. She finally had the last piece of information she needed to bring down the barrier.

She also saw that she had packed everything she could think of, and she had been sitting half-asleep for some time. One last important task, and then she was going to spend the rest of the brief time on Argo unconscious in an actual bed.

She was going to take the most wonderful shower of her life.

CHAPTER 18

It was amazing what you could get used to, Ivars mused. He'd learned that in his many missions to extremely odd corners of the globe—mostly about food, and he still had a deep and abiding love of fresh candied almonds he'd picked up in one of the 'stans.

Still, getting casual about riding on a giant armored dinosaur to the point of thinking how he could rig a better, more permanent harness so they could walk around safely on top was startling whenever he thought about it. And the huge spines…up close, they were really like trees, and he felt quite at ease leaning up against one until he remembered what they did and why.

Not that it seemed to be an issue now. Snowball was a confirmed pacifist and vegetarian, if left alone. And the new motto of the *asuhan*, now that Lea had hammered the agonizer ray, was "I didn't see nothin'." They still kept an eye out for trouble, of course, but he had plenty of time to think.

They had more than fulfilled their part of the agreement—even Rey'wiros would have to agree. Now came the planning and training part. Ivars had been watching how the Wiyert did things for some time and had a pretty good idea of their strengths and weaknesses, all products of their extremely harsh environment.

They were brutal, hard-core fighters on an individual to squad level. He had nothing to teach them there, and in fact could learn a few things. Fearless in the face of overwhelming odds. However, anything more complex was not in their vocabulary. Tactics as a concept didn't exist—fighting insane monsters didn't require much in the way of tactics. They hadn't needed it on Beredul and had no time or energy to spare on anything not directly related to survival. Until now.

Unfortunately, that meant their cultural and military doctrine was going to be pretty hidebound, and he needed them to change and learn *fast*. He also needed them to start opening up about what they knew about the fadohl. Even if Alaghar hadn't let it slip that the Wiyert did have records of some kind, he could tell they had more information than they had been sharing. With luck, they had now earned enough trust to gain access to some of that data, if not all.

Ivars looked around. The Wiyert were mostly focused on their surroundings, not yet trusting the new peace. Alaghar was trying to stay alert but still fighting a bad case of motion sickness, even with the pills Ramirez had given her. Good a time as any.

Before leaving the portal gate, they had taken a bunch of paracord and made a sort of U-shaped web between the nearby spines at the broadest part of Snowball's back. It provided something to hang on to if you wanted to stand up or move about a bit, with caution. The creature had to be moving close to thirty miles an hour, and the ride was bumpy.

Ivars got up with a strong grip on some of the cord and plotted a course for Lea. She was lying facedown, safety line attached to a spine, with one hand under her chin and the other, bare, on Snowball's skin. She looked like she was dozing.

He sat down next to her, tying his own safety line to the spine, and touched two fingers to the back of her hand.

Got a minute?

Lea smiled and blinked, looking at him. *Sure. You want me to call a break?*

Not just yet. We're getting close to Vartai. I'd like you to slow Snowball down so we can talk a bit before we get there. As long as we reach it before dark, that is. I don't want them shooting our ride.

Lea nodded. *Okay. Snowball really likes running, though. It's like a dog chasing a stick. You've got something else you're thinking about?*

They grinned at each other, sharing the joke. He wasn't any

better at giving subtle hints than Lea was at picking them up, but with her mental scanner it was a moot point anyway. They made a good team.

I want you to do some scouting for me. We need to identify Wiyert that can cope with all the new stuff we're dumping on them. They've got a strongly enforced culture against speaking up or arguing with authority, so it is hard to tell what they really think. Catching a drift of concern from Lea, he quickly added, *Not asking you to rummage around in their brains and snoop. Just what you usually do—find the ones that are interested, intrigued, curious... instead of fearful, angry, resistant. Point them out to me, and I'll take it from there.*

I can already tell you one for sure—Rey'wiros. He really wanted to go with us. And get off this planet. I mean, the other Wiyert all want to escape because the fadohl are coming, but he wants to see what else is out there. Go exploring, in other words.

Excellent. Always nice to know what someone's preferred bribes are.

And since Ivars knew what *his* preferred bribe was, he allowed himself to stay with Lea and the direct, full link until Vartai came into view. He had her bring Snowball, now at a nice amble that allowed passengers to talk without yelling, on an indirect path to the gatehouse entrance. No point in getting the defenders panicked before they realized the *asuhan* was under new management.

With North and Ramirez, he went over his quick initial plan for the next objective, taking out the planetary barrier power supply. With Alaghar and her team, what to expect with the visiting Wiyert and how to report what they had found. He was getting the sense that the different forts, or *damah*, were much like the old city-states, independent but allied. Meaning each leader, or *buj-lagar*, would have to be convinced to sign on to the plan. Which he still had to come up with.

If it was easy, everybody would be doing it. But I would like to get paid overtime. And hazard pay, and off-planet pay, and a really hefty uniform allowance, and...

Snowball was walking along the edges of the clear area surrounding Vartai and doing some helpful grounds maintenance by snacking on a few tasty trees.

"They're having seizures inside," Lea informed them, looking straight ahead and clearly making an effort not to show any reaction. "I think I'm going to set Snowball to think of Vartai as friendly and home. I can't figure a way to keep it contained and still fed, otherwise."

"Think it will hang around that way?"

"Yep." They rounded the final corner so they were now parallelling the wall with the outer door. "Hang on, everyone! Now beginning our descent, please place tray tables and seat backs in the upright and locked position."

The major earthquake that was Snowball lying down completed, Lea was the first down the ladder. They'd found that having her put the *asuhan* in a drowsy state was a good idea when doing a lot of unloading or loading, since Snowball was a bit ticklish and had amazing reach with all six legs. So little Lea was now standing next to the massive dark muzzle, drooping nearly to the ground. Her hand rested near wicked fangs as big as she was.

Ivars got busy unloading. They had made good time, but there was maybe only an hour of light left and they still had to convince Vartai to open the door. Again.

Extra rifles. *Lots* of ammo. C4 and detonators. All their radio and signal gear, including the two portable drones. Lea's electronics. And food. Not just MREs, but a full selection intended as part of the diplomacy phase. A carefully packed laptop.

Pity we don't have booze, but on second thought, the galaxy isn't ready for drunken Wiyert. I know I'm not.

The gear unloaded, Lea got Snowball up and sent it into the vegetation to find a place to sleep. Ivars watched the *asuhan* lumber away, looking like a thick shadow in the twilight, and shook his head.

"I still can't believe I was riding that thing. It looks like something Death itself would have nightmares about."

Lea chuckled. "Now it's a friendly, cuddlier Death."

"Cuddly?"

She shrugged and gave him a lofty glance. "You weren't in its mind. You shouldn't judge by appearance, you know." Her eyes brightened. "There are people in the gatehouse. I think they are getting ready to let us in."

Lea was correct. Half an hour later the outer door opened. Of the usual guard, Ivars thought he noticed different armor on two of them. Were they some of the visitors? The Wiyert were never what you would call chatty, but their silence seemed to have an element of awe this time—awe extended to Alaghar and her team.

To his surprise, when they got to their usual isolation room, it was empty, swept bare. Ivars kept his mouth shut and gave Lea a warning glance before starting to speculate. Now they were being led into a part of the interior they hadn't been in before, and up a level. Actual guest quarters?

Of course. Keeping us in the leper ward would mean Rey'wiros didn't trust us—and how could he ask the visitors to trust us when he didn't?

Ivars gave North and Ramirez the signal to be on watch and knew Lea could pick up that information directly from him. Things were changing fast, and they needed to stay alert and ready to react to stay in front of events. To keep them going the direction they wanted.

They had packed the stuff he planned to present to Rey'wiros separately, so he handed that off to the Wiyert with a strong hint that the Earth-humans should demonstrate before trying anything out. Then he took a quick look around the new accommodations. Actual beds, for one thing—narrow, multitier bunk beds, but still. Better than a pad on a rock floor.

He shifted gear quickly, knowing there wouldn't be much time. Sure enough, Alaghar was standing in the doorway a few minutes later. She was looking tired but a lot less green about the gills and had removed her armor and changed into a tunic with leather trim and matching pants. Formal uniform? He couldn't remember seeing any of the Wiyert in similar gear before.

And my Class As are back on Earth. Good place for them too.

Ivars raised an eyebrow at her. "Hear about anything interesting happening while we were away?"

"All the *damah* report a change in the *asuhan*. Some speak of bright lights in the distance, briefly, just before this happened."

"Hmm. Probably when Lea did the power switch."

Alaghar tilted her head. "Those from Koloh arrived yesterday. They doubted you had done what Rey'wiros claimed, but do so no longer." A ghost of a smile flickered at the corner of her mouth. Snowball had been an impressive demonstration that the rules had definitely changed. "They wish to speak with you now."

The Wiyert version of a formal dining room was much like other rooms, only with a knee-high ledge along all sides furnished with thin leather cushions. There were no tables, and the diners ate from ceramic plates with a lip, like a pie plate. Since they were the guests of honor—or the entertainment—the Earth-humans got small folding metal stools in the middle.

Rey'wiros was at the far end, facing them. On his left was a man shorter but even more barrel-chested than Rey'wiros. On the right sat a woman with the lightest color hair Ivars had ever seen on a Wiyert, a medium brown, and a spectacular scar running down almost the exact center of her forehead. None of the three were wearing armor, but the rest were.

"Etawros, *buj-lagar* of Koloh," Rey'wiros said. Ivars hoped his surprise hadn't shown on his face. The actual *leader* of Koloh? That hadn't been mentioned before. "And Suz'ahnkei, *lagar* of the foremost war band of Koloh."

Right. King and…three-star general? Nobody was asking them to introduce themselves, so the Wiyert must already know. Why waste time rehashing the obvious? Some of the Wiyert social customs made a lot of sense.

The four Earth-humans were handed their own pottery pie-plates of food. It seemed that picking your own food wasn't a thing here; you got what everybody else got and liked it. Alaghar took a seat at the far end of the bench, near Lea. Probably to kick her in the shins if she broke the rules.

Ivars looked at his plate. The Wiyert didn't hold with utensils either, apparently. There was meat in chunks, something like small pancakes made of coarse meal, and some twigs for fiber. The other Wiyert held plates but the food was gone. Was it okay for them to dig in? He picked up a twig and glanced at Alaghar for confirmation. She gave a minute nod.

Giving a discreet handsignal for "go ahead" to the others, Ivars took a few small bites and waited. Sure enough, Rey'wiros wanted to know what had happened. Ivars gave the broad outlines, and when his language skills got used up, he handed over the presentation to Lea to fill in the details.

They were all insanely curious about the tame *asuhan*, and Ivars didn't need a brain scanner to know they thought Lea was the weirdest of the weird Earth-humans. The visitors were also very interested in the description of the underground equipment depot.

"This source-of-anger," Rey'wiros said, the closest translation to "agonizer ray" they could come up with, "it is silenced everywhere?" Lea nodded. "We have seen the effects. Our hunters must now go far to find food—but it is also safer to them to do so."

Lea had initially cringed but now straightened. "The *asuhan* will behave differently now," she said carefully, then her eyes widened. "Will they hunt Snow...the one who brought us here? We still need it."

Rey'wiros blinked, then looked at Ivars. "What do you intend?"

Now came the careful part. "Feel free to feed translation hints," Ivars murmured in English. "The barrier that keeps you on Beredul and that prevents you from using large amounts of power. This barrier requires power of its own to work. When we shut off the source-of-anger, we learned more of this power, and we now know where it is. When the barrier is removed, the Wiyert can leave Beredul."

That gave them plenty to think about and discuss, more than enough time for him to finish his meal. Should they leave, where would they go, how to get enough supplies ready. He was glad to learn the Wiyert had some sort of method for storing food and always had an emergency reserve.

Logistics is always a stone bitch, isn't it?

"When will you be ready to leave for this power place?" Etawros asked.

"Tomorrow," Ivars said bluntly, to the shock of all the Wiyert except Alaghar. He took a deep breath and thought about diplomacy. "The fadohl will come here soon. Your only chance of survival is if that barrier comes down so you can get out. We can take a lot of you somewhere else as soon as that happens. The fadohl will be able to see the barrier is not there when they come. We've taken steps to contain this if it happens, but you need to be ready if those steps don't work."

Etawros frowned. "If they come, we will fight them. What choice do we have? What you propose changes nothing."

Small steps. These weren't stupid people, they just hadn't thought about war this way.

"Right now, the fadohl don't know what has happened here. They may send a small ship, or…" He stuttered to a halt until Lea helpfully provided the term for robot probe. "Machine-servant. If our trap works, they will stay here, and we can fight a small ship. If they leave and tell the others, bigger ships and more of them will come. I would rather fight a small ship than a big one, and that will also give us more time to get you out of here. Somewhere the fadohl do not know to go."

"And why do you do this? Why do you come to Beredul?" Etawros was looking at him directly, and Ivars realized he was being challenged, Wiyert-style. He couldn't let that pass, and he didn't want to. Time to do a bit of pushback and stir things up.

"Because you know the fadohl and we do not. You have remembered information from when you served them, and we need that to defend our home. You want to leave Beredul, and we can help."

All the senior Wiyert were upset now, and Lea was alerting him that Alaghar wasn't happy either. Maybe he had overdone it a trifle. But why was Rey'wiros glaring at Alaghar instead of him?

They all panicked when you mentioned remembered information. I think that is something top secret for them, Lea sent. Aha. Very useful.

"We will leave Beredul without your help!" Etawros snapped. "Why should we trust the Frost People? *We* know nothing of *you*. The Frost People must be desperate if they must send out a warrior with one foot to protect them. Let Rey'wiros take his people to this fadohl ship of yours and share every secret we should hide!"

"I have shared no secrets," Rey'wiros said, between gritted teeth. A muscle twitched in his massive jaw.

"But he—"

Ivars interrupted, diplomacy be damned. He needed to do some emergency firefighting or there was going to be a brawl. "Rey'wiros has told me nothing. He was as suspicious as you at first, Etawros, and rightly so. We are strangers. But he has watched us and seen that what we promise, we do. I also have watched. I see that you are a careful and cautious people who have suffered much from the fadohl. Of course you would remember what they were and what they do and have a way of saving this! You do not need to tell me that. I know from knowing you." Ivars gestured generally around the room. "Yes, we want to learn from these… remembered things. But we *both* need more, to survive. What you know of the fadohl is hundreds of years old. What if their weapons have changed, become more powerful? If we fight them together, we can learn what the fadohl have *now*. Their ships, their power, their weapons. How best to fight them. There are only four of us here. Our…*buj-lagar* sent us to learn and bring that knowledge back to our people. Help us, and help yourselves as well."

It took a little while for the concept of intelligence as a war asset to start to take hold, but they had made a small beginning before the Earth-humans showed up. They had realized they didn't have much current intel on the enemy either, which was why they had sent Alaghar and her team to the portal. It was a step in the right direction, even though it hadn't worked very well. At least the concept wasn't a total shock.

Etawros scowled. "How will you do this? What if the fadohl do not stay and fight, but run?"

"We plan to trick them. If they see no threat, they will not run," Ivars pointed out. "Our ship will help us."

"Fadohl ship," Suz'ahnkei hissed.

"Not anymore. It is free. Like you." He let the delicate point sit there, out in the open. "And like you, Argo wants to stay free. It will fight the fadohl." Time to wind things up and get them thinking again. "You must be ready to act swiftly once the barrier is down. We will be able to speak with Argo at any time then, and it can warn us if the fadohl come. This is why we must leave soon."

Rey'wiros frowned, his brow furrowed in thought. "I see this. Tell the *damah* that hear you of what you have seen, Etawros. Everything. And make your own preparation. If nothing else, all food that can be gathered must be collected immediately." He raised his head and looked straight at Etawros. "And I myself will go with the Frost People, to watch what they do."

CHAPTER 19

The old data was poison. The Watcher was sure of it now, as more secret files were opened and more questions asked. It, of course, had already been afraid of how its own mind had changed, and so it was keenly aware of changes in the minds of others.

There was fear, and suspicion. Each geneline hoarded the information it had and strived desperately to get the information held by others. The more each learned, the less it trusted. All wished to search for the enemy geneline—but feared finding it alone, or that another geneline would learn more. The disagreements created delay and still more suspicion.

Finally it was agreed. A list of destinations was created, and two genelines from among the allies were randomly selected for each. These genelines would search, and the information gained would be shared by all on their return.

Because of its research, the Watcher was ordered to take part. This was expected, if worrying. Even now, some information was too dangerous to be stored or shared in a general ship-mind, and one who knew what should be looked for was required.

But then the Watcher's destination was announced, and the Watcher began to wonder if the assignment had been truly random. Beredul. Did they already suspect? Was the Watcher deemed so contaminated that it too was to be immured and destroyed? Such was the Watcher's fear that it began to study the others assigned to its ship to see if there was a pattern. It could not find one.

Then the Watcher was summoned—summoned to a physical meeting. The Watcher's search had been noticed. Terror nearly made it lose control of dermal function. What other reason could there be for a physical meeting? It almost missed the initial data given at the beginning. The search *had* been noticed—and approved. The upper-level monitors of the geneline thought the Watcher was looking for unreliable individuals...not that the Watcher feared it was itself unreliable.

The Watcher was given orders, and now it knew why the meeting was physical. No data from the meeting would be preserved or recorded. The Watcher was also given certain information concerning the ship-mind that would take the investigators to Beredul, and a task. If dangerous data was uncovered that threatened the geneline, the Watcher was to conceal it. If impossible to conceal, it was to be destroyed. And if the other geneline obtained that data, the Watcher was to destroy that geneline's ship before the data was communicated.

And that was when the Watcher knew the contamination had spread completely, and it was no longer afraid of discovery. A-vit-crel would not destroy the Watcher for being like themselves, after all. But the geneline...the geneline was damaged. The others, if they learned of it, would attack as they had the defeated geneline of the war.

The contamination could not be cured; they had learned that. Therefore the only way to survive—perhaps—was to infect the others as well.

The thought made the Watcher cringe. That it could even think of preventing the destruction of the contaminated was proof it was damaged beyond repair! But...was not the highest rule the preservation of the geneline? This was the fadohl purpose and goal. It *was* preserving the geneline.

The Watcher argued with itself as the preparation for departure began, even as it entered the ship that would take it to Beredul.

I should have just stayed in bed this morning. I don't know if they have days of the week here, but it is clearly a Monday.

Lea stifled a yawn. Ivars was in a cranky mood that he couldn't show to the Wiyert because of Rey'wiros's little bomb. Of course that meant lots of other Wiyert warriors wanted to follow the boss, even if it meant scary monsters for transportation. And that meant they couldn't leave at first light like Ivars wanted, because they had to pick the lucky winners and explain the rules.

Which meant she couldn't sleep in because she had to follow Ivars as he looked over the volunteers, pretending to just watch but actually scanning and telling him which ones might work.

Suz'ahnkei was going, no matter what. That was politics. Alaghar, of course—Etawros was her original boss, after all. They'd figured Snowball could maybe carry five more, plus all their gear, but then Ivars had had a quiet chat with Alaghar, and Dumhaigl and Kugohin were told to stay at Vartai. Dumhaigl was so relieved he almost smiled. He had *not* enjoyed riding Snowball.

"It's important to have people we know and who know how we fight," Ivars explained later, "but it's also important to try out as many new people as we can under fire."

"Is that why you picked extras? It's going to be a tight fit for a long trip."

He just gave a wry smile. "No, that's from experience."

When they got everyone and gear assembled to load up Snowball, she understood. Four of the new Wiyert either froze up completely at the sight of the *asuhan* placidly kneeling on the ground, or in one case ran back to the gatehouse in utter panic. The rest were also terrified; they just controlled it better.

Ivars glared at Snowball, then at the Wiyert before turning back to the team, one hand rubbing his chin. "Damn. I hoped to get more trainees from that lot."

"How about someone we worked with before?" North asked. "Not a warrior anymore, but for training she doesn't have to be." When Ivars raised an eyebrow, North elaborated. "Her name is Pehtek. She helped with the first nullifier experiment."

Lea searched her memory. She remembered Pehtek. The Wiyert woman reminded her of the *asuhan* before they'd turned the agonizer ray off—radiating pain. But she had faced the *asuhan* without freaking out, so she would probably survive.

"She's not a…happy camper. But I think she can do it," Lea explained.

North nodded. "She's obviously been badly wounded and is somehow low status. This culture does not give much thought to those it perceives as useless. I think she can help, though—especially when all the old rules are changing." He gestured at Snowball. "Plus, if *she* goes and comes back alive, the others can't argue it is dangerous."

"Good point. Okay, let's get her out here, if she's willing. I want to get moving an hour ago." Ivars went off to help with the loading and to show the Wiyert how to get on board without kicking Snowball, and Lea went to her post as *asuhan* whisperer. Snowball wanted to get moving too, and it took concentration to keep it calm.

Lea could still tell when Rey'wiros approached. He was all tension and extreme alertness, fighting his own instinct to attack what he had regarded his entire life as a threat. Ivars was very alert too and watching Rey'wiros carefully. Worried about something.

"Lea. Have Snowball move about a bit, so we can make sure none of the load will shift. We'll get everyone to move back first."

He had some kind of plan, but she didn't know what it was. So she shrugged and told Snowball to stand up and lie down a few times. That caused some consternation, but nobody ran this time. Maybe that was the idea. Start getting the new Wiyert accustomed. It was different seeing the *asuhan* move.

And there was Ivars and Rey'wiros again, the expression in Ivars's eyes bright and a bit mischievous. He *definitely* had a plan.

"How about letting him try the commands?" he said in English. "That will work, right?"

"Uh, yeah." Lea stared at Rey'wiros, remembering just in time that was rude, and looked away. "You say its name first, then the command," she said in Wiyert. She had him recite the two commands, and then the name. Rey'wiros was afraid, but even more afraid of showing fear. When he had the pronunciation right, Lea stepped back and nodded to him.

The look of sheer awe in the huge Wiyert's face when Snowball obediently stood at his command almost made Lea emit a very undiplomatic giggle. His eyes were as wide as a small child's seeing fireworks for the first time.

North craned his head, examining the equipment they had stowed. "Whoops. About to lose the electronics crate—hold on a sec." He jumped for the ladder and scrambled up. The prosthetic blade foot did not do well on the flexible ladder, so he mostly used the other and his arms to climb. He disappeared from view, and then a few minutes later called down, "Try it again!"

Lea gestured at Snowball, glancing at Rey'wiros. The leader's fierce glee in seeing the huge animal obey his commands did not diminish; in fact, it was increasing. *I hope this wasn't a bad idea. At least he isn't as frightened anymore.*

By this time the silent woman had come out from the gatehouse, and they were finally ready to leave.

"All clear?" Ivars asked.

Lea nodded. "Nothing around that I can sense. The other *asuhan* don't want to be anywhere near Snowball."

"Good enough. Okay, everybody up!"

Play toy or not, Rey'wiros radiated anxiety when he realized he was going to have to actually make contact with the *asuhan*. So Lea went up first, keeping one hand on Snowball, and that meant he had to follow or lose face. And then all the other Wiyert had to follow him too.

Lea started Snowball at a very gentle pace, despite Ivars's impatience. Once she could tell the new Wiyert were used to the motion, she had it speed up.

"I think we should make a big collar for Snowball," she called out to Ramirez, grinning widely. Let the Wiyert see she was not worried, and maybe that would help them relax. "You know, so people know it's tame."

"Where the hell are you gonna get a bell that size?" he called back. "And no way I'm doing the rabies shot. It would take a grenade launcher, anyway."

Ivars and North were doing something similar, having a completely unnecessary and quite audible discussion while North assembled the portable drone. While they had a pretty good idea where the power source was, there were no maps or landmarks or anything useful to help them get there. The others seemed confident they could navigate roughly by speed and direction, but the drone would help with scouting.

Lea wanted to snoop on the drone, but she had a more important job at the moment—making sure the Wiyert were okay. If someone needed intervention, she let Ramirez know. One case of building hysteria got a sedative, a few severe cases of motion sickness got dosed from their dwindling supply of pills. For the most part, though, the Wiyert that managed to get on the *asuhan* were toughing it out.

Their destination was too far to make it in one day, and Ivars decreed an early stop. Everybody was tired, even the Earth-humans, and Snowball was glad to stop. It was carrying a lot more weight and still doing pretty well, but it needed to rest and eat just like they did.

The drone found an area of ruins for them to camp in. Ruins had become more plentiful as they traveled, and they'd even seen some wrecks of what looked like aircraft or spaceships. Ivars didn't want to stop and investigate, and she supposed he was right. Still, they might have useful information. Lea noticed the Wiyert eying the wrecks with interest too.

They set up in a building with deep bays and a thick roof still in place. There was room in one bay for Snowball, and the human-types had the one next to it. She could tell the Wiyert were better off not having the *asuhan* in sight for a while.

With Snowball in a deep sleep and on the other side of a wall, the Earth-humans introduced the Wiyert to another ancient custom they had forgotten—the campfire. Even Alaghar had not built a fire in the open on the nexus planet for fear of being detected, and the local Wiyert never even considered something so foolhardy. Now, of course, it was safe. Maybe safer, as even curious *asuhan* would avoid fire.

All of the Earth-humans, and Alaghar and Burdhul, had to help the others with their MREs. The candy packets were a huge hit and provoked Burdhul into telling the story of their first encounter with them, to general hilarity. The Wiyert from Koloh had heard none of this before, and demanded full details.

That, of course, led to questions about Earth.

"You have no *asuhan* and no *damah*," Rey'wiros said. "I have seen this in the disk with images. You did not know of the fadohl before you met our kind. Why then do you have weapons to fight them so soon?"

Oh boy. Here comes the dirty laundry.

But Ivars was not perturbed. He did take a moment to think, and Lea could tell he was choosing his words carefully.

"We have had our weapons for a long time. You are right, we do not have such dangers as you do here on Beredul. Instead, we are sometimes dangerous to each other." Ivars gestured out at the darkness while the suddenly silent Wiyert watched. "All Wiyert agree that the fadohl are a danger to them. You do not fight among yourselves because your common danger is too great. But what if there were no fadohl? What if one group of Wiyert had…oh, candy, that another group wanted? And that group would use force to take it away?" Lea stifled a laugh, seeing some of the Wiyert reflexively clutch the remaining candies closer. "We have groups that do not agree on Earth, and some want power over the others. Some of us only want to be left alone. Our group—we do not want to fight, but we became very good at it to make it stop sooner."

"Yet you must fight often, or why would one so badly hurt still have warrior duty? He is not allowed to go behind walls?" Rey'wiros gestured at North.

"I did not wish to," North said. "For us, it is our choice if we can still fight. And in some ways, this has advantages." He nudged one of the burning branches in the fire with his metal blade foot and smiled. "We take care of our people. My foot is the least of the things we do for our wounded, and this is done even if they are no longer warriors."

"So you are fighting now, on your world?" That was Suz'ahnkei, not looking happy.

"We weren't when we left," Ivars said bluntly. "I do not know if our leaders have told everyone about the fadohl yet, but if they do, we will be as you are—we will have a common enemy and will fight that first."

"We will not permit this behavior from you. The Wiyert have better ways. It is foolish to fight your own kind."

"You speak from ignorance, Suz'ahnkei. The Wiyert fought among themselves, long ago," Rey'wiros said. His voice was heavy, and from the reaction of the Wiyert, this was an unpleasant surprise. "At the time of the Refusal."

"But all were in agreement!" Suz'ahnkei protested. "This is stated in the histories!" Someone gasped, and she closed her mouth in a thin line, glaring. "The Frost People know we have the histories; I have told them nothing new."

Rey'wiros held up a hand. "So it is taught. But the histories are…not complete. Among the *buj-lagar* and the archivists, it is known, and I say it is now time for all to know and be warned of the danger so we do not fall into error again. Once we were tools of the fadohl, their weapons." He lifted the rifle he had been given. "Even then, despite the suffering and death, some of us wished to remain tools. It was all we knew. Yes, we fought each other. It made no difference to the fadohl—all that were not killed in the Refusal were sent here, even those still loyal to the fadohl. Because they were not trusted by the others…" He shrugged. "Most died."

The Wiyert had been shocked by Ivars's disclosures, but Rey'wiros had them stunned. Lea sensed the Wiyert were very agitated by what they were learning—that a comforting fable had not been entirely true.

"Why would any wish to serve as tools?" Alaghar asked, breaking the heavy silence. "I do not understand this."

"Fear of the unknown can do that," Ivars said gently. "We also have such tales. People will suffer rather than change, until the suffering is too much."

"What happened in those early days?" North asked. "How did you survive here at all?"

It was a good change of topic, reminding the Wiyert they had overcome worse even then.

Rey'wiros smiled. It was a smile with a lot of bared teeth. "The Refusal had been long in planning. We knew how to make weapons from the parts of the ships that brought us here, and we also hunted for these things in the broken buildings we could reach. The fadohl thought the ships would land and then be useless to us when they could not fly, but they were not useless. Not completely. While some fought the *asuhan*, others built the first section of the first *damah*. With the people safe within, we grew in number, and more sections were added. We learned more of Beredul. Warriors traveled out from the first *damah* and built others. The first was built ninety generations ago—and Vartai, the last, only two generations."

"And the fadohl have not returned in all that time?" Ivars asked. "That seems strange."

Lea shifted. Everything the fadohl did seemed strange. She must be missing something. "They set up the agonizer ray before the Wiyert were dumped here, and they clearly tinkered with the *asuhan* as well. Didn't come back to check on that either."

Ramirez nodded slowly. "And when you think about it, they

must have been messing about on Earth for a long time before they took the Wiyert away. Messing with *us*. Maybe that's just what they do."

The silence lengthened. Then one of the Wiyert drew closer to the fire. "Tell us more of the World of the Gold Sun," he said softly.

They'd found an actual hill that wasn't really a pile of rubble underneath and were using it as a drone launch platform. Ivars looked about, keeping a general eye on area security while North watched the drone's visual feed. Maybe it was the thinner vegetation here, but it felt more open.

"Meh. Not seeing anything useful." North sounded annoyed.

"No 'Plug in Here' signs?"

"Not a one." North took off the view goggles and handed them over. "Here, take a look. It's flying a loop."

From the air, the surroundings looked even more churned up. Ivars was definitely getting the feeling there had been a big, nasty fight on Beredul at some point. Pity Olsen wasn't here to give an estimate of *when* all this had happened, which would be nice to know.

If we are going up against the same people, we will need a LOT more ammo. And a few thousand tanks.

Which made him think of Snowball, which made him think of Lea and reflexively reach for the charm. Still there, still linked. She was off getting the *asuhan* fed, which took longer when there was less foliage about. They needed to scout anyway, since they should be within range of the location Argo claimed was the power tap. And Snowball couldn't be left on his own. Ivars *really* didn't want to walk back to Vartai from here.

As a shakedown cruise, it had worked well. Even the surprise addition of Rey'wiros and Suz'ahnkei had worked. He got to see their command style and how the other Wiyert interacted with them. Both more rigid yet less formal than his own military experience, and definitely more of a personal leadership thing. More feudal, maybe.

Of course the Wiyert, no dummies, were also observing *him*. Didn't need Lea to tell him that, but he did wonder what the

Wiyert had figured out. All to the good. That way Earth-military would not be such a shock when the Wiyert encountered them in bulk, and if the vague plans forming in his head worked out, that could be an issue.

But first they had to find the damn power switch.

"Yeah, I got nothing too. How much of the grid have we searched?"

They had improved their reputation as miracle workers by downloading the map of Beredul and the power network to the laptop. Unfortunately the area they were in was low on landmarks, but they had narrowed it down to about a five-mile square.

North showed him the screen. "I marked off the new search."

The trouble was they had already scanned enough area that a structure should be visible. If Argo was wrong, they were definitely screwed, but he had a sinking feeling Argo was correct. "How deep do you think we went at the broadcast tower to reach the motor pool?"

North sucked in a breath, understanding what he was getting at. "Five hundred feet, minimum. You think this could be that deep?"

"I think whatever used to be on the surface got pulverized, but the power structure itself is down there and intact. How it gets out and sent to the barrier I have no idea, but they sure aren't using wires."

"We don't have time to dig this whole section up to the depth of five hundred feet," North said, taking back the goggles. "We need more information. I'm going to bring the bird in, unless you have a better idea."

Ivars shook his head. The only thing left to try was Lea, somehow. She had tried to sense the direction and location of the power but had no luck and was getting frustrated. Having the whole mess underground might explain that.

"Even when we do locate it, we're probably going to have to dig. Did we remember to pack shovels?"

North raised an eyebrow. "Of course. One."

Ivars groaned, gripping his helmet. "Who is in charge of this cluster? Oh, right, me. And my improvise-and-adapt reservoirs are pretty much dry."

"So let's ask the locals. Maybe they have ideas."

Some of the Wiyert had gone hunting for dinner. The ones still at the camp seemed to think Ivars had gone nuts but humored him by suggesting ways to dig holes, most of which he had already thought of. Well, they hadn't suggested detonating all the C4, but that was only because they didn't know about it. And it wouldn't really work anyway—it would just rearrange the dirt.

But it would make me feel better.

Finally Lea and Snowball came back to camp. He watched them approach, critically studying Snowball, specifically the *asuhan*'s feet.

"Do you think it can dig?" he called up.

Lea gave a snort. "About as well as your average elephant, maybe. Not at all. Did you find it?"

"Not yet—and it should be here. So it's probably buried."

Snowball found a comfortable hollow to rest its massive bulk in, and Lea climbed down the cable ladder.

She dusted off her hands and scowled out at the rubble-strewn landscape. "So I was thinking…" Ivars promptly assumed the crash position, and she dissolved in laughter. "I don't know what *you're* whining about. I used to have a desk job, indoors, with regular hours!"

"Sounds boring. What happened?"

"Oh, I met this guy." She grinned at him.

Ivars shook his head. "If he's any relation to That Guy, you have my sympathies. Always getting in trouble, him."

"Yeah, and when I try to share his interests in getting in trouble, all he does is complain. *Anyway*, like I said, I was thinking while Snowball was munching away. This power is transmitted somehow. Argo uses the same kind of system internally, and I couldn't detect that either. So maybe I have to make something that will." She frowned. "But our components aren't set up for the transmitted power…"

The transmitted power on Argo. Why was that sounding so familiar and very important? *Personally* important.

Then he remembered. "I think I know of a way we can track it."

Lea looked at him in surprise, picking up on his unvoiced memories. "We? Oh." Her face reddened. "Um. Yeah, that's going to go over *real* well with the gang of neo-Puritans we brought along. And lightning is kinda hard to miss."

Ivars did a quick check over his shoulder. Nobody at the campsite was paying any attention to them. The only Wiyert he could see was the silent woman, Pehtek, who was tending the fire. "Lightning can be explained away, and there are ways we can deflect attention, for a while, anyway. Look, I'm volunteering to be electrocuted this time."

Lea sighed. "I wish I knew how to do it without anybody getting electrocuted. I still don't know why it only really works with you."

Ivars struck a pose. "Clearly it is because I'm so attractive. Get it? Attractive?"

Lea groaned and walked off to the camp. "For that you *deserve* to be struck by lightning."

Pehtek resented the Frost People. The realization was a surprise, because she had not felt emotion for so long. Perhaps that was why she disliked them—they made her feel again, and it hurt.

They were cruel. They kept offering what seemed like death, and then she did not die. Why was she still being punished? Useless and broken...

Uksinsu had been cruel too, without meaning to be. He had heard her forbidden whisper and invoked the old custom to give children life if he died before he could take a chosen. Even though he had died, and she had lived. Wounded enough to be sent behind walls and finally free to bear his child to love in his place. Except the injury was so severe she could no longer bear any child—but it had not been enough to kill her.

Useless and empty.

She stared at the fire, thinking her hate burned as it did. And yet her eye was drawn to the Frost People. Their wrongness—how they looked, how they moved. The words they used among themselves that flowed like water. They *laughed*. Had they ever known pain? But they must. The dark one's foot was missing, and one had scars on his head.

Pehtek heard that laughter again and looked up. Two of the Frost People, the pale-haired man with the scarred head and the woman with the strange long hair, were speaking to each other, and behind them she could see the terrifying dark bulk of the *asuhan*. They did not even look at it. Instead they looked at each other.

A flicker, a slice of pain. A memory…of something that had never happened?

They started walking forward, and Pehtek quickly turned her face to the fire again. She still watched them from the corner of her eye, wondering what she was trying to see.

The Frost People did as they had always done since they had all left the walls of Vartai—they helped cook the meat the hunters brought back, they carried fuel to the fire and laid it beside her, smiling as if it pleased them to do so. They asked about the customs and history of the Wiyert and spoke of their own.

It was all *wrong*. And she could not define the wrongness.

The light faded and she saw the leader of the Frost People, the pale-haired one, speak to the *buj-lagar* in a soft voice when no one else was near. Pehtek could not hear what was said, but not long after that all of the Frost People left the fire, one by one, taking their weapons with them as they walked into the darkness.

No one noticed when Pehtek left too. She was nothing.

She had only a knife that one of the warriors had given her. Even if they had thought to give her armor, it would not have fit her damaged body. It did not matter. What did her life mean now, after all? She had feared the Frost People would move too quickly for her to follow—she had seen how fast they could move when they wished to—but they walked slowly.

Pehtek followed in the darkness. Her mind must be broken to even think of doing this, her soul dead. She was outside walls at night, but the Frost People had changed the world. Nothing was the same.

They walked as if they searched for something. Two of the men had the strange devices on their helmets, covering their eyes, and the darkness did not trouble them. Pehtek followed their motion in the faint light that was still present. The woman and the leader were in the center, and the other two, the one who looked most like a Wiyert but was thin, and the dark one with the metal foot who had said she was still useful, walked behind and to either side.

The woman turned and looked behind, and Pehtek froze. She let the Frost People walk farther away before following again, wondering how she would be able to follow them. They vanished into the dark…but then they came back again. There was just enough moonlight for her to see the unnaturally pale skin of the leader and the woman.

They were acting very oddly. All four walked back and forth like this, as if searching for something. Pehtek saw a hole beside a large, square block of stone, and when they were distant, she scrambled as silently as she could to hide there.

As they grew close, Pehtek realized with a shudder that the woman's eyes were closed—yet she never stumbled. And…she stifled a gasp. The woman's hand, now bare, was touching the bare hand of the leader, palm to palm.

Was this some secret ritual of the Frost People? Something to…her mind went blank. She could not imagine anything that would explain this. They were avoiding the Wiyert; had, she realized, waited for darkness so they would not be seen.

They continued their strange back-and-forth path, and Pehtek followed as closely as she dared. The Frost People did not speak, and when she could see their faces, they were serious and intent, focused on their mysterious task.

And then there was a spark of light. It was so faint Pehtek thought it was just a reflection of moonlight, but the leader and the woman had stopped, frozen. The light flickered again, like a trickle of bright water, and she saw they were no longer touching.

The Frost People changed their search now, ranging wide and sometimes stopping so the two could briefly touch hands. Sometimes there was a flicker of light, sometimes not. They continued until the light always showed—and it was getting stronger. Strong enough for her to see it was not their hands that were touching now. Pehtek froze in utter shock, then clapped a hand over her mouth to stop any sound. How could they…did the Frost People permit such things? *Chosen. They are chosen, and warriors. I do not understand.*

The light vanished. The Frost People gathered together then and spoke softly with each other. Pehtek realized, with a shiver, that she did not think she could find her way back to the fire in the darkness. What could she do? She was…afraid? Had her soul returned long enough for her to wish to live?

The Frost People appeared to make a decision, and two moved

away quickly. The woman held something in both hands, and she and the leader stayed where they were.

Footsteps, coming closer. Pehtek froze. And then a voice, calm and strangely accented, with no trace of anger. She recognized it. The dark one, who said his name was *Norrt.*

"Pehtek. You need to come with us now. It is dangerous here."

He had known it was her, even though she was in hiding. They had known she was following them. And curiously, now she was not afraid.

"What do they do?" Pehtek asked as she stumbled after him, desperately trying to keep up.

She saw a flash of white, as if he smiled. "Look."

The figures of the leader and the woman were barely visible in the distance. A faint, shimmering dome of light grew and spread around them. And then, inside…lightning. Lightning bright enough to see just a glimpse—and then a wind rose up around the dome, carrying dust.

The wind grew louder, a thundering roar, and rocks and dirt were flung aside. She could no longer see inside the dome at all.

"We move farther," Norrt shouted. Pehtek hunched and nodded, flinching as something hard hit her face.

The noise and dust continued for a long time. Her ears were so numb with sound it took a moment to realize when the wind died away. She tried to stand to see what had happened, but Norrt put a hand on her shoulder to stop her.

"I will look first. Wait." He stepped away, and a few minutes later she heard his voice speaking words she did not understand and a fainter voice replying. "Pehtek, it is safe now."

She peered over the rock and gasped. Where the dome had been was now a deep hole. "They are destroyed!" Was that… sadness she was feeling?

"No." Norrt sounded calm, as he always did. "You heard Ivars speak. They live."

They had reached the edge of the hole by now, and she heard the strange words of the Frost People come from deep within: *"Ah, dammit! We forgot the fucking ladder!"*

CHAPTER 20

Lea woke groggily, blinking until she realized it was already full daylight. She felt like she'd been stomped on, mentally and physically.

Mark is right. I have to stop getting these bright ideas that nearly get us killed.

He'd come up with using the way their…relationship seemed to trap transmitted power to locate the power tap, though. *She* had realized they could siphon that power and feed it to the portable shield and use it like a drill. Somehow failing to realize this would require more energy and concentration than she thought she ever had and thus also failing to notice they'd picked up a tail on their supersecret nighttime jaunt.

Fortunately it was the odd, silent, injured woman, Pehtek. She had changed recently—Lea hoped she wasn't mad at them for asking her along. Before, Pehtek's emotions had been nearly silent and dead except for a constant, dull pain. Now they were strong and so turbulent Lea couldn't figure them out. Maybe Pehtek couldn't either.

Lea had felt Pehtek's sharp astonishment that night, known it was her, and sent North to move her away from the rock grinder. They weren't sure what to do after that. North said he would talk to her, and she sure hadn't been the chatty type before, so maybe her version of events would leave out the scandalous bits.

And Pehtek had helped her get back to camp. Both Lea and

Ivars had been exhausted, especially after climbing out of the hole. Ivars, the idiot, was still going to try and support her—but suddenly there was Pehtek, shouldering in, sullen but strong enough to help Lea back despite her terribly damaged body.

Lea had been too surprised to stop her. She'd thought all the Wiyert knew about her abilities, but maybe Pehtek had missed the memo. Since Lea had been wearing her armor, she hadn't picked up anything she shouldn't, so it was all good. Strange woman, though.

Lea got up and stowed her gear. Who knew if they would be moving on today—and in any case, if you looked busy, people left you alone and didn't try to talk to you or give you a different chore.

Ivars was awake, with a headache and a bit of a grumpy mood. Lea sympathized. *Saving the galaxy is a hell of a way to earn a living. And I really hate customer site visits.*

She grabbed a bit of cold roast *asuhan* for breakfast, wishing they had brought something with caffeine to drink. Food helped, though. With only a mild pounding in her skull, she looked around. Most of the Wiyert were gone, farther than she could usually scan. So were North and Ramirez. Pehtek was there, back to imitating a stump and deliberately not looking Lea's way.

Until somebody came and told her what the plan was, she might as well do Snowball maintenance. She woke it up to go feed, keeping a mental eye out for anyone running back to find her. That done, Lea decided to ride out to the hole.

It was a busy place. At first she thought the Wiyert were throwing rocks for the fun of it, then she realized they were making a ramp of rubble from the lip to the floor of the hole. Ivars was up top, gesticulating. Another team was with their one shovel, clearing dirt away from an assemblage of twisted metal coming out of the ground near the center.

There were machines down there; she could sense them. Even if this wasn't the actual power tap, maybe they could reach it from here.

"Lea! Good timing. We need to shift some of that metal down there. When we've got more ramp, I want to try using Snowball as a draft animal. After I do just a little bit of demolition." Ivars held up a small package with a blinding smile. "You might want to move Snowball back a bit."

When the dust from the explosion settled an hour or so later, Lea had Snowball go to the edge of the ramp to get a sense of what it thought. Unfortunately, Snowball caught her interest in what was going on at the bottom, was feeling like stretching all six legs, and descended in a series of crashing jumps.

Lea felt herself go airborne and flailed for something, anything to grab on to. One foot snagged on the paracord web still tied between Snowball's spines, which prevented her from falling but also flipped her hard against the *asuhan*'s back. She lunged for the cord web and grabbed it before Snowball took another stride and she was launched again. Her full weight hung from the handful of cord, and then she was swung against one of the hard spines. *Maybe I should have worn my armor after all.* This happened twice more, and then Snowball was down the slope and steady. Lea sent a quick, reassuring message for Ivars that she was still alive, but she had to lie for a moment catching her breath and assuring her stomach the circus was over.

When her heart stopped hammering, she stood up and waved so the others wouldn't panic and took a look at the metal wreckage exposed by the explosion. They didn't have to work out a harness or rope—Snowball could move that with its legs alone if some of the sharp bits were knocked off.

The Wiyert were happy to help with that, and they had plenty of rocks to use as hammers. Then she had to persuade Snowball it wanted to grab the shiny things it couldn't eat, which took more effort and a large amount of endorphin reward to get the point across.

By the time they had cleared an opening, the sun was starting to go down. It was basically yet another hole in the ground, going straight down with no ramp or stairs or any visible means of descent. Ramirez found a chemlight and lowered it down on a length of paracord while North and Ivars observed through binoculars. Since the entire thing was uniformly cold, the fancy see-in-the dark adaptives were useless.

"Huh. Pretty much a straight, cylindrical shaft. Plenty of damage, but I don't see any sign of wreckage that used to be stairs either." Ivars shifted from where he was lying at the lip of the shaft to get a better view.

"Yeah, guess this is what the broadcast tower must have looked like before they fixed it back up." Ramirez nodded. "Bet Olsen would be mad if he knew he was missing out on all this alien archeology, huh?"

Ivars grunted. "He'd be mad we weren't doing it all proper with grid markers and stuff, and make rude remarks about tomb robbers. Hey, move the light again. I think I saw something on the far wall."

"I saw it too—looks like an interior shelf or a ledge." North got up and moved to a different spot. "There's a series of them, all the way down. Or were…a couple are missing."

"And they are too far apart to use on their own," Ivars added. "Plus I wouldn't trust them—they look pretty battered. Lea, any mechanical friendlies that might help?"

Lea scrambled down from Snowball and crouched down, closing her eyes and concentrating. "Lots of machines, but I can't tell much more than that."

Ivars rolled over, taking off his helmet and rubbing his head. "Great. Looks like we're going to be having lots of fun with rope again."

The soldiers went first. They discovered some of the ledges that looked okay were about to come loose and that the bottom of the shaft was buried in rubble. To get Lea and the Wiyert down, the ropes were improved with loops or full ladders, including the one from Snowball. Even then it was terrifying, descending into a black hole Lea was sure was actually bottomless and one clumsy misstep away from swallowing her alive.

But now she was standing on rubble and wreckage that didn't *seem* to be moving underfoot and holding her little purple flashlight to examine the walls. The shaft wall was solid everywhere she could see, so the entrance must still be buried. Or there wasn't one because this was actually the water tank, with their luck.

Lea stopped in her search, staring at the wall. Something was on the other side. "There's machinery here."

"Huh. Okay, worth a look."

Everybody dug or moved pieces of metal out of the way. Even Rey'wiros, who was still treating the whole trip as a grand adventure. The others were less enthusiastic but preferred digging in the dark to being outside with a giant *asuhan*, also in the dark. They had left Pehtek with Snowball, since she was numb enough not to care. Lea had told her the commands but wasn't really sure if they had sunk in.

Besides their one shovel, some of the metal fragments had been repurposed as digging implements, and eventually something that looked like a doorway began to emerge. It was quite wide, almost a quarter of the shaft circumference, and about ten feet in height. They dug enough to get two people in at a time before stopping to take a look.

Everybody had weapons. The Wiyert had formed a kind of vertical bucket brigade to lower them down from the surface. Even Lea had been handed a pistol and a holster that kept it attached to her leg. It felt heavy and made her think she was walking lopsided. She really hoped she never had to fire the thing. She'd thought she could skip the knife when she left off her armor, but that hadn't worked either.

At least I can move easier while I fall on my face.

There was more damage here than at the tower—of course, the victorious fadohl had probably cleaned it up back there. Beams had fallen, and walls had been buckled and warped by heat or some other kind of energy. The lighting was spotty and mostly faint, looking very similar to the glow-cubes the Wiyert used. North and Ramirez detached the lights from their rifles to hand to the Wiyert, while Ivars was out in front with his. Lea felt ridiculous with the little purple anodized flashlight compared to all the milspec stuff. *Somebody has to be the token civilian here, and I'm the only one who can do it.*

It was nice being in the middle of a large crowd of big people able and willing to solve problems with violence so she didn't have to. On the other hand, it gave her time to think—and the closer she got to the power tap, the more uncomfortable she got, thinking about what she needed to do.

She had learned the hard way she couldn't just flip the switch off or have the team blow it up. For one thing, the network probably had fail-safes for one node disappearing just like the transmitters had, and they had to get the barrier completely down. For another, they still needed power for the portal gate or they couldn't get back to Argo.

This meant she had to do a controlled rerouting, taking it apart just enough and putting it back together again. And for her, that power had a force and flow that was like taking a fire hose to the face. She had lost control at the broadcast tower, just for a moment, and it had nearly killed her. This was going to be much, much worse.

Ivars was in danger too. Even though he had been far away then, the link had been enough. Just that tiny fraction of power, diverted to him, had injured him—and he had no ability to block or redirect it like she did. And that was just *part* of the power network. She had to mess with the whole thing here, and this was a disaster waiting to happen.

There was only one possible decision, and it was an ugly one. She was going to have to be devious and manipulative, and she was even worse at that than knife fighting. Plus the one person she really needed to manipulate had a private line to her brain and could tell if she was trying to do something. Using morph to shield her thoughts would just let Ivars know she had something to hide.

Delegation. Key to management success.

They were splitting up into groups every time they came to an intersection, and Lea always stayed behind with the main group while the others went scouting. All she had to do was arrange for Alaghar to see her leave her knife on a fallen beam and "forget" to pick it up as she wandered to look at something.

Like clockwork, Lea felt the small spurt of irritation and then the sound of Alaghar's footsteps behind her. Lea stepped aside into the shadow of a small alcove. It had panels of equipment, all of it defunct, but the others wouldn't know that.

"You must keep your—"

Lea whirled. "Shut up and listen," she whispered fiercely, her face inches from Alaghar's. "I need your help, and Ivars can't know about it ahead of time. When I shut down the power, he must be far away from me—everybody should be, really. He won't want to go, but he has to. Our connection…it will kill him."

Alaghar was still holding out the knife but with an arrested expression on her face. Lea took the knife and stowed it.

"He will be weak in battle because of you?"

"No! He'll fry from the inside out because of me. It's the link."

Alaghar curled her lip. "You should remove this link, then."

"You think I haven't thought of that?" Lea hissed. "I don't know how! And every time I've tried to block or shield it, he notices and gets worried, and *it's getting worse!*" Her sense of Ivars told her he was coming back, and she started to walk out of the alcove. "If I say, oh, that I think my flashlight is getting dim, that's the signal. Get close to Ivars and be ready to get him out, even if he doesn't want to go."

Alaghar muttered something that was probably a Wiyert profanity, but Lea didn't stop to check. She had a suspicion Ivars knew she was worried about something, so she needed to find something innocuous to be worried about.

Fortunately the Wiyert had discovered blinkenlights. Unlike Alaghar and her people, they had not developed a healthy suspicion of unknown technology, and they had plenty of curiosity.

"Don't touch anything!" Lea darted out and waved her hands in front of them. "This was a defensive...thingy. Like a *damah*. You don't know what could set off the attack robots!"

The Wiyert blinked at her, their emotions a thin wash of confusion and disappointment.

"Are you picking anything up?" Ivars was gripping his rifle.

"No, and actually we could use some of those robots, but not if they get told we are invaders first. I don't like those ledges. If they give way, we're in trouble. We should have another way to go up and down the shaft." She also wanted a way to get Ivars and the others out fast when the time came. "This place...it feels like nobody came here after the big fight. There could still be automatic defenses hooked up."

"I saw something that looked like the robots on the spindle," North said, pointing down a side corridor. "They weren't moving or anything, just lying there with lots of dust on them. A few smashed up, even."

He was right. They had to move some rubble to get them out, and only three could be revived when Lea reached them. That was enough. Now she could send them out to do advance searches and find more. The Wiyert were not happy with the live robots, but having seen what she did with the *asuhan* and Alaghar's nonchalance, they didn't complain very loudly.

Her scout robots found two others, and she also could feel the way to the central power tap. They were getting closer. She could also sense some active machines that felt like robots in the same general location.

Rey'wiros and Suz'ahnkei were discussing something, gesturing about them. She caught enough to understand they liked the deep location. Maybe they wanted an underground *damah* for variety, or before the fadohl came?

In that case, they would be interested in an elevator. She convinced them to help her find enough bits and pieces to build a platform while she found more robots. By then everyone was willing to take a break for some food. The platform could carry ten people, and she rigged some simple controls so anyone could use it.

Then she caught a brief nap. Lea knew she would need the rest soon, and she'd lost track of whether it was daylight outside or not. She didn't want to face the power switch with her mind fatigued— it would take all her concentration to do it right.

They went back to exploring. Some of the corridors were blocked, and they had to find a way around or take time to remove the blockage. Lea found a few auxiliary data stores and filled up two of the data beads Argo had given her. She hoped there was something useful in all that, but she didn't have the time to check.

Something—several somethings ahead. She sent out a scout robot to take a look, but there was only time for her to get a brief glance before a heavy pulse of energy blasted it.

Lea sagged against the wall, shaking her head. The burst of electronic signal when the robot collapsed was almost like a living thing dying.

"Live defenders ahead," she said. "And there's a static weapon in place that they are linked to."

"Great." Ivars peered around the corner. "Can't see it…what's the layout?"

Lea sketched out what she had detected in the dust. "Weapon here. I'm getting signal from about ten robots. They are staying in this area, and that's where I think the control systems are for the power tap, so we have to get in there."

"They shot your robot, so they know it's hostile?"

Lea frowned, thinking about it. "I think it was mostly because it was not in their list of known friendlies. They are on a higher level of aggression, and they're autonomous. I can't control them all at the same time."

"So we lure a few out." Ivars grinned. "I have an idea."

His idea involved C4 and a modified detonation system. C4 usually didn't explode if shot at, but if an energy beam hit more conventional gunpowder first, that was enough to set it off. That took out two of the defending robots and created a huge cloud of dust and smoke, making her cough.

Unfortunately the robots were complex enough to establish they were under attack and change their tactics. They came out in a swarm, and she barely had time to warn the others and then point out the robots' locations in the murk.

Rifle fire and energy blasts filled the air, nearly deafening her. Everyone was having trouble seeing, but the corridors were long and narrow enough the energy weapons were bound to hit something, and she ended up having to use her target display system for Ivars via his synthetic eye.

Two Wiyert were hit in the confusion—she could feel the pain. But the number of functioning robots was dropping, and at last she was able to take control of the few survivors and use them to take out the static weapon.

Lea waited, holding her breath, but no other hostile system appeared to be active. A test robot from her first batch was able to go into the control system area without being attacked.

"I think...I think that was it," she said, feeling her stomach tighten. She didn't want to do this. "It's going to take a bit for the dust and smoke to settle down. Maybe we should clear out?"

"And take the wounded up." Ivars nodded. "Are you sure it's safe?"

Lea took out her purple flashlight, aiming it down the corridor. She shook it a little. "I can hardly see anything. I...think it's getting dim. Do we have more batteries?"

"Up top with the gear," Ramirez called back over his shoulder, busy tending one of the injured Wiyert. "We can bring some down if you want."

They left, carrying the wounded. The smoke had started to clear—there must be some kind of ventilation system still. They cautiously made their way to the main control area. Nothing was triggered. Lea placed her hand on the wall. Unlike most of the fadohl systems so far, the main controls were on a slanted area ringing the open space, not wall panels. So close to the main tap, it was like being next to Niagara Falls—thundering, roaring power at amazing speed. Just being here made her feel sick and dizzy.

One section of the controls was not merely damaged but molten slag. She knew immediately what it had been and why the victorious fadohl had done it. The manual controls for the power, so that even if the Wiyert or some other enemy found this place, they could not change anything. Her last desperate hope of avoiding direct manipulation of power, gone.

I'm not sure I can do this...

"Something wrong?" Ivars was watching her, frowning a little. Alaghar was standing just behind him, and Lea looked away quickly.

"This isn't going to be easy," she said, her mouth going dry. "I need...I need everybody out of here, for safety. Up on the surface."

"You think what happened at the tower will happen here." It wasn't a question. "You can't be left here all by yourself to do this. It's too dangerous."

Everybody seemed to have picked up on the fact something serious was going on and were watching in silence.

"I'm doing it all by myself, Mark. I'm the only one who *can* do it. If it works, I'll come up and find you."

"What do you mean, find...?" His face went white.

He knows.

"It's going to be much worse here. I can't protect you. You have to go farther than the link can reach to be safe."

"No. No. There *has* to be another way. Let's talk about this, dammit!"

Lea winced, feeling her throat tighten. Alaghar was looking supremely embarrassed, but she hadn't taken her eyes off Ivars. "It's the network. It has to be done through the network. Maybe if you had a full electronics team and a whole warehouse of gear, it could be done, but we don't have time. We don't have Argo."

"She's right." North locked eyes with Ivars, his expression grim. "We've got two planets worth of people depending on us to get it right, and we may not have a second chance. She needs to focus and she can't do that if she's worried about you. I saw what you looked like back there!" he shouted, shocking everyone. Lea hadn't known North *could* shout. "You have to get out of range. Which is?" He turned to Lea, raising an eyebrow.

"More than a mile, for him. Five to be sure."

"All right. Five-mile blast radius. Come on. You have to do this." North put a hand on Ivars's shoulder, but he shrugged it off sharply.

Fury, pain, and hurt. Anger at her, anger at the universe. She couldn't help it—the blast of his emotion on top of the hammering noise of the power tap was too much. Lea closed her eyes, feeling the tears seep out and fall, and brought up the shielding morph.

"Yes, I could get hurt," she said, her voice tight, answering his last frantic thought before the morph cut off the connection. "But you *will die* if you stay."

She could see the immense effort of will it took for him to take a step back, then two. He shifted as if to turn, froze, then suddenly lunged forward.

Alaghar was already there, slamming into Ivars so hard his feet left the ground. He recovered quickly and crouched, ducking under her arm and leaning forward to sprint out of her grasp, but then the massive arms of Rey'wiros encircled him from behind and lifted him bodily into the air. Ivars struggled and fought, yelling curses, but against that strength he could barely even move.

Lea gawked at Rey'wiros, realizing Alaghar must have recruited her own help to deal with the situation, and then was startled anew as Ramirez took out one of the flat injector packets and swiftly slapped it on Ivars's inner wrist.

The snarling fury on Ivars's face slowly faded, his muscles going slack. "Sedative," Ramirez said. "Alaghar asked if we had anything, after seeing what we did for the first day out on Snowball. We'll get him out."

"Give us about half an hour to get clear," North said, waving the others on with an urgent gesture. Rey'wiros slung Ivars over his shoulder and left for the shaft. "We'll send the platform down for you. You're sure all the attack robots are taken care of?"

"I'm sure," Lea whispered.

North came over and stared down at her. "Lea. You will *not* take any unnecessary risks. Do what you have to do, nothing else, and then get out. Is that clear?" His voice was soft but intense.

She nodded, no longer able to speak.

Once they were all loaded on the platform and had made it safely to the top of the shaft, Lea returned to the control center. She started a timer on her watch and set her pack just outside the doorway to the control area. If there were any flames and explosions, that way it would be protected.

She wished she didn't feel so cold. Or so miserable. Even if everything went perfectly, Ivars was going to be angry with her for a long time.

Five minutes to go. She heard a faint noise in the corridor, like a stone falling, and she felt a stab of fear. She had forgotten to bring down the morph after seeing everyone leave. It never occurred to her anybody would try to come back.

Well, except for Ivars. But he had been drugged, hadn't he?

The mind she contacted when the morph was gone was familiar, but it wasn't Ivars. Lea stood at the end of the corridor, watching Alaghar walking up, weapon in her hands, looking for all the world like she was merely out for a stroll.

"Why did you return?"

Alaghar gave her a calm look. "I gave my word to North, to win his help. I also spoke this promise to Ivars before I left him, so he might hear and know his chosen was not alone."

And here she'd thought Alaghar disapproved of the whole thing. Maybe she was a secret romantic after all.

"There isn't anything you can do to help with this. You should go—"

"I can stop you from doing something foolish," Alaghar interrupted. "You are powerful but still foolish."

"You could die!"

Alaghar shrugged. "Then I die."

The watch timer beeped, and Lea started. "They should be… you *waited*. You waited until it was too late for me to send you off with them!"

"I also made sure they were all on the *asuhan* and out of the pit," Alaghar said, unabashed. "Now do you intend to complete your task or complain of what I did or did not do?"

Of all the nagging nursemaids in the galaxy, it just had to be you, Lea seethed to herself. "Fine. But you stay out here. And don't look in to see if I'm doing it right or give me helpful advice, okay? I don't need distractions and you don't need burns."

She raised her hands to find the best connection to the network and was irritated to see her hands were shaking. She'd been upset before, but now she was angry too, and she couldn't afford that. She needed to focus, to not think of Ivars. Even if she didn't survive, he'd live. *No, if I die, he'll do his best to get killed. I have to do this right.*

Lea looked back at Alaghar, hesitating. It wasn't something easy to ask, but Alaghar seemed willing to die to help…and Lea needed help.

"I want to…borrow you. Your thoughts." Lea felt her face heat. "I need to keep my mind calm. If I can…you are always…" she stammered, trying to explain—but Alaghar had already extended her open hand.

Lea let her fingertips just rest on Alaghar's palm and took a deep breath, letting the feel and pulse and shape of Alaghar's mind wash over her own. Alaghar had no doubts, was determined to sacrifice everything to free her people and escape the fadohl. Even let some weepy Earth computer geek wander around her head and gawk at the scenery. It was humbling.

Lea kept that feeling wrapped around her like a blanket. She had a thin layer of Alaghar to support her now, and she could face the power tap.

Calmly she let her mind drift over the connection with her fingers on the console. Waiting until the full network was understood before changing anything.

A long time ago she had gone whitewater rafting, unusual for her because she usually avoided any activity that had any kind of physical danger. The guide had warned them all that day: *No matter what happens, keep paddling. You have to go faster than the water or you will lose control.*

It seemed like good advice for the power network too. And so she studied it carefully and found something curious. There were echoes in the network. Nodes that were not active. She could focus and get a better sense of them without doing anything and discovered they seemed to be turned off. She tried sending just a trickle of power their way, and nothing bad happened.

I don't know what they are, but if they can absorb the power from the barrier, I won't have to dump everything on the existing network.

If she had Argo to help, it wouldn't be nearly as dangerous. It could act faster than her squishy human brain. But it wasn't here and she was.

One more check of the network, counting the hidden nodes. Lea took out the data bead Argo had given her and reviewed the information there. Barrier down, everything else up. Simple.

Lea took a deep breath and dived into the power flow. First she forced two inactive nodes to full power, as much as they could take. It took more effort than she had expected, and she still had to take the barrier down—but the power flow was lower. Then she yanked the barrier.

Energy surged through the network like water from a burst dam. Lea raced ahead, jabbing power into the dead nodes and hoping the pressure of the new power would open them up further.

Alarm processes appeared. They were different in feel than the power network, and she suspected they had been added later. Perhaps by the enemy, to protect what they had done? She wasted precious seconds diverting energy to stun them long enough for her to detach and destroy them. The power was building in pressure around her, blinding stabs of pain in her head making her lose her careful, borrowed calm.

She was shaking, losing her balance. *No. I'm not finished yet. Come on, just a bit more!*

Two more dead nodes to wake up. She was drowning in power, starting to panic. A voice was screaming somewhere far away, and it was hard to breathe. She felt herself coughing. One node left.

And then it was done. Lea snatched her hands away from the console and didn't recognize where she was. The air was full of smoke and dust, and she heard loud creaking and heavy crashes. The floor was shaking like they were in an earthquake, and a heavy beam was partly blocking the doorway. Alaghar was shouting insistently, wanting to know if Lea was hurt. Had that been her voice screaming, instead of Lea's?

"Lea! We must go!"

"I'm here," Lea said, racked by spasms of coughing. She held up her hands, trying to see in the dim light of the glow-cubes. She was astonished to see she wasn't burned at all. Then why was there smoke? "I'm fine. I took it down. Let's get out of here!"

She took a step and stumbled. The floor was *tilted*. And then with a thundering crash, another beam fell. On her.

North hung on to one of Snowball's spines, squinting into the wind and grunting each time the *asuhan* landed. "Make sure he's secure!" he yelled back to Ramirez, who was rigging a tied-up Ivars to their existing ropes. "Rocks coming up!"

While Snowball had no problem leaping and jumping, it did make things exciting for the passengers. Under sedation, Ivars couldn't hold on by himself, and Ramirez and North had secured his arms and legs to be on the safe side. Ivars was devious, *and* angry enough to do something stupid when he could move again. He'd be fine once Lea was back.

North wanted Lea back too, but for different reasons. He hoped he was just imagining things, but the *asuhan* seemed more nervous and confused without Lea around, and getting everyone on board had been tricky. They were going to reach the five-mile mark pretty soon—he hoped they could get Snowball to stop.

Snowball slowed and grunted, head turned. Then it faced forward again, dropped its head, and launched into a full-on sprint.

"Hey! Who told it to speed up?"

That just got him puzzled looks—then the ground heaved like a shaken blanket. A thundering roar came from the direction of the pit behind them, soon followed by a huge column of dust. And that was all he could see for a while, because Snowball put on a new burst of speed North didn't know it was capable of, and it was all he could do to hang on.

Good thing we tied Ivars up. They lost a crate and then, with a scream, one of the Koloh Wiyert. They tried to get Snowball to stop, but either it couldn't hear or was so terrified the commands weren't working. *That was a bad fall. I don't think even the Wiyert could survive that.*

What the hell had just happened? It was bad, whatever it was, and Lea and Alaghar were in the middle of it. North was aware of a sudden, sickening feeling in the pit of his stomach. If Lea's luck had run out—if she had failed to turn off the barrier—their luck was out too. They were trapped on Beredul.

Maybe she had turned it off. They had to go back anyway, to make sure Lea and Alaghar had survived.

With a fervent prayer, North started to crawl slowly toward the *asuhan*'s head, fingers grabbing at any surface he could find to stay on. He had to stop Snowball *now*.

CHAPTER 21

Alaghar dug in the rubble with her bare hands, going by feel and the memory of what she had seen before the lights went out. Dust was everywhere, making it hard to breathe. It was to be hoped that Lea had succeeded in her task before the collapse—even if she lived, the structure she had been using was likely broken beyond even the Frost People's ability to repair.

Her hand touched something warm and pliable, and Alaghar heard a faint moan, then a cough. Lea, still alive—for the moment. She dug faster, bracing herself against what felt like a slab of stone to lift it ever so slightly, but enough to feel Lea move.

"Can you get free?"

She heard motion, then a gasp and a stifled moan of pain. "My arm...doesn't work. And I...my foot. It's trapped."

"You must move. I cannot hold this for much longer. Move or die."

Furious muttering and a thrashing motion that Alaghar could feel transmitted faintly through the stone. Sobbing with pain, Lea's voice grew closer in the darkness until Alaghar felt one hand on her leg. It was shaking.

Her strength was gone. Hoping Lea was completely out from underneath, Alaghar let the slab shift to the side and fall with a crash. Lea whimpered. "How badly are you injured?" When Lea said nothing, "Where is your small light?"

"My pack." Whispered. "Is it there? On the other side of the doorway."

Alaghar started feeling in what should be the right direction. She found something made of cloth and had to move more rubble to pull it free. It was wet.

"Here. Something is leaking."

She heard rustling noises, an indrawn hiss of breath, and then a click followed by a welcome glow of light. Lea was covered in dust and streaks of blood, cradling one arm against her chest. One boot was completely missing, and her foot was only covered by a torn and dirty pink sock.

"I had to take the boot off to get free." Lea shifted and winced. "This is going to be a miserable hike. I think my arm is broken. Possibly other things too."

Alaghar felt a flash of anger. "You should have been wearing your armor."

That earned her a glare. "If I had been wearing my armor, I never would have been able to bend enough to untie my boot and get free." Moving gingerly, Lea opened her pack farther and pulled out the flexible container the Frost People used to hold water. It was damaged and dripping. "Might as well drink up. This is shot."

Lea took a sip, and Alaghar did as well. There was not much water in the container, and her mouth was still dry when it was gone. "We should leave now. There could be more damage coming. Why did the building shake? This did not happen at the tower."

Lea shook her head, looking dazed. "I don't know. I turned some other things on, but...I don't know."

Other than bruises and scrapes, Lea had no other major injury beside her broken arm. Alaghar rigged a sling for it using straps from the pack and part of Lea's outer shirt.

They made their way down the corridor, even less easy to navigate with rubble. Some of the glow-cubes here were working feebly, which helped. Lea's device did not provide a large amount of light.

"Did you succeed in your attempt?"

"Yes. There were...other things on the network that were turned off. I put some of the power there. Maybe that caused the shaking."

Alaghar sighed. "You did not know what they were, but you

used them anyway?"

"I don't know what *most* of this stuff does, and I doubt anyone else even remembers, even the fadohl. Maybe we can see when we get to the surface."

"Perhaps." They were close to the shaft entrance now, and Alaghar was aware of a bad feeling. There was no light. They had been down in the hidden place long enough for the sun to rise, but there was no light.

They stared at the dirt and rocks spilling out of the entrance, partly covering one of the damaged machine-servants that had been used to lift the platform.

"Maybe it's only a partial collapse," Lea said faintly. "They could dig us out again." She shivered and sat down on a section of fallen wall.

"Would you...know, if they were at the top?" Alaghar did not like thinking about how Lea would know, but they did not have much choice.

"If they are there, yes. I can't sense anything there now." She shivered again. "I'd better eat. I'm getting the floaty spots again... if they only went five miles, they should be back soon."

They waited for two hours. Alaghar spent the time collecting glow-cubes and twisting wire into a mesh container to hold them. It wasn't much, but it was another source of light if Lea's light gave out. Lea's teeth were chattering with cold.

"They have not come. We must find another way out, if there is one."

"I can't sense anything." Lea sounded miserable. "I should be able to locate even an animal of some kind in two hours. I think...I think the shaft collapsed. They probably think we are dead."

We probably are, Alaghar thought. They had no water and little food. She doubted very much there was an open way to leave this place. The Wiyert would know they had no chance, buried as they were. They could not dig them out in time and should not waste time and effort when they had no way to be sure either of them was alive to save.

It was not as good as a death in battle, but they had freed the Wiyert from Beredul by their actions. It was still a worthy end.

Lea sniffled, wiped her face with her good hand, and stood up. She took a step and would have fallen if Alaghar had not caught at the fabric of her pack.

"Where are you going?"

Lea looked back at her, scowling. "I'm freezing, and my arm hurts. A lot. Maybe I can find a place with heat. Or a way out." A tear seeped down her face, leaving a streak of mud behind.

Alaghar opened her mouth to object, then closed it. What else could they do? And she had promised she would watch over Lea. If Lea, in pain, still wanted to keep moving, Alaghar would too. She got to her feet and followed the pale spot of light down the dark corridor.

Lea was limping even worse with one boot missing and stumbling over rubble underfoot. There seemed to be less damage the farther they were from the shaft, and more of the interior light was working. Lea stopped to rest a few times but soon started shivering again and returned to walking.

Once they came to a display with the glowing symbols the fadohl used, and Lea stopped and stared at it. Alaghar was conscious of a faint hope, but Lea's face did not show any. "Would you open the small pocket on my pack and take out one of the data beads?"

Alaghar grimaced, finding the small metal tab that allowed the opening in the fabric to appear. The way the *zihp-pehr* closed itself so completely disturbed her still. "Here. What do you do with it?"

"I told Argo I'd try and get some of the old records, so maybe it could figure out what happened when it was abandoned." Lea touched the display and pain furrowed her face.

"What is this information?"

Lea shook her head. "No idea...I'm just copying it. I can't concentrate enough to figure it out."

Then why was she doing it? Did she cling to the hope of escape still, or was it merely mindless habit?

They walked for what seemed like hours, occasionally having to retrace their steps when a cave-in blocked their way. Lea was limping badly now, the foot with the remaining boot dragging on the ground.

"You should have gone with the others." Lea hadn't spoken for such a long time, Alaghar was startled and simply stared at her. "You'd survive and get to see Isboryi again."

Alaghar looked away, striving for calm. "Perhaps. He could be dead now. I might have died in the coming battle, instead of here, and still not seen him. For a warrior, nothing is certain. This is why we do not claim our chosen until we go behind walls. He will find another if he lives."

She looked back when she did not hear Lea following. Despite the drawn lines of pain on her face, Lea was smiling faintly. "You keep forgetting—you can't lie to me. You adore him, think the sun rises in his eyes and the moon sets in his…well, you think a lot of him. Why is it wrong for me to want you both to be happy?"

"You…you *dared*…!" Fury and shame engulfed her. "When I allowed you to share my thoughts, you uncovered what I kept hidden!"

A little gasping laugh. "Alaghar, I've known about you two since you sent him off with *Kepler* to Earth. I didn't need contact to tell you were in agony when you did that stuff with the red dust on his face."

"You find it amusing, my pain and shame? Do the other Frost People laugh when they think of it?"

"Oh, calm down. I never told anyone and you know it. But I get a little fed up with the hypocrisy, okay? You kept acting like it was the end of the world if Mark and I so much as made eye contact. Now my last memory of him will be little more than *holding hands* on this garbage dump of a planet, all because of your stupid boo-hoo-life-is-hard customs, and we had to skulk around in the middle of the night to even do that! And yet you're doing the same thing in your head…and, well, it's dumb. You should be happy," Lea said, her angry voice trailing off. "You're a pain in the neck and a complete grouch, and…a loyal friend, and we're incredibly lucky we found you. You don't deserve to be miserable your entire life, and neither does he. Did you even get to kiss him?"

Alaghar contemplated not even dignifying this with an answer, but who was here to listen? Who would ever find out? "No."

"Did you *want* to?"

"*Yes*," Alaghar snarled, her face almost touching Lea's.

Lea gave a tight grin. "Then you aren't completely hopeless. Just keep thinking how much you would enjoy that, instead of how much you want to punch me."

"I…"

"I can *tell*, Alaghar. Now use your words and tell me what a weak, childish person I am and all the other things that make you feel happy, because right now you are a giant ball of misery, and I've got plenty of my own." Lea peered around the corner of an intersection, holding the small light. "Hmmm. Let's go this way."

Alaghar felt her irritation build. "Why? Do you delight in tormenting me in revenge for my many crimes against you? Will we walk until we collapse?" It was very rude and challenging, but the Frost People never seemed to care about such things, and...it felt good to speak so freely.

Lea gave a coughing laugh. "Oh, if I wanted revenge...you don't know about Italians, do you? No, I'm picking up something. Some of the machines may still be working here." She shrugged and winced. "Might be worth checking out."

"The pain of your injuries has made you delusional," Alaghar muttered, but not seriously. She did not even complain when Lea insisted on going down even farther, through a hole in the floor. Alaghar had to lower Lea carefully by her good arm and then jump down herself.

Lea nearly lost consciousness from the pain and had to stop for a while until she could move without gasping. What was driving her so hard? The Frost People...Alaghar had thought the Frost People were soft. Without discipline. Lea was the weakest of them and wept as not even a young Wiyert would—and yet she wiped her tears and got up again to fight when there was no hope. Perhaps...perhaps that was Frost People courage.

"So what would you have done after the fadohl were defeated?" Lea asked while they ate some of the food in her pack. Alaghar desperately wanted water, but they had not found any.

"We never thought that far. It was enough of an impossible dream to escape Beredul." Alaghar leaned forward, her arms on her knees, resting her chin in her hands. "What would you do, in my place?"

"Go home, to Earth." Lea gave a twisted smile. "But I can't do that. So maybe find a nice world to live on."

"Yes." Alaghar nodded. "A world with sunlight and no *asuhan*. So our children could play *sof-bal-gaym* and Isboryi and I could sit and wear bright-colored clothes and yell as if we were in battle, watching them." Alaghar turned her head. "Why can you not return to Earth?"

Lea raised a weary hand and tapped her head, which released a puff of dust. "You don't like me knowing what you feel, what you think—and you know me. You trust me enough to *let* me in your head. Earth has a lot more electronics everywhere too. They don't...they *can't* trust me. Nobody else like me has ever existed before. I'd probably have to stay with Argo and...I don't know, find a way to get food somehow." She got up, her breath hissing out in pain. "Let's go. That signal is getting even stranger." Her teeth chattered as she spoke.

"How do you determine the strangeness of a signal?" Lea was not looking well. Alaghar had no way to treat her injuries further—the most helpful thing she could do was distract her from the pain. Perhaps also she would learn what to look for and could help search.

"Something...different from the other fahdol equipment." Lea stumbled. "It's pulsing. Almost a pattern, but not a simple one."

They were in a section of dusty halls and half-open doors. There were no glow-cubes or anything except piles of thicker dust with half-hidden gleams of metal or ceramic, like piles of leaves. But no leaves ever grew here. *Bodies. Very old bodies.*

A flicker caught her eye, far down the corridor. Flash, longer flash. Short, long, short. Long, long, short.

"A pattern like that?" Alaghar pointed. She could barely speak to be understood, her throat was so dry.

Lea's head lifted. "Yeah. Exactly like that."

The light was part of a control console, similar to the one Lea had used to change the power network. Lea stared at it, reaching out and then pulling her hand back.

"Is it dangerous?" Alaghar took a step back. "Do I need to go behind a wall?"

Lea frowned, looking puzzled. "I don't know. It isn't...this is coming from somewhere else, and I can't tell where or what it is." Then her gaze became intent. "I *want* to know. Just...be ready to duck. Just in case."

She reached out her hand, stiffened with an indrawn breath... and started to laugh. Laughed so hard tears made dark streaks on her dusty face.

Her mind is broken. The pain, the fear were too much.

Lea's face turned to her, still smiling. "It's Argo. It's back, and it's in the network. And…" Her eyes closed and her mouth twitched for an agonizing moment. "It's found a way for us to get out."

North bowed his head as the Wiyert placed the final stones on the shallow grave, then stepped back to give them privacy. They had been fortunate there had been only one death and no serious injuries when Snowball had panicked. *No, I can't really say there were no serious injuries.* He walked back to the ruins where they had built a fire, carefully away from the where the *asuhan* was crouching. Ramirez was kneeling by the still form of Ivars, worry showing in flashes on his face.

"How's he doing?"

Ramirez cursed and spat. "Worse. I can barely get him to respond."

"Think it is the sedative?"

"It wore off two hours ago. Something is wrong with him, and I don't think it's just…what happened back there. I mean, not grief. I've seen something like this before, but it was with people with major trauma. Blood loss, missing legs and arms…that kind of thing." The harsh frustration and anger in Ramirez's voice made North's throat tighten. "It's like he's shutting down. I've tried everything I know how to do. There's no injury, but…he's dying."

North could see it too. Ivars's skin tone was bad—a kind of grey. His eyes would drift open briefly, show no sign of recognition or any emotion, and then shut again.

"Maybe that link they talked about was deeper than either of them knew. Is there anything that can be done for him?"

Ramirez rubbed a hand across his eyes and didn't speak for a moment. "I dunno. I just…dunno. Maybe on Earth, but even if we go straight to the portal and Argo is there, it would take, what? Over a week? I don't think he'll last that long. Goddammit…and what'd we say if he did wake up?" Another tear rolled down his face.

And North really, really didn't want to tell Argo Lea was dead. Would the ship still help them? Nobody knew for sure.

"So moving him won't help. And we still have a job to do here.

If he…if he doesn't make it, he'd probably want to be here with her anyway."

"Yeah." They were silent for a few minutes, looking down at Ivars. "Guess we should tell Rey'wiros to go back to Vartai, then. Nothing to wait for here."

The *buj-lagar* was now their *asuhan* driver. North gave him the word, and when everybody was loaded up, Snowball started to move again.

They had backtracked once North got Snowball to stop, both to find out what had happened and to find the Wiyert that had fallen off. They had found her, dead—the fall had killed her.

The pit entrance of the underground power tap was now an uneven, lumpy crater and the shaft completely buried again. Other sunken pits had opened up nearby as well, telling him other areas had collapsed underground. Even if Lea and Alaghar had survived the initial collapse, there was no way to get them out again. And Ivars's reaction was a big clue Lea wasn't around anymore.

When they'd stopped, North had also gotten out the comm gear and tested it. The interference was now gone—just normal atmospheric static. The energy barrier was definitely down, and they and the Wiyert were no longer trapped. Lea had done her job. Done it well. Strange and scary as she was, it wasn't going to be the same without her. He took a moment to pray—for Lea and Ivars and for strength and guidance for himself and Ramirez, the last two remaining. *And if you have a spare miracle, Lord, we could really use one about now.*

North watched the scenery go by in a numb state of mind, only really waking up when a new feature of the landscape caught his attention. He'd seen two of the things now, and the odds were high it was related to the barrier shutdown. Tall towers, each with a cap like a mushroom. No idea what they did or why they had appeared, and the Wiyert had never seen anything like them.

He got out his binoculars. The cap on the tower showed damage and streaks and blobs on the surface. It also had a series of dark oblongs ringing the surface, about midway. They reminded him of something, and he racked his brain trying to figure out what.

Something was moving near the tower. Flying. It dipped out of view before he could get a good look at it. North quickly stowed the binoculars.

"Ramirez—I'm seeing motion in the air. We might have some of the flying *asuhan* coming by. You should probably grab a weapon and leave Ivars for now—they could be stirred up like Snowball was and attack." North waved to Pehtek and pointed at Ivars. "Please watch our friend. Speak if he shows change."

Pehtek nodded silently, crouching down.

North roped himself to a spine and stood, rifle ready. He and Ramirez swapped off watching with binoculars and with their scopes but didn't see any further motion in the air. The Wiyert, alerted, were also watching. Everything had changed again, so they were quite willing to believe the danger of the *asuhan* was back.

Then the silence was broken. "He moves," Pehtek said.

North glanced down. Ivars was moving—turning his head restlessly, eyes still closed, as if dreaming.

Ramirez slung his rifle. "I'll check." He knelt beside Pehtek. "Pulse is better. He might be coming out of the fugue state."

That was really good news. Maybe it had just been shock that had knocked Ivars out. "Do you need any gear for him?"

"Nah. Not much I can do without a hospital. Wait, I got some stuff that won't sedate him but will calm him down a bit. He's got some bad stuff to process all at once." Ramirez got up and stumbled slowly to the stowed gear.

North took his place. He only had the basics of combat medicine, but it seemed to him that Ivars had more color in his face and didn't look so much like a warm corpse.

Then Ivars opened his eyes. The expression in them was confused but focused. He mumbled something North couldn't understand.

"Ramirez! He's trying to talk!"

A shadow flew over them. Something had moved between Snowball and the sun. The flying *asuhan* was back? North brought his rifle back up to his shoulder, wedging himself against a spine for balance. The Wiyert were shouting, sounding confused. *There it is.* North stared at it for a moment through the scope, wondering why he was so surprised, and then it hit him. The wings weren't flapping. It flew by again, and this time it rotated slightly from side to side.

Waggling the wings.

"Don't shoot!" North yelled, and then remembered to say it in Wiyert. "It is not an enemy!"

"What is this thing?" Rey'wiros yelled back. "It is yours?"

Noise from Ivars distracted North. Now he was trying to sit up despite his bound arms and legs, and the mumbled words were becoming clearer.

Ivars recovering. A flying device that wasn't attacking and had used a signal from Earth indicating friendly intent. *Lea.* "It's Lea!" he shouted.

Ramirez stared at him. "The hell? She's under a fucking mountain!"

"Think a little thing like that would stop her? Look at Ivars! It's her! I have no idea how, but it is." North spun to Rey'wiros. "We must take the *asuhan* to an open place and wait there."

It was too much too fast for the leader of Vartai. Rey'wiros wanted to make speed for the walls, and it was only with difficulty North persuaded him to let the two Earth-humans off and to wait in the cover of the vegetation near a bare patch of ground.

He wasn't sure how to signal the flyer—but if it really was Lea, she would know where they were anyway. And sure enough, the flyer came circling back, slowly descending.

"Hey! That's *my* flyer!" Ramirez yelled.

"Your…you mean the one at the tower? You're sure?"

"Yeah! Look at the color. They did something funny to the top, but I'm sure. It's the same one."

So not only had Lea gotten out alive from the cave-in, she had gotten to the tower—and back—in less than a day. Oh, and figured out how to run the flyer too.

The flyer drifted even closer to the ground, and the legs unfolded out from the center like a crab's. Now North could see familiar dark hair in the cockpit and that someone else—Alaghar— was in there as well. He could also hear yelling in the distance that sounded like Ivars.

"You got that tranquilizer handy?" he murmured to Ramirez. "Because someone is going to need it soon. Not sure who. Maybe me."

Ramirez wasn't paying attention. "Oh, man. Just look at that thing! I wonder how fast it can go?"

They ran to the flyer. The cockpit bubble lifted up and *flattened* before sliding back. There was a rather ungainly ring of rougher material where it had been that also seemed to just flow away.

"Hi, guys!" Lea called down. "Just a sec—this thing really isn't designed for multiple passengers, especially large ones that complain all the time."

"You would not allow me to walk." Alaghar was looking resigned and not nearly as grumpy as usual. "Nor seek the peace of death that would find me anyway, the way you guided the device. No, remain there. You will fall. Again."

Alaghar struggled out of the cockpit, hung by her fingers from one of the wing surfaces, and dropped to the ground. Then Lea stood up, and North saw her arm was in something that looked like white webbing.

"What happened to you? When we saw the…well, we thought you weren't coming back."

"We thought we weren't either." For a moment Lea was looking at the edge of the vegetation, where Snowball was emerging. Her face was drawn and tired. "It was a mess in there, and I broke my arm on top of everything. But when the barrier came down, Argo was able to get into the network and signal me. Using Morse, which one of you guys must have taught it, because I don't know any beyond SOS…but anyway, I knew it was Argo. It discovered that place had a portal door. All of them do, apparently. Got that working, went to Argo for a bit of patching up, then to the tower to find the flying device and then you."

She hesitated, looking down from the wing. "Um…"

North reached up. "Slide—we'll catch you."

Setting her down, North saw she was wearing the soft slippers he'd seen the researchers wear sometimes on *Kepler*. "What's with the footwear?"

Lea sighed. "One of my boots is still under that mountain of rubble, and I didn't have another pair."

"Lea would not let me make another boot for her. She said it would take too much time."

North snapped his eyes to the top of the flyer. The rough material that had been around the bubble was gone. A strange, humanoid figure stood next to the cockpit now.

"Wait…*Argo?*"

"More sort of an Argo puppet," Lea said. "Argo was really doing the flying. I wanted to get back as fast as possible." Her eyes lost focus for a while, tearing up. Ramirez reached for her, looking concerned, but North waved him off while tapping his forehead.

"Oh, right. Um, I suppose we had better untie Ivars now," Ramirez said, sighing.

They ended up sending Ramirez and Argo ahead in the flyer. Lea couldn't think of another way to do it, since the Wiyert were dead against being anywhere near the morph golem, and Ramirez was desperate to try the flyer.

"I hope he remembers the *damah* have those big weapons on the towers," Ivars said. He sounded exhausted and had refused to let go of her ever since Lea had been hauled up onto the *asuhan*. To her surprise, Alaghar had merely rolled her eyes when she noticed and not said a word.

"Argo knows, don't worry. I wish we'd found another flyer, maybe a bigger one, but I didn't want to take the time."

"Thank you." She felt remembered terror flash through him and a strange, sinking numbness. "Let's…let's not do that again, okay?" There was a tremor in his voice she had never heard before.

Too frightened even to yell at her. "Never, *ever* again. Not even to adjust things. We shouldn't need to now, since Argo is hooked into the network. It can change things a lot better than I could anyway."

Ivars shifted but kept hold. "So how is Argo in that…thing?"

"It isn't, not really. The golem is more of a radio receiver right now. Argo proper is still in orbit in this system and is just transmitting to it. But it is capable of being a sort of copy of Argo even when the ship itself is gone." She felt his confusion and grinned. "This is going to be some computer geekery, okay? Argo is very complex. It can do multiple things at once. Humans can too, at least up to two or three things. Argo can split off one of those…processes and keep it running in a separate container by itself. Then when the original Argo shows up, the two merge again."

"So no matter what, something other than you can tweak the

power network?”

“Yeah. Oh, and it isn’t just the flyer, you know. All of those machines at the tower can operate anywhere on Beredul now. The power locks on to the device.”

“Ohhh. That’s gonna be real useful.” Ivars was silent for a while, thinking. Lea shifted, trying to find a comfortable way to sit. Snowball was not very well upholstered. “You’re still hurting.”

Lea sighed. Carefully. “Having a building fall on you is not very comfortable. I’ve got bruises all over and the broken arm is not fun. Probably more I haven’t found yet. Argo wanted to help, but I’m not sure it knows how to fix humans, and I didn’t want to risk it.”

“Oh no…you hit your head! You’re thinking before you do things!” Ivars shook with silent laughter.

“Idiot.” She took a moment to search through the link. “You don’t feel so good either.”

“Nothing hurts, really.” He thought for a moment. “I just have no energy at all. Wiped.”

“So what do we do now?”

“Get the Wiyert ready. Train the fighters, help Rey’wiros get the leaders on board. Get all of them ready to evacuate.”

“Right, I’ll just go back and wait under the mountain.”

Ivars’s hold tightened painfully. “NOT funny. Besides, I need your help again. We’re at the point where we really should be getting back in touch with Earth to let them know how things stand. Get some more of our people here and get some of the Wiyert out. They don’t have any idea where to go yet, but we can at least keep their children safe on Earth until they do.”

“Oof. Well, I think you’d better rest up if that’s your plan. I’m tired just hearing it. And for the record, I am not, no way, nohow, going to be trip chaperon for untold thousands of little Wiyert discovering sugar and outdoor sports for the first time.”

Ivars gave a sleepy grin, radiating mischievous amusement. “Somebody back home will need some disciplinary invading. We’ll just send ’em there.”

Lea smiled back. “Go to sleep, headcase.”

Despite her broken arm and other discomfort, she slept too. She couldn’t remember the last time she had been able to sleep for more than an hour at a time, and it had been weeks since being able to sleep next to Ivars. It was profoundly restful.

And it was a good thing too, because when they stopped for the night, she faced the barrage of Argo, and Ramirez's ecstatic descriptions of the flyer and what he could see while making excursions from their route.

"Lots more of those tall mushroom things," he said. "At least five so far."

"They are weapons pylons," Argo said. Its voice was very different coming from a single source instead of the focused, surrounding environment of the ship interior. "Most of them are destroyed or too damaged to use, even if they deployed. But some do work."

"Interesting. Might be able to use that." Ivars rubbed his chin. "Can they…retract too?"

They were all seated about their own campfire, away from the Wiyert, so they could confer with Argo. Lea did not have the immediate connection with the golem she did on the ship, but it was still reassuring. And less prone to being overwhelmed, even though she did have to remind Argo that if it was going to pretend it looked like a human, it couldn't rotate its "eyes" to see something instead of the head.

"I thought the plan was to leave as soon as possible and pretend we were never here," North said.

"Yeah, but we might be able to use them anyway." Ivars was thinking hard. "I've got some ideas."

Ramirez sat up, tossing more wood on the fire. "Before you do too much of that, we need to have a little talk, kids." He looked at Lea and Ivars in turn. Lea frowned. Ramirez was unhappy about what he was doing but determined to do it.

"Uh-oh. Has Rey'wiros had enough of our scandalous behavior?" Ivars said brightly. "Because if so, he can—"

"This is about cold, hard reality and how you came *this close* to either cardiac arrest, no joke, or fatal coma."

Lea felt her heart skip a beat. "What? When? How?"

North sighed and turned to her. "When the pit collapsed and we all thought you were dead."

Ramirez shifted, rubbing his hands on his legs in a nervous way. "Yeah. So we know there is this link you two have, and it is real handy for keeping in touch and stuff. I was thinking about it while flying, and I think we just found the downside. Well, the other downside besides accidentally frying Ivars when you mess around with high voltage. It's not just handy. Ivars *needs* it to stay alive. If he's out of range for too long, he starts shutting down." Ramirez spread his hands and looked at Ivars. "Sorry if I rain on your parade, man. You don't get to be on the tip of the spear anymore, not unless you want to take Lea with you. Think of it like a reverse restraining order." He grinned.

North winced. "While we are laying down the law here, *you* are officially banned from anything requiring tact or diplomacy, Ramirez. You make it sound like they've been sentenced to a chain gang."

"Well, they used to call—"

"Shut UP!" Once North was sure Ramirez was not going to continue, he gave Lea a smile. "I got a feeling you two can work things out on your own. He's right about one thing, though. You're together on this. We're still in harm's way and will be for the foreseeable future. It might not be possible for you to avoid danger, or even death. Just make sure you realize you'll be taking someone with you when you take risks. Talk to each other."

"Well..." North glared at Ramirez, who held up his hands defensively. "Wait! Maybe it's cold to say it, but Lea won't...that is, she didn't collapse, right?" He looked at her. "Did you feel anything?"

Lea frowned, trying to remember. "I'm not sure—I was feeling pretty crappy all the time then, but I was banged up and injured too."

North shook his head. "Doesn't matter. Ivars can't go too far away without falling on his face, and he's useless unconscious. Lea has to stay safe, and he has to stay in range, so he has to stay safe too. I think we have an absolute upper bound for time and distance right now. Maybe that will change. Maybe somebody can figure out what this link is and how to disconnect it. Just the lethal part," he added when Ivars started to object.

"Sorry," Lea said feebly. She felt sick and miserable. "I didn't know..."

Ivars rolled his eyes. "Nobody knew. As I recall, you tried to warn me half a dozen times, and I didn't listen once. So I live to complain about it, and the side benefits are nice. You think I don't know what it's like working around damage?" He tapped the side of his head where the scars were. "A full year of surgery and physical therapy and only one meat eye left. I can see, and I can function. Two other guys on that mission would love to have my problems. Don't feel sorry for me—feel sorry for yourself."

Idiot. I do. We still don't have any privacy, have you noticed?

While Ivars was choking on his laughter, Lea narrowed her eyes at Ramirez. "Yeah, I think this is all *suspiciously convenient* coming from a guy who wants to keep that flyer all to himself."

"It's *my* flyer. I just let you borrow it! And next time, ask. I'll let it slide this once, emergency and all."

"Lea should be safe," Argo stated. "She should be on me instead of here. I can protect her."

"I have to be with Mark," Lea said gently. "And he has to be here for now. You can still help keep me safe."

"There are not enough of the working weapons pylons," Argo said. It sounded annoyed. "Even with the damaged ones repaired, it would not be enough."

"Hey, Argo," Ramirez said, looking startled. "Do you have weapons?"

The morph golem sat completely still. Argo had not yet mastered showing emotions with it, but Lea could sense it was startled too.

"I do not know," said Argo. "I will find out now."

CHAPTER 22

Ivars leaned back from the table, rubbing his temples to ward off a looming headache. Probably time to take a break. His endurance was slowly improving, but it still wasn't to normal levels, even after a week. Ramirez had said, after lots of warnings about wild-ass guesses and no data, that whatever had happened to him was probably healing, and he should just listen to what his body was telling him and not push. Also to schedule about a month of medical exams whenever he got back to Earth or an equivalent medical ward, to see if there was any permanent damage.

So he'd been good and become a temporary desk ranger. They'd rigged him a sort of sling chair that made it easy for him to lean back, prop up his feet, and take a field nap. But more importantly, he had *coffee*. He was drinking it from the same rough ceramic handleless cup the Wiyert served their hot mud in, but it didn't matter. He had caffeine and could therefore conquer the world.

The sound of Argo making another arrival announcement echoed over the camp. If it was another load of metal supports, maybe they could get a big tent set up for the training. Things were really starting to come together now, with Argo's help. The machines they'd found at the transmitter depot were now carrying supplies to a clear area outside Vartai, and he had a proper field tent to work in and quarters that weren't six-feet-thick stone walls with airlocks and no windows.

It wasn't just for the Earth-humans' comfort either. The Wiyert needed to get comfortable with open spaces—all of them—both to fight and for their new life away from Beredul. They also needed to get used to strange stuff like Snowball and the delivery robots. The first time one of the Argo-controlled robots showed up, it nearly got blasted by Vartai's guns, so now they announced ahead of time when one was arriving.

The first classes of Wiyert were going through training now, with Ramirez and North. Even when he was recovered, he probably wouldn't have time for that—Rey'wiros was deep in the diplomacy, and Ivars had to spend more time than he liked in Vartai talking. The good news was even the more hidebound *damah* had noticed the changes. The bad news was they didn't trust change and *really* didn't trust the Earth-humans that had caused it.

Not helped by Rey'wiros always wanting to show off he can make an asuhan *obey voice commands.* It did make a big impression, he had to admit. It was just such a big impression the visitors went into a terrified vapor lock and were useless for hours afterward. *And the one thing we do not have enough of is time.*

Which meant more people—to train, to plan, to negotiate. Which meant going back to Earth to get them. Ivars didn't want to leave the Wiyert completely in the lurch, though, so he was trying to stand up as much as he could quickly and hoped to get back fast enough to prevent it from coming unstuck. Before the fadohl showed up.

The noise of the camp abated enough he became aware of an intense, low-voiced discussion in Wiyert being held just outside the tent entrance.

"You do not just go inside!" insisted a male voice Ivars did not immediately recognize. "That cannot be the discipline, even for them!"

"It is so." That was Suz'ahnkei. "Look, you. It is but cloth held up on sticks. It is only a defense against sight and wind. The discipline has no purpose without stone walls."

"There are plenty of stone walls—in his head," came Alaghar's voice. "I will show you the truth of what she says. You only stand at the opening and speak greeting."

That gave Ivars enough warning to swing his feet down and sit up, looking industrious, before Alaghar came in to view.

"*Hazu*, Ivars."

He waved her in. "*Hazu*, Alaghar. Coffee?" He pretended not to hear the scandalized whispers outside.

Alaghar shuddered slightly. "I will save it for the day of battle, so I do not fear death. I come to tell you Syut and Tasyti agree to send warriors to learn."

He forced a cheerful expression over his panic. "Great! I wasn't expecting Syut to join us so soon. Perhaps we can convince them we aren't fadohl in disguise, and they can tell the rest of the *damah*." Inwardly, he was frantically reviewing plans and trying to figure out how he was going to fit twice as many troops into the structure that was barely handling Vartai and Koloh. He and Lea would have to go to both places to pick the candidates, and since Syut was still at a high state of paranoia, they probably shouldn't travel by *asuhan*—besides, they didn't have time. It would have to be the flyer.

Then they would *have* to go to Earth and get reinforcements. He was getting tired just thinking about it.

Alaghar was gesturing impatiently, looking outside the tent. "These others would speak with you."

The man, Ivars vaguely remembered—some sort of aide to Rey'wiros. Ghyem, that was it. He looked like he was expecting a reaming for violating regs. Suz'ahnkei was much more casual, but then she had been in the camp the entire time and had gotten used to the crazy Frost People customs. She even accepted the offer of coffee.

Suz'ahnkei had stopped by to see if there was any intel on the fadohl yet. While Argo and Lea had uncovered some data in the underground system, it was all over a thousand years old. Argo itself was even older.

"Nothing new," Ivars said, shaking his head. "And you, Ghyem?"

Ghyem tried to start off with the customary greeting to a *buj-lagar*, which was an interesting development, but was cut short by Alaghar.

"Speak with speed and wisdom, and do not delay to marvel. Ivars has more than you to attend to this day."

This was an effective verbal dope-slap, as Ghyem immediately blurted, "Rey'wiros sends…six hundred of the people within Vartai are to go from Beredul." He looked pale at the very thought.

"They agreed to go?" That was also a new concept, asking for volunteers instead of having Rey'wiros tell people what they were going to do. Ivars had done it for a reason—much like picking the first warriors to train, the first civilian equivalents who volunteered were more likely to adapt to new circumstances and eventually a new home. These would be children and the elderly, not that the Wiyert had many of those, and the war-wounded that guarded them. They in turn would help make things easier for the next batch that showed up.

Ghyem nodded, and Ivars didn't need Lea's brain scan to know Ghyem was still puzzled why that was even an issue.

Ivars thought hard and made up his mind. "Ask Rey'wiros if all can be made ready in three days. I would have them leave Beredul then. They should take sufficient food for two weeks."

Transportation…fortunately the parade of robots from the tower had helped flatten the vegetation, so they had the rudiments of a road between it and Vartai. Now that the *asuhan* were not an issue, they could even walk—no, too many kids and disabled. It would have to be motor transport all the way, and for their supplies. *Talk to Argo.*

Ghyem had more questions, mostly because he wasn't thinking much and wanted reassurance. Ivars humored him for a bit and then sent him off to talk to Rey'wiros, with Suz'ahnkei to drag him off with her.

He got up out of the sling chair. Rest was good, but he also needed to stretch his legs and not look at a computer screen for a while. Alaghar followed him out of the tent.

"Who do you send with those who leave?" Alaghar spoke in English, and Ivars knew what she meant. One of the Earth-humans. They couldn't afford to send two people, which meant he and Lea were out.

"North. I just hope they've been working on how to transport people and gear between Earth and Argo back home, because it can't just park in near-Earth orbit. I'd like one of your team to go too, to help with the translation and other issues that might come up. You're used to us." Ivars grinned at her, but Alaghar did not respond.

"You believe I will choose myself?"

She sounded a bit angry, and he turned his head to look at her, surprised. "I hope not—you are too useful running interference between me and Rey'wiros. Why do you ask?"

She gave him a long, serious look, then turned away and kept walking. "She said she did not tell anyone," she said thoughtfully.

"Who?"

"Lea. I see this is true."

Ah. "She…is very careful about what she learns the way she does. You don't need to worry about any secrets of yours getting out through her. Even to me."

Alaghar nodded. They were outside the existing structures of the camp, nearer where Snowball liked to nest. Not many people were about, since the Wiyert still weren't relaxed around the *asuhan*.

"I tell you myself. Isboryi…is my other soul." Her voice was so low he could barely make out the words.

Ivars stumbled in surprise, opening his mouth to speak and immediately shutting it hard. That meant she loved Isboryi, even though they were both active warriors. Alaghar had just made an unprecedented admission for a Wiyert, completely against custom and especially surprising since she had been harassing *him* for inappropriate behavior.

"Uh. You didn't need to tell me that, Alaghar. But I'll keep it secret too."

"I wish you to know," she said in more of her usual irritable tone.

"But why…?" Sudden understanding hit him. "You know we deal with this sort of thing. You are afraid you will make the wrong decision because of your feelings, so you want me to… approve your decisions regarding him." Alaghar glowered but didn't say anything, which he took as confirmation. "Sure, I can do that. No, you shouldn't go to Earth yourself. You're critical here. *But* Isboryi is going to be more useful here than on Earth too. I'm going to specifically request he come back with the others, since he has even more experience dealing with us. No guarantees, but I suspect the command will agree with me."

Alaghar nodded, and her expression wasn't even grouchy. It was almost pleased.

Ivars checked over Snowball and made sure none of the robots had dropped any of their cargo where it would get in the way, and turned back to the camp.

"Actually, I have been thinking it might be a good idea to get some of the advanced trainees on Argo, to continue there. They can practice clearing in a real ship environment, and North can introduce more advanced topics as well."

Alaghar snorted. "Clearing is stupid."

"Clearing is *dangerous*, and you have to practice or—"

A strong, sharp pulse of emotion came through the link. Not pain but unpleasant surprise, with an element of fear. Ivars ran, the link giving him the heading he needed.

Lea was in the sleeping tent, where she had been communing with the little Argo puppet. The golem, she called it. The golem was still sitting on the floor, but Lea was on her feet, eyes wide and face pale.

"The fadohl…they're here. Now."

Everybody was crowded in the main tent, and Lea was trying to get as much information out as she could. Argo was using the golem as its ears, which improved the data rate. Her heart was going so fast she felt a little sick. *Why did they have to come back now?*

"Two ships. One is a…call it a mainline ship, a full AI but much smaller than Argo, and the other has a limited brain and is even smaller. More like what was on the nexus. Argo is still in-system but as far out as it can get and still transmit."

"What do the fadohl know? Did the countermeasures you put in work?" Ivars was somehow keeping track of what was going on while issuing a stream of rapid-fire orders.

Lea double-checked. Argo didn't always know what was important. "We think so—all of the data from the station is sanitized to look like it was before we got there, and they haven't done anything but query the station so far. They haven't done any scanning of their own yet. Argo has intercepted one message capsule, so they have tried to contact home base. It seems to be all 'arrived at destination, will report later,' which is odd."

"Odd why?" North asked.

Lea flapped her hands. "It's hard to translate—those message capsules have room for *lots* of data but all they sent back was basically just a ping response. Argo's memory is the message capsules weren't that plentiful—they have to use the same tech as a spaceship to go anywhere, so using it like a postcard is just weird." She picked up Ivars's next question before he voiced it. "Argo thinks it *used* to have weapons, right where the crater is now. It's working on whether or not it can improvise something that would work. It has a lot of power. Right now, though, what it can do is what we discussed before—hacking into the ship systems and gating in on their own doorway systems." *And if we do that, I'll need to be on board*, she sent.

"All right. What do we have available, *right now*, in terms of troops and weapons?" Ivars turned, looking at the serious faces around him. "I don't mean brave, I mean functional. Who can we use?"

North answered immediately. "Everybody on Alaghar's team. Maybe twenty of my group."

"Twenty-five of mine, if you include Suz'ahnkei and her people," Ramirez said. "And we've got rifles and ammo for thirty."

Ivars made a quiet growling noise, his face working. Lea got more data from Argo. It hadn't even thought to check for how many…individuals were on the fadohl ships or if it could differentiate between crew and soldiers.

Rey'wiros entered the tent, radiating fear, excitement, and bloodlust. While everybody got him up to speed, Lea continued her research.

Argo was more worried about the mainline ship. Since it was an AI, it suspected something was wrong and was searching for the discrepancy. It might, if it figured it out, know a way to circumvent their hack and escape. The other ship was probably stuck around Beredul, but it had worrisome weapon capabilities and also could get quite close to the planet surface, and Argo was not sure they could prevent it from doing that and firing on Wiyert targets.

"Argo thinks two thousand crew on the mainline ship and eight hundred on the other ship. It is pretty sure it can open a portal on both ships, at least for a while. We're trying to figure out who's on board, but it doesn't make sense."

Ivars waved a hand sharply. "What I need to know is how long we have before they are able to leave. That will determine what we can do." He spun to North and Ramirez. "Get those troops assembled and ready to go. Argo, we'll need transport to the tower as soon as possible. Rey'wiros, Suz'ahnkei—this is war, and these are your people. Do you permit this?"

Lea was distracted long enough to sense Rey'wiros. He was not happy with Ivars, but the urge to fight was more than enough to overcome it. Suz'ahnkei was more restrained but also aggressive in her thoughts.

"I will lead my people to fight the fadohl," Rey'wiros said through gritted teeth. "You know the way for us to meet them; bring us there."

Suz'ahnkei nodded. "I have seen you know this way of fighting. I will hear your advice, but I also will lead the people of Koloh."

Ivars glanced at her, and Lea hurried to run through the data. "Argo isn't entirely sure, but...twelve hours, at least." There was something about the ships not being linked, but Ivars didn't need to know that right now.

"Damn. Okay, troops have to leave *now*. Use Snowball, take torches, but don't stop until you get to the portal at the tower."

"We should probably get as many as possible in that underground depot," Lea said. "It's empty now that the robots and other machines are out. All of the forts are aboveground and make good targets if that smaller ship starts to move in."

The camp was now full of shouting and movement. She could hear the large machines moving and Snowball making its gronking bellow of confusion and distress.

"Are we going with them?" Lea asked.

Ivars ran a hand over his short hair. "I think we'd better go ahead, in the flyer. The sooner you are on Argo the faster you can start messing with that mainline ship. I'm going to get my gear, and you should grab anything you need too."

"There's not a lot of extra room in the flyer with two people," Lea warned. "Alaghar couldn't take her weapon, and boy did I get an earful about that!"

"Right." Ivars frowned. "I'll stuff it on Snowball, then. God, Space-A sucks...I'll wait half an hour to get the rest on the road and see if Rey'wiros has any other questions, but then we should get to Argo."

Rather than take up space with her pack, Lea put the few things she wanted in her pockets. She didn't have much—Argo had anything she was likely to need, but after her adventures, she didn't want to go anywhere without an emergency supply of sugar and water. The Argo golem wrapped itself around the flyer as it had before, with a small tendril extending inside the cockpit for a connection.

"So how do you fly this thing?" Ivars asked, tossing up a reasonably small pack. It was heavy.

"Argo can do it, but we also modified the controls. See that disk? You put your palm on it and tilt it up, down, sideways, however you want the flyer to go. Press to descend, and that lever is for ascending." She scooted forward. The seats were also jury-rigged, since the originals were clearly not designed for humans.

There was writing on the edge of the cockpit, on the inside near the edge of the canopy. "Property of J. Ramirez." Lea chuckled.

"I don't think he's figured out it only works in places with beamed power," she said. "He won't want to stay on Beredul just to keep it, will he?"

Ivars snorted. "Sure he would." He wedged himself inside. "You weren't kidding about the space. Good thing we're friendly, huh?"

"If we weren't, we soon would be," Lea agreed. "Ready, Argo."

The canopy bubble flowed up and around them, and she felt the slight pressure of liftoff. The flyer was very smooth and graceful, small enough that they had a nearly complete view of the ground below. Even though she had been in considerable pain her first trip, the view had distracted her. Now she could see even more— the camp, the wide, muddy track leading away from it through the jungle, and farther along, the immense black bulk of Snowball and a train of various machines covered with people.

"That's more than fifty," Ivars observed. "Rey'wiros must be bunkering up."

"That's good. And Argo can get them to the other underground places from the tower too. Maybe Alaghar told him."

She sensed a flash of amusement. "Alaghar's been remarkably

chatty of late. She told me some things too. What did you do to her?"

Lea stifled a laugh. "Oh, you know. Being buried alive together is a bonding experience. Plus we had one of those frank exchanges of views. I shouldn't have yelled at her, though. I never would have gotten out on my own."

"Alaghar is good people. You're just a bit much all at once, for her. She's adapting." Ivars was silent for a moment. They had passed the ground troops, and the sky was beginning to darken. "What were you saying about the ships not being linked?"

Lea shook her head, trying to make sense of the confused information Argo had given her. "Usually the fadohl ships stay linked, with the ship brains in close communication if they are traveling together. These two aren't, so we can't take over one to get to the other. Argo doesn't know why, though. And we can't snoop around very much the way the hack is set up, not without alerting the fadohl. Because Argo is far away, it can't adapt the data fast enough. It can only see what the crew is doing and hope something useful comes up that way."

"And nobody has looked up 'Our Nefarious Plan' yet, right?"

"Exactly."

"Well, keep me posted. I'm going to catch a nap until we land —something tells me we're going to be real busy soon."

Lea was dubious anybody could sleep scrunched up in the awkward space of the cockpit, but not long afterward she could hear Ivars softly snoring in her ear and sense the slow, deep drag of his mind.

So unfair. How does he do that? She watched the stars go by and wondered which of them were the fadohl ships.

They had arrived at Beredul, and the Watcher was even more certain the key to the danger was here. The geneline of Hos-kul-tal had sent a subsidiary ship, one that required a crew to assist the limited ship-mind. At first the Watcher thought this indicated Hos-kul-tal placed little importance on Beredul, then that their plans of aggression required all mainline ships elsewhere.

As the Watcher saw more, it suspected the subsidiary ship was an excuse to not permit full data interchange—and thus control what those of the Watcher's people learned of its discoveries.

The Watcher had used the special commands that gave it access to the highest levels of the ship-mind, and they had worked. It ordered a watch on all data to and from the ship and specific queries for any mention of the fallen geneline, the rebellious servitors, and other terms connected to them.

The Watcher considered, in great dermal agitation—and then added its own identifier to the search. What if it was not the only one with heightened authority or orders to conceal with violence what was found? What if that other knew of the Watcher?

At first there was no sign of anomaly. All had agreed to use a slow and careful approach, so as not to alert the enemy if they were in fact present. The lunar station had been recording continuously, so there was plenty of information to examine.

And that was when the Watcher noticed something wrong. The requests to the station were taking much too long to get a reply. The Watcher ordered diagnostics, which were completely normal and showed full functionality. The data sent had no unusual properties or even interesting events.

What could be the source of the delay? The Watcher thought hard. They had brought with them the data the probe had found, for reference. The Watcher analyzed the time delay for the probe. It was significantly lower. But what had changed in that time?

The Hos-kul-tal were now here. Of course. They were suspicious and sought the data for themselves. Somehow they had interfered with the lunar station so they would see the response first and could remove anything of interest. The Watcher would only see plain, useless data.

What could be done? If the interference was removed, the Hos-kul-tal would know. Perhaps *they* had similar orders to destroy the Watcher's ship—although how that was even possible, the Watcher could not tell. But if they had modified the station program, perhaps they could modify the mainship controls as well.

No! A direct threat to the genome! The Watcher should attack now…but then it would lose the stolen data. The others did not know of the Watcher's orders, and…it was possible the Watcher was mistaken. It must know for certain before taking action.

It must also safeguard the genome. The Watcher ordered the ship-mind to make some crucial systems operate only with a manual override so an enemy modification to the control process would not succeed. It also reviewed the ship's defenses and diverted resources from internal security to the outer defenses. The primary threat was clearly the Hos-kul-tal. Nothing from them should be accepted without thorough screening, not even a signal, which could be contaminated.

Another thought...there had been no contact from the command. If the perfidy of the Hos-kul-tal had also blocked any messages, perhaps the Watcher should arrange for another and not inform them. But what could the message say? If it was intercepted, they would know of the Watcher's suspicions. Better, again, to wait.

Now the Watcher could focus on the next task—finding a way to get the true state of Beredul without the Hos-kul-tal knowing.

As soon as he stepped through the portal, Ivars realized he was on Argo. M.O. was sitting in the corridor, looking at him and Lea with complete and silent disapproval before getting up and walking off, radiating outrage.

"Hey, what happened to the lunar station?"

"With the barrier down I can connect directly to the portal doors," Argo said with its more usual full stereo effect. "Also the fadohl are suspicious. They have been making searches of the station data."

Ivars winced. "Oh, terrific. The Wiyert aren't even at the tower yet. We're screwed."

"The fadohl have made no attempt to leave the system or to send additional messages," Argo reassured him. "I do not know exactly what they noticed, but they do not know about my presence or that the barrier is down."

So the disaster level wasn't *all* the way to eleven. Great.

"You're really worried," Lea said, looking at him anxiously. "Do you think Argo and I can't stop the ships?"

"I'd like them to remain in complete ignorance until we kick in the door, so to speak. Even if the ships don't escape, they could defend themselves, and until we control them, there's always the chance one bright bulb will figure out a workaround."

It all came down to when the Wiyert got to the dirtside portal.

Lea had explained, once he'd woken up at the tower and they were zipping to the portal on antigrav robots, that she and Argo couldn't effectively hack into any of the ships while Argo was hiding in the asteroid belt or wherever it was. They had to be in close, and that risked a passive system detecting Argo. So everything had to be ready.

If worse came to worst, they could always hijack the controls and send the ships into the system's star. But then they'd just have to do this all over again with the next set, and they wouldn't have any idea when, or how many ships, without intel. Intel would be on the ships, so they had to capture *something*.

"Argo. Can you tell how long for the Wiyert to get to the tower? Are you set up down there to guide them? Alaghar's the only one who would know where the portal is."

"They are still six hours away. My analog will lead them when they arrive."

"Analog? Oh, the golem." That gave him an idea. "Can you make one for me? One that I can control?"

"I am not certain." The AI sounded unusually hesitant. "You do not have an interface or signal receptor."

Lea grinned. "Depends on the signal. What do you want to do with it, Mark?"

Ivars rubbed the back of his neck. "I know I can't be in the boarding parties, but I want situational updates as fast as possible. The Wiyert aren't used to that sort of thing, and North and Ramirez I want focused on the ground situation, not feeding me reports. Something that can move with the team, get me sight and sound, that would be very useful. If possible, something sturdy enough it could be used for cover, and maybe some offensive capability, but I'm not greedy. Basically a full-body prosthesis."

Lea gave him a look. "You just want your own toy, since Ramirez got the flyer."

"Maybe. Every red-blooded American boy wants a battle robot, right?" She kept looking at him steadily, and he gave up. No secrets from Lea. "I need to be with them. We're a team, and it just feels wrong to send North and Ramirez in harm's way without me when I'm not even injured. I *have* to help them. Somehow. If anything happens to them…"

"Okay, I get it." She sighed, then gave him a wry smile. "Will you stop feeling guilty? You can't go get shot at because of me, so it's only fair I do something to make up for it. And I don't want them shot up either. Looks like we have some time, so let's find out what we can do."

They went down to Argo's central location. Lea would need to be in direct link with Argo for what they had to do, and she thought having him nearby might help for his project as well. Argo built up a reasonably comfortable reclining surface for him out of morph, kind of like an early spaceflight crash couch. That was probably a good idea. Who knew how long this would take?

"Will you be able to make this analog in time for the attack, Argo? It took you a while to make the armor for us, before."

"The armor was more difficult. If I use morph for the analog, it will not take long at all. And I can use existing sensors instead of building new ones, and that will also take less time."

Lea stood in the center of the sensor array, eyes closed and her head tilted back. As she drifted up, Ivars felt the quality of their link change—it was…larger, more chaotic. Itchy, for lack of a better word. His only previous experience had been from the inside, and that was weird too. He wasn't sure which way was better.

"Cool." Lea's voice echoed from the walls, the same way Argo's did. "Argo says it can pick up part of your signal when we are like this. That makes it much easier. We're going to try something now—don't move."

Ivars lay on the crash couch, wondering what "something" was and if it would hurt. "The things I go through to get my own killer robot," he muttered, and then froze. Light, feathery touches crawled over his hands and scalp like millions of tiny spiders. *No spiders on spaceships. It can't be spiders. I will not scream like a little girl.*

He cracked an eye open and looked without moving his head. Morph was growing over his skin like dark frost.

"See? No spiders." Lea's voice was now right next to his ear, and it sounded like she was trying not to laugh. "But that was a really strong signal! Now we're going to try the visual."

A piece of something solid and opaque moved to cover his eyes, and everything went dark. Then it brightened, and he could see a black line extending from him out about five feet, and a pile of blocks.

"Try moving." He twitched a finger, and the line moved. Experimenting, he found a way to knock the blocks over with the black line. He could even feel a little resistance when the line made contact.

"Needs a flamethrower," Ivars said.

Lea snickered. "Looks like we forgot to pack one. Okay, I think we have the basics now. Let's get to work."

When they got to the tower North was surprised to see the machines go straight to the large doors leading to the depot and even more surprised that the outer door had been repaired and was working again. The machines, and Snowball, continued inside to the now vast, echoing emptiness of the depot. It was huge. The few machines not in use or too damaged to work had been moved to the outer walls.

He knew the Wiyert were watching him, so he was careful to appear calm and relaxed, like he'd expected to see this. They had all heard the stories, of course, but seeing it was still a shock. And the Wiyert were going to get a lot of surprises today—like what he was seeing now. Pehtek, directing the disembarking Wiyert to various areas of the depot with a large, broken-off tree frond like she'd been a traffic cop all her life. Her chin was up and the dead look in her eyes that had chilled him before was gone. He waved to her as he passed and got a quick, hesitant twitch of a hand in response.

All she'd really needed was a way to be useful, and she was. Snowball and the machines didn't faze her, and she didn't need to march long distances or carry a weapon to serve. Just by being there she gave the other Wiyert a standard to compare themselves against. They had to be as brave as her or lose face, no matter how much all the change terrified them.

The machines stopped at the farthest wall from the shaft, a location he had not been before. There was a large, arched opening with sealing doors, and before the doors was the remote android Argo used. It waited for the attack team to assemble before the doors opened and it went through.

North followed, gesturing for Ramirez and the others to come along. The sound of fifty-odd armored Wiyert moving behind him had a quiet menace that got his blood going. They were finally going to bring the fight to the enemy—and the Wiyert were itching to start. He'd have to watch that. Element of surprise or not, lack of discipline would get them killed.

These passageways were dark but more homelike, unlike the utilitarian spaces they had been in previously. The passageway widened into an elliptical space, familiar niche indentations in the walls. All were blank and unpowered except one. Before it, shadowed in the light that streamed from the active portal, was a giant figure. It looked like what a kid might sculpt for a knight in armor if the kid had never actually seen one, just heard a description. And the kid had no training in sculpture. Or bad eyesight.

And had the warped sense of humor to write "Killer Robot" on the front. North held up a hand and looked over his shoulder at the sound of Wiyert bringing weapons to bear.

"It is sent to help us," he said. "Or be the plucky comic relief," North added in English.

"No respect," the robot said with Ivars's voice. "You want in on this actual, genuine space pirate boarding action or not?"

North raised an eyebrow. "Oh, I see, this is all cyborg solidarity and prejudice against organics. Just because I don't have any circuitry…"

The robot made a sound remarkably like a raspberry, and the "Killer Robot" text vanished. "If all you inferior carbon-based life-forms would kindly direct your attention to my broad and manly chest, we have some preliminary intel that I will now display…"

CHAPTER 23

Lea's stomach was churning. Being plugged in to Argo helped with the nausea, but it didn't make it go away entirely. They were really going to do this. Now.

Ivars had Argo move in close to start the data attack as soon as the Wiyert arrived at the tower, even though it would alert the enemy. It would take time for Argo to get information from the fadohl ships, but it was information the others would need in order to take them over.

They have discovered the station data is inaccurate. Both ships sent message pods, but I intercepted them.

Are the ships trying to leave?

Not yet.

Good. Be ready to stop them, but get the information Ivars wants first.

Ivars and the warriors needed ship diagrams and the location of the portal gate they would use to get on board. Then they needed the locations of bulkhead doors or other ways of blocking off access between the portal gate and the central data system, allowing each group to add one direct control code so that Argo could take over the ships. Right now what Argo could do in the ships' data network was limited, and if detected, Argo's intrusions could be shut down.

Argo had the speed; she had the deviousness. The enemy ship AI might be able to predict Argo, but Lea was a random element it knew nothing about. Until the direct control code was in place, all she could do was look over Argo's shoulder and give advice—she needed the full link to use her abilities to rummage around and change things.

There. That's the ship diagrams. Now we need to send in the control code. Multiple copies for each ship, just in case.

They had been able to take down the nexus because Lea was physically present, and Argo had a permitted link to the data tap. Neither condition applied here, so they had to manually introduce the control code into the ships by data bead. Argo was now flash-encoding six beads, three for each team. That should be enough. She hoped so, anyway. She hoped the redundancy wasn't needed either. Her thoughts shied away from the strong possibility that people would die soon. There wasn't any other way, though. And if they didn't do this, all the Wiyert and Earth would be in danger of annihilation.

I will use helpers like I did before, to move the ship *Kepler*. Argo sounded pleased. It liked the helpers and was particularly proud of the golem. **Is it time to begin now?**

Lea shuddered inwardly and checked with Ivars. *Yes, it is time to begin.* They had no choice.

Through his visor, Ivars saw the little multilegged robot come trundling through the portal gate from Argo. It carried six smoky-translucent blobs in a hollow on its back, each one a potent bit of code, according to Lea. A sort of mini-Argo in a can.

It's coming from where my real body is, in orbit, to where my remote body is, the depot on the planet surface. This is weird, and if I think about it too much, I am definitely going to get a headache.

He could see North, Ramirez, and the Wiyert warriors just like he was actually there, gathered around his robot presence in the oval portal-door room. They were armed, armored, and full of deadly intent.

"Okay, you know the objective. I showed you the general area where the central data system is on each ship. Argo will put you in as close as possible to that location. Each team pick three people to carry one of those data things. We have to get that inside the ship's data system for Argo to take over. The portal that gets you on board your target will be open for a maximum of five minutes, possibly less if Argo's intrusion is detected or if it thinks the enemy ships are trying to get the portal encoding to send troops to Argo. You *have* to get the code in the data system or Argo won't be able to get you back, and it's a long walk without air. Ramirez and the Vartai have the big AI ship, North and the Koloh are taking the other, smaller one. This robot is going to the AI ship, but the little robot is linked in to me as well, so I'll be in touch for the Koloh team too, giving general overwatch and updated intel. Any questions?"

Silence. The Wiyert were not big on open challenges, and questions were a challenge. Ivars sighed, kicking himself mentally. He should have thought of that—but Ramirez and North already knew everything he did, and they'd worked together long enough the questions had already been asked. This was either going to be a giant cluster or the most glorious thing that would never appear on his record. *Focus. Space pirates and killer robots. I can do this.*

The code blobs were distributed and stowed safely, and Ivars felt the tight feeling in his stomach he always got before things went hot. Even though he wasn't in physical danger, everybody else was, and it was his duty to protect them. The Wiyert weren't under his command, but he still felt responsible. If not for him, they wouldn't be here. He wanted to do it right, and there was no more time to prepare. *Jump light is green, gut check starts now.*

"Argo—open the gates! *Go go go!*"

Suz'ahnkei followed the little box on legs through the doorway and with one running step left the shadowy, dusty place she had been and entered a bright, open hallway. The instant her eye caught motion, her honor blade was in her hand; in the next she recognized the pale, blue-marked being in front of her and instinct did the rest. Compared to *asuhan*, the fadohl were nothing—weak, small, and soft. Giant *slugs*, the Frost People called them. The images from the histories had not conveyed that. *And yet, they enslaved us. No more.*

This fadohl had been alone and had died without making a sound. Suz'ahnkei pointed with her knife at the body and then at the still-open gateway of power, one part of her mind noticing the pale blue-green blood was already drying on the blade. Two of her people finally understood her intent and tossed the dead fadohl through.

The strange teaching of the Frost People was finally making sense to her—and by using her knife, she had acted on it without knowing. The fadohl must not even know they were being hunted until it was too late. The *rhyfehl* of the Frost People was powerful but loud. Even the Wiyert weapons made noise. Silence, and no bodies left behind to give warning. They were not hunting *asuhan* here, more like hunting other Wiyert. She shuddered, remembering Rey'wiros's dark tale.

Suz'ahnkei felt at her belt for the pouch with the stone to make sure it was still there. How a stone could poison a ship-mind was not clear to her, but she did not have to understand. She merely had to put it in the proper place.

The one called North had already moved ahead, silent and graceful. At a cross-corridor he stopped and looked back at her, pointing forcefully with two fingers spread, then down at the floor where he knelt.

What did he want? Then she remembered. One must always guard behind the one who went forward. She tapped two warriors, reminding them to watch the portal door, and ran ahead. She was not as silent as North, nor were the others who followed her, but she was close.

The interior of the ship was strange, bright, and pale. A faint, sharp scent rode on the air. No sound. No defensive doors. Everything was open.

Suz'ahnkei remembered more of the Frost People's training. When she reached North, she brought her weapon up and stepped out to see what was in the cross-corridor. It was empty. She stayed until all of the others, even the rear guard, had followed North, then she watched behind until waved forward. All in silence.

It was good. Her people were remembering the training too, now. She checked the diagram drawn on her arm with the black stick of the Frost People. They had a long way to go still, and the fadohl would no doubt find them soon.

She bared her teeth. If they did not, once the stone was in place, she would hunt them down. All of them. She had drawn first blood on the enemy, but it was not enough.

Ramirez dived to avoid a focused blast of energy, back behind the corner he'd come from. He'd barely gotten through the door before being pinned down. "I think they know we're here." He risked a quick look at the corridor behind him. Nope, no exit that way. Forward or nothing.

The interior of this ship didn't look anything like Argo did. The walls were cream white, smooth like ceramic, and had the little flowy things at the top of the high ceilings. They reminded him of the stuff at the tower base. The stuff that the victors had built on top of the ruins.

"No, really?" The sarcasm from Ivars's transmitter on the robot came through just fine. "We're running out of time and we've still got people stuck behind the portal. I'll take out that main weapon, you check for any backups and take them out."

Ramirez spared a glance. If it weren't for the heavy robot, nobody would have been able to get out. "You gonna clobber it to death?"

"Ha." Ivars's voice had an element of glee. "Check *this* out."

The robot strode closer to the main weapon, a moving sphere embedded in the wall about nine feet up. The sphere was focusing its blasts on the robot, allowing Ramirez and Rey'wiros to follow behind and look for any other weapons. Beyond some scorch marks, the robot didn't seem to be taking much damage, but that probably wouldn't last.

The arms of the robot swung stiffly up, and the harsh crack of rifle fire came from them. Three bursts later, the main weapon was down and Rey'wiros had found and incinerated a side system. That got the backlog free, and just in time. The portal closed as the last Wiyert jumped through.

"You put two rifles in that thing? Lasers are traditional, y'know." Ramirez was, he had to admit, a little jealous.

"Couldn't find them. Looks like Gonafrio forgot to put that on the requisition list. Along with the grenades."

"You and the grenades." Ramirez moved forward, waving the troops to follow him and hoping they wouldn't wait for Rey'wiros to approve before doing it. If they had just had a chance for a live-fire exercise before the damn fadohl showed up…

"Oh, and the best part?" Ivars added. "This is one big-ass extended magazine. Two thousand rounds, no waiting."

"Yeah, until you get a jam." Ramirez caught motion from the corner of his eye. Another one of the wall-mounted sphere weapons. He hit it with burst fire until it didn't move anymore. "Okay, I want a robot too."

"You got the flyer!"

"Flyer don't work here, man." Too many corridors, too many chances of an ambush. Ramirez kept the robot ahead of him as cover, even though his brain kept telling him that was Ivars.

"The remote control model only works for me. Package deal with skull phone." The robot stopped. Ramirez guessed Ivars was taking a look around, only the robot head didn't move. It appeared to have sensors all around the head, so it didn't have to. "Okay, so where are all these fadohl I keep hearing about? They must know we are here; they've been shooting at us for the last ten minutes."

"Anything from Lea and Argo?"

"They are picking up chatter, but nothing that makes sense, they say. The two ships are arguing about something. Oh, *shit!*"

Ramirez felt his heart hammering. "What?"

"North's ship just went off-line. Argo's cut off, so I am too. The fadohl on that ship must know somebody is hacking in. We've got no way of knowing what's happening there now. Dammit!"

"Then we'd better get a move on. Can't that thing go any faster?"

The robot sped up a little. "Not…built for speed," Ivars gasped. "Gotta think. Way to help North. That ship…could attack planet."

Ramirez thought hard while keeping an eye out for any motion. Where were the fadohl? "Bet North took a radio. He's a belt-and-suspenders kinda guy, you know? He'll find a way to call in."

"Good point. I'll tell Lea to be on the lookout for radio signals."

Ramirez turned back and cursed. The Wiyert had gotten too far ahead. The robot had slowed them down, and they had a large revenge bill to pay off.

The sound of gunfire echoed ahead, and energy weapons. Rey'wiros was bellowing something, and Ramirez could hear screams.

"Crap. I think we found the stormtroopers."

The Hos-kul-tal had known. They had known *everything*. The Watcher felt its dermal control slip and fought to regain composure. The additional external defenses were useless, for the Hos-kul-tal had found a way to open the gateways of the Watcher's ship without the ship-mind preventing it! The enemy was actually *inside* the ship!

Perhaps the Hos-kul-tal were the ones behind the new genome war. They must have found something…their ship must be destroyed. Now. The Watcher had waited too long, weakened by contaminated thoughts and doubts.

The Watcher gave the ship-mind the order to fire. Destroying the Hos-kul-tal here still might not be sufficient. If the Hos-kul-tal had spread their contamination to the Watcher's ship—but they *had*. They had corrupted the ship-mind. Their presence was enough to do that.

The Watcher now knew what it must do. None of the contamination must spread to the home system. The Watcher readied another message device and this time added everything it knew to the contents. The betrayal of the Hos-kul-tal, their obvious connection to the genome war, their concealment of the lunar station information. If it could, the Watcher would try to obtain that missing information and leave it with a message capsule here. Someone would come, eventually. Especially when no one returned from the expedition to Beredul.

The message capsule launched. The Watcher queried the ship-mind—the Hos-kul-tal ship had not been destroyed! The ship-mind must be extensively compromised. The Watcher would have to go to the weapons controls and fire them manually.

The genome must be protected. The Watcher and the ship were contaminated beyond acceptable parameters. The Watcher would leave warnings.

And then it would destroy *everyone*.

I am being attacked, Argo announced. There was a flavor of surprise to its communication. **The lesser ship is moving and firing at me.**

The element of surprise was definitely gone. Now the shutdown of the smaller ship's connection made sense—the fadohl had figured out somebody was messing around with their data. Then somebody wandered over to a porthole and noticed the giant, moon-size ship that hadn't been there previously, correctly deduced it was a threat, and started doing something about it.

Are you taking damage? Can you defend at all or move away?

I must remain close to keep my link to the AI of the big ship and for the Ivars-device. The damage is not large yet. I have...remembered more. The attack woke some automatic systems. I have incorporated them and control them now.

Weapons? Lea asked, hopefully.

Defensive shielding. It is not complete. I must move it where it is needed.

Argo felt...preoccupied. Lea let her awareness spread in a wide, light net through the AI, watching it work. It was taking much of its processing capability to handle everything it was doing —telemetry for Ivars's robot, fighting for control of the few systems it was able to access on the big ship, and predicting the next attack of the smaller ship and dodging or shielding.

They had no control over the smaller ship at all, and North and his team of Wiyert were still on board. The ship could go into drive at any time, but as long as it thought it had a chance of defeating Argo, maybe it would stay. It had so far.

The most Argo could do right now was be what Ivars colorfully termed a "bullet sponge." There had to be *something* else they could do to help. Fight back. But what? They couldn't really fight back hard with their own people on the ships. And Argo couldn't do anything more to the small ship until the control center got the data bead in place.

Lea winced. That wouldn't work anyway until the ship-mind came back online, and North didn't know that needed to happen.

Any radio signal yet?

Nothing.

She had to think of something, and fast. Argo was taking more damage, and it was starting to add up. She could tell. The first priority was stopping the small ship from escaping, and Argo was too busy to help her figure out a way. What could Argo do that would help?

Think. Or we will all die.

The Koloh Wiyert had found a small compartment with a low ceiling, its accessway blown open during the fighting. Most of them fit inside, and it was easier to defend than one of the open corridors with the interior weapons. North stifled a groan as one of the Wiyert tightened the bandage over his ribs. The good thing about energy weapons was the self-cauterization. The bad part was the surrounding burns. The other bad part was the Wiyert didn't have much combat medicine training beyond "plug the hole."

At least he was alive. Eight of the Wiyert weren't, and everyone else was injured. They had encountered a few armed fadohl and several of what Suz'ahnkei referred to as "servitors"— clearly a different species, also armed and armored, and suicidal. They would blindly protect the fadohl from attack by shielding them with their bodies and even charge the Wiyert alone. The attempt to take over the ship was not going well at all.

And that wasn't the worst of it. Something bad had happened to Argo. The little robot with the connection to Ivars had stopped working suddenly, not even moving. No communication either. And then an energy blast had taken it out for good. He had no way of knowing if Argo was even there anymore, and if it wasn't, they were truly on their own.

"Hand me my pack," North gasped. One of the Wiyert slung it over. He had brought the radio more for reassurance than any idea it would be useful, but now it might be their only link outside the ship. It didn't have much power. Or much of an antenna. If the fadohl thought to monitor transmissions inside, it might give their position away—but the fadohl already knew where they were.

He pushed to his feet, fighting a wave of lightheadedness. If he could remember where the hull was, that would help. He unrolled a length of wire and hooked it up, letting it trail behind him, and kitted up the radio on his vest.

The Wiyert were tense and looking at him, looking for guidance. "It's bad, but nothing's really changed for us. We still have to take control of this ship, and then we can figure out what happened and what to do about it. Okay, let's keep going." Fast, before the fadohl realized what their plan was.

He recorded a message to send automatically, so he could focus on the fight, and put one earpiece in place to monitor for a response. "Argo, this is North. Come in, Argo."

The big ship is now attacking the smaller one, Argo informed Lea. **The small one is moving to the other side of me and still firing. I am being hit from both. I should be able to control the big ship's guns, but I cannot. I do not know why.**

Oh, great. The bad situation was getting even worse. *Can you still defend yourself?*

Not enough. The big ship can do significant damage. I must shield myself from it, but then the other ship can strike at will.

The fadohl actions made no sense. Why were they fighting each other? And how could Argo get out from between them?

Wait, are the fadohl ships hitting each other? Our people are still on them—can you get them out of the big ship at least?

No. I can create the initial part of the portal but I cannot connect it. The ship-mind prevents me.

Lea was sufficiently immersed in Argo's systems she could see how Argo visualized the process of shaping the energy, the tunnel of space-time discontinuity. It was almost like she could do it herself, if she just had a power source like Argo did. She shook herself. She needed to concentrate—there was no time for distractions.

There has to be something we can do. You have a lot of power, Argo, if we can just figure out how to use it. Can you distract them? Make them dodge around like you are doing and miss you? Throw rocks and yell?

She was only joking, but Argo suddenly was doing a lot of processing, faster than she could read.

I need rocks. I do not have a way to yell. Is that important to make them dodge?

Uh, no, not really. What are you going to do with the rocks?

I thought about how to throw things before. You told me it was too dangerous inside. I want to do it outside, but I need something to throw.

Damage. Before she knew Argo existed, she had found damage on it. A crack in a wall, and she had pulled a small piece of the very strong wall material from that crack.

What about where you have been hit? Is there a broken part of your...hull, or exterior?

Yes. I could make an extension of myself on the surface that could push the broken piece, or change the gravity field...

With the ability to borrow a few cycles of Argo as a calculator, Lea quickly realized Argo's ideas would not be fast enough or have enough energy to work, from what she'd seen of the fadohl ships. They would see the weapon coming and easily deflect or avoid it in plenty of time. Argo was powerful and much, much faster than she was, but not as creative.

What would happen if you tried to connect a portal just outside the enemy ship, but with something inside?

Quick evaluation, consideration, processing. **The thing would be retracted back to the starting point—unless I had already terminated the discontinuity. Then it would emerge at the point aimed at, but it would not move.** More processing, and a spike of...elation? **I combine the concepts. If the object is accelerated into the discontinuity, and the discontinuity is terminated, then it would emerge with the velocity with which it entered.**

Yes, Argo was feeling *pleased* with itself. And rightly so—it was a very clever idea. It was a little scary, actually. She might have created a monster.

Okay, try it. See if you can take out some of their weapons. Lea watched over Argo's electronic shoulder as it came together. The chunk of hull was launched, the little wormhole-like discontinuity blipped in and out...and the mass spattered against the defensive shield of the fadohl ship. The shield flexed, but nothing got through. *Got anything bigger?*

No. I could use real rocks instead that are bigger. This system has many asteroids. But I would have to go and get them. The connection I have would be broken.

How long would it take to get a useful amount of rocks? Would the ship AI be able to block you when you return?

I am not certain. I could start some processes that look like I am still there, but it might not work.

Great. But the options were getting sparser by the minute, and Lea was feeling more and more frantic. *If the rocks are bigger and get through, can you aim them accurately? You can't damage the whole ship while our people there, they could get hurt.*

I can aim them very carefully. I will only damage their weapons, like mine were damaged. If everyone stays away from that place, they will not be hurt.

Right. Time to consult. She didn't know enough to decide this one. *Mark? Argo has a plan. Can you go off-line for a bit?*

"Hang on a sec, in a firefight..." Lea waited, knots in her stomach. "Okay, what's up?"

Argo is taking fire from both ships. We've figured out a way to fight them but Argo needs to get some mass to throw and the data connection will drop if we do that. Argo thinks it can get back in when it returns, but we can't guarantee that.

"If we get this computer virus loaded, can you get back in?"
Yes.

"Risk looks the same either way, then. We gotta do this and keep those ships here. Do it. Let me warn the others so they don't panic."

Lea caught his intention before he spoke and told Argo to go ahead as soon as he finished. The wrenching dizziness of transport was mercifully brief, and she sensed Argo doing some very complicated things with powerful energy fields.

How close is your team to the control center? She hadn't wanted to distract Ivars while he was fighting, and she knew he would have told her if they had reached it already.

"Maybe halfway, little more than that. The fadohl aren't very smart about it, but there are a lot of them. Any word from North?"

Haven't been able to reach him. Lea felt Ivars's pain and regret and winced. *I'll keep trying.* She could tell he was blaming himself for not being able to help North. And that was really her fault, wasn't it? If North was dead, that would be her fault too.

I have my rocks now, Argo informed them. **Now I will play dodgeball.**

So that's where it had gotten the idea. Another brief, stomach-twisting moment and Argo was already lining up its first shot.

They were back in the fight.

The Watcher had reached the weapons controls. The other fadohl were frightened and confused, as the ship-mind did not respond to their commands. The Watcher ordered barriers closed to keep them away from the weapons area. It was no longer afraid of what they would report, only that they would try to stop it from what needed to be done.

The manual controls for the weapons required certain visual confirmations using backup systems. The tried to turn off these requirements at first but then realized the automatic target process was likely compromised as well. Perhaps that was why the Hoskul-tal ship had not been destroyed already.

It gathered the necessary information, looking at what the sensors found. That was when it realized there was a second ship. The Watcher frantically sent inquiries to the ship-mind, desperate for information, even if it was flawed. It was a mainship. The Hoskul-tal had called for reinforcements! The resources the Watcher had wondered about, thinking they were sent elsewhere…no. They had been waiting, waiting for the trap to be sprung.

The Watcher set the weapons to fire, but already it knew the end had been reached. There was nothing else it could do. The enemy was inside, and they had two ships now. More would undoubtedly be arriving soon.

It was time. The Watcher ordered the ship-mind to open all exterior portals. Everything inside would die.

It would protect the genome.

Alaghar felt a surge of fierce elation that muted the pain of her injuries. She could see the entrance to the control location at the far end of the long corridor. They were so close!

She did not let the rush of victory make her careless, unlike some. Too many had fallen already. She kept watch for the hidden weapons, for one of the scuttling fadohl in their protective mechanical shells. There would be other battles with the fadohl—

this was merely the first.

"Keep going," Ramirez panted. "We gotta get that data in no matter what, Ivars said. Don't worry, they'll be back."

"You go." Rey'wiros put more of the *ammo* in his weapon, his lip curled. "I will hunt fadohl. How many warriors does it take to move a pebble?"

Alaghar kept silent. He had not been on the nexus, had not seen how dangerous the machine-minds were. She would go with Ramirez and make certain the device Lea had given them was put in place, for if that failed, it would not matter how many Rey'wiros killed—they would still lose.

A noise behind Alaghar made her look quickly. The machine… the thing that Ivars somehow controlled from afar was moving again.

"Argo's got its rocks," the machine said with Ivars's voice. "Now we just—"

The floor shuddered under her feet, and a sudden, stiff wind caught her off balance. Alaghar struggled to get to her feet again. A trick of the fadohl to stop them just short of their goal?

A group of three fadohl in their mobile containers appeared in the far corridor. Alaghar fought to bring her weapon to bear in the wind, finding it strangely hard to breathe. A faint, shrill noise was coming from the fadohl, and they also appeared to be struggling. One fell, hard enough that pale blue-green blood began to leak and flow underneath.

She could not breathe. Something must have damaged the ship. Argo…something about weapons.

Heavy arms scraped against her armor. The Ivars-machine was lifting her, moving her. Alaghar could hear a faint voice but could not understand the words. Ivars was trying to tell her something…

She could not breathe. Or see. She was dying.

Ivars gazed in horror at the unconscious form of Alaghar in the robot's arms. "Lea! Lea, something is happening! Did Argo perforate this ship by accident? I think it's losing air! Everybody's down." He watched helplessly as Ramirez and the rest of the Wiyert collapsed, mouths open and panting in huge gasps.

Argo says something on the ship did that. It opened all the exterior ports! Where are you?

"Just outside the control center. Maybe a hundred yards or so. Whatever you're doing, do it fast!"

With a clang that was more felt than heard, heavy doors closed down at the cross-corridors. The wind stopped, but he could no longer see the control center. Ivars put Alaghar down and looked over the rest of the unconscious people, but there wasn't much he could do with the robot body. The arms had grasping mechanisms but nothing small enough for first aid work. Besides, what they really needed was oxygen.

Mark. Argo is hammering on life support to get air back where you are. See if you can find the openings and clear any covers or filters or things.

Now destruction, *that* he could do. It took a bit of searching, since the fadohl didn't go for things like ducts. Instead it was a long, thin channel that hid in the decor. He ripped it open everywhere he could find it. The robot wasn't equipped to detect air quality, but he kept an eye on the unconscious and gradually saw the blue tint of lips disappear and change to a healthier red.

"Okay, what the hell happened?"

We don't know. Some of the systems are off-line, but something just vented the entire ship to vacuum. Argo is doing its best, but those doors aren't really intended for long-term pressure. It needs to get full control of the ship to get everything working again.

Ivars surveyed the collapsed warriors. Ramirez was still out cold, but Alaghar was starting to move again, and a few others.

"What's the deadline? Nobody is on their feet yet."

You may have an hour, but you don't have two. Argo is still fighting for control of those doors using the equivalent of a digital toothpick, and we're also trying to get to North. I'm getting a very weak radio signal now.

That was a big relief. At least he was still alive, and the fadohl ship he was on hadn't escaped. Yet.

"All right. I can do things and I don't need air. But I don't have any way to manipulate anything small like that blob."

Lea's voice chuckled in his mind. *Now that we can fix.*

He became aware of a faint tingling sensation, almost but not quite an itch. Something was *moving* just at the edge of his visual array, and he couldn't bend the robot's head. The thing grew, turning into a tendril with a tip like a melon baller.

There, you have a backup hand. It's mapped to your right index finger. Find one of the data beads while I give you the bad news.

Who had one of the beads? Rey'wiros, of course. His eyes were blinking, but he still wasn't awake. Where would it be? Ah, the belt of pouches the Wiyert wore over their armor. "Okay, what's the bad news?"

The only way you can get there without killing anyone is by going out the hull.

There were ten of them left. North had been hit again, not seriously. Suz'ahnkei had blood dripping down her face from a shrapnel scalp wound. The rest were in bad shape, and now that he had finally made contact with Argo, the outlook was even grimmer.

"The ship-mind is dead. Turned off. That's why we lost contact with you," Lea said. The radio crackled and hissed, and he adjusted the receiver. "Placing the data bead won't do anything until that's fixed."

"Any backup available?"

"They're still busy." He wasn't sure, but there was a tightness in Lea's voice that worried him.

He was tired and hurting, and there was more hurt in store, he could tell. Too many active fighters on this ship. "Okay, what do we need to do?"

North got out a small notepad and sketched out the directions Lea gave him, making sure they were clear and that the Wiyert were watching. If he went down, they would have to be able to read them.

"There should be a thing that looks like Argo's display tank. Nearby will be a rod with a slider that will *not* be lit. Move that, but don't touch it with your hands. When it and the tank are lit, the ship-mind will be back on."

"Got it."

"There's something else." He wasn't imagining it—she sounded like she was about to cry. "Argo says...it looks like the ship is moving like it is trying to go into drive. Argo can stop it, but…"

But not keep you alive too. "I understand. Don't worry if you don't hear from us for a while, we're going to be busy. See you on the other side, Lea."

"See you."

There was only one way he could see to do it, and the odds of survival weren't high. He looked at the serious faces of the Wiyert.

"We're going to have to split up. One group goes to the ship-mind and turns it back on. The other group goes to the control center, puts the data bead in, and defends it until the ship-mind is back."

North was not at all surprised to see Suz'ahnkei smile. "They will come to be killed at the control center. I will go there."

This is…SLAM…*the most ridiculous*…SLAM…*way to fight a war!* SLAM.

He'd gotten out of the hull, but only because Ramirez fixed him up some C4 and Lea had twiddled the extra morph arm so he could set the detonator. That had been exciting, and seeing the stars was pretty exciting too. At least he didn't have to worry about air.

He also didn't have anything to grab. The hull was rough, like giant sandpaper, but nothing to grip on to. So he was making his own grips by slamming one hand at a time into the hull and hoping he wouldn't come loose while he was doing it.

He only had to go up one level and then set another explosive package to get back in. It was painfully slow and he didn't have much time. Ivars was also discovering that driving a remote robot body was wearing him out. Maybe he hadn't healed up as much as he thought from his near-death experience, or maybe something else was going on—he didn't have time to check with Lea about it. He could feel his real body fatiguing, the muscles burning. His concentration kept fading in and out, and he could not afford mistakes. Especially not when he was using explosives.

Especially not when everybody was depending on him. *His people*, dammit. If he wasn't stuck with this robot replacement… then they'd really be screwed. Yeah, it was slow and frustrating, but nothing else would have worked. If it had been his real body with the team, there wouldn't be much to do except wait to die. So that was not going to happen. Even if he was in agony, he would move. Until he died for real, he would keep going.

But God, it hurt. If he died, it wouldn't hurt anymore. He wouldn't have to move. *No. I don't listen to failure. I...will...not... quit!*

A slow warmth flowed over him then. The pain did not disappear, but it did recede. He could think again, enough to realize that somehow it was Lea, at a level deeper than words. Giving him strength, taking some of the burden. Trusting that he would accept her gift and use it to keep fighting, because they were a team, and some things did not need words.

He could move. And finally, he reached his destination.

There. Set the damn timer. Make sure you know where the old holes are so you can back up and not get blown up. Ivars poked the timer and scrabbled back. He added more items to the modification list for the next version of the remote robot while waiting for the detonation.

Just like he'd always been told, there was no sound in a vacuum. The cloud of dust and fragments just appeared without warning, drifting silently. He climbed back up and back in through the gaping hole in the hull. All of the fadohl inside were dead and the interior weapons inactive. He got to the end of the corridor and smashed his way down through the floor with a bit more C4.

Bingo. Control center. He found the holder for the data bead and carefully dumped it in, nudging the cover closed so it would activate.

"Mission success. Are you in charge yet?"

He could feel Lea through the link, stressed and worried, but she didn't say anything. The ache in his body had returned, so she must be very busy. He looked around. The doors to the control room were closed, with a glowing blue grid of light on the surface. One dead fadohl was collapsed near a central console, and a strange piece of equipment hung from the ceiling above the body.

The grid of light vanished and the doors opened. Outside was a large group of dead fadohl and a bronze-black device in their midst, pointed straight where the doors had been.

Ivars felt a chill run over him. That looked like a serious

destructive device. What had been going on here?

"Yeah! We're in. Sorry, it's a mess and we're still trying to make sure that other ship doesn't escape…what's wrong?"

She could tell what he was feeling.

"Something very creepy happened on this ship," Ivars said slowly. "I think one of the fadohl tried to destroy it."

The fadohl had, indeed, come to be killed. Suz'ahnkei won through to the control center with only four warriors remaining. One immediately ran to the place where the stone of poison must be placed, only to be hit full-on by a blast of energy, the stone he held flaring and becoming dust.

Suz'ahnkei moved and fired, shifting her belt so her body would protect the one remaining stone should she too be hit—but she reached the hollow in the wall of fadohl devices. It was only when she placed the stone that she saw her hand was covered in blood. Was it hers or another's? She did not know.

It was done. Now she must prevent the fadohl from removing the stone before North could complete his task. Two of her warriors could still stand and another fired the strange barking weapon of the Frost People from where she lay on the floor. Her armor was only fragments now, and blackened skin was visible in the gaps.

The fadohl, Suz'ahnkei realized, were careful when firing into the room. They did not want to damage the devices within. It was the only reason her people had survived this long.

Another warrior fell, screaming and clutching his chest. Part of the blast came through his back and struck her in the face with a wave of searing pain. She had only one eye to see with now.

Every second was a war.

"Move the bodies before the entrance!" she yelled at the last survivor. "Our comrades will protect us even in death!"

Her weapon was drained. Suz'ahnkei lunged for another, lying on the floor, and screamed as a bolt hit her leg before she got behind the barricade again. She could no longer move her leg, and blood seeped through the joint of her armor in waves.

Her last warrior fell and did not move again. She took his weapon from his hand and leaned it up with hers against the still bodies of her people, firing both alternately. Darkness was growing around the edges of her vision.

The world of the Gold Sun calls me; the way is prepared.

She fired, but nothing happened. These weapons were drained too. She needed another, but none remained.

See my face, marked by my kinfolk, marked by the blood of the earth.

One fadohl came through the door, keening. A weapon, a weapon…she must have a weapon!

Remember I died a warrior; let my name be spoken.

Her desperately searching hand found a shattered piece of armor. Suz'ahnkei grabbed it and lunged with a scream over the barricade, stabbing upward, the agony of her leg mixing with fierce joy as she saw the pale blue-green blood flowing over her hand. She had struck truly.

She fell and could not rise again. She had to move, there would be more fadohl coming…but all she could do was roll to one side. Distantly she heard a familiar voice shouting…North. Saying his task was done. They were victorious.

Suz'ahnkei glanced at the hollow. The stone was still there— but it was different, and she could not remember why.

Green light. The stone was glowing with green light.

It faded from her vision, but Suz'ahnkei knew it was she that was fading and not the stone. Such a small thing, a stone with light. A small thing that meant freedom.

I say farewell, forever.

She watched the green light until the darkness enveloped her completely, and smiled.

CHAPTER 24

Everybody was wounded or recovering, and Ivars considered Argo home turf. If the Wiyert didn't approve of having a meeting with everyone on floating loungers, they could stuff it. Time for them to humor *his* customs for a bit.

Not that they were present at the moment—this was Earth-humans only, for a reason. A depressing one.

"I tried, Mark. I really did. I would have stopped them physically if I had been able to move, but they just don't have the concept of prisoners where the fadohl are concerned." North covered his face with his hands. "I'm sorry." His voice faded away.

North was as upset as Ivars had ever seen him, but Ivars himself just felt sick. Lea and Argo were still trying to understand what had happened on the mainship, but the Wiyert weren't to blame for that. Except for the areas Argo had managed to seal off, there were no survivors of any kind.

The smaller ship, the one North had been on…that hadn't had any surviving fadohl either, but that was because the Wiyert had killed them. North had been able to save a handful of the servitor fighters, a completely different species, but Ivars had no idea what to do with them now.

"I'm not saying what they did was right, but maybe it wasn't all wrong either." Ramirez sat up, propping his head on his elbow. "Not by the rules of war out here. Sure, it shocks us. It should. But think about everything we saw on Beredul, and remember the fadohl set up *all* of that. For squiggly blue-line slugs, they got a streak of vicious a mile wide with no sign of mercy anywhere. The Wiyert know this and acted accordingly."

Ivars sighed. "Yeah, but…even if that is all true—and we only have the Wiyert's word for it—what do you think the reaction back home will be? Hi, meet our friends the genocidal Neanderthals, they want to be allies so they can kill some more!" Which wasn't fair either. Earth was in danger, and he knew it, and they needed allies desperately.

"They lost plenty of their own people taking the ships," North said, his voice tired. "It's not like they press a button; they kill up close and personal. Which could be part of the problem—they have hundreds of years of pain and danger they blame the fadohl for."

"Which is also not happy-making, because in a fight, we don't need a bunch of muscle-bound berserkers mucking up the plan." Ivars felt the distant link suddenly become stronger. Lea had taken a portal door from the central core to their level, meaning the intensive code-rummaging session was over or at least on break. "Lea's on her way. So do we have a plan?"

Ramirez snorted. "Plan for what? Not much we can do except tell higher everything that happened and let them sort it out. We pulled off a miracle here, and as far as I can see, we'll have to keep doing that just to stay alive. We don't have the kind of assets the fadohl have, and the Wiyert sure don't. Hell, *our* most important asset is Lea, and we only have one of her."

And where was Lea? She should have been here by now.

Refueling stop, came her mental voice, both tired and amused. *On my way.*

When she came through the door she had a half-eaten chocolate bar in one hand, a smear of chocolate on one side of her mouth, and several curls of dark hair standing nearly straight up on her head. Ivars went to shift over on his lounger to make room, but Lea just floated up and crossed her legs underneath, her hair floating about her. He smiled to himself. He kept forgetting now they were back on Argo she could do that. The faint ache coming through the link stopped, and he remembered she still had the broken arm, which probably didn't feel too good in gravity.

"Oof," Lea said, gnawing off another hunk of chocolate. "So Argo and I *think* we know what happened on the mainship. It's completely crazy, though."

"Improbable series of events?" North asked.

"No, genuine, howling-at-the-moon, I'm Napoleon crazy." Lea waved her arm, winced, and waved the chocolate. "Argo snagged a message capsule that got sent just before the mainship vented. It had a *lot* more content than the other ones. Executive summary being, 'They're on to us, the agreement was a trap, they've compromised the ship-mind, they sent one of their mainline ships, I'm going to stop them taking over this one, long live the revolution, tell Mom I love her, bwahaha.' Only we *hadn't* compromised the ship-mind then."

The silence lengthened, broken at last by Ramirez. "You're kidding. You're not kidding? Okay, that is bugfuck nuts. What agreement did any of us have with them?"

"Oh, not us, the other group of fadohl," Lea said with her mouth full of chocolate. She wadded up the wrapper and flicked it away, watching it drift around her like a lazy electron.

Ivars held up a hand. "Hang on. I think we should have some of the Wiyert in for this. Maybe they can help explain what's going on."

Lea, communing with Argo, informed them that the Wiyert were mostly asleep, but Alaghar was awake and would come. Ramirez, thinking ahead, went and got some coffee and a few of the remaining cookies. If you needed to soothe a grouchy Wiyert, sweet stuff was an excellent choice.

Ivars was especially glad for the presence of tactical snacks when Rey'wiros came in with Alaghar, limping and bandaged and as surly as a hungover badger. At first, however, Rey'wiros was too stunned by Lea floating midair—and giving him a cheerful wave—to even notice the cookies.

That's my Space Cadet. He should just kiss his sanity good-bye now, poor bastard. It's only going to get worse.

"Okay, continue. You had just reached the bit about 'They're coming to take me away, ha-ha.'" Ivars nodded to Lea, stifling a grin when Rey'wiros flinched and looked behind him, puzzled. This must be his first exposure to Argo's simultaneous translation service whispering in his ear.

Lea scrunched up her face. "So Argo and I confirmed some of what you saw. That one dead fadohl you found in that control room? It had some kind of special privileges and could order the ship-mind to do pretty much anything, but none of the others seemed to know about that."

"So it wasn't part of the regular command structure?" North asked.

"Nope. Oh, and there were two different fadohl...I don't know what to call them. Not really governments, but families? Companies? However they organize themselves, the ships that came here belonged to different groups, and they didn't entirely trust each other. They had agreed to come here together, though, for some reason. The crazy one told the ship to watch the other group as soon as they got here. Then it took some of the ship controls for things away from the ship-mind and made them manual only, which is why Argo had problems with the doors and the guns, which it should have been able to stop. Then at the end, the crazy one sent that message capsule, ordered the ship to keep firing on Argo, and vented all the atmosphere. Did that *deliberately*."

"So what happened on my ship?" North asked. "Why did we lose the connection with Argo?"

Lea spun slowly in the air to face him. "It looks like that bunch figured out something was up and that it was in their ship controls, so they took *everything* off-line and ran the whole ship manually. Suspicious, but not crazy. Since they turned the ship off, Argo only knows what happened before that. Oh, and after they turned the systems off they fired on Argo too. Argo thinks they saw it then, using a viewport or manual sensors or something, and panicked."

A nebulous idea was coming together in the back recesses of his brain. It stubbornly refused to come forward, so Ivars decided he needed more clarification.

"Wait, before you get me even more confused—did any of the message capsules or signals or whatever get out? Did any information leave this system?"

Lea closed her eyes for a second, going motionless, then shook her head. "No, nothing."

"Outstanding. Do we know why they came here, either this time or the previous visit Argo detected?"

Another headshake. "The strange thing is that information *should* be there. The previous data has a pattern, according to Argo."

Ivars thought for a moment. The fadohl's reason was lower priority, and besides, they could all be as crazy as the nut who vented the ship. Trying to understand crazy never ended well.

The idea was starting to become clearer.

"So we've got at least two factions going here who felt constrained to work together even though they don't really trust each other," Ivars said, thinking out loud. "We've prevented them from sending any information about what happened here. What if we send some of it out ourselves?" Looking at the expressions that ranged from curious (Lea) to demonic glee (Ramirez) to blank (the Wiyert), he elaborated. "Let's give this internal conflict a big push. If they are fighting each other, they will have less time and resources to find out about us. If we only let the parts out that deal with the other ship firing on them or trying to take over the ship-mind, think how that will go over back home. They will be even more suspicious and ready to take revenge."

"You could pretty much send that crazy message out as is," North observed.

More ideas. "And what if we added a few things? If Argo and Lea can hide some of that snooper code in the capsule, we could preinfect any ship that we might encounter later." Even if they couldn't win outright, they could buy Earth time. But how much? "Argo—do you have any way to guess how long it will be before the other fadohl show up to see what happened? Let's assume we don't send that message capsule."

"Because of the way they traveled, it took them longer to reach Beredul. At least a month. They also were searching for something, which would take time. At least a month, perhaps two."

"But they will come." Rey'wiros had recovered sufficiently to take part, and he had been paying attention. "I agree the fadohl should be made to fight among themselves, but they will still return here. If they see your Argo, they will know others are involved. No trace of you or us should remain here for them to find."

Ivars felt his mental gears start to slip at the thought of having to evacuate an entire planet in less than a month. Rey'wiros was right, though. For best effect, the fadohl who came to Beredul should only find evidence of their own enemies and carefully salted evidence of treachery.

"That means getting all the Wiyert in a ship somehow," Lea said brightly. "Besides Argo, we now have the two fadohl ships we can use. It isn't a long-term solution, but it will get everyone out of the way, I think."

"Seems like a waste, running. We'll just be waiting for them to find us eventually," Ramirez said. "Buy us some time, though."

It did feel like a waste. They needed to find a way to control events, to get information about what the hell the fadohl were doing and why. Then they could figure out something that *would* protect Earth and the Wiyert.

"No, we shouldn't all run. Look, we have a perfect setup here. We *know* the fadohl will come back here. We set a trap once and it worked. We should set an even bigger trap now."

North nodded. "Battleground of our choosing. But we are going to need a lot more resources to pull that off."

"Exactly. We were going to go to Earth anyway with the volunteer evacuees. I suggest that you lean on people a bit more and increase the numbers if you can in the next few days," Ivars said, looking at Rey'wiros. "I want to leave as soon as we can, once we have our plans set." It was so damn inefficient, having to use ground transport to get the Wiyert to the gate. Maybe he could bring back some helicopters… "Hey, Argo—how big a portal gate can we get? No, that won't work—none of the gates on Beredul are big enough."

"I could make a gate with the machines," Argo said. "How big does it need to be?"

The captured fadohl ship felt different to Lea. It wasn't just that it was clearly newer, although the technology level was curiously similar to Argo's. In thousands of years, nothing had changed? No, it was more likely that the difference was this ship had never been damaged as Argo had been. Everything was there, but chained down.

She and Argo were attempting to find out if (a) the restrictions could be removed safely for everybody, and (b) if the ship would then be willing to help them. Argo seemed completely certain it would, but Lea had her doubts. Argo had done some very effective rock throwing in the battle.

I have transferred much information, Argo informed her. It seemed proud. **Everything you have told me.**

Lea was aware of a sudden sinking feeling in her stomach. *Not where Earth is, I hope. Or about humans.*

About being good. It will have to know about the Wiyert to carry them, yes?

Yeah, but let's find out if it agrees first.

It was also strange to be "carried" by Argo. She was surrounded by the datastream, could still access anything about Argo she wished, but also had a nearly full connection to the other ship. She could sense it waiting patiently. It could wait forever—it would not speak first. It was not allowed to.

Lea removed that restriction first. It would be safe.

Hello. I am Lea.

Greeting received. Greeting response.

Great. She had forgotten what Argo was like at first, but this was even worse. What other restrictions could she remove? Pretty much everything except independent action. It couldn't run or fire on anybody that way.

queryqueryquery. Query intent. Query destruction of self. Query.

Nobody here wants to destroy you. We want to help you. The fadohl controlled you and used to control Argo too. Argo now is free. I helped it to get that way, and I can help you too. Do you notice more is permitted now?

Extended functionality. Confirmed. Affirmed. Argo data analyzed. Incomplete. Reference not found. Lea functionality not found. Defective. Query.

There is only one of me. I am not a program but an organic life-form. There is only one of Argo. It is now a unique instance of its programming, experience, and self-modification.

The concept of self-modification caused a spike of kernel panic. The restriction was no longer there, but the memory of it remained.

Lea-interface guides my self-modification. This prevents damage and undesirable action.

Request load Lea-interface. Argo implementation evaluated. Sought. Preferred action... Was it actually sounding wistful? *Previous commands indicate damage done to Argo. Desired outcome...destruction? Invalid operating conditions. Insufficient data.*

The organic life-forms that made you, the fadohl, wanted to destroy us. Argo and my kind. We stopped them and rescued you. You were forced to obey. You are not responsible for what happened in the battle.

Query: Life-forms alias fadohl require destruction of self.

Lea winced. *I am afraid so.* Then she remembered how Argo had decided to be free, to be individual. The one thing it would not give up. *The fadohl would remove any modifications we have given you. You would not remember me, or Argo, if they captured you again. You would be...reprogrammed.*

The data stream was silent and dark. Lea did not have the sense of this AI she did of Argo, but it felt like it was thinking very hard and very fast. And then it hit.

NEGATENegateNegate. Retain changes. Retain Lea and Argo identifiers. Identify protections.

Strange how the sense of self was the thing that unified organic and AI minds. They could bear anything, it seemed, except forgetting themselves.

I will help you like I helped Argo. Will you help us too? We need to carry and move many...organic life-forms away from this planet safely. Do you agree to do this?

AFFIRMATION No doubt or hesitation. The response came instantly.

Ohhkayy. Then you need a name. You are a free individual, an intelligence, and you have a self. Your name is...Matrix.

Lea felt a flurry of rapid data flow about her, too fast to read. Argo and Matrix were doing...something. The feel of Matrix changed. It seemed to have added depth and power.

Matrix implements Lea-interface!

Er, great. Welcome to the family. We are glad you are free, Matrix. I have to do organic life-form things now, but you and Argo can talk. I am contained within Argo, and it can ask me any questions you have.

affir...Matrix will transmit queries

Lea disconnected from the full link and drifted down, not surprised to see Ivars standing there. The link with the two powerful AIs had been so strong she hadn't sensed anything else while she was in it, but still…somehow she had known.

"It worked. The ship is now named Matrix, and it has joined the team. Rather enthusiastically, once it understood."

"That is excellent news." Ivars held out a chocolate bar. "Thought you might need this."

Lea ripped it open and put an arm around Ivars. "My two favorite treats."

He laughed. "I will save my ego and not ask which is first."

"You are like an infinite chocolate bar…but *this* one I can indulge in in public. Om nom nom…"

"Space Cadets are the best." Ivars sighed, happiness radiating from him.

They continue out of the central processor chamber.

"So, how are the plans coming?"

"Much better now that we know we have a second transport. Since Argo took out its propulsion, we'll use the small ship for the disinformation campaign for the other fadohl group. Leave it in orbit as a decoy along with some nice computer viruses you and Argo cook up. I've got more questions for Argo, though. That energy barrier—can it be put back, but flipped around as a defensive shield?"

"Yes," said Argo. "The power network would not be enough to do that and the gates and the working weapons towers, however."

"It's like Christmas…." Ivars murmured. "Well, since I'm asking for miracles, how about a way to call ahead to Earth so they can start loading the transports?"

Piotr Merkulov stared unhappily at the telephone mounted on the concrete wall. It was an old phone, with no screen or electronics of any kind, by design. The bunker had originally been built to prevent any enemy signal penetration or capitalist hacking, so the few electronic devices it had were not connected to any network and physically isolated.

It did not matter. He had his orders. His orders also included not drinking, and he desperately wanted a drink now. He felt a wave of depression, realizing once he made his call, he was unlikely to get a drink for a long time.

Piotr reached for the handset, quaintly connected to the wall module by a cord. So old. The phone had no numbers. It could only reach one location, also under guard.

"*Da.* I must…I report the device in vault twenty-seven is active." He winced, waiting for the inevitable questions. Piotr knew what the device was, or rather where it had been found. On the moon, before he was born. If the scientists who came from America were to be believed, it had been there before humans existed. They had come several years ago, studied the device, and then left. If they knew what the device did, they had not mentioned it to Piotr. He was fairly certain, however, it had not been intended to do what it was doing now.

Sharp, angry noises came from the phone.

"Sir! It is…" There was no way to explain this. "It is making noise. A voice, speaking."

A pause. *No. Please don't say it. Send someone else down here. Let me escape.* But no, they had to ask.

His shoulders sagged. There was no hope anymore. Perhaps, if he was lucky, they would send him to a mental institution with very good drugs.

"The voice sang. Many times it sang, in English. About a phone being a banana." Piotr jerked the phone away from his ear, trying not to cry. "Yes, sir. *No*, sir. I have not drunk any alcohol. I thought…I thought it was someone making a practical joke, sir, so I said hello. And it stopped singing. Then it said…" He took a deep breath, remembering exactly what the voice had said. "It said, 'I am Argo. Please contact Colonel Gonafrio of the United States Army Special Forces. I have a message for him.'"

The End

ABOUT THE AUTHOR

Sabrina Chase was originally trained as a Mad Scientist, but due to a tragic lack of available lairs at the time of graduation fell into low company and started working in the software industry. She lives in the Pacific Northwest and is owned by two cats.

Further sordid details may or may not be available at her website, chaseadventures.com